You're so vain,
you probably think this book is about you . . .

Acknowledgments

I am particularly grateful to Judith Curr, Brenda Copeland, and Eric Shaw Quinn for their contributions to this book and for their faith in this project, which surpassed my own.

To my family, my friends, and my children, who clearly get my sense of humor and tolerate the rest.

To Marrianne, who spoiled Eric and me every day we worked on this book (and for the ten pounds we both put on—thanks a lot!).

And to the real star in my life—Star, my fifteen-year-old golden retriever, who has stuck by me through thick and thin . . . the keeper of all my secrets.

And of course to all the men I've loved before . . . ha!

St⭐r

Theresa, the friend who named her. Little by little, she was saving up enough money for formal cosmetology training so she could earn some real money burning hair at a nice salon.

As she made her way up the Dixie Highway from her day job at Talon's Nail and Tan Spa to her night job at Mother Pearl's Steak and Oyster Emporium, two rarely seen creases appeared between her brows. She worked hard. Two jobs took most of her time, and the few hours she didn't spend working were filled by constant activity with her friends and her boyfriend, Adam. It wasn't that the work bothered her or that she'd have traded in a single volleyball game, beach party, bar crawl, or wild night at Adam's apartment. It was a spider sense that something was missing, like that feeling you get when you stand looking into the refrigerator, not really hungry, but unable to stop looking. The feeling that this time, it might be there, right behind the ketchup and the pickled beets.

Talon's had been particularly trying that day. Miss Elliott, the rather terrifying Eurasian mistress of the establishment, who'd taught Star everything she knew about nails, was breaking up with her Cuban boyfriend, Adolpho. All day in between monsoon-sized crying jags, the scissors hadn't been sharp enough, the nail polish had been sorted wrong, the tan accelerator wasn't stocked right, and the tanning beds weren't clean enough.

"Go home and call in sick" had been Star's advice to Trudy, the second-shift girl, when she arrived.

As Star caught the long light at Calle Ocho, she began changing into her "uniform" for Mother Pearl's. The "uniform"—the girls all laughed at the word—was a pair of silky, pearl-colored, onion-skin running shorts, white cross-trainers, a pair of light-toast Danskin shimmery tights, and a too-tight T-shirt with SHUCK ME, SUCK ME, EAT ME RAW emblazoned in red across the front. Mother's made almost as much from the sale of the T-shirts as from the oysters. And Star did her part to sell the shirts.

She may have been a late bloomer, but when she did finally bloom, it was with a vengeance. Star was used to the boys' teasing nickname—Pirate's Favorite, code for "sunken chest." Since she could take most of the boys in her class best two falls out of three, the teasing was always good-natured. For her part, Star was perfectly content to be MVP and couldn't really see what all the fuss was about anyway.

And then came puberty. The onset was so abrupt that it frightened her. All she knew was that one day there was a lump on the right side. Convinced she was dying of cancer, Star took the bus to the Broad Key Public Library and confirmed her worst suspicions. The bus ride home was long, and it took her all evening to get up the nerve to break the sad news to her mother.

"Mom," she'd said quietly, sticking her head in her parents' bedroom door. "Can I talk to you a minute?"

"What is it, honey?" Lucille Leigh said, looking up from her Stephen King novel. "You look like someone licked all the red off your candy." She patted the bed beside her.

The tears came even before Star got the words out of her mouth. She piled onto the bed beside her mother and buried her face in Lucille's ample bosom.

"Honey," Lucille said, stroking her daughter's hair. "What's wrong?"

"I . . . I found . . . a lump," Star managed to choke out.

"A lump?" Lucille asked, confused.

"Right here." Star took her mother's hand and placed in on the poisonous node. "I think it's cancer."

"Oh," Lucille said, drawing back suddenly and laughing as she wrapped her arms around her beloved daughter. "Well, well, well," she said, rocking Star gently. "You're not dying, you're just growing up. Looks like you're finally going to get some boobs. You're becoming a woman, honey. You're blooming!"

And bloom she did. Her breasts came on suddenly and tenaciously, as if trying to make up for

estly, if she doesn't find a boyfriend soon, I'm going to break into my savings and hire her the biggest—"

"Mother's looking for you," Theresa said, cutting her off. "And you just missed Adam. What's he so pissed about?"

"I don't know." Star shrugged. It was only a half-truth. She didn't really know what it was this time. "He seemed okay yesterday." Star sat heavily on the bench beside the lockers where the staff stowed their purses and street clothes.

Just off the kitchen, the dingy room reeked of old sneakers, foot powder, and fried seafood. The only ornamentation in the windowless cell was the "Choking" poster that detailed the Heimlich maneuver and a hand-lettered sign exhorting employees to wash their hands. On the far end was a sink, a medicine cabinet, and the door to the toilet. A bench was bolted to the floor down the center of the room, and on one side of that was a bank of old gray-green lockers that Mother had bought as surplus after a hurricane had leveled a local junior high. They had survived the storm, but only just. Opposite, the rough wooden shelf bolted to the wall served as vanity table to the lighted makeup mirror affixed to the wall above. Depending on which way you faced from your seat on the bench, you were either in the "dressing room" or the "makeup room"—but really, you were just in a glorified broom closet.

"Well, Adam was plenty pissed and slamming

around, let me tell you," Theresa said, sitting on the bench beside Star and facing the makeup-room side as she checked herself in the mirror. "Came back in the kitchen screaming out your name. Mother picked him up by the shirtfront and set him beside the Dumpster out back. Said next time he'd be in the Dumpster if he came in the place acting like trash."

Mother was Bernie Weintraub, a great grizzly bear of a man who defended and guided his girls with similar bruin ferocity.

"Now he's looking for me," Star said, biting the side of her lower lip.

"You bet your tights." Theresa sighed. "Star?"

"Yeah."

"Do you think he's worth it?"

"Mother?"

"No, Adam."

"Ladies," Vanda, the senior girl, said, popping her head into the locker room. "Just a reminder. We keep the customers in the dining room, so there's no point waiting for them back here."

"Sorry, Vanda, coming," Star said, glad of the interruption. She tested the bow on her apron as she made her way to the kitchen.

"Well?" Theresa asked, pursuing her. "Is he?"

"Oh, for heaven's sake, Theresa." Star giggled. "That's like saying, 'Quick, what's the meaning of life?' You only find out after it's over."

"That seems like a mean trick," Theresa said, arms folded.

"Star!" Andre, the head cook and shucker, hollered as they passed through on their way to the dining room. "Dinnertime," he called, tossing her an enormous chocolate chip cookie, Frisbee-style.

"Thanks, Andre," Star said, catching it between two hands and backing through the swinging door into the dining room. The cookies were a shared joke. Star's vegetarian diet was at odds with the steak-house menu at Mother Pearl's.

"Star!" the bartender called to the busy room as she took up her cork-topped tray.

The crowd took up the greeting. "Star!" they called, not together but in fits and starts as they spotted her, like a syncopated echo, erratic and startling but totally endearing.

"Star, there you are," called a familiar voice.

"Randy, Andy," Star said, dropping off a couple of beers before making her way over to their table. "Hi, boys. Are those clamshells in your pockets or just the best you can do?"

"You know better than that." Randy grinned. "You've been in our hot tub before."

Randy and Andy were the world's oldest living frat boys. They'd made a career out of being good-looking beach bums, always hustling some angle to keep themselves afloat without actually having to work. Their most successful scheme was getting the Zax beer company to pay for their Jeep, gas, insurance, and all by designating it the Zax Mobile and turning it into a rolling billboard for the company. Their backyard Jacuzzi was also the scene of frequent Zax promotions, which kept the hot tub bubbling and the coolers full of complimentary beer.

"So, what'll it be?" Star teased. "A couple of Buds?"

"Never," Andy said, clutching his throat dramatically.

"Maybe some iced tea?"

Both guys slumped over, tongues lolling out of their mouths like a couple of dead bodies.

"How about the refreshing, smooth taste of Zax?" Star said, mocking the commercial. "The only brew that could tame old Rough and Ready?"

"Zax you say?" Randy said, stroking his chin. "That sounds interesting."

"Yes, let's try some of that," Andy suggested.

"All right then." Star laughed.

"So, Star, you got plans tomorrow night?"

"I have plans every night." Star winked. "It just depends on what kind of mood I'm in as to which ones I end up keeping."

"How about spending the evening with the Miami Dolphins?"

"Oh, I don't know," Star began.

"We really need you," Randy put in. "It's a Zax thing and we need more bodacious babes like yourself."

"So you two won't look like losers?" Star teased, crossing her arms.

"Exactly," Andy agreed. "We want to show people that if they drink Zax, they can come to the Dolphins games with you."

"But you're not going to promise them that, right?" Star asked to make sure. With Randy and Andy it was never wise to leave such things to chance.

"Well, if you put it like that . . . no," Randy said with a little pout.

"I don't know, guys," she said with a toss of her hair. "I haven't been spending enough time with Adam lately."

"Oh, come on, Star," Andy urged. "You have to embrace what life has to offer you."

The phrase she'd heard so often from her grandfather stopped her in her tracks and stunned her into silence. Here was a small but very real opportunity to say yes to life.

"So, we'll pick you up tomorrow evening?" Andy asked tentatively when she said nothing else.

"No tricks?"

"Zax honor," both guys said, raising their bottles.

"And two more?" she asked, writing down their order.

"Always," Randy said.

"As luck would have it, I'm off tomorrow night and I'm pretty sure I saw two more cold Zax in the fridge, so you guys get both your wishes," she said, turning to go.

"Pick you up at six," Andy called after her.

Time passed with no sign of Mother or Adam. Star was having a pretty good night of it. Along with the Miami tourists, there for the T-shirts and what was in them, one of the regulars had a birthday party. That meant the traditional Mother Pearl's Gob Smack—a Polaroid of a kiss on the cheek from one of Pearl's Girls and, of course, a souvenir T-shirt the birthday boy was required to wear in the photo. Star was just presenting the birthday party with the Polaroid in its cardboard oyster-shell frame when Theresa brushed by and whispered in her ear.

"You might want to take your break now," Theresa said with a note of warning in her voice.

Star's head snapped to the front door in search of Adam, and to the office door in search of Mother. Spotting neither, she caught up to Theresa, already on her way to the back. "What's up, Ter?"

"The leech," Theresa said, moving on.

"Theresa," Star sighed, following her. "You have got to stop calling Brandi that."

"Okay," Theresa said, raising her shoulder mockingly. "The mooch then. Is that better?"

"Theresa," Star warned.

"Okay, lookit," Theresa began. "When was the last time you heard from Brandi—*there*, I said her name. Are you satisfied? When was the last time you heard from her that she didn't want something?"

"I don't know. I don't keep track," Star said as the two turned in their drink orders at the service bar.

"Yeah? Well, how about never? She's always borrowing your clothes, your time, even your boyfriend."

"Alvin was not my boyfriend," Star cut her off. "He had a crush on me but I was not interested. I'm glad they got together."

"But she only wanted him 'cause he was with you," Theresa said, exasperated. "Why do you refuse to see it? She's a loser and a leech."

"She is a figure skater and she has all her badges," Star defended. "That can't be a bad thing."

"Yeah, right. Tonya Harding turned out okay." Theresa laughed. "And remember her modeling portfolio? Borrowing your clothes and wearing them to get her pictures made in the photo booth in front of Kmart? And then passing them out to people at school and sending them to magazines and modeling agencies?"

"That was a little odd," Star agreed reluctantly.

"Everything about her is a little odd," Theresa said, starting to get herself wound up. Theresa was protective of Star. She loved her best friend dearly but worried about her tendency to trust people too readily. "Those underwear shots her step-dad took of her and sent into the *Star Search* spokesmodel competition?"

"They were *lingerie* shots," Star corrected without much conviction, as she loaded up her tray with beers and drinks.

"No, lingerie shots are sexy and provocative and tasteful and, most of all, professionally done," Theresa insisted. "These were just sleazy snapshots of her lying on her Sears French Provincial canopy bed in her bra and panties."

"I always liked that bed."

"Star!"

"It was the best they could do."

"You are always trying to find the best in people," Theresa snapped irritably.

"And that's a bad thing?"

"No." Theresa sulked. "It's one of the things I like best about you."

"Star, there you are," Brandi called, approaching.

"Hey, Brandi," Star said with a little hug. "How've you been? I haven't seen you since the Miss Dade Mall contest. Too bad about your baton catching that hairpiece on fire."

"Well, at least I met that cute fireman," Brandi said with a snort of laughter.

"Did Alvin get to meet him too?" Theresa asked primly.

Star gave Theresa's shoe a little kick.

"Oh, hi, Maria," Brandi said with a little smirk

of a smile. "I'm sure one day if you ever get a boyfriend, you'll understand."

"It's Theresa. And maybe I'll just ask Alvin to explain it to me, Shotzy," Theresa said, dodging the second kick from Star. "Excuse me, ladies."

"What was that all about?" Brandi asked, rolling her eyes. "Oh, before I forget, new shots." She reached into her backpack and pulled out a strip of photo-booth pictures. She tore off a couple and handed them to Star.

"These are nice," Star said, squinting. "Isn't that my vest?"

"I'm so glad you think so," Brandi said, hopping nervously and exuberantly from one foot to the other. "I've got a test shoot tomorrow for *Mann* magazine."

"Shut up," Star gasped. "That is so cool!"

"Yeah," Brandi said, continuing her dance. "I sent in some of those shots my step-father took. The test is tomorrow."

Both girls squealed with excitement.

"That is *so* great," Star said, joining in the little dance.

"I'm really nervous though. And I was wondering . . . could you help me out?"

"Sure," Star said, trying to wipe Theresa's words from her mind. "If I can."

"Would you come and do my hair and make-up?" Brandi asked, suddenly still, taking both of Star's hands in hers. "You're the only almostcosmetologist I know, and you do such a great job with your own. I really admire your taste. Please?"

"Of course I will," Star said, trying not to let on that she'd just given away pretty much her entire day off. "I've got to go the Dolphins game with Randy and Andy at six though."

"No problem," Brandi said, embracing Star. "This is so great. I don't know how to thank you."

"You gonna drink all those yourself?" Vanda asked as she breezed by, pointing at Star's full tray sitting on the bar beside them.

"I gotta work," Star said with an apologetic shrug as she turned and hefted the overloaded tray onto her arm.

"I'm sorry, of course," Brandi said, climbing onto a nearby stool. "I'll just wait at the bar and we can talk about it all on your next break."

"Thanks I—" Star began, but that was as far as she got. The tray full of drinks was knocked violently out of her hand. The room was filled with the sound of breaking glass, and then a shocked silence.

"There you are!" Adam shouted. "Why the hell haven't you called me back?"

"You didn't call me, Adam," Star said irritably. "Look at this mess."

"I left a message on your machine."

"Well, when I get home at two o'clock in the morning, I'll be sure and call you back," Star snapped, leaning down to pick up her tray off the floor. "Meanwhile, I haven't been home since seven this morning so there's no way I could have heard your message, let alone called you back."

"Always a smart answer," Adam said, knocking the tray from her hands again. "And why couldn't you call last night? Tell me that. Was it because you were at a party half-naked?" he demanded, grabbing the front of Star's T-shirt and ripping it straight down the front. "There. Now you can run around naked at work too." As he reached for the waistband of the onionskin running shorts, Adam's feet left the ground. The silence more than the sound of breaking glass had alerted Mother's trained ear, and he had emerged from his office, mama bear on the charge. Adam's legs wiggled helplessly in the air as Mother bore him toward the glass doors that opened onto the restaurant's crowded bayside deck. Andy held the door for them as the ambivalent weeknight crowd looked on in horror and satisfaction. The patrons on the deck, unaware of the disturbance inside, had almost no time to react as Mother emerged from the main dining room under full steam, made his way to the railing, and threw Adam overhand into Biscayne Bay.

"There," Mother called down as Adam splashed and spluttered in the water below. "That should cool you off a bit. Stop by later and you can settle up with me for that tray of drinks."

The crowd stood and cheered.

"Quick," Theresa said, grabbing Star. "You've

got to get out of here. Mother is going to kill you."

"Oh, he is not," Star said, clutching her gaping T-shirt. "He'll just yell and tell me Adam can never come in here again. And then at the next big party all will be forgiven."

"Maria's right," Brandi said. "You should get out of here now. Even if you're not worried about Mother, Adam isn't going to be too happy with you when he does get out of the water."

"I do have to get dressed," Star said as they hustled her into the back and toward the rear exit. "Although I kind of think this is a cute look."

Arcady Key was a little spit of land in the Gulf of Mexico, just west of Key Largo between Buttonwood Sound and Spoil Banks. Brandi and Star had both grown up there along with Theresa and Adam. Despite its more famous and prestigious neighbors like nearby Key Largo or, far to the south, Key West, life in Arcady Key was more like the small-town life of southern and central Florida than anything else.

The town's only nod to being island dwellers was the annual bathtub race across Buttonwood Sound to Pelican Key. Star's father, along with the other drunks and would-be engineers on Arcady and the surrounding keys, added motors and sails and all manner of shade-tree mechanical inven-

troleum products. It was the sort of room that could only accurately be described with terms like *woodtone* and *leatherette*. The chair made farting sounds as Star sat down.

"No problem," O.Z. said, flopping down on the chair beside hers, oblivious to the embarrassing noises. "You want a beer?"

"Yes, that would be nice," Star agreed, still shaken from the events of the evening and not feeling the least bit calmed by the change of scenery.

"Well, here you go," O.Z. said, opening the lid on the cooler beside his chair and pulling out a couple of bottles of Zax.

"Thanks," Star said, a little startled by the gesture and the cooler. The Leigh house may not have been the center of sophistication, but unless it was Super Bowl Sunday or the Daytona 500, coolers full of beer were not kept in the living room.

"Well, certainly," O.Z. said, patting her knee with a cold, clammy hand straight from the cooler. "Brandi, you want a beer?"

"No, thanks, but roll us a fat one for the road, would you?" she shouted back from wherever she was.

"You got it, little missy." O.Z. took out an old metal Zax beer tray already strewn with a packet of papers and a lid of dope. "You all will have to forgive me for a little while," O.Z. said apologetically as he began to clean a joint's worth of dope on the metal tray, tapping it gently with his index finger to separate the stems and seeds from the buds. The seeds rolled free down the smooth metal tray as he tapped and then scooped the partially cleaned dope, moving it up the slant of the tray he had balanced in his lap, before tapping again. "I've got a couple of associates coming by and they prefer to keep their business confidential, so if you two can give me a couple of hours here on my own, why that would be great. Then we can have ourselves a high old-time when you get back."

"Well, Brandi has her shoot tomorrow, so we'd probably better make an early night of it," Star suggested.

"Brandi? Early?" O.Z. guffawed. "That'll be the day. It's good of you to help her out with the shoot tomorrow."

"I'm glad to do it," Star said, moving her knee in time to avoid a grateful pat from O.Z.'s big paw.

"Okay," Brandi said, returning with a couple of bags of chips, a small Playmate cooler, and a man's dress shirt, which she tossed to Star. "Here, this will be better than that galley-slave uniform. Put this on and let's get out of here before O.Z.'s creepy friends get here. How's that jay coming?"

"Just a little spit and it's ready, muffin," O.Z. said, licking the paper with his pointy lizard tongue.

"Where can I change?" Star asked Brandi.

"Oh, right here's fine." Brandi shrugged. "I do it all the time. Nothing he hasn't seen."

"Well, I can think of a couple of things he hasn't," Star giggled, using her Mother Pearl's tableside manner to manage a moment that made her blush. She stepped just out of view into the hallway and slipped on the oversize shirt as she tossed the smock back through the doorway, Gypsy Rose Lee style. Star tried not to die as she tied the excess of what was clearly one of O.Z.'s oxford-cloth shirts at her waist and re-emerged with a flourish.

"Looks better on you than it ever did on me," O.Z. said, his tongue still flicking lazily at the joint.

Brandi drove out to Sunset Point and parked the car. "This is my favorite spot to watch the sun set," Brandi explained, leading the way. "We can burn this and kill some time until the coast is clear back at *casa mía.*"

They spread out their picnic on a recently felled palmetto log.

"So, you've never smoked pot before?" Brandi asked incredulously. "What's the weather like on your planet?"

"I've never even smoked a cigarette." Star shrugged. "Remember, I was a jock in high school, so none of that."

"You're doing okay with that beer," Brandi snorted. "Okay, so watch me. You breathe in a little smoke through your mouth . . . careful, not too much. You hold it for a minute and then blow it out. Like this." Brandi demonstrated a couple of hits and then passed the joint to Star.

Star accepted the joint and the challenge. Taking a big manly puff, she dissolved into a huge coughing fit. Brandi laughed, losing her toke.

"Nice job," Brandi said, recovering. "Try just a little ladylike toke this time."

"I don't know," Star said, a little light-headed.

"Aw, come on," Brandi urged, taking another for herself and then insistently pushing the joint Star's way.

Star made another attempt, this one more successful and coughing-fit free. The two sat silently on the log to watch the sun sink into the glowing orange waters of the Gulf. It didn't take too long for the joint to do its work, and it soon went out from neglect as both were too stoned to remember they were smoking it. Brandi laughed and tucked it into the cellophane of her Salem Lights cigarette pack.

"What's so funny?" Star asked, finding herself unable to resist the urge to laugh anyway. "I'm hungry." She giggled, though she couldn't have told you why.

Brandi laughed again and tore open a bag of chips. "Here," she said, offering. "You won't believe how good these are."

"I've had these before." Star shrugged. "They're all right." She took one. The taste exploded on her tongue. The texture, the salt, the almost burnt qual-

"Brandi," Star said urgently.

"Shhh," Brandi soothed, working a second finger under the panty line and gently raking the tender flesh with her fingertips, just brushing. "It's okay. Don't tense up now."

"But, Brandi, I think you should know—"

"It's okay, it's perfectly natural," Brandi urged, silencing her with tiny hungry kisses. Star fought and then succumbed, soft lips on soft lips. "It doesn't mean a thing . . ."

"Brandi, look around us," Star hissed, reawakening from the pleasure. "We're in a fucking Alfred Hitchcock movie."

Brandi looked up and gasped. One of the gulls let out a harsh cry and Brandi screamed. That was it. Suddenly the whole flock exploded into flight, surrounding both screaming women with the beating wings of hundreds of startled and frightened gulls.

Star abandoned her bra, the chips, and even Brandi as she wrapped the shirt around her face and ran. By the time the two were back to the car, they were laughing so hard they could hardly breathe. They sat on the warm hood of the Gremlin and leaned against the windshield as they watched the last of the sunset and caught their breath.

"Well," Star said, cutting the uncomfortable moment short and dusting herself primly. "I've never had sand there before."

The two girls lay back on the hood and laughed the laugh of the stoned.

"Thank God nobody else was around for that," Star chuckled.

"It'll be our secret," Brandi said with a Cheshire grin.

2

"louie louíe"

Star's eyes came open suddenly. For a moment she didn't know where she was or how she got there. But it all came back when she tried to sit up and her skin made that awful ripping sound as she detached herself from the cheap vinyl sofa.

Silently, she surveyed the room. Brandi was nowhere in sight and O.Z. was asleep with his face in the rolling tray, slumped over the edge of the hideous "Mediterranean" coffee table, the one that matched the hideous Naugahyde sofa. The light of the TV, playing with the sound down, made the room feel like that scene from *Poltergeist*. "They're here," Star wanted to scream.

"Oh my God," she cried out, realizing from the VJ miming on the screen that it was after nine. The photo shoot.

"What the fuck," O.Z. said, sitting up abruptly, bits of pot and a single wide paper stuck to one side of his face.

"Brandi," Star called, jumping to her feet. "Brandi, we're going to be late."

"Jeez," O.Z. said, rousing himself. "I'll get her. She'll die and take all of us with her if she blows this."

"I'll make some coffee," Star said, looking around for the kitchen. She seemed to recall its being behind some louvered doors on the far side of the living room, but that had been years before and the louvered doors now opened into a greenhouse of some sort. Puzzled, she looked around, opening a few doors until she happened on a closet with food-like things and a coffeemaker.

"She'll be right out," O.Z. said, startling Star as he came back into the front room.

"Where's the water?" Star asked, looking around for the sink.

"Oh." O.Z. laughed. "We've been batching it for so long that I just turned the kitchen into my office. There's a hose over by the far end of that rack of cuttings," Oz called, peeling the paper off his face.

Brandi's elbow and led her into the light toward the rest of the crew. "Let's meet Ron, the photographer you'll be working with today."

"You know you've only got on one earring," Star said, trying to be helpful. Skip looked up from his copy of *W* and dispatched her silently with an eyebrow. She'd been trying to make conversation ever since Billy had deposited them both in the hydraulic makeup chairs and dashed off to get them coffees. The silence was killing her. Star tried again. "It probably came off around here somewhere. I'd be glad to help look. It's really too nice a set to let it go—"

Skip's laughter brought her up short.

Once again, Star had no idea how to react.

"You're serious, aren't you?" Skip asked, tossing aside the magazine. "Are you for real?" He rose and embraced her.

It didn't really make her feel any better, but it was less menacing than everything else he'd done so far.

"I see you two have made up," Billy said, backing through the swinging doors into the room, his hands balanced with coffees and a few purloined cookies and doughnuts. He turned balletically to face them as he carried on. "I'm glad. This way we can have *so* much more fun."

"Star just offered to help me look for my other

earring," Skip said, putting his arm around her and dragging her across the room to where Billy was laying out the coffee and treats. "Is she just the deal?"

"I love that!" Billy exclaimed, giving her a little peck on the cheek. "Cream, sugar, or dangerous chemicals?"

"Dangerous chemicals?" Star asked, wary after her night with the Fescues.

"Sweet and fake? Nondairy whitener?" Billy offered, clarifying. "Or high test?"

"Oh, got it," Star said. "Real sugar, no dairy, please. I read somewhere that it really never gets digested and just turns into mucus."

"That's horrific," Skip groaned. "Let's make a deal not to talk about the food we eat while we're eating it."

"Or after for that matter," Billy added, stirring vigorously.

"I just try to be careful," Star said with a shrug. "Sorry, no offense."

"Oh, darling," Skip said, squeezing her shoulder with one arm as they made their way back over to the makeup chairs. "You'd need a year of very specialized training to offend me. Food facts just make me queasy."

"Got it," Star said.

"Okay," the assistant with the clipboard announced from the door as she led Brandi in. "We're going with a smoldering-brunette thing. Put her in black lace. Put the hair up, but make it easy for her to take down."

"We could put a bone in it, Wilma," Skip suggested nastily.

"Along those lines," clipboard lady said. "Maybe a touch more sophisticated and a little less masticated?"

"You are a wit today, Miss Flintstone," Skip said, taking Brandi's hand and leading her to the chair. "Now let's have a look at you. Perhaps there's hope."

"Play nice," Billy warned. "Star, why don't you help me pick out a few things from the rack and then we'll get started on your friend's face."

"That would be great." Star nodded like one of the bobble-head spaniels in the back window of her Impala. Keen to learn what she could, Star set her coffee aside and followed Billy into the next room, where a few rolling racks of surprisingly small clothing had been staged as a sort of make-do costume shop.

Star had a really great time helping Billy and Skip. The two were funny with one another and really brilliant at what they did. She took it as a chance to learn and asked questions about each step of the process.

"Okay," Star reviewed as she worked with Billy on Brandi's face. "It's concealer, foundation, and then contour."

"Well, not everyone needs contour," Billy said

as he drew in the bone structure that Brandi had
not been born with. "Sometimes you can just use
the foundation. But the trick is contouring just a
couple of shades darker than skin tone. Along the
sides of the nose, the tip, cheekbones—"

"Or where you wish you had some," Skip put in
nastily.

"—the temples, under the chin," Billy went on
narrating as he performed the task. "And then take
one of these little sponges and blend."

"And you do the whole face before you highlight?" Star asked, fascinated by how much better
Brandi looked already.

"Exactly," Billy said, dabbing at Brandi's face
with a tiny sponge. "It's like you're drawing in the
idealized face, drawing attention to what's best and
taking focus off what's not."

In the end, Brandi was transformed and Star
was ready to stay on for the rest of the day and
help out with the other girls who were coming in.

"How did you guys end up with these great
jobs?" Star asked as Brandi was swept out of the
makeup room and onto the set.

"Well, someone had already been elected president," Skip said, shrugging as he pushed a broom
in her direction and began sorting and preparing
his equipment for the next session.

"*Queen* is an hereditary title," Billy corrected,
giving Skip a little poke.

"And someone had already filled the job fitting

the football teams for jockstraps," Skip concluded. "So, this was the next logical choice."

"Actually," Billy said with a little laugh, "the first time I did this was for a man. A friend was doing drag for this competition in L.A., 'The Battle for the Tiara.' I was already doing hair and I helped him put his whole look together—Judy Izzem. Turned out my process works even better on real women."

"Oh my God," Star said, pushing the hair off her forehead. "You guys are gay, aren't you?"

The guys broke up.

"Did you just, like, come out of some sort of a waking coma?" Billy managed.

"You are a treasure," Skip said, grinning like Alice's cat.

"So you are then?" Star asked again.

"Umm-hmm," they answered her, nodding.

"No offense," Star said hurriedly. "I just never met anyone who was gay. Not that I was sure of, anyway. There was this one guy back on Arcady Key, Mr. Arden. He taught drama classes in a studio his roommate had converted out of their garage. I always thought maybe he was, but he never said for sure. And it seemed impolite to ask."

"And Mr. Arden's roommate?" Skip asked, eyebrow raised.

"Chuck? He did contracting work." And then Star got it. "You think he was too?"

"Who's house was it to begin with?" Billy asked knowingly as he cleaned makeup brushes.

"Chuck's," Star answered readily. "They met when Mr. Arden came through Miami with a touring company of *Grease*."

"I'm thinking," Billy said, nodding.

"Sounds like the sort of guy who might offer to push in your stool," Skip said cryptically. Star missed the joke, but Billy smacked him on the back of the head anyway.

"Cool," Star said. "So, you're *not* my first."

"Or the last, if you stay in this line of work," Billy said with a little laugh.

"I just hope that I'll be as good as you two one day," Star said, sweeping around the chairs. "Brandi looked fantastic. I'm working a couple of J-O-Bs saving for cosmetology school. How did you get the job with Judy?"

"Well, it was a lot like you helping Brandi," Billy suggested. "I think it's the same course. You learn as you go. The more you do it, the better you get."

"We've got some time to kill between setups," Skip suggested. "We could start now."

"You mean it?" Star said, clutching the broom handle like an award.

"If you can make Billy pretty, the sky's the limit," Skip said with a vicious little laugh.

"Bitch," Billy cackled. "And with what you've already got to work with, we can make you look like a movie star."

"Climb aboard," Skip said, patting the seat of one of the chairs. "We'll start with you and then you can practice on us. I'm dying to get my hand on that hair. What color is this anyway?"

"Oh." Star blushed. "I call it manila, like the envelopes?"

Skip laughed as he starting running his hands through. "That's it all right."

"Brandi and I went out to Key Biscayne to work on our tans and there was this sale on Sun-In," she said, wincing from the incident.

"And how much did you use?" Skip asked, letting the damaged strands sift through his fingers.

"Well, we didn't have a lot of time," Star admitted. "So, I used a whole bottle."

"And you know now that that doesn't speed it up?" Skip pointed out as gently as was possible for him.

"Now." Star nodded.

"Well, fortunately, I've got a few tricks that will help cover it. But they're temporary."

"Perfect," Star said, climbing into the chair.

"So, how old is she?" the photographer asked under his breath.

"Just, ummmm," the assistant said quietly as she flipped through the forms on the clipboard. "Just twenty-one, barely that."

"Seems older somehow." Ron shrugged, observing as the stylist and the lighting designer got Brandi settled in. "Not looks, but seems, you know?"

"She's been around, you mean?" the assistant asked.

"Not really the *Mann* type," he said by way of an answer.

"How's this, Ron," the stylist called in their direction.

"Let's see." Ron moved over to look at the scene through his lens. "Fan out the drape a little more to the right. Good. Now, Brandi, turn to look at me."

Brandi turned to him, wet her lips, and gave a little kiss toward the camera, which made Ron's blood run a little cold. He pulled back from the viewfinder.

"Okay then," Ron said. "Let's burn some film."

Ron got the shots and Brandi was a pliant and ready subject . . . a little too ready. She lacked a certain girl-next-door quality that he knew Jayne, the creative director for *Mann*—which was to say Marsten Mann—was looking for. This girl didn't have it. She looked great. She was a good model too. But something about her technique suggested she might work better with a pole. He was beginning to think that the whole trip to Miami was turning out to be a waste.

Ron tried to be fair and took her through a couple of setups, but he knew that she was never going to work out. Most girls they shot didn't. He was skilled enough to know that that day's shoot might be the best Brandi might ever get, and in the end he was only phoning it in.

"And one more for fun," Ron called as he always did at the end of his sessions.

Brandi playfully tossed him the camisole she had been wearing as he reeled off the last shot. The crew broke up around them as the camera began to rewind itself. Between the laughter and the mechanical whirring, no one but Ron heard Brandi say it as she rose from the bench where she'd been posing and embraced him.

"I can be a lot more fun than that," she said, her bare breasts rubbing not so subtly against his arm.

"I bet you can."

"Perfect," Star called. "Hold it."

Skip and Billy struck their best vogue and held it. The Polaroid groaned and spit out another plate. Between the wigs and the makeup, Star's skills, and their coaching, they were a presentable spectacle, but a spectacle nonetheless.

"If I didn't know better, I'd say you two had done this before," Star said, admiring the shot as it centered itself in the white square.

"Okay, now you," Billy said, recovering from one of a hundred fits of laughter Star had provoked since they'd started. He grabbed another camera out of his bag. "You look amazing. I want to get some thirty-five-millimeter of you."

"Oh, come on," Star said, waving off the flattery.

"Look in the mirror, Star," Skip said, taking her hand and turning her. He stood just behind her, his lips near her ear. He scrunched her hair a bit and let it fall. "See? You're beautiful."

Her face lit up just as Billy's flash filled up the room. "That's the shot," Billy screamed. "Now, baby, work it for me. Hit the fans."

Skip turned one of the blow-dryers on cool air and blew it in Star's direction as Billy continued to shout out absurd and stagy photographer's suggestions.

"Bleed for me, baby," Billy cackled. "Make love to me. Make me a sandwich."

They were all laughing so hard that they didn't hear Brandi come in.

Frozen, she watched Star play at being a model.

"I'm ready to get out of this," Brandi said, clearing her throat.

"One of your arms broken or something?" Skip answered disdainfully.

Billy got a couple more shots and Star insisted on taking a couple of Billy and Skip, as well as Brandi.

"We'll send you copies," Billy said, tucking away the camera. "We've got Brandi's contact information already."

"Great," Star said as Brandi went to get changed. "And can I have one of these Polaroids of us?"

"Sure, take a couple," Billy said. "It was fun. And here's that list of the things you should get for your kit. Though I'm telling you, you're on the wrong side of the camera."

Brandi visibly stiffened.

"He's right, Star," Skip said. "You should think about it."

"Well, my boyfriend is a photographer and he's never even offered to take my picture at my birthday party, so I'm doubting that," Star scoffed. "But thanks for the vote of confidence. I'll show him one of these."

"Meanwhile . . . ," Brandi huffed, throwing herself into a chair and pointing at her face.

Billy handed her some cold cream and a box of wipes. "What about you, Star?"

Brandi's sigh was just short of a growl as she leaned forward to take off her makeup. This was always how it was with Star. She'd hoped that at her own shoot she'd get to be the center of attention. But, no. Not with Star around.

Star waved him off. "I'm keeping my masterpiece as long as I can."

"You know how to do it now, but don't give away our secrets," Billy chided.

"Maybe you can help us out if we're ever back this way?" Skip suggested. "Do you have a résumé we can keep?"

"Résumé? Me?" Star laughed as she tucked the Polaroids into the yellow tackle box, next to the Aqua Net and the Lucite fish-head lures. "What would I put on it? Mother Pearl's Steak and Oyster Emporium? Or Talon's Nail and Tan Spa?"

"How about assistant to lead hair and makeup, *Mann* magazine?" Skip suggested.

"That could work." Star grinned. "Not really true."

"You were here and we'd swear to it," Billy said, handing her their cards. "Send us your first draft when we send the photos."

"You got it," Star said, hugging them both as Brandi struggled to put herself back to rights.

The ride back to Star's car had been largely silent. Brandi said she was tired from it all and wanted to get home and get a nap. But in truth she was anxious to get home and get cleaned up to meet Ron for her follow-up interview at his hotel later. She wasn't about to miss a second chance to get into *Mann* magazine.

"Thanks, honey," Brandi said as she pulled into the lot behind Mother Pearl's. "Sorry they didn't really need you today."

"Are you kidding?" Star said, giving Brandi's shoulder a playful shove. "I had a ball. They did my hair and makeup and I got my first professional job credit. It couldn't have gone better for me."

"Oh, Star, you always make the best out of everything," Brandi said, taking Star's hand gently. "And don't you listen to a word they said. You'd be great behind the camera." She gave Star's hand an understanding squeeze and then leaned across and popped Star's door open for her. "I'll see you soon."

"Sure," Star said, in far too good a mood to be brought down by Brandi's tactics. "And you let me know the minute you get those pictures."

"You bet," Brandi called, pulling away even before Star's door was closed.

Star was blissful crossing the parking lot to her car, swinging her makeup kit like a little girl with a lunch pail on her way to school. Then she saw the note under her windshield wiper.

Star—

Baby, you know I love you so much it makes me crazy sometimes. I waited all night for you to come out, and when you didn't, I didn't know what I'd do without you. Call me or better yet come home.

Adam

P.S. If I'm not there, I may be at Marci's, try me there.

Star crumpled up the note and tossed it on the floorboard beside the *I forgot your birthday* bouquet.

Marci. Adam's model. He had put it in just to get at her. And it had worked.

Adam was trying to get Marci into *Mann* magazine—to help both their careers, he said. And even though Marci was married, and even though Adam assured Star that there was nothing between them, finding those nude pictures was just more than she could take.

Star slammed Rusty's door, gunned the engine and went looking.

By the time she got to Adam's she had already worked herself up to the fight, arguing with him in her head the whole way. It was a bit of a letdown when she let herself into the apartment, flinging the door open and storming through the house looking for Adam and for trouble. No sign of either.

She flung herself onto the sofa and waited. His car had been in the space downstairs so she figured he couldn't have gone far. Probably around the corner to the Dash In. The "Inconvenience Mart," he called it. Star softened, smiling as she thought of how much she enjoyed him. The arguments in her head seemed to fade as she thought about spending time with him and his family. Adam had been her high school sweetheart, and she'd spent so much time with them that being together just felt natural. But it had started to come apart when he'd moved to Miami to strike out on his own.

When Star and Theresa had gotten a place and moved to the city, things had gone from bad to worse. Bad was locking her out of the apartment with no clothes. Worse was driving into an outdoor restaurant where she was having dinner with some friend, a stunt that had gotten his license suspended for six months—though that never stopped him from driving. Star didn't know what the problem was, but she was sure there was a problem. He was jealous and possessive, and yet he didn't seem to want her around. He wanted her on his terms, which meant back at his mom's house on Arcady Key.

Should she marry him? she wondered. It seemed like the right thing to do. She could kind of say that she'd waited until she was married 'cause he was the only guy she'd ever done it with. Well, except for those two times before Adam, but neither was real sex. And Brandi . . . well, girls don't count. It wasn't a good enough reason to stay, though, and there were plenty of good reasons to leave.

But when she thought of leaving him, she thought of the time they'd gotten stuck at the top of the Ferris wheel at the Dade County fair and he'd made love to her to stop her from being afraid. Or the way he'd come to find her when she'd been lost on the beach in a storm; he kissed her like he'd never let her go. Or just his gentle way with his nieces and nephews. He could be so tender, it was hard to believe that he was the same Adam as the wild man on the rampage.

Maybe it was because she hadn't said yes to his proposal. But how could she? Life with Adam was the Bavarian Mood Swings. What kept her around was his family. She loved being at their place. They did the kind of things that families were supposed to do on holidays—and regular days for that matter—and Star couldn't get enough.

On the Fourth of July, Adam's family would barbecue ribs and grill burgers outdoors, playing lawn games until dark, when they could light off a few Roman candles and bottle rockets. The last time Star's family had celebrated the Fourth her father had staged an impressive exhibition of his homemade rockets. They had lit up the night sky with chrysanthemums of purple and gold and silver—and their neighbor's roof. What with the fire department, the sheriff, and the police force stopping by, it was quite a turnout. Not exactly Norman Rockwell, though.

For Thanksgiving, Adam's family gathered at the family home, and the boys played touch football on the lawn while Star helped Adam's mom and sisters make green bean casserole, sweet potato pie, and a turkey so huge it took two of them to carry it in for Adam's father to carve. Star's family never did an official Thanksgiving because her mom was always working. Turkey Day was a particularly lucrative holiday for waitresses, and

Lucille couldn't pass up the extra money. She'd cook turkey and trimmings the day before and leave them for Star, her father, and her brother, Hank, to enjoy. What Lucille didn't know was that as soon as she left for work, Rick called his "poker buddies"—his euphemism for drinking cronies. Each Thanksgiving, Rick and the poker buddies got drunk, ate the food, and passed out on the porch. Star and Hank made a game of throwing pebbles and small shells at the unconscious guests, with various point values for scored hits. But it didn't make Thanksgiving special. They could play "bean the drunk" anytime their father's friends came to visit, which was often when her mom was at work. But it wasn't all bad. The visits often included swimming in the ocean in their underwear, the occasional beer, and trips to local bars and nightspots, all of it kept in strictest confidence from Lucille.

The fact was, Star's father was a genius—a frustrated genius, but a genius nonetheless. Never satisfied simply working for someone else, he was always busy with some scheme or other. His schemes were always brilliant, but they never really came to anything other than another visit from the police or the county health inspector. Rick could balance the checkbook in his head, keep track of all the cards in a poker deck, and do the crossword in ink. He never missed a question on *Jeopardy!*, and *Wheel of Fortune* hadn't come up with a puzzle to stump him yet; but he'd never found a practical application for his genius that didn't blow up in his face.

Star's thoughts drifted back to Adam. His family was the main reason she stayed: "the Adam's Family" she lovingly called them. Their dull and predictable dinner table was the closest that Star had ever come to feeling safe, she realized with a sad smile. She put down the photo she had been looking at, the one Adam had taken of them all the previous Thanksgiving.

Still no Adam.

Stretching out on the sofa, tired from a late night and a busy day, Star felt something jab her. She reached into the pocket of her tightly fitted jeans and pulled out the Polaroids Billy had taken of her. She really did look good. Star lovingly placed the pictures on her chest and was just drifting off when she saw it.

There on the wall of the living room was a collection of *Mann* magazine centerfolds hung along with nude photos of Marci, clearly from a variety of shoots. She'd seen the pictures before. The ones of Marci were not new, and the centerfolds were just a part of the landscape at Adam's. But that afternoon, it was as if she could hear them laughing at her. She felt that she'd never be enough as long as Adam kept comparing her to them. Star raised a photo of herself again and held it up so that, in her line of sight, it was next to the centerfolds and nude studies.

The nap was over.

She tore up the pictures of herself from that afternoon and threw the bits up into the air like bitter confetti. And then, as if she were watching it happen, she was up and shredding the magazine pages and photos of Marci as tears streamed down her face.

She didn't even hear Adam come in.

"What are you doing?" he demanded, grabbing her wrists and shaking her.

"I'm . . . I don't . . . How many shoots did you do with Marci?" she said finally, finding a voice for her anger.

"Tons." Adam shrugged, pulling her over to the sofa and pushing her onto it. "We're trying to build her a portfolio and I—"

"How many nude shoots?" she demanded, jumping up from the sofa only to be pushed back down.

"Five. What's it to you? It's a job. I'm trying to be a photographer. Look, Star, I like you just fine. Just the way you are. Just because you don't look like Marci or those other girls is no reason to get all jealous. So just let it go, okay?"

Adam's words took the fight right out of her. It was true. She didn't care about the photo shoots. She didn't care that Marci was nude. She wasn't even sure she cared about Adam. It had nothing to do with them. It was how unsure she felt about herself. He wasn't comparing her to the pictures, she was.

She regarded Adam a moment, looking down at her as she rocked on the sofa, her arms folded around her knees. She smiled up at him.

With the speed that had made her the setter for the state champion Double A girls volleyball team for five straight years, she was over the back of the sofa and out the door before Adam realized she was leaving. Her lead was so great that she was already down the stairs and running across the parking lot toward Rusty when she heard him calling down to her from the second-floor gallery.

"Don't you walk out on me like this, Star," he called, shaking his fist. "If you leave like this, don't bother coming back. Do you hear me?"

It might have sounded pretty serious if you were hearing it for the first time. But Star and the neighbors had heard Adam's rant so often that it had become a standard farewell between the two. Star waved genially as she pulled away.

"Dude," Randy called as Star pulled into the driveway beside the little duplex in Miami Springs that she shared with Theresa. "It's almost time for the game."

Fresh from the fight with Adam and still tired from her adventures with Brandi, Star had pretty much forgotten about the Dolphins game.

"Oh, guys," she said, getting out of the car. "I'm

really sorry, but I'm exhausted. I don't think I can make it."

"Really?" Randy questioned, genuinely surprised as he stepped out of the Jeep filled with fellow Zax-enhanced partyers. " 'Cause you look amazing."

"You *really* do," Andy agreed, nodding vigorously. "I mean, you always look great, Star, but I mean, like, wow! You look like you spent a lot of time getting ready to go out. Doesn't she look great, guys?" he called to the five other people stuffed into the Zax Mobile.

There were cheers and whistles from the men and women packed into the Jeep and hanging from the crash bar.

"Oh, right," Star said, realizing she'd come straight from the updo at the photo shoot. And Adam hadn't even noticed, she thought disgustedly. "I did kind of get my hair and face done a little while ago."

"Be a shame to waste it," Randy said, extending his hand.

"Come on, suit up," Andy said, tossing her a Zax T-shirt as they climbed into the overloaded Jeep. "Put this on."

"Here," Randy said, cracking open a cold Zax. "Have a beer, you'll feel better."

"And by the time we get to Robbie Stadium, you'll feel like a new woman," Andy said. "You already look like one."

"Oh, what that hell," Star said, taking the beer. "This one's for you Papa Jens."

It was one of those perfect Miami nights. A cool ocean breeze was blowing just enough to balance the tropical heat that made Miami, Miami. Star was exhilarated. It had been a great day for her. Meeting Skip and Billy had been a real break, and she let her mind wander through all the possibilities of where her life could take her. She imagined herself doing hair and makeup for the famous and celebrated. Maybe even Hollywood. The promise of something new infused her with excitement.

She felt free. Free from Adam. Free from thinking about work and saving for beauty school. Free just to be herself with people who didn't want anything more than to spend a couple of hours with her at the ball game and then later at Zax Party Central—Randy and Andy's hot tub.

By the time they got to Joe Robbie Stadium nothing could have spoiled Star's mood. She ducked behind a conversion van in the parking lot and slipped into the Zax T-shirt to earn her place inside. Their Zax seats were on the club level, and while they were not exactly box seats, they were the best Star had ever had for a ball game. Dave Ryan, the Zax sports promotion guy, met them at the gate and escorted them to their section. Far from its being private seating, maybe as many as a hundred people were got up in various Zax garb, waving signs and banners cheering for the beer and the twelfth president of the United States for whom the beer had been named—Zachary Taylor, fondly known as Old Rough and Ready.

It was a pretty good idea. For the cost of the seats, Zax beer got a national commercial every time the TV cameras panned past their section. Those, like Randy and Andy, who were good at getting the camera's attention, were asked back.

"Here, you, what's your name?" Dave asked Star as he surveyed the group.

"Star Wood Leigh," she said proudly, extending her hand to greet him.

"That T-shirt looks great on you," he said slyly, taking her hand and leading her to the first row of seats in the section. "Why don't you sit right down front." He indicated a seat as he handed her a sign that said *I Can Tame Old Rough and Ready.*

"Well," she demurred, shoving her hands into the pockets of her jeans like the shy little girl she in so many ways still was. "I came with Randy and Andy and a couple of their friends, so I'd want to sit with them."

"Of course," Dave said, turning to the group at large. "Who's in Star's party?"

Andy and Randy grinned at their own success in inviting Star as they raised their hands along with the other occupants of the Zax Mobile.

"Okay," Dave said, moving them into the front row as he handed her a clipboard with some forms on it. "You take these seats here. Sign these photo releases. And be sure and stay up on your feet for big plays, and especially during time-outs."

"Way to go, Star," Randy said, raising his hand for five.

"Primo seats, dude," Andy concurred. "You're my hero."

The others agreed, thanking her for their good fortune as they settled in to enjoy the festivities. They had their own private bottomless Zax supply, so by kickoff the party was well underway.

The game got off to a slow start. The home-town crowd cheered the team onto the field, but little had happened and the score was tied at noth-ing to nothing when the ball went out of bounds and the clock stopped. Mindful of their instruc-tions, Star led her little party as they rose and cheered for the Dolphins, but it was halfhearted and died quickly.

Star leaned forward slightly, placing her hands on the railing in front of them, as she took in the view of the stadium and the perfect night.

When wild cheers erupted in the stadium, she looked down at the field to see what was happen-ing. Players and officials were milling around as the Dolphins quarterback conferred with the coach. Nothing to cheer about. Even the cheerleaders were just standing there. But when she leaned back and shrugged, the cheering got wilder. She looked to Randy and Andy to see what was going on and they were giving her the thumbs-up, which only puzzled her more. Beyond them she could see Dave running toward her, shouting, "The logo, show the logo," as he pulled at his own T-shirt to demonstrate. Still not getting it, she imitated his action, grabbing her T-shirt by the hem and tugging it down. The stadium came to its feet. The cheers were deafening. Again, Star looked to the field to see what was going on and saw that not only were the players not playing, but they were looking up and pointing at the giant video screens stationed strategically at either end of the stadium.

And there she was.

Star turned to see what they were looking at and saw herself staring back down from the Jumbotron. Thrilled and amused by the moment, she jumped up and down and waved. Pandemonium! Someone punched up "Louie Louie" on the stadium's sound system and the dance was on. Star tugged down the front of her shirt to show the Zax logo, and the cameras went off around her.

Everyone in Joe Robbie Stadium danced with Star that night.

The deafening roar seemed to fade as she saw the girl on the giant screens overhead.

Is that really me? She waves when I wave, jumps

when I jump. *She seems so old,* Star thought of her twenty-one-year-old face on the big screen.

The crowd continued to cheer until at last an amused voice came on the loudspeakers echoing through the stadium. "If the young lady in the club section is ready to take her seat, the Dolphins would like to resume play now."

Star laughed and blew the team a kiss. The team waved back from the field and the crowd gave one last salute as she sat down.

"Well, that was amazing," Star said to Randy. "Didn't I look kind of old?" she commented, pointing at the screen, which was by then flashing the word *DEFENSE* over and over.

"You looked old enough," Andy said, laughing at his own crass joke.

Star gave him a friendly punch in the upper arm, and they returned to being part of the thousands of fans in the stadium that evening. It had been a bit of fun and a laugh. It would make a great story. And then the game resumed and Star and the little group went on with their evening.

Both teams managed to score and the Dolphins pulled ahead as the half approached. Star and the boys were talking about what they felt Marino should do next when Dave approached them.

"Star," Dave said, leaning down to interrupt.

"I'm sorry," Star said, jumping up. "We should be on our feet. We were just wondering if Marino should keep it on the ground or risk going airborne—"

"Star." Dave laughed. "You do not have to apologize to me. You already earned your free tickets tonight—and my salary for the year for that matter. You can sit and read a magazine for all I care. I would like to ask a favor, though, if you don't mind."

"Okay, sure," Star said. "If I can."

"Oh, you can," Dave said, leading her away with his hand on the small of her back.

Randy and Andy exchanged a look of concern.

"You think?" Randy said.

"Dave's a good guy," Andy countered, shaking his head.

"He's still a guy."

"Nah," they said in unison, shaking their heads.

Marino decided to keep the game on the ground and ran out the clock, taking the Dolphins into the half with a lead, and still no sign of Star.

"Okay, I'm starting to remember that Dave is still a guy," Andy said.

"Should we go look?" Randy said, also a bit concerned.

"Where?"

"Down there." Randy jumped to his feet and pointed at the field.

"Ladies and gentlemen," the announcer's voice boomed. "The Miami Dolphins and Zax beer are pleased to present Miss R&R, Star Wood Leigh, who will draw the name of one lucky fan out of the dolphin tank to receive a truckload of Zax and season tickets to . . ."

The crowd was no longer interested in what the announcer said, what the winner would receive, or even who would win. Star was on the field and the crowd was on its feet.

3

to be real

Jayne Hersfield was the first woman to be named executive editor and creative director of *Mann* magazine. Starting as a lowly copy editor in the ultimate boy's club, through her own determination, shrewd judgment, and an unerring eye for what the *Mann* reader wanted, she had risen to be the most powerful person in the empire, second only to Marsten Mann himself. She personally selected each girl for the cover and the gatefold—subject to Marsten's approval of course. So far, neither he nor the readers had ever disagreed with her choice.

The Miami shoot had turned out to be a disappointment. The girls had been good. They might even use some of them inside the magazine. But none had turned out to be the one in ten thousand who was cover material. Another scouting shoot was planned in St. Louis the following week, though, and Jayne stopped by Skip and Billy's "office" to talk with them about the look she was going for.

"Billy? Skip?" she called, leaning in as she knocked on the makeup room door off Mann's in-house studio.

Billy looked up from some photos he and Skip were sorting through at the light table. "Jayne, hi."

"What brings you down to the factory floor?" Skip asked snidely. "Are you fired or are we?"

"Just keep it up." Jayne laughed a friendly warning. "Who is *she*?" Jayne asked, spotting the photos of Star spread across the light table.

"That's our new best girlfriend. She helped us with hair and makeup at the Miami shoot," Billy said. "Isn't she great?"

"And here I thought the Miami shoot was a complete waste," Jayne said, a smile splitting her face.

O.Z. was in the midst of watering his hemp plants when the phone rang again. Covered in mulch and water, he continued with what he was doing, ignoring the ringing as he had all morning.

"Brandi," he called when the ringing didn't stop. "Brandi, phone."

No reply.

"Brandi!"

"What?" she said, emerging sleepily from her room, clad only in her oversized acetate panties and midriff baring tee.

"Phone."

"Yeah, I know. And like it's not hard enough to sleep around here with the phone ringing off the hook, you have to start yelling my name?"

He checked the VCR to make sure it really was after one in the afternoon.

The phone continued to ring.

"As long as you're up?" O.Z. shrugged. "Could you get that?"

Brandi sighed, put her hands on her hips, and regarded him a moment.

And the phone continued to ring.

"Yeah? What is it?" Brandi said into the receiver.

"Hi, this is Sami in Jayne Hersfield's office at *Mann* magazine. Is this Brandi Fescue?"

"*Mann* magazine?" Brandi said, suddenly much friendlier and more alert. She pointed at the phone for O.Z.'s benefit. "This is Brandi."

"Can you hold for Jayne please?"

"Sure, I'll hold."

"Thanks," Sami said cheerfully.

"Oh my God," Brandi screamed when the hold

music began to play. "I can't fucking believe it. It's *Mann* magazine."

"Well, it's been ringing like that all morning," O.Z. said. "I guess they must really want to talk to you."

"It has?" Brandi growled. "Well, why the hell didn't you—"

"Hello? Brandi?" Jayne asked.

"Hi, yes, this is Brandi," she said sweetly, trying her best to be calm.

"Hi, Brandi, this is Jayne Hersfield. I'm the executive editor here at *Mann* magazine."

"I know who you are," Brandi said with a little snort of laughter that made Jayne wince.

"Great," Jayne said enthusiastically. "Couple of things. I just wanted to tell you how much I enjoyed your photos."

"Oh, Miss Hersfield, that means so much coming from you," Brandi said graciously, despite squirming as if she needed the ladies' room.

"Call me Jayne," she said kindly. "Yes, you're certainly under consideration, and we'll be letting you know just as soon as we make a definite decision." An experienced hand at her job, Jayne knew how to sound hopeful without promising anything.

"Thanks, Jayne," Brandi said, trying on the first name.

"You bet," Jayne went on, ready for the business at hand. "Listen, there's one other thing I need.

You brought a friend who worked with Billy and Skip on makeup and hair?"

"Un-huh," Brandi said, teeth gritted, her eyebrows shooting up.

"We need to get in touch with her and I was wondering if you'd have a number?" Jayne asked, pen poised, ready to be done with Brandi Fescue once and for all.

"Hmmm," Brandi mused. "That girl from the nail salon. What is her name?"

"Star," Jayne suggested, knowing full well that it was and wanting to kill Billy and Skip for putting her through this.

"No," Brandi said. "I don't think that's it. Esther maybe? No, it's Ethel I think."

"Billy and Skip seemed quite sure."

"Maybe. I'm not sure exactly how to get in touch with her."

"The name of the nail salon perhaps?" Jayne suggested helpfully, wishing she could reach through the phone and choke Brandi.

"She was fired from there," Brandi confided. "So that wouldn't help. It's kind of why I said she could come along. She got fired for being drunk on the job and I just thought she should have another chance. I hope that nothing turned up missing after we were there."

"Just her phone number," Jayne said, giving up and ready to try sailing into this wind on a new tack. "Well, the boys were just crazy about her and

I like to keep them happy. We've got a shoot coming up in Dallas, and I'd like to hire her. So if you see her, I'd be very grateful if you'd give her my number. Perhaps a finder's fee of some sort."

"Oh, that's not necessary," Brandi said, seething but not letting on. "I'd be delighted to give her that number if I see her. . . . Uh-huh, yeah, got it," Brandi said, picking at a nail. "It's on the pad right here," she assured Jayne as she patted the paneling next to the wall-mounted phone. "As soon as I see her, I'll get her to call you. Thanks for calling and I look forward to hearing from you soon about the shoot. Thanks again, Jayne. . . . Yes, I'll have her call you.

"In hell," Brandi said, hanging up.

"So, what did they say?" O.Z. asked, looking up from his pruning.

"I'm going back to bed. Answer the phone, don't answer the phone, but don't wake me up again."

"You got it, muffin," he said, going back to his horticulture. He knew better than to ask anything else.

Star shivered nervously as she waited outside Dave Ryan's office at the local Zax beer operation. It was springtime in Miami and the AC had been cranked up to accommodate the heat.

"Star," Dave said genially as he emerged from

his office, his arms extended in greeting. They exchanged a friendly hug and he ushered her into the mahogany and leather office, stacked with Zax T-shirts, hung with neon beer signs, and crowded with a surprising number of people, all of whom stood and applauded as she entered. "Ladies and gentlemen, I give you the people's choice for Zax's official Miss R&R."

Star gasped as a couple of the executives stepped aside to reveal a life-size cutout of her, made from one of the photos taken at the game. "It's me" was all she could manage.

"It sure is," Dave said, ushering her into a seat. "Star, I've got to tell you. I've been doing promotions all my life and I've never seen anything like the other night. You owned that place."

"Oh, everybody was just having a good time." Star blushed.

"No, really, Star," a sophisticated-looking woman, one of the executives, added. "I'm Brenda Copeland, vice president for nonmedia marketing. And I think I speak for the whole Zax organization when I say we were more than a little impressed with what you were able to do. We want that kind of excitement around our whole product line."

"That's right, Star," Dave said, indicating the others in the room with an expansive gesture. "These people are Zax beer, and we have not talked about anything but you since that game."

"We're already planning a whole campaign around you," Brenda said, indicating the stack of photos and illustrations on Dave's desk.

"We want you to come to work with us," an elderly man said, helping Star into a chair. "My family has owned Zax beer for a very long time, and I believe Zachary Taylor himself would be proud to have his name associated with you, Star. Even though we're now a publicly traded company, I still take great care about the company name. I'd be honored to work with you, young lady."

Star's head was spinning when she left them for work at Talon's. She'd had to switch shifts with Trudy to be able to make the meeting, but it had been so worth it. As things were looking, she'd have the money for cosmetology school much sooner than she'd planned. In fact, if things went as Dave was predicting, she might be able to quit work and go to school full-time. She was giddy with the prospect of it all.

Pulling her car into the lot behind Talon's, Star tried to talk herself down a bit as she made her way around front to the entrance. She didn't want to get her hopes up too high. Zax was offering to pay her to use photos they technically already owned. They didn't have to do that since she'd signed releases. If the campaign went well, they'd planned a whole series of promotions around Star. Lost in thought, she rounded the corner onto Ponce de Leon Boulevard, almost colliding with a couple of businessmen on the sidewalk.

"Hey, you're the R&R girl," one of the men said. "I saw you on TV at the game the other night."

"Hi," Star said, grinning and laughing nervously.

"You were great," one of the other men said.

"Thanks," Star said as she ducked into the salon a little unnerved. "That was so freaky."

"Freaky?" Miss Elliott said, looking up from the mag lamp mounted to the side of her manicure station. She was poised over the ludicrously long, jungle-red nails of a customer. "What freaky? Call cops?"

"No, no," Star gushed. "Good freaky, great freaky. I was recognized from being on TV the other night at the Dolphins game. Did I tell you?"

"Now you mention it, I recognize you too," Miss Elliott said, squinting an eye at her and pointing at her with an orange stick. "You used to work here, didn't you? You the girl who supposed to clean the tanning beds a half hour ago."

"Yes, ma'am," Star said, stowing her purse and grabbing a roll of paper towels and a spray bottle of Miss Elliott's secret antibacterial degreaser. "I'm on it."

"I thought that was you," Miss Elliott chuckled, returning her gaze to the lens in front of her.

★

Thursday's American Grille was dark. Even at noon there was no sign of daylight. Stained-glass windows, dark paneling, red rugs, oxblood leather booths, and whiskey-barrel chairs—about the only bright thing in the place was the brass bar rail.

Adam took off his obligatory Wayfarer's and squinted as he waited for his eyes to adjust. It took him a moment to spot her seated in the back of the bar, illuminated faintly by one of the tiny bistro lamps that adorned each table. He grinned and waved as he crossed to her.

"Hi, honey," Adam said, leaning across the booth to give her a kiss. "I'm glad you could meet me for lunch. I know it's hard to get away in the middle of the day, but I just needed to see you." He took her hand. "I just don't feel like I've been getting enough time with you and I want to try and change that."

"Well, I've got some time coming at the club, and my husband is going to be away on a sales trip—" she began, but stopped as he gasped, grabbed a menu, and held it over his face. "Adam? What is it?"

"It's her," he hissed, sliding down the banquette. "She's here."

"What?" Marci said, ducking, and then, trying not to look suspicious, holding up her hand along the side of her face in a pathetic gesture. It would have been comic had it not been sincere.

Adam leaned forward over the menu. "You know she can still see you even with the hand," he whispered sarcastically.

"Like you look normal slouched down below the table with that menu over your head. Besides, why do we have to hide? We work together."

"I guess," he said, peeking to see Star's head bobbing through the restaurant. "Hold on a minute," he said, rising to get a better look.

"Are you crazy?" Marci said, grabbing his hand. "You don't have to flag her down."

"There's something strange." He stepped out of the booth and walked toward the approaching Star. "She's not that tall and her hair's not moving . . ."

The bartender came into view with the life-size cutout of Star. A banner had been affixed to her hands that read, "Meet me at Thursday's for Zax *Monday Night Football*." Adam collapsed with a sigh.

"It's only a cutout," he said, relieved.

Then it hit him.

"Jayne?" Sami tapped gently on the door to her boss's office. "This ad layout just came in for one of our regional editions. I thought you should see it."

"Sami," Jayne said, trying for patience. "Did you have wine at lunch today?"

"No, ma'am," Sami said, treading carefully. "But I still thought you should—"

"Then perhaps you've had a stroke or a grand mal seizure?" Jayne suggested, looking up. "To refresh your possibly damaged memory, I'm in the middle of an editorial meeting. Moreover, I am not the ad manager. I never, ever look at the ads. Never. So, I couldn't possibly care less. Is any of this sounding familiar?"

"Yes," Sami said with a little smile. Jayne was such a good-natured boss that even getting in trouble was funny. "I am sorry to interrupt. I do know this is an important meeting. In fact, that's one of the reasons I decided to interrupt. You really should see this."

"Sami," Jayne said, just before genuine anger. "Bring it here, but if I don't get it right away, you will."

"Sorry to interrupt, sir," Sami apologized, nodding to Jayne's guest as she crossed the expansive office and handed over the ad.

"We don't pay you enough, Sami," Jayne said, taking the ad. "Get the advertising agency this came from on the phone. I want to speak with the ad exec in charge of this account right now."

"Have a look at this, sir," Jayne said, handing the Miss R&R ad to Marsten Mann.

★

"Star!" Adam screamed as he burst into her apartment, the cardboard cutout under one arm. "Star, where the hell are you?"

"Be quiet, Adam," she called back from the kitchen. "I live in a duplex, not the Australian outback. I can hear you just fine and so can the neighbors."

"Don't you get snotty with me," he ranted, dragging her likeness into the tiny kitchen. "What the hell is this supposed to be?"

"Well, duh, it's me," Star said, looking up from the veggie lasagna she was layering with toejack soy cheese.

"I know it's you, dimbot," he said, tearing off the cardboard head and tossing the body aside. "What the hell are you doing in a Zax beer ad?"

"I asked you not to scream," Star said, ignoring his question.

"God damn it, Star," he shouted. "What the fuck are you doing in this ad?"

No answer. Star hummed as she laid the fresh pasta across the shredded toejack.

Adam trembled with rage as he made a strangled and exasperated noise, his hand clutched over his mouth.

"Star," he said sweetly, his color rising. "Honey?

What are you doing in this Zax ad?" He held up the head, both hands wrapped around the throat as if to clarify.

"Well, I'm glad you asked." Star started to slice mushrooms. "You know Randy and Andy, right?"

"Star," Adam warned, fighting to keep his voice down.

"Right, of course you do," she teased, ladling sauce over the noodles. "Well, they won free tickets to the Dolphins game the other night from Zax. Well, of course they did, right?" She laughed at her own little joke about the two Zax fanatics.

Adam gave her a look.

"You are going to be so cracked up when you hear the rest of this," she said, shaking a handful of mushrooms at him. "Anyway, I went along on one of their free tickets—I mean, why not? And during a quiet moment in the game the camera picked me out of the crowd and put me on the giant screens. Well, turns out I was a hit. People have been stopping me on the street all day!"

"Star," Adam said hoarsely. "That does not explain how you wound up on this."

"I'm getting to that." She sprinkled mushrooms over the lime and cilantro marinara sauce that was the secret to her special veggie lasagna margarita. "I was such a big hit that the Zax promotions guy called me into a meeting with the owner and everyone. They offered me a job as the official Miss R&R. Isn't that great? I'm official." She giggled. "I was making us a special dinner to celebrate."

"No, it is not great," Adam said, hurling the cardboard head at her like a Frisbee. "Where did the photograph in this ad come from?"

Star stepped back to dodge the cardboard, but it hit the back of her arm. "I don't know," she said irritably. "That hurt, be careful. I guess it was one of the photographers at the game."

"And what is it that I do for a living?"

"You sell tan accelerator." Star shrugged.

"God damn it," he howled, raking the lasagna onto the floor. "I'm a photographer."

"Damn it, Adam, just look at this mess." Star bent down to begin to pick it up. "Why do you have to be so destructive?"

"Star, you're not listening to me."

"I heard you. I know you're a photographer. Don't get your dandruff up. There'll be other photographs."

"Did you already sign something?" he snarled, grabbing her by the wrist and dragging her toward his face.

"Yes, I did today," Star said, struggling to pull away. "That's what we're celebrating here tonight." She pointed with her free hand at the flowers and candles on the table.

"Well, stupid," he explained, snatching her even closer and hurting her wrist, "if you'd talked to me about it, we could have gotten me written into the contract as your photographer. Now it's their choice, moron."

That was enough for Star. She hooked her foot behind his ankle and, stepping toward him as she'd learned in self-defense class at the Y, knocked him off-balance and threw him face first onto the lasagna-splattered floor.

"I seem to remember some moron telling me that I wasn't good enough to be in any ads like your precious Marci and your precious Miss April," Star said, darting onto the dining-room side of the counter to put it between them. "But it seems like the folks at Zax don't agree. So who's stupid now?"

Star shrieked as Adam leaped to his feet and dashed around the counter after her. She countered and dashed down the hallway toward the front of the house.

"What I said was that you didn't have the looks to be in *Mann* magazine like Marci or those girls who already are," he hollered, pursuing her down the hall and back into the living room as she circled back through the swinging door that connected the living room with the kitchen. Technically, there was a more formal dining area in the living room, hence the swinging door—but she and Theresa only had the one table, so they used the extra space in the living room as their study area. Theresa kept her desk there. Star had set up a small in-home beauty station, with a nice secondhand chair she'd gotten from Miss Elliott, and even an old hooded dryer her mom had given her. To be fair, the living room was only one old sofa and a television, so it wasn't all that formal either. The good part was you could watch TV while you got your hair done. The bad part was, there was nowhere to run.

Star dashed back through the kitchen to the hallway and into the living room again to keep ahead of him. It wasn't a large house, and there was only a basic circuit that they could run: around the island cabinet that separated the kitchen from the dining room, down the hall into the living room, and back into the kitchen through the beauty station and the swinging door that joined the two rooms.

It wasn't much of a chase, but it was on.

"This is Dave Ryan, can I help you?"

"Dave, hi," Sami said from her end. "I'm relieved you're still at the office."

"Well, that makes one of us," he said with a good-natured laugh.

"I'm Sami Rankin. I work for Jayne Hersfield, executive editor of *Mann* magazine. Are you by any chance in charge of the Miss R&R campaign?"

"Well, the head of the marketing department is in charge around here, but it was my idea. Or rather, the ad agency's idea. But I came up with

Miss R&R. Best thing that ever happened to me really."

"Hold for Miss Hersfield please," Sami said, hitting the hold button and raising both arms above her head, touchdown style. "Yes!" she exclaimed victoriously, then said into the intercom, "Jayne, the man with the information you're looking for is on line one."

"Yes!" Jayne said, pulling a fist. "Marsten, you'll excuse me a minute?"

"For this?" He smiled at her. "You bet."

Sami's voice issued forth from the intercom: "His name's Dave Ryan. He's the sports promotions coordinator for Zax beer."

"Dave," Jayne said, hitting the button as she picked up the receiver. "Jayne Hersfield, *Mann* magazine. How are you?"

"Doing great," he said. "And I know I speak for all my fellow readers when I say, so are you."

"Well, thanks, Dave," Jayne said affably. "It's always nice to hear. I'll be sure to pass that along to Mr. Mann the next time I speak to him. I'm sure he'd love to have you up to the Castle next time you're in L.A."

"I could leave now," Dave said with a little laugh, only half-kidding.

The bragging rights of an invitation to the Mann Castle were one of the most coveted trophies in the showcase of the red-blooded male. Famed as the headquarters of the sexual revolution, Marsten

Mann's opulent hilltop home had become a symbol of the good life and good living. Constantly peopled with the world's most beautiful women, and the richest and most famous men, the Castle was as much a place of power as it was of hedonism. As time and the sexual revolution had passed, the Castle remained a symbol of the all that was desirable, a legend of the best of times.

"Anytime, I'm sure," Jayne said, knowing full well the power and cachet that came with being one of the three people in the world who could issue such an invitation. "Listen, Dave, I'm wondering if you could help me out here?"

"Sure, Jayne, whatever I can do," Dave said, glowing from his open invitation to the bastion of testosterone.

"Well, I'm interested in getting in touch with your Miss R&R—Star I believe it is?"

"Star Wood Leigh," Dave said, proud to be able to help out the folks at *Mann*. "I'm sure I have her number right here on the Rolodex. Hang on a sec. . . ."

"Right, got it," Jayne said triumphantly, writing it down. "Talon's Nail and Tan Spa, uh-huh. Mother Pearl's you said, right. Okay, okay. Great, well, surely one of those numbers will work for her. Dave, thanks for helping me out here. You're a lifesaver. I'm going to switch you back to Sami now. She can give you the contact information so we can arrange that visit the next time you're on the coast. . . .

Perfect. Can't be too soon. Don't work too late now, hear? . . . All right, hang on," she concluded, putting the phone on hold and hitting the intercom. "Sami? Talk to Dave. He needs your contact information so you can set him up for a visit to the Castle. But make it snappy. Then get in here. We've got some important calls to make."

"You got it, boss lady," Sami's voice came back.

"You want to pick this up later?" Jayne offered, turning to Marsten, who was looking over the preliminary proofs for the next month's layout. "Or would you like to stick around for this?"

"I wouldn't miss it for the world." He grinned, looking down at Star's photo.

"You missed me," Star shouted, popping up over the counter as the cereal bowl smashed against the wall behind her. "Now you gotta kiss me."

"I'll kiss you, all right," Adam said, giving chase as they took up the circuit—down the hall, rounding the living-room turn, through to the kitchen, and back again. Adam fell farther and farther behind each time they ran it, until finally he was waiting for her when she rounded the turn and came back into the kitchen.

He body-blocked her, but she hit him with enough force that they both lost their balance, slipped on the lasagna, and fell, smashing into the kitchen cabinets.

"Well, Adam," Star said, breathing heavily from all the running. "You got me. Now what are you going to do with me?"

"This," he said nastily as he pulled the drawer out above her and dumped the silverware over her head, drawer and all.

"You son of a—" Star said through clenched teeth, breaking off. "No, I like your mother too much to blame her for an asshole like you." She scooped up a big blob of the uncooked lasagna and smeared it in his face.

"Ow, my eye," he shouted, clutching his face. "That lime juice burns."

"Good," Star said, rising.

"Oh, no, you don't," he said, grabbing at her, but the sauce made her slippery and she slid through his fingers.

"You had your chance with me and you blew it, Adam. If you want work as a photographer, go ask Marci for a job."

"Oh, give me a break," Adam said, struggling to his feet. "Marci is a professional. You're just a fluke. This whole thing is a fluke."

"Marci is a waitress at a topless cocktail lounge," Star snarled. "She may be a professional, but I'm not sure she's a professional model."

"You wait and see. This whole Zax flash in the pan will be over at the end of football season and you'll be a has-been before you're twenty-two. Nobody will want you. In fact, they wouldn't want you now if you weren't such a drunken whore that you waved your tits at an entire stadium full of people. You're not a real model. This isn't for real."

"You know, Adam, you're right. I am pretty stupid," Star said with a huge shrug, her arms slapping against her sides. "I actually thought you'd be happy for me."

The phone rang.

"Happy for you? That's a laugh. I'm embarrassed for you. Making such a fool of yourself. Have you seen these things? Now you can realize your lifelong ambition and be in every bar in Miami at the same time."

Star flipped him the bird as she answered the phone.

"Hello?" she said sweetly.

"Star Wood Leigh?"

"Yes, it is."

"Star, I'm so glad we found you. Can you hold for a minute for Jayne Hersfield?"

"Jayne whose field?" Star asked, picking a mushroom off her cheek.

"I'm sorry, my name is Sami Rankin. I work at *Mann* magazine. Jayne Hersfield is my boss; she's the executive editor of the magazine. Do you have a minute to talk?"

"Sure, I guess."

"Sure, I guess," Adam imitated, making fun of her as he opened the refrigerator and took out a beer.

"Thanks," Sami said. "Hang on a sec."

Star put a finger in her ear to ward off Adam's taunting. The music on hold came on as Cheryl Lynn belted out a couple of lines:

What you find
What you feel
What you know
To be real

Angry and more than a little confused, she couldn't decide if the call was for real or just someone pulling her leg.

"Hello, Star?"

"Yes," she said suspiciously.

"Star, this is Jayne Hersfield, can you hear me all right?"

Adam shook up his beer and walked through the lasagna to where Star stood, her finger still in her ear.

"Are you trying to sell me a subscription?"

There was laughter on the other end of the line. A man's laughter, Star thought.

"No, Star," Jayne said, still laughing a bit. "I'm the executive editor. I saw the pictures Billy and Skip took of you when they were out in Miami. I'm considering you for the cover."

"Really?" No one would know about the photos Skip and Billy took of her, she reasoned, so she could at least trust that.

"Really?" Adam mocked, popping the can and spraying her with beer.

Star swung wildly to get him to back away.

Stepping back to avoid her reach, Adam's foot hit a patch of sautéed zucchini and he went down again.

"That's right," Jayne said. "I see a real quality in you that I think could work for us. I'd like to fly you out to L.A. for a test."

"Could you hang on for one second?" Star said.

"Um, sure," Jayne said, not really accustomed to being put on hold.

"It's *Mann* magazine," Star hissed at Adam, who was lying on the kitchen floor drinking what was left of his beer.

"Sure it is," he scoffed with a snort of laughter.

"Okay, do you know the name of their executive editor?"

"Of course," Adam harrumphed.

"Is it Jayne Hersfield?"

"Anyone could know that," Adam said, unconvinced.

"Well, they saw my pictures and they want to fly me to Los Angeles for a test shoot for the cover of the magazine," Star taunted. "What do you think of that?"

"I think you'll fall for anything," Adam said, laughing cruelly. "They only want a test. They've seen your picture and they're still not sure. You're a fluke. You're not a real model."

"Fine. We'll just see about that," Star said, taking her hand away from the phone and in effect broadcasting the words into Jayne's office from the speakerphone. "Jayne? You still there?"

"Hi, Star, yeah, still here."

"It's just a test, right?"

"That's right, Star. We'd fly you out here for a full professional shoot."

"Yeah, I don't think so, Jayne. Thanks for thinking of me, but you've seen my photos. Call me back when it's for real."

The dial tone filled Jayne's office.

She and Marsten exchanged a look and then broke up laughing.

"She's something," he said.

"What do you think?" Jayne said.

"Let me see those pictures again."

"There," Star said, hanging up the phone. "Now we'll see once and for all who's for real."

"What?" Adam asked, avoiding a little kick as she passed on her way to get the mop off the service porch.

"I told them that I wasn't interested in a test, that they should call me back when it was for real." She plopped the bucket into the sink and began to fill it with warm water as she rummaged underneath for some Spic and Span.

"Who was it really?" Adam asked, leaning back

against the cabinet doors. "Theresa? Randy and Andy? Some of that other trash you hang around with?"

"She said she was Jayne Hersfield." Star shrugged, shutting off the water and hefting the bucket back down onto the floor. "If you see my picture on the cover of *Mann* magazine, you'll know it was her."

She knelt, picking up the pieces of the broken Corningware and scooping the ruined lasagna into the trash. "You know, Adam," Star said calmly, "this was actually a really great day for me."

Adam shrugged and took another pull at his beer.

Star dipped the strings of the mop into the sudsy water and wrung it out before slapping it against the tile floor. For a few moments the only sounds in the room were the slap of the mop and the slosh of the water. The rhythm was soothing.

Star wondered if the magazine would ever call her back. She wondered if it was too late to call and tell them that she'd changed her mind. She wondered if she would kill Adam if she hit him in the head with the mop.

Slowly the mess dissolved into a bucket of blood-colored water and she set the bucket and mop aside. She knelt and tossed the silverware into the sink, slid the drawer back into its pocket, and began to wash the silver, the last evidence of their fight.

The phone rang.

Star looked at it and then at Adam.

It rang again.

She turned off the water and dried her hands on her jeans.

Another ring.

She crossed to answer it.

She was afraid and let it ring.

It's probably somebody else she assured herself as she let it ring again.

"If you don't answer it, I will," Adam said.

She picked it up.

"Hello?" she said, gesturing for Adam to come listen in.

He stood next to her, their faces side by side.

"Star?"

"It is."

"Star, this is Jayne Hersfield again."

"Hi again, Jayne," Star said tentatively, giving Adam a look.

He shrugged skeptically.

"Yeah, well, I've never done this before, Star," Jayne explained. "After we talked, I had another look at the pictures, and I've only got one thing to say to you."

Star held her breath.

"It's for real."

4

don't leave me
this way

"For she's a jolly good fellow, for she's a jolly good fellow," the chorus of drunken voices rang out at Mother Pearl's. Mother was leading the song, tears in his eyes. Star couldn't help but cry a bit herself.

Originally her plan had been to go to Los Angeles, do the cover shoot for the magazine, do a little sightseeing, put her feet in Marilyn's footprints at the Chinese Theatre, then come home and bank the money. That much more for cosmetology school. But as with all important decisions, she'd wanted to discuss it with her parents. The cover of *Mann* magazine was not nearly the same as Miss R&R or even the shorts and T-shirt uniform from Mother Pearl's. It was a national magazine and it was about sex, no kidding around.

Star knew *Mann* magazine and thought it was well done. The women were beautiful and the layouts were what Theresa had called "sexy, provocative, tasteful, and, most of all, professionally done." Where the Hooters mentality that fueled the tight T-shirts at Mother's was a dirty giggle, *Mann* magazine was a celebration of sex; Star was even a fan of their sister publication, *Mann Talk,* which specialized in erotic fiction. She figured she'd do it no matter what her parents said, but she'd rather hear about it before than after. She expected some opposition, but she was completely unprepared for what happened.

"Mom? Dad?" she called, making her way inside. "Mutley!" she cried as her beloved dog bounded into the room to greet her. Star fell to her knees and the two wrestled around on the living-room floor for a minute.

"Well, my God, Star," her mom said, coming into the room. "Get up off the floor. You're a grown woman."

Star tackled her mom, grabbing her around the knees. The three of them wound up on the floor, laughing and rolling around.

"Did I miss the first round of drinks?" Star's dad asked with a teasing grin, catching them.

"Help me up, Rick," Lucille said, extending her hands. "Thank God you've come to save me from these two." Of course he fell for it, and of course she pulled him down with the rest of them.

Breathless and laughing, they all ended up sitting on the floor, leaning against the furniture, Mutley making his way joyfully from one to the next.

"Well, Star," her mom asked, catching her breath from the horseplay, "what's got you so frisky?"

"Aw, Mom," Star said, giving her mom's ribs a little tickle. "I've been in trouble for roughhousing indoors since I was old enough to walk. I'm just old enough to get away with it now."

"Get away with it?" Rick said, rising to his feet and hoisting Star over his shoulder in a fireman's carry. "What makes you think you're old enough to get away with it now?" he asked, playfully spanking her as she lay helpless over his shoulder, kicking and squealing. Mutley began jumping and barking, unsure of what this all meant or what his duty was.

"All right, all right, all right," Lucille said, raising herself off the floor and holding up her hands like a traffic cop. "That's it, that's enough; my God, the neighbors will think we're the trailer trash that they've come to know we are over the years. But there's no point in confirming it for them."

Star and her father fell laughing onto the sofa.

"Who wants an RC?" Lucille said, making her way to the fridge. "We're out of root beer, Star."

"Me," Rick called. "And I think Star only

drinks Zax now," he said, tickling her as he teased.

"Here we are," Lucille said, returning with three Royal Crown colas.

"Thanks, Mom," Star said, taking the soda. "Sit down, will you? Listen, you two; I came out here for your advice about something."

"Who are you and what have you done with our daughter?" Lucille asked, sitting heavily in the nearby recliner, still a bit winded from their games.

"Now, Mom," Star said. "You know that's not true. I always ask you all what you think about what I should do."

Both her parents choked with laughter.

"Star," her mother cackled. "You always ask us about what you should do about the mess you've made doing whatever it was you wanted to do in the first place."

This only made her parents laugh harder, and Star couldn't help it.

"Okay," Star said, raising her hands in surrender. "This time, I'm actually asking you before I make the huge mess."

More laughter.

"Princess," Star's father said, reaching out to stroke her chin with one of his big, callused fingers. "I believe in you, Star, whatever it is you do."

"I'm waiting to hear what it is this time," Lucille said, breaking the moment. "And if it's that

Miss R&R thing with the beer, people on Mars have already heard."

"No, it's not that." Star grinned, realizing that with one thing and another she'd kind of forgotten to mention the Zax job to them.

"I can't walk down the street in this town without someone saying something about it," Lucille said, taking a sip of her RC.

"It's true." Rick grinned. "You're a regular local celebrity. You're everywhere! I think it was the Taylor boys who started poaching those things. Now it seems like everyone on the key has taken to stealing those cardboard cutouts from the bars and putting them on the front porch or in the window, or on the seat beside them in the pickup. I passed you in three Chevys just this morning. It's the damnedest thing. Like the whole town is one big photo album."

"Well, I'm glad you two are pleased, 'cause I've been asked to do another photo. For a magazine this time," Star said, easing into it. "It'll be on the cover, and they assure me it'll be a beautiful shot."

"What magazine?" Lucille asked flatly.

"And they'll do my hair and my makeup and clothes," Star went on with her rehearsed speech.

"What magazine?" Lucille asked again, as expressionlessly as before.

"And I think the key word here is *clothes*," Star continued undaunted, a trait she'd clearly inherited from Lucille.

"What—"

"It's for *Mann* magazine," Star relented.

Rick whistled.

"There going to fly me out to Los Angeles for a couple of days, and they're putting me up at a hotel so it shouldn't cost a bunch," Star went on with her speech. "And it'll pay almost a whole year of tuition for cosmetology school."

There was a moment's silence when she finally ran out of steam and stopped talking.

"Well, it'll be nice to see some other photos of you around town," Rick said with a little shrug to break the silence. "I was getting kind of tired of just the one."

Star's mom upended her RC, finished it off, and left the room.

Star exchanged a look with her dad. He winked and patted her shoulder. She gave him a smile and then rose to follow for the final and official verdict. She was more nervous about her mom's reaction than she was about the shoot itself. And she was plenty nervous about the shoot.

"So, what do you think, Mom?"

"Honey, what's going on with your hair?"

"Mom," she pleaded, making it two syllables.

Lucille rinsed the empty RC bottle, then put it in the plastic crate she'd return with the empties to the Pancake House. She looked at her daughter thoughtfully as she dried her hands on the towel that was threaded through the mismatched drawer pull. "Well," she said at last, "if it was me, I'd do it."

"It's too good an offer to turn down," Star began, continuing with the argument she'd rehearsed. "It's as much as I can earn in six months at the two jobs . . . What?"

"I said, 'If it was me, I'd do it.'"

"You think I should do it?"

"Yeah," Lucille said with a tight nod.

"Well, me too. And I figure it can't hurt this Miss R&R gig when I get back—"

"I don't think you should come back," Lucille said, cutting her off abruptly.

Silence.

"Come again?" Star said at last.

Lucille took a deep breath. "I don't think you should come back here, Star." She dropped into a chair at the kitchen table and put her face in her hands. "I hate to say it. But if I didn't, it'd just be selfishness, 'cause I want you here, in your old room if I can get it, but for your own good, Star, you should get out there and use this money and any you've got saved to get yourself started. Hell, you can wait tables in Los Angeles as well as you can here." There were tears in her eyes, despite her laughter.

"Mom," Star said, taking her mother's hand.

"I just think you'd have more of a chance there, Star. A chance for more. There's a lot going on and I'd hate to see you stay here and marry that Adam and wind up waiting tables at the Pancake House." Lucille patted Star's hand.

"Don't, Mom," Star began, shaking her head strongly.

"Don't get me wrong. I don't feel sorry for myself. I'm having a great life. I live on an island paradise and with a sailor in my bed. It's great for me. But you're not an extension of me or this pissant town. Star, you are your own person."

Star stared into her mom's eyes. Once again, Papa Jens's words came back to her. It was as though he were speaking to her through the people around her.

"Papa Jens used to say that to me," she said quietly, near tears.

"Did he?" Lucille grinned, remembering him. "Well, he was usually right, so maybe that's a good sign. I just figure you can always come back. Adam and the Pancake House will still be here."

"I love you, Mom."

And that had been that.

She and her mom and Theresa had been crying off and on pretty much ever since. Star had cried moving her stuff out of the duplex, and she'd cried moving Vanda's stuff in to take her place. She'd cried when Miss Elliott had slipped her a hundred-dollar bill on her last day at Talon's.

"For emergency," Miss Elliott said, hiding her own tears as she thrust the bill into Star's hand. "Sew it in your bra for just in case. You good girl. You always got job here."

And she was crying with Mother as they sang

the final strains of "For She's a Jolly Good Fellow" at her going-away party.

"Speech, speech," the little crowd called out to her.

"Oh, God," she said, wiping away the tears. "If this keeps up, I'm going to be too dehydrated to travel."

There was a little laughter.

"I don't have a speech," she said with a shrug. "I feel like I'm going off to war or something. I'm just moving to Los Angeles and I don't want to make too big a thing out of it in case I fall on my face and have to come back here. So, I'll just make a toast."

She looked around the room at the faces of her family and her friends; everyone was there with one conspicuous absence. No one had heard from Adam.

"I'm not leaving you all behind. Everything I am, everything I do, all that I believe, is made up of little bits of all of you. So, in a way, you're all coming with me. Here's to us. Bon voyage, life is but a dream."

Everyone cheered, and of course, there was more crying.

No one cried harder than Brandi.

"God, we haven't been separated since you were kicked out of tenth grade for staging that prison break in biology class," Theresa said, laughing at the old memory and trying to keep up a brave front to support her dear friend.

"Lord," Lucille cackled, rolling her eyes. "My child the activist."

"Prison break?" Randy asked.

"Well, they had all these poor little animals in cages in that awful room," Star said, bemoaning their fate all these years later.

"They were more like house pets than prisoners," Theresa said, laughing. "Bunny rabbits and guinea pigs and hamsters and this moldy old garter snake who loved to wrap himself around your arm and nap. They all had names, but I can only remember we called the snake Bogart because someone found him on Key Largo."

"It was inhumane," Star insisted.

"It was a petting zoo." Theresa giggled.

"So I did what I had to," Star asserted.

"She sneaked in at night with the cleaning crew and let them all out of their cages."

"They were free at last," Star said, raising a fist without much conviction.

"The trouble was, none of them wanted to leave," Theresa said, breaking up. "So for weeks after Star's conviction—"

"I claimed responsibility," Star insisted.

"You got a week off from school," Lucille edited. "I never get why they thought that was punishment. You want to punish kids, make 'em go to school on nights and weekends."

"Anyway, the school was overrun with mice and hamsters and bunny rabbits," Theresa said, riding herd on her story, knowing full well that Star and Lucille were shameless rustlers. "You'd be going about your business on a normal school day and there'd be a bloodcurdling scream. Someone would have found a white rat in their locker or a gerbil in their book bag. It took a while to catch them all, but slowly the menagerie in the biology lab was restored. Not one animal left the building. The last and most persistent was Bogart."

"The true radical." Star nodded, making fun of her ninth-grade self.

"No one could find him," Theresa went on. "We all thought we'd lost him for good. We thought we'd never see him again. And then one day during lunch, Miss Veda, the lunch lady, stuck her hand into a box of lettuce and Bogart wrapped himself around her wrist. I swear they heard the scream in Tallahassee—"

But that was as far as she got. At first they thought Theresa was just laughing, but she looked up and they realized she was hysterical. It was that kind of crying that comes on so hard and so intense that you can't get your breath to stop. Her mouth was open in a silent scream, tears pouring. She threw her arms around Star until the spasm passed and then finally managed to croak, "Who will take care of everyone? What will happen to all the stray dogs?"

Star didn't get a chance to answer her. As she hugged Theresa, rubbing her back, she spotted him, standing on the deck, watching the party through the window. "Mom," Star said, pushing Theresa's tearstained face toward Lucille's. "Could you two look after each other for a minute?"

Without waiting for an answer she made her way out to the deck.

"Hi," she said, leaning in the doorway. "I was wondering if you'd come to say good-bye."

"Well, I haven't," Adam said, shoving his hands into his pockets belligerently.

"I see that," Star said, folding her arms and giving him a look. "So, what did you come to say?"

"You'll be back," he said with a little shrug. "But if not, I hope you do good, Star."

"Well, thanks for that at least." Star shifted from one foot to the other. "You know, Adam, thank you for asking me to marry you. It was sweet of you and it made me feel special. I'm sorry I didn't just tell you no. I didn't because I didn't want to hurt you, and I think I hurt you even more this way. I'm sorry for that. I wish you good luck, Adam."

She kissed him abruptly on the cheek, then turned to go inside.

"See you on the rack at the 7-Eleven," he chuckled.

"Thanks," she said with a quick turn.

As she opened the door to go back inside, Thelma Houston's voice cut into the night, and though she didn't see it, Adam cried just a little before he turned to go.

Oh baby please, don't leave me this way . . .

"Come listen to my story 'bout a girl named Star," her younger brother, Hank, sang into the door of her old room as she tried to pack. "Had a magic T-shirt that took her very far."

"Cut it out, Hank," Star said, throwing a pillow at him off the bed.

"The kinfolks said Star move away from h'yar."

"Mom, make Hank stop it."

"Said Californy is the place you ought to be, so they loaded up the truck and they dumped her in the sea. 'Swim,' they said. 'It's not so far.' "

"Mom!?"

"Star," Lucille shouted back. "Shut the hell up and kick your brother's butt. You know you can take him two falls out of three. Besides, it might be a long time before you have the chance again."

Star only had to run as far as the door to her room and Hank was already across the front porch and running down the street. She only smiled after him. She knew the teasing was just his way of saying he'd miss her.

Star decided she would say her good-byes to everyone at the house and that Lucille would take her to the airport in the pickup so Mutley could ride along. Varmints were strictly forbidden in

Lucille's ancient but spotless Thunderbird with the suicide doors. Star was more than a little nervous. She'd never been on a plane before, none of her family had, and they were not well acquainted with the process.

The airport was just north of Star's old place in Miami Springs, about forty miles north of the key. So it had seemed as if they had plenty of time. What hadn't really occurred to them was that, unlike the Greyhound station, you didn't just drive alongside the plane and toss your luggage in the open baggage compartment underneath.

Unaware, Star lingered on the porch, hugging her father and even Hank, who tried to act as if he didn't mind her leaving nearly as much as he really did.

"You kidding?" Hank had said. "Now you'll be far enough away that I can really have your room."

Star felt protective of her brother. He was younger and couldn't seem to manage their parents the way she could. Star was the official family peacemaker—sometimes with sweetness and sometimes with saber rattling—always managing to still the battles and shield her brother from becoming a casualty in her parents' wars.

Hank had moved out after high school mostly just to get away. He'd gotten a place in Florida City with a buddy from the Gulf station where he worked.

"You don't even live here anymore," Star chided.

"I might if I had a good room like yours," Hank said, kicking dirt in the drive with his toe.

"You're going to be okay," Star said quietly, giving him a reassuring hug. "You've got your own place now. Remember, it's just how they love each other is all. It's got nothing to do with you."

"I'll miss you," he said just as quietly.

"Not a bit," she said, pinching his chin.

"Well, honey," Rick said, taking her in his arms, "I guess this is it, till the next time anyway. You can't come home with your dirty laundry anymore. But you can come home anytime you want. I'll be right here waiting for you. I'm proud of you, Star. I'll always believe in you."

"Thanks, Dad." She hugged him.

"Well, my God," Lucille said, climbing into the cab of the pickup. "You're draggin' this out like a Debra Winger death scene."

"Up you go," her father said, lifting his daughter up onto her seat, something he hadn't done since she was a little girl. It was a touching and sentimental gesture, especially for her father. "I got this for you, in case of emergency." He handed her the Miami Dolphins phone card he'd gotten as a premium when he'd bought a bed liner for the truck. "So you can always call home."

"All right then," Lucille said, choking the engine to life. "You boys don't burn the house down. I'll be back soon enough."

Mutley barked some orders from the truck window before settling down to weather Lucille's unpredictable driving to the airport. Riding with his head out the window was one of Mutley's favorite things, and Star had wanted to give him the treat one more time before she left.

They rode in silence for a bit, up the Overseas Highway, a rather improbable series of bridges and roadways that strung the keys together and made them a part of Florida. Star took the rather miraculous roadway for granted most of the time; it was so much a part of her life. But today, everything seemed rare and special.

"Well," Lucille said, ending the quiet. "I feel like I should say something wise. I don't know that my life is any picture or why anyone would want my advice about it. I love your father but I can't stand him. Maybe that's the advice. Don't do what I did unless you want what I got." She laughed and wished for the first time in years that she still smoked.

"Oh, Mom," Star said, not sure how to respond. She was on the record and now didn't really seem the time.

"I don't know." Lucille shrugged. "Life is not a box of chocolates. I do know that much. That is the stupidest thing I ever heard. I mean, imagine how dull that would be? If you have watermelon every day, it takes some of the fun out of summer when it comes. Life is like sex. It's not always good, but it's always worth trying."

"That's the one, Mom," Star said, laughing as she squeezed her mom's knee.

They got to the airport with fifteen minutes to spare. They were a little surprised that you couldn't get any closer to the business end of the place, what with security being what it was, but they stopped and unloaded Star's bags. Mutley was up and down and barking at anyone who offered to help, so Star was left to fend for herself pretty much.

Star said good-bye to her mom at the curb.

"Thanks for this, Mom," she said, hugging her. "I don't think I'd have had the nerve without your push."

"That's how you learn to fly," Lucille said, giving her a hug. "Try not to turn into one of those Hollywood fools whose picture is always in the wrong places."

"I won't, Mom," Star said with a little laugh at the idea. "Bye, Mutley. You be good while I'm gone." She let the dog take her seat and closed the door. "Here we go," she said with a little forced laugh, lifting the bags onto her shoulders and trudging into the airport.

She looked around.

"Excuse me?" she said to a passing man in uniform. "Do you know where Concourse D is? For that matter, do you know *what* Concourse D is?"

The skycap laughed gently and pointed down a long hallway. "Look for the yellow. Just keep going this way down a ways," he explained. "You okay with all those bags?"

"I'd be better if they didn't put the plane so far from the door," she said, shifting the weight and striking out again. By the time she got to the American counter at Concourse D, she had two minutes to get on her plane.

The line of passengers snaked like the Suwannee toward the check-in counter: bedraggled tourists, sunburned and laden with raffia bags of crap made out of seashells; lizard-skinned retirees who'd baked themselves into leather on the golf courses; and of course the requisite number of screaming little kids.

"Excuse me," Star said, raising her voice to be heard from the back of the long line. "I'm supposed to be on my plane in two minutes and they tell me I need to have my bags checked. Do you suppose I could go first?"

There was some laughter.

"Let's see your ticket, ma'am," an agent said, heading her off.

"Oh, thanks," Star said, volunteering the ticket to the uniformed agent. "I don't know where I'm supposed to be. I've never flown before and I'm not sure what they need to check my bags for. There's nothing in them but clothes and a few personal items from home."

"Right this way," the agent said, unsnapping the turnbuckle that held the velvet rope in place. As the now less than amused passengers in the long line watched, the agent led Star to the first-class check-in station. "I've got some good news and some bad news," the agent said, heaving Star's bags onto the scale. "The good news is, you're in the right place. The bad news is, your plane leaves in thirty seconds and it's too late to stop it."

"You mean I've missed it?" Star asked sadly.

"I'm afraid so."

"Could I leave my bags here for a minute?" Star asked, stunned. "I need to make a phone call."

"Of course." The agent smiled indulgently as he began to check them in.

"Do you have some change?" Star asked, fighting back the tears.

"Change?" the agent asked, weighing the word as though unfamiliar.

"For the phone," Star explained, forcing a smile.

"Oh." The agent laughed. "I'll get these squared away for you here. If you'd like to step into the first-class lounge, they have phones you can use."

"It's long distance," Star explained, rummaging through her bag hurriedly for Jayne's number.

"We deal primarily in long distance here." The agent smiled, trying to reassure an increasingly agitated Star.

"Okay," Star said, making her way into the lounge.

"Hi," the hostess said. "Welcome to American first class. Can I help you?"

"Um, yeah," Star said, still looking for the number as she pulled things randomly out of her bag and put them on the reception desk. An extra dog collar, a box of tampons, sparkle body gel, nail polish remover, a bag of lime Gummi bears, and at last her wallet emerged from the seemly bottomless canvas bag. "There it is," she crowed triumphantly. "The guy in the coat at the thing said I could use the phones in here? I need to make a long-distance call."

"Oh, of course." The hostess helped Star gather her things and took her gently by the arm as she led her to one of a series of phone stations. "Here you go. Would you like something to drink?"

"Oh, God, I'd kill for a root beer," Star said with profound gratitude.

"No problem," the hostess said with an amused smile. "I'll send someone over."

"There it is," Star said, pulling the paper with Jayne's number and instructions on it from her wallet as though unearthing the Holy Grail.

"I'll leave you with it then," the hostess said, taking her leave.

Star was truly brokenhearted. All the farewells, all the good-byes, her parents' hopes for her, her dreams of Los Angeles, dashed just like that. She wondered how much the plane ticket had cost, but she resolved to pay it back no matter how long it took. She was sure Mother and Miss Elliott would take her back. They probably hadn't even had time to find replacements yet.

She took a deep breath and dialed.

"Card number, please," a pleasant voice said to her.

"I'm sorry," Star said, confused by the odd question. "Could I speak to Jayne Hersfield?"

"I need your long-distance calling card number," the operator explained briskly.

"Oh," Star said, her hopes falling, and then suddenly remembering. "Oh, okay, I have a Miami Dolphins phone card, will that do?" She pulled the card from her pocket. She wouldn't be needing it.

"Who's the issuer?" the operator asked.

"Well, I think he got it from the Dodge place."

"Okay," the operator said, starting to get amused. "You have the card?"

"Mmmhmm."

"Turn it over and tell me what it says on the back."

"Okay, it says 'Southern Bell'?"

It took a few minutes, but they placed Star's call to Jayne's office.

"Jayne Hersfield's office. This is Sami, can I help you?"

"Hi, Sami," Star said as brightly as she could muster. "This is Star Wood Leigh."

"Oh, hi, Star. How are you?"

"Not so good," Star said sadly, her mask slipping. "Something bad has happened. I need to talk to Jayne."

"Okay," Sami said, alarmed. "Hang on, let me get her."

"Thanks," Star said, trying to be as cheerful as possible. It wasn't their fault that she'd screwed everything up.

"Star?" Jayne said on the other end of the line before Star could even recognize the song on hold. "What's wrong?"

"I'll pay you back for the tickets," Star said, rushing into it headlong. "I didn't know it would take so long to get on board. I'm really sorry. I missed the plane and ruined everything. But thank you for giving me the chance. Everyone here was so excited for me. I don't know how I'll face them now that I've let everybody down—"

"Star, Star, Star," Jayne cut in, a bit less alarmed than when Sami had buzzed her through. "Are you telling me that the terrible thing that's happened is that you've missed your flight?"

"Yes," Star confessed, distraught. "I'm so sorry. How much was the ticket? I'll pay you back every penny."

"Oh, Star," Jayne said with a little laugh, hugely relieved. "It's going to be okay. Go ahead and check your bags and go to the Admiral's Club."

"I'm at the Flagship Club now," Star said, looking around. "Should I go look for the admiral?"

"No, no, wait right there and Sami will get you some new tickets. Have a drink, order what you like, I'll see that it's taken care of, just sign for it."

Jayne was so relieved after the fright Star had given her, it had actually improved her spirits. "You scared me, Star. I thought something bad had happened to you or your family. I'll see you soon. Hold on for Sami."

"Your root beer, ma'am," the waitress said, stopping by. "Can I get you something else? Would you like to see a menu?"

A couple of beers and a club sandwich later, Star had settled in to watch the *Jeopardy!* marathon on one of the giant televisions in the largely abandoned lounge.

Her father was a big fan, hardly ever missing a question. Star did her best, but she was never a match for her father's bottomless pit of information. She had been a straight-A student, but she'd had to work for it.

Things didn't come easy for Star. She wasn't a natural at anything. She studied hard for every A she got. She had to practice extra hours just to get on the volleyball team let alone play setter and win the South Florida Double A Championship. In many ways, it was because Star wasn't a natural that helped her to succeed. She was never able to rest on her laurels so she was always willing to work harder, try harder, go the extra mile. Not being naturally the best had turned out to be her edge.

"Miss Leigh," the agent said, gently touching her shoulder on the sofa where she'd fallen asleep in front of the TV. "Your flight is boarding now."

"Oh, yes, dear God," Star said, leaping to her feet. "How long do I have? Where are my bags? Oh, God."

"Relax," the agent said, laughing. "You have plenty of time and your bags are already checked."

"So where are they? Was there some problem?"

"No," the agent said, uncertain of her meaning. "There was no problem."

"Then where are they?"

"They're already checked."

"So, when you checked them, you didn't find anything wrong?" Star asked again, trying to be patient with the uncommunicative agent.

"Oh, no, no, ma'am," the agent said, grinning and not letting on. "They checked out A-OK and we went ahead and put them into the luggage hold of the plane for you. You just give these claim tickets to the gate agent on the other end," he said, pointing to the tags he'd stapled to the inside of her ticket folder.

"Well, that's a relief," Star said. "I wasn't sure what you'd be checking for. Nobody warned me."

"Here's your ticket," the agent said, deciding not to get on that ride again.

"And where's the plane?" Star asked, a bit excited again. "I've been at the airport all morning and I haven't seen a single plane."

"Well, let's just take care of that right now. Follow me and we'll get you up close and personal."

"Miss Leigh," the waitress called as the agent and Star made for the door. "There's a call for you."

"Really? Who?" Star asked, amazed that anyone would know she was there, let alone call her.

"Star, it's Jayne." Jayne said. "Sami said she got
you on a later flight."

"Thank you so much," Star said. "I really appreciate you being so understanding about all this."

"Not to worry," Jayne said, touched by Star's
sincerity. There was a certain naïveté that made
Jayne feel protective toward the girl. She understood
why Skip and Billy had taken to her so quickly.

"All the same," Star said with quiet firmness, "if
there's any difference in the cost, you can take it out
of my paycheck."

"Okay, well, we'll see," Jayne said, trying not to
laugh. "But I think you actually saved us some
money by taking a later flight. Look, here's the
deal. You'll be getting in to Los Angeles later
than we'd originally planned, so I'm going to have
a car meet you at the airport and bring you straight
to the Castle. We'll get you to your hotel later on.
But, it's fight night and I don't want you to miss it."

"Oh," Star said, suddenly serious. She'd seen ads
for wrestling on the flashing sign next to The Booby-
Hatch, the two pink domes just off Highway 1.

"You don't mind too terribly, do you?" Jayne
asked. "It'll be a good chance to be seen and to
meet Marsten."

"Well," Star sighed, a bit overwhelmed. "Okay,
but I won't do mud or oil."

"What?" Jayne asked, completely at a loss.

"Maybe I can arm wrestle or something?" Star suggested, not really knowing what to suggest. "I did a wet T-shirt contest once at the Coppertone beach promotion. But mud wrestling just seems to be, I don't know, a little too low-rent."

Jayne was near hysterics. "God, you are an original." She laughed. "I can see I'm going to have to keep my eye on you. Star, darling, we will be watching a boxing match on closed-circuit television in the Castle's theater. It's actually kind of dressy."

"Oh, thank God," Star said, giggling at her mistake. "I was wondering. I mean, I've heard wild stories . . . you never know."

"No, darling," Jayne assured her. "Marsten lives at the Castle with his wife. Now you go get on that plane and I'll worry about the rest."

"Yes, ma'am," Star said, and hung up.

"That girl," Jayne said aloud, shaking her head as she hung up the phone. "What will become of you in this place?"

5

welcome to the
hotel california

Star could see the storm clouds rolling in as she looked out the window by her seat on the plane. She was glad that her mom and Mutley would have had time to get home before the rain started. As she sat there, it really started to hit her, what she was doing, where she was going, how far away. She was a bit nervous about flying for the first time, but the butterflies in her stomach were not from that. It all seemed so final, so complete somehow. Los Angeles was so far away both in miles and in ways that couldn't be measured. It was a city of dreams both a source and a destination, the goal and inspiration of many. Brandi hadn't stopped crying, and Star knew in her heart that it wasn't over losing her friend. It was losing L.A.

The feeling of leaving was more like breaking up with someone. You know it's the right thing to do, but it just keeps hitting you again and again that you won't be there anymore. She'd lived within about fifty miles her entire life. She'd never even been to Orlando. Now she was headed for the original Disneyland.

"Would you care for something to drink?" the handsome young steward asked, leaning down to her.

"Oh, I don't know," she said, startled, looking away from the window. "I'm so full of root beer I'm about to burst. Tell the truth, I'm a little nervous and I don't think all this sugar is helping."

"Well, how about a little champagne to calm you down?"

"Does that calm you down?" Star asked, not sure of the logic.

"I don't know, but I think you don't care so much," he suggested with a smile and a shrug.

"Couldn't hurt," Star said, really noticing his beautiful eyes. "I'm Star, by the way."

"Of course you are." He grinned. "I'm Croix. Good to meet you. So, that's a yes to the champagne?"

"You talked me into it," she answered with a wink.

His look lingered on Star even as he turned away, almost colliding with an oncoming passenger on his way to the galley.

Star got her purse, rummaged for her wallet, and had just come up with it when Croix returned with her flute of champagne. He leaned in and deftly flicked the latch, causing her tray table to drop into place, eliciting a startled cry from Star.

"Oh! I didn't see that coming," she said, slightly embarrassed.

Croix just winked.

"How much do I owe you?"

"Owe? Ohhh," Croix said, realizing. "The drinks are complimentary. Is this your first flight?"

"Is it that obvious?" Star blushed deeply.

"Not a bit," he fibbed chivalrously. "I'm sort of an expert."

"Sure," she said, then sipped her champagne. "You're up here all the time; I bet you've seen it all."

"They ask us not to say," Croix said with a musical laugh that Star found attractive.

"You know, I trained to be a flight attendant," Star said, regretting the story at once. She'd signed up for a correspondence course she'd seen on a commercial with Sally Struthers. It was geared to flight attendants and travel agents, though what one had to do with the other she was never sure. Star hadn't studied hard and couldn't really remember whether she'd finished the course requirements.

"Oh, really?" he said, leaning on the seat back ahead of her and ignoring the other passengers. "What airline?"

"What?" Star asked, unclear on the concept. "Oh, no, I never got as far as an actual airline."

"I see," Croix said skeptically. "Well, you let me know if you need anything else."

"It was just a correspondence course," Star admitted, blushing again. "I saw it on TV with that lady from *All in the Family.*"

"Really," Croix said, sounding more alarmed than skeptical as he backed away. "I didn't know you could do that."

"Well, I didn't really," Star confided, taking a big gulp of the champagne. "I mean, do I seem experienced at this?"

That musical laugh again.

"No, not really," he said, smiling and giving her a wink that made it all better. "I'll check on you in a minute. I have to look in on the other passengers."

"Thanks," Star said, turning to the window. It was beginning to rain, and heavy, dark clouds were forming in the sky. Star was pleased to be safe and sound inside. She took another sip of her champagne and watched the luggage handlers working below.

"Star?" Croix said, stopping by. "You about finished with that?"

"No." Star laughed. "Are you trying to get me drunk?"

"As long as you're not flying the plane. Knock

yourself out. But I do need to get your glass for now. I'll get you a fresh one as soon as we're airborne."

"I think I remember that from the safety module." Star giggled. She started to hand him the half-filled glass, then thought better of it. "What the hell?" she said, then turned up the last of the wine.

"What the hell," Croix agreed, toasting her with the empty glass. "I'll bring you a fresh one right after takeoff."

"Whee!" Star giggled. Was it possible that Croix was cuter than he had been earlier?

"Ladies and gentlemen," the head attendant's voice crackled through the cabin speakers as Croix took up his position to perform the safety demonstration. Their eyes met and he smiled. As the head attendant narrated, Croix went through the balletic routine, revealing the safety card, demonstrating the oxygen masks, and pointing out lights and exits. He might just as well have been dancing the lead in *Swan Lake* for all Star knew. All she could think of were those eyes and that laugh—and those shoulders, that chest, those arms . . .

At the end of the demonstration, Croix disappeared to take care of his duties and Star's focus drifted out the window. The clouds looked even angrier and she was pleased that they were leaving just in time to miss the storm.

The plane lurched away from the gate and Star gave a sharp cry.

"You okay, ace?" Croix asked, flipping up her tray table. "You need to put on your seat belt now. And after we take off, remind me and I'll show you how that seat reclines so you can be more comfortable."

"Thanks," she said, digging for the ends of the seat belt as the plane rumbled across the tarmac to the runway. Despite the rather pronounced effects of the champagne, by the time the airliner was poised for takeoff Star was braced for impact, clutching the armrests as if the plane were going down rather than up.

The engines revved and the plane took off down the runway, picking up speed until the scenery outside was just a blur. Star clenched her eyes shut and held on as they ascended and gracefully took flight. A smile spread across her face as she remembered the sensation of cresting the top of the first hill on a roller coaster when it felt as if she could fly. Only now, on the plane, it wasn't followed by that alarming downward plunge. She was flying. She was really flying. Giddy, Star squealed with delight and the joy of her new adventure, and then a fierce shaft of lightning streaked past her window. The plane pitched as though it had run into a wall.

The joy and elation of only a moment before were immediately replaced with terror as she once again gripped the armrests and held on for dear life. The plane was buffeted about in the Miami sky, and it became clear that they hadn't missed the storm, but had rushed to join it. The reaction was mixed. Some passengers went dead quiet, while others gasped or screamed in the challenging ascent. It was more like the familiar roller coaster rides, but the problem was there were no tracks underneath.

An overhead bin sprang open and passengers were pelted with carry-on bags, blankets, and airline pillows. And the bronco ride continued. Star tried to look out the window, but the dark clouds surrounding them offered no point of reference. She had no sense of up or down, or anything for that matter. It reminded her of the tornado from *The Wizard of Oz* and Star half-expected to see Miss Elliott fly by on her manicure station. She remembered that the safest seats on the plane were in the back and was suddenly resentful that she had been forced to sit way up front. What she could not remember was the rest of her safety training from the Sally Struthers school for stewardesses, and she cursed herself for not studying harder, convinced that she was going to die. If only she had better study habits. Star was terrified. And all she could remember from Croix's demonstration was what pretty eyes he had, which she would never see again.

She wondered why people flew at all if it was like this.

And then it was over.

They broke through the clouds and the late-afternoon sun shone through the window. The plane leveled off, and aside from the occasional lurch, the flight became a whole different experience. Once they had attained what the captain called "cruising altitude," Croix reappeared with her champagne.

"Thanks," she said breathlessly, still a bit overwrought from takeoff. "I can sure see now why they're free."

"Excuse me," Star said, looking up from her ticket folder.

"Yes, ma'am, may I help you?" the agent said, eyes intent on the TV monitor above Star's head.

"Can you tell me where I can find lax?" Star asked, craning her neck to see what was on.

"Find . . . what?" the agent said, actually looking at Star.

"I'm looking for lax." Star pointed at her baggage-claim tickets.

"This is it, honey," the agent said with an expansive gesture to include the airport around them.

"It's called lax?" Star asked, trying not to laugh in her face.

"No, it's actually Los Angeles International Airport," the gate agent explained. "*L-A-X* for short."

"Short for what?" Star asked, more puzzled than before.

"It officially stands for nothing. Back in the thirties airports were only identified by two letters. The Los Angeles airport was known as L.A., which may be where people got started calling the city itself L.A. Well, there weren't many airports then, but after a while, they needed go to three letters to identify the larger number of airports, and so a third letter was added and it became LAX. The X officially stands for nothing."

"Okay." Star nodded ruminatively. "Then could I please have my bags?"

"Your first flight, huh?" The gate agent smiled at Star.

"That's right." Star smiled back. "How'd you guess?"

"You get a feel for these things," the agent said with a nonchalant shrug. "Your bag will be waiting for you by the exit. Just go along here and then take the escalator down. Follow the pictures of the suitcase," she offered, pointing.

"Well, that's better than Miami," Star said with a sigh of relief. "They make you carry your bags for miles. Right by the exit, huh?"

"You got it." The agent smiled, charmed by Star's wide-eyed appreciation of LAX.

"Thanks," Star said as she headed along the concourse. She got lost once looking at the shops rather than keeping an eye out for the pictures of the suitcase, but it was easily corrected and soon she was on the escalator heading down.

She saw him before she reached the ground. He

was standing in a sort of official-looking outfit holding a sign that was getting him laughs and remarks from passersby in the status-mad capital of the world.

The sign said simply STAR.

Star couldn't hear the remarks he was getting—she was about five steps up from the bottom of the escalator—but it caught her attention and made her wonder if there was some kind of problem. Maybe the lady at the gate had called ahead and this man had her luggage. Tentatively she walked toward him.

"Excuse me," she said. "Are you looking for a Star?"

"Very funny, lady," the young man said, looking past her.

"'Cause I am," Star said, not really understanding his joke.

"Great. Could I get your autograph?"

"Well, I'm not famous yet, but I guess—"

"Look, lady," the young man said, frustrated that she was still harassing him. "I've got work to do. I'm waiting to pick someone up and her name happens to be Star and that's why I have the sign, so if you could just let me do my job. Have a great visit to Los Angeles."

"Well, my name is Star. Star Wood Leigh. And I was wondering if you maybe had my luggage, but maybe you're my ride to the Castle?"

"*Ay, Dios mio,*" the driver said, tossing the sign aside. "I'm so sorry, Miss Leigh. I didn't realize, but of course I should have. You will be perfect for the Castle. I'm an idiot. So many people were giving me trouble about this sign. But you, truly, are a star," he concluded with a little bow.

"So, does that mean you don't have my bags?" Star clarified, ducking her head in a halfhearted bow of her own.

"Allow me," he said, extending his hand to her. "Your claim checks?"

Wordlessly, she handed him the ticket, folder and all.

"I will be right back, Miss Leigh," he said, bowing again.

"Call me Star," she said, smiling at his continued fawning.

"Yes, Miss Star," he replied, walking backward toward the luggage carousels as he continued to face her. He had intended to say "I'm Carlito," but as he began to speak, he tripped over a passing luggage cart and did a backflip over the trolley. "I'm Car-LITOOOOOOOOOO . . ." was what he actually said.

"Lito," Star exclaimed, rushing to his aid. "Are you okay?"

"Yes," Carlito said, brushing himself off as he scrambled to his feet. "I am fine. Not to worry about me. I'll be right back with your luggage, Miss Star."

"Lito," Star said, following him. "How will you know which bags are mine?"

"Well, I will check the claim ticket," Carlito explained, too embarrassed about the whole incident to correct her misapprehension about his name.

"Wouldn't it be easier if I came with you?" she asked as she pursued him across baggage claims. "I mean, I have seen my luggage before."

Lito stopped still and Star caught up with him.

"Miss Star," he said, hanging his head. "There's something I need to tell you."

"They've lost my luggage?" she gasped.

"I don't know, maybe," Lito said noncommittally. "But, Miss Star, this is my first day."

"Oh, Lito, that's perfect." Star beamed. She could not have been more relieved. At last someone with whom she did not have to be on her guard. "This is my first visit to L.A. Really, it's my first day too. We can figure this out together."

Eventually they found the carousel. "Kind of boring without the horses," she said, amazed at what passed for a carousel in Los Angeles. In due course, her bags were disgorged and collected.

Lito, of course, insisted on carrying all of them, over Star's strenuous objections, which slowed down their progress considerably. As they finally reached the car, the police were just about to tow the limo out of the loading zone where Lito had left it.

"What are you doing?" Lito cried, vaulting the last couple of steps.

"You can't leave your vehicle unattended here."

Having grown up in good-old-boy country, Star knew just how to play with the local boys in blue. They never knew what hit them.

"I am so sorry," Star said, tugging shyly at the vee in the front of her T-shirt. "This is all my fault," she went on, twisting the tee and biting her bottom lip. "This is my first time in Los Angeles. I'm here to have my picture made for the cover of *Mann* magazine, and they sent this nice gentleman over to pick me up. We're actually on our way over to the Castle now. Only I couldn't find the carousel 'cause there were no horses. And he had to come inside to rescue me."

She could have quit after *"Mann* magazine." In short order, the tow truck was dispatched and Lito got off with a warning.

"Thank you, Miss Star," Lito said, trundling the various pieces of mismatched luggage to the rear of the car and heaving them inside. "I'll just get this loaded and we'll get you to your party." He slammed the trunk and moved to hold the door for her. "Miss Star?" he called, looking around at the gritty underpass that was the pickup porte cochere.

The whir of an electric motor caused him to turn just as Star leaned out of the window on the passenger's side in the front seat.

"Oh, Miss Star, this is for you," he said, gesturing to the rear coach. "There's champagne and strawberries and TV and video games."

"This is my first time in Los Angeles. You think

I want to watch TV? Come up here and show me around. And bring the strawberries. Do we have time?"

"A little bit." Lito grinned, closing the door and coming around to get in the front seat with her. "We can see the blimp field and PCH and the sights along Sunset."

"The blimp field?" she exclaimed. "Blimps grow in fields?"

No one can tell anymore, but underneath the city of Los Angeles lies one of the most amazing pieces of real estate ever. A coastal desert plain, it is met at the shore by a mountain range that runs like a backdrop along the northern boundary of the Los Angeles basin. That means there's a broad and almost perfectly flat plane fringed on two sides by the ocean and broad, sandy beaches, and overlooked by a mountain ridge that appears suddenly along the edge of what would otherwise be a completely uninterrupted expanse. It must have been breathtaking for the first Native Americans, and later the conquistadors and missionaries who made their way over the Hollywood Hills to drink in a completely unobstructed view of the 3,000 square miles below.

Even today, after the paving of the basin, the Hollywood Hills and the Santa Monica Mountains afford that same expansive one-eighty view of the city.

Running along the spine of Los Angeles' private and self-contained mountain range is the legendary Mulholland Drive. The road is the zenith undulating along the high sustained ridge above the city spread out like a cloth below on both sides. The views are among the best in the city.

Perched along this crinkle formed by the collision of two tectonic plates, poised like the birds of prey that frequent the neighboring trees, the Mann Castle watches over the city below. Like a penthouse, the castle affords its guests pristine and unobstructed city views and the freedom and private isolation of Olympus.

The flatlands of the basin were a part of the landscape of Star's life, like the familiar monotony of the endless south-Florida tidal plain. But as the limo began to climb into the overgrown hills that were the Santa Monica Mountains, Star felt giddy and more than a little afraid of the winding roads and sheer drop-offs that cleaved alongside them.

The gate to the property was formidable but unobstrusive on a roadside grown thick with gates. "Miss Star Wood Leigh," Lito spoke into the intercom, reading her full name from his clipboard. The gates opened with a low hum.

"This is it," Star said through a gritted smile, her fists clenched in excitement and apprehension. "I've arrived."

The drive wound through a wooded area to

open out onto a broad rolling lawn and a view of
the massive main house—a formal French château,
not unlike the palace at Versailles. The yellow gran-
ite walls and blue slate roof, the perfect symmetry
of the two flanking wings balanced on the central
body of the house, even the formality of the
sculpted shrubbery of the front garden wrapped in
the oval drive, gave the place an air of propriety—
ironic given its reputation.

An amazing array of cars spilled out of the
motor court into the drive—Rolls, Bentley, Ferrari,
Porsche, Mercedes, Corvette, Cadillac, Lincoln, and
a seemingly endless line of limos.

Star gave a low whistle as she took it all in.

"This place is bigger than my high school," she
gasped.

As they drew near, the massive front door
opened and a tall, handsome woman emerged.
With an athletic body that her well-tailored business suit did more to enhance than conceal, she carried herself with an air of confidence and purpose
that was at once reassuring and intimidating. She
reminded Star of her old gymnastics coach. As they
drew up to the curb, the woman walked to the back
of the limo and opened the door to the rear compartment.

Lito leaped out and ran around to the passenger
door.

"Where is she?" the statuesque woman demanded of Lito.

"Well, she didn't want to ride in—"

Star cut him short, opening the passenger door and emerging backward onto the front steps of the Castle, hands filled with smaller carry bags.

"Star?" the woman said, puzzled and amused.

"Yes," she said, turning and trying to focus on the woman. There was so much to see and it felt as if she were trying to see it all at once.

"Star," the woman greeted her warmly as she approached, her hand extended. "I'm Jayne Hersfield. Welcome to Los Angeles."

"Hi," Star said shyly, taking Jayne's hand.

"What are you doing sitting in the front seat?" Jayne asked as she enclosed Star's hand in both of her own.

"I like to see where I'm going." Star shrugged it off. "Besides, it's lonely back there."

Jayne smiled.

"This place is amazing," Star exclaimed, throwing her arms wide and spinning to include as much of her surroundings as possible.

"Ah, yes, Mann Castle," Jayne acknowledged their opulent surroundings.

"Oh, yeah, it's a great house," Star said, nodding vigorously. "And this city, I mean what little I've seen of it. Driving up the coast and then up Sunset Boulevard and into the mountains. Why do they need Disneyland?"

"Just for fun." Jayne smiled at Star's complete lack of artifice. "Kind of like this place. We have to get you a tour, we've got a few minutes before the fight."

"That would be so awesome," Star agreed enthusiastically.

"You can just leave the bags here," Jayne said to Lito. "We'll stow your things and we can get you a car to your hotel when the time comes."

"I'll be here for Miss Star when the party's over," Lito said with a polite nod.

"Oh, that won't be necessary," Jayne assured him.

"I know," Lito said. "But it will be my pleasure. I've promised a bit more tour and I'm off the clock in ten minutes. The car can sit in my driveway or Mr. Mann's just as easily."

"Thanks, Lito," Star said, giving him a quick hug and a peck on the cheek. "That's so sweet."

"Okay then," Jayne said. "I guess you can just pull around behind the other limos. I'm not sure how long we'll be going tonight, though. If you change your mind, you can leave the bags and we'll take care of it."

"I'll be here," Lito assured her with his patented little bow.

"Well, let's go meet everyone," Jayne said, inclining her head to him respectfully as she ushered Star inside.

The Mann Castle and its singular resident, Marsten Mann, were legend. Originally based in an opulent Knickerbocker mansion in New York City where the magazine was founded, Marsten had gone West as his fortunes became more closely aligned with Hollywood, moving into the forty-four-room 1920s French Empire castle, bringing his entourage and legend with him. With the New York Castle turned condo and long forgotten, the Mann Castle West had gained a place in the American imagination, a symbol of the sexual liberation and libertinism that Marsten and his publications had come to represent. The truth and the legend of the place had become blurred, creating a reputation where fact and fiction were hard, if not impossible, to separate.

For Star, the tour was even more amazing than the stories she'd heard from Adam and her brother, Hank; they were more intoxicated with the "secret" deeds that had reportedly taken place in the Castle than with the halls that held the secrets.

The place was incredible. A stream ran the length of the stately front lawn, connecting a series of elaborate fountains before running through the living room and out the back of the house to the Castle's notorious lagoon, which was stocked with naked women.

"Marsten doesn't allow swimsuits in the lagoon," Jayne explained with a knowing grin. "He says it keeps lint out of the filters."

"Very sensible." Star nodded, following her across the patio to the cabanas on the far side.

"These dressing rooms were built by the first owners in the twenties and were used by many famous silent-movie stars as was the pool," Jayne explained. And with that, one of the doors sprang open and a naked couple raced across the flagstones and disappeared under the waterfall.

Star wondered why they needed dressing rooms if everyone was skinny-dipping.

"It was Marsten who replaced the original pool with this lagoon," Jayne explained, pausing near the French door that led back inside. "That rocky cliff and the waterfall beyond are man-made, catacombed with dozens of little private pools and nooks when you want to get away for a more intimate moment."

Star paused to marvel at the flock of nude women in and around the pool. They were so beautiful. Why had she been chosen for the cover of such a storied magazine?

"Come on, Star," Jayne said, taking her arm. "Lots more to see."

"Lots more" turned out to be a bowling alley, a nightclub-size discotheque, and even a full-size movie theater. An arcade-quality game room was filled with all manner of diversions, from pool table to video games, and along its perimeter ran a series of small, windowless rooms, each completely and totally awash—walls, ceiling, floor, and furnishings—in a single color. There was a red room, a blue room, a green room, perfectly upholstered little bedrooms offering a place for games of a different sort.

It was perhaps these small rooms that seemed most in keeping with the reputation of the place.

Peeking into the red room, Star reached into a crystal candy dish and took a mint. Without paying much attention she began unwrapping it . . . and was startled to find that it was a condom. They were everywhere: in bowls, jars, and dishes all throughout the house. An ounce of prevention, she thought.

The more of the Castle Star saw, the more amazing it seemed. Tennis courts, swimming pools inside and out, a gym, a wine cellar hidden beyond a secret passageway left over from Prohibition, playrooms, a formal ballroom, a television studio, and Marsten's two-story bedroom and office from which he ran the empire.

More remarkable still were the stars, sports figures, and celebrities who adorned the already lavish rooms and settings.

Many of the celebrated guests were lost on Star. She had spent her childhood and most of her adolescence either on the beach, the volleyball court, or in school. The movies were a sometimes treat, and the TV was usually tuned to some game or game show or other, though she did have her favorites. If Alex Trebek or Wayne Gretzky had walked in, she'd have known him right away, but George Plimpton and Ivana Trump might as well have been the caterers.

"Want something to drink?" Jayne asked as they

made their way around the grounds. "Or maybe some food? Here I am showing you around when you may need some refreshment after your trip."

"Yeah, that would be great," Star said, knocking into a distinguished-looking gentleman who looked more than a little familiar. "Oh, I'm so sorry."

"Don't worry about it, young lady," the man said, grinning at her mischievously. "At my age, I welcome any contact with young women that I can get."

"Say, don't I know you?" Star asked, cocking her head playfully.

"Star," Jayne began the introduction. "This is—"

"Stoney Curtis," Star said triumphantly. "From *The Flintstones*!"

"Why, yes, I am," he said graciously, even more charmed. "And who might you be?"

"I'm Star," she said, offering her hand. "Star Wood Leigh."

"Star is here to do the cover for our back-to-school issue," Jayne explained. "Oh . . . there's someone who we've been looking for, if you'll excuse us."

"Why, certainly," Tony said, turning back to his companions. "And I'll be here all evening if you'd like to run into me again." He smiled and kissed Star's hand.

"Thank you, Mr. Curtis," Star said with a little shiver. Her first celebrity kiss.

"My pleasure," he said.

"Oh my God," Star confided as they made their way up a broad flight of stairs, "I love *The Flintstones*. And look, isn't that Elizabeth Taylor?"

"Joan Collins," Jayne corrected as they emerged onto the massive formal deck that ran behind the house.

"This is killer," Star said, dashing to the elegant stone balustrade that bordered the precipice and showcased the astounding view of the city spread out below. "It's like we're in an airplane up here."

"There's Los Angeles," Jayne said.

"Did you know this place is named after the airport?" Star asked proudly.

"I did not know that," Jayne admitted, puzzled.

"The lady at the flight gate told me that."

"No kidding."

Jayne smiled. She spent so much time around people trying to be sophisticated and smart and generally trying to impress her for one reason or another, Star's ability to be completely herself was almost unnerving. She was like a week in the country. "Come with me, Star," she said, offering her hand. "There's someone I want you to meet."

Star gave her hand reluctantly, not ready to turn away from the breathtaking view. Glancing back over her shoulder at the gradually setting sun, she allowed herself to be led toward an older gentleman wearing his pajamas and his bathrobe. Still in her T-shirt and jeans, Star was relieved to meet someone at the party who was dressed even more inappropriately than she was.

"Excuse me, Marsten," Jayne said, interrupting his conversation with several other people, one of whom Star recognized from his days on her favorite cop show.

"Jayne," Marsten said warmly, turning to put an arm around her shoulder. "I believe you know everyone?"

"Yes, indeed," Jayne said, putting an arm round Marsten's waist. "Marsten, I want you to meet our back-to-school cover—"

"Star Wood Leigh," Marsten said, lighting up. "I'd recognize you anywhere." He extended both hands and enfolded both of hers. "I'm Marsten Mann. Welcome to my home and to the family."

"Hi, Mr. Mann," Star said, beaming, thrilled to meet the man she'd be working for. "What a great house. Thanks for inviting me." Star found Marsten delightful and charming. He made her feel as though they were alone together on the deck rather than surrounded by hundreds. Had she truly known whom she was speaking to she would have been far too intimidated to make the impression she made. But he was her new boss—and not for very long at that—and she spoke to him with the friendly respect she might have used with Mother on her first day at work.

"Well, you're welcome and please call me Mars, all my very best friends do," he said, still holding both her hands. He spread his arms and hers and looked her up and down unabashedly. "It's wonderful to see you. Come by here anytime you want."

"That's very kind of you, sir," she said, a bit shy of his gaze.

"Call me Marsten," he said, dropping her hands and taking her under his arm. "Let me introduce you to my colleague here. This is Van Pursens."

"From *Hip-Hop Cops*," Star gushed. "I know. I never missed an episode."

Van was clearly less than thrilled. He got his start as a teenager on the show, but had since made a respectable career for himself on film, in front of, and more especially behind, the camera.

"Hello, Star," Van said, doing his best to hide his irritation.

"So, what are you doing these days?" Star asked with a fan's interest. "It's not been the same since you graduated."

"This and that," Van said, increasingly irritated. "Directing mostly."

"Oh," Star said with a sympathetic nod, though she'd never really understood what a director did exactly. "Well, I hope you'll get cast in something again real soon."

"Thanks," Van said tightly. "Excuse me, won't you?" He turned abruptly and left.

Marsten chuckled.

"Here you go," Jayne said, handing Star a glass

of champagne and a small plate of finger food. "A toast," she proposed.

"To Star," Marsten said, raising his glass.

"Here, here," Jayne agreed, raising hers.

"Skoal," she offered. Papa Jens's toast was the only one she knew that seemed to suit such a nice party.

"This your first visit?" Marsten asked Star, trying to get her on familiar turf.

"Here and Los Angeles." Star grinned. "The farthest I've been from home before was a field trip we took to the state capital in Tallahassee."

"So, what does everyone think of you back home?" Marsten asked jovially. "Coming to the big city. Doing the cover of the magazine."

"Frankly my mother told me never to come back," Star said for effect.

She got it. Jayne and Marsten exchanged a troubled look.

"She thinks I should make the most of this big opportunity," Star said with a big smile.

"Oh," Marsten said with a little laugh. "Good for her. As well you should."

"Between you and me though," Star said confidentially, "I just think she wants me away from the guy I've been dating."

"A lot of parents want that," Marsten agreed, nodding.

"He's not so bad," Star said, not wanting to make Adam out to be too awful. "But it was time."

"Fallen out of love?" he offered.

"I'm not sure I ever was," Star said, opening up to this gentle and sensitive man. "He asked me to marry him, but I never gave him an answer. I think it hurt him. He started doing mean stuff. Meaner."

Marsten tightened his grasp and gave her a reassuring pat on the shoulder.

"Jayne?" A Jayne junior—but with red hair—inquired quietly to attract Jayne's attention without interrupting.

"Oh, Sami," Jayne said, catching Jayne junior by the elbow and drawing her more fully into the conversation. "This is Star Wood Leigh."

"Oh, yes, we spoke on the phone. Glad you got here okay," Sami said, shaking Star's hand. "Listen, I hate to interrupt, but the satellite feed begins soon and we need to bring folks into the theater. It would be great if you two could set an example."

"Right, of course," Marsten said. "Let me just freshen my drink and I'll head that way. Star, we should talk more. Jayne, you'll see we get a chance, huh?"

"I sure will, won't I, Sami? And I'll head in now," Jayne said. "Star, you coming?"

Star gazed at the fiery explosion of orange as the sun hit the sea in the distance.

"I've never seen the sun set on the Pacific."

"Well, you take your time," Jayne said. "You remember the way. I'll save you a seat for the event. Just listen for the gong."

"Thanks. I'll be right in."

As the others went their separate ways, Star returned to her favorite part of the Castle. It wasn't the art or the pools or the electronics or even the star-studded guest list that enchanted her. It was the view. She leaned against the broad stone railing and breathed it all in. She could feel the warmth of the stone under her hands. It was amazing to be outside and this high up at the same time. Miami had tall buildings, but above sea level was considered altitude back home.

As the sun dissolved into the ocean and the rays ricocheted off the clouds, the lights below began to twinkle as the city came to life.

And then a firm hand on her shoulder brought her gently back to the party she'd already forgotten behind her.

The gentle touch went with an inquisitive smile and kind gaze, but not a word. This man was deeply tanned and his face lit up with laugh lines as he smiled. Slowly, he began to walk a crescent around her. Their eyes locked. Star turned with him as he shifted suddenly back in the other direction in a playful effort to get behind her. She wheeled, more than a little unnerved. Turning again, she was startled to find him back at her side, staring still.

She laughed.

"I knew it," he said finally. "All teeth and a halo."

"And that's a good thing?" she asked, still laughing at his strange behavior.

"Oh, yeah, a very good thing." He reached for her hand. "I'm Peter."

"Hi, Peter," she said, taking his hand. "I'm Star."

"You certainly are," he said, not letting go. "There's no doubt about it."

"My *name* is Star," she explained, trying unsuccessfully to get her hand back. "Star Wood Leigh."

"I see," he said, holding just her fingers. "And what brings you here to the party tonight, Star Wood Leigh?"

"Jayne and Marsten invited me," she said, feeling like a real star just saying it.

"Old friends?"

"Yeah, we were in high school together," she said, breaking up and hiding her face behind her hand.

"There it is again," he said, putting an index finger under her chin and tipping it back up. "You mustn't hide that light from the world."

"Are you with the magazine?" Star asked, shy of his intensity.

"I'm a movie producer."

"Really? Like Steven Spielberg?" she asked, her interest piqued by the strange world of moviemaking. She'd been in Los Angeles only a few minutes really, and already she was meeting people in the movie industry.

"No, Steven does some producing, but he's a director," Peter explained. "Directors are in charge of all aspects of the shooting of the movie."

"Oh, I see," Star said, not really seeing. "So you manage the money side?"

"I have people who do that," he acknowledged. "But in a manner of speaking."

"Do you promote the movie once it's made?"

"Really that's marketing."

"So, you hire the people who work on the movie?"

"Not exactly."

"Well, you don't act in the movies, do you?"

"No, of course not," he chuckled.

"Or do lighting or makeup or paint the scenery?" She was laughing again.

"None of those things."

"So, what do you do exactly?"

"I can show you if you've got some time."

She'd heard that one before, though admittedly never from a Hollywood producer.

The gong sounded. Star turned around to see a large Amazon of a woman, wearing a couple of pieces of what looked like leopard skin tied in just the right spots, pounding the gong with a large padded mallet.

"Saved by the bell," Star said with a mischievous grin. It was funny; it really wasn't so much different from the guys at the tables at Mother Pearl's back home. They were all got up here and had fancier jobs with fancier titles and nicer cars, but guys were guys all over. It was sort of reassuring.

"You can sit with me for the fight," Peter announced.

Typical.

She let him take her arm and lead her inside.

"Star, there you are," Jayne said, threading her way skillfully through the crowd to rescue her from Peter Rodick. "Hi, Peter, thanks so much for bringing her back to us."

"Don't be stingy, Jayne," Peter said with a little pout as he released Star into Jayne's firm grip. "I was just about to show her what a movie producer can do."

"Is that right?" Jayne inquired archly. "I'd be happy to have Sami set up an appointment for the two of you at your office."

"Well, that's really going to limit my demonstration." Peter grinned with just a hint of malice.

"That's exactly what I had in mind," Jayne said, matching his grin.

"Till then," Peter said, clicking his heels theatrically and bowing to kiss Star's hand. "I'll count the hours."

"Don't you have people to do that?"

It was Peter's turn to laugh.

"This one's something, Jayne," Peter said, nodding and pointing at Star with both index fingers.

"I'm getting the idea," Jayne said. "We'll call you."

"I'll call if you don't."

"Nobody wants to see that happen, Peter," Jayne said, giving him a glancing kiss near the cheek before guiding Star across what was, in fact, a full-size movie theater.

"I can't believe there's a movie theater in this house," Star said, marveling.

"Do you know who that was?" Jayne asked when they were a safe distance away from Peter.

"Peter," Star said, searching to remember if he'd given her a last name. "He didn't tell me his last name."

"He's a mogul."

"A mongrel?"

"That too. He's a major player," Jayne said as she led Star down the aisle to the front row of seats.

"Well, you couldn't judge it by me," Star said. "We talked for ten minutes and he couldn't come up with a single thing that he actually does. Maybe he only plays."

"Trust me. He does a lot more than play." Jayne pointed to a vacant seat. "He used to be a studio chief. He's put together some major, major movies. He does plenty, even if it's only spend the studio's money. Almost nobody's allowed to spend more."

"Nice work if you can get it," Star said.

"He's also such a legend with the ladies that they made a movie about it," Jayne said with a motherly tone. "So heads up."

"Oh, duh," Star said, rolling her eyes.

"Here's your seat," Jayne said with a little laugh. "I'll have someone check on you later. More champagne?"

"Thanks, Jayne," Star said, truly grateful as she sank into the seat. "No more champagne or I'll be asleep in the first inning. But a root beer would be amazing."

"Root beer? Anything's possible. I'll see what I can do."

Star curled up in the oversize velvet seat and closed her eyes for a moment. It had been a long day. Only that morning she had woken up in her old room on Arcady Key. The sun was just setting on the same day and she was at the Mann Castle, rubbing shoulders with movie mongrels. Star drifted off, lulled by the constant roar of the hundreds of voices raised all around her, and vaguely aware that her shoe was slipping off her foot. She reached to grab it before it fell, but her eyes flew open when, instead of her shoe, she caught someone's hand.

"What the . . . ?"

Star wheeled to face the shoe thief.

"Vince Piccolo," he announced, as if it were the way people always met.

Star lost her breath for moment. All she could do was gasp and wonder if she was still asleep.

"Oh my God," she said incredulously. "This has been the most amazing day. I'm so pleased to meet you."

She gave him her hand and he handed back the shoe. "Oh. Um, right, thanks, I think."

"You have really lovely feet," Vince said, running two fingers professionally along the arch. "And let's see," he went on, raking her hair back with the same two fingers. "Very well-formed ears."

"Thank you, do you really think so?" she asked sincerely, too starstruck to react to the bizarre remark. Vince Piccolo had starred on one of the few TV shows to take her off the volleyball court. The encounter was like having him leap off the poster on the back of her bedroom door. He could have complimented the bumps on her head and she'd have been flattered.

He trailed his hand behind her ear and down her arm to where it rested at the elbow.

She shivered at his touch.

"I'm Star."

"And you've fallen from heaven into the seat beside me."

"No, just American Airlines. And it was a pretty smooth landing, actually," she said, immediately wishing she could take it back. Stupid, stupid, stupid. "I really loved *Family Daze* and *Hi There High*," she gushed, trying to save herself, but only making it worse. "I don't get to see *He's the Boss* nearly as much as I'd like to, but I watch it as often as I can."

"Well, thank you," Vince said, signaling the

waiter, who lowered his tray so that Vince could take two glasses of champagne. Star took the glass he offered, her root beer long forgotten. "Now what brings you here to the party tonight?"

"Oh, Marsten and Jayne invited me," she said demurely, using her great line from earlier.

"Well, that's how we all got here, didn't we? How do you know them?"

"Oh," Star said, brought up short. "I just flew in from Miami to shoot a cover for the magazine."

"Excellent," Vince said, lighting up. "I may catch up with James Caan's record yet."

"What kind of record is that?" Star asked, innocent of the salacious legend.

"Nothing important," Vince said, waving the topic away. "I'd be honored if you'd let me take you out to celebrate."

"On a date?" Star said, too stunned for a moment to realize that she'd actually said it out loud.

"Or we could go whale watching," Vince suggested, aware of the effect that being on television since puberty had on the residents of the real world. "Yes, a date, but only if you want to, I just thought it might be—"

"Oh, yeah, that would be great," Star said, hoping that she really had woken up from her nap.

"Terrific." Vince smiled, unconsciously touching her foot again. "Where are you staying?"

"I'm not sure." Star shrugged. "I came straight from the airport. Jayne made arrangements."

"I'll give Sami a call tomorrow. Meanwhile, we've got all evening to get to know each other."

"Ladies and gentlemen . . ." the fight announcer's voice cut through the crowded theater, and people took their seats as the lights dimmed.

Vince took Star's hand and gave it a squeeze.

It was all too perfect. The most perfect night of her life so far. She sank into the rich red velvet seat and drank it all in.

6

freeze-frame

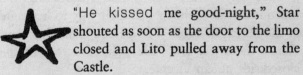 "He kissed me good-night," Star shouted as soon as the door to the limo closed and Lito pulled away from the Castle.

She sighed as they made their way down the drive and off the estate. As the spectacular views of the city lights from Mulholland Drive rushed past the window beside her, Star cast her mind back over her evening with Vince Piccolo.

It seemed like a dream. And like a dream, as soon as it was over, it was hard to remember. It was a lot like cotton candy—lovely, sweet, and enjoyable, but hard to sink your teeth into. As she tried to recall the exact details of her romantic evening, she hardly noticed as the mountain roads gave way to the broad boulevards and skyscraper palm trees of Beverly Hills.

Then Beverly Hills dissolved into West Hollywood and they approached her hotel, where suddenly the streets were thronged and the lights glared with an outrageous festive air that Star could not resist.

"That guy doesn't have on any pants under his chaps," she said, pointing at one of a number of people strolling the main boulevard of West Hollywood. "Those guys are holding hands. Those two are making out. And that woman doesn't have a shirt on. Lands! This place makes South Beach look like Cypress Gardens."

"It's gay pride," Lito said, negotiating the hideous traffic as they made their way to her suite at the Hotel Bel Age. "The parade is Sunday. And there's the street fair." He pointed across to the closed side of San Vicente.

"There's a fair?" Star said, plastered to the window searching for signs of a fair. "There aren't any rides."

"There are different kinds of rides at this fair," Lito said with an odd smile.

"Look at those pink hot pants," Star said, glued to the glass. "And handcuffs as an accessory? Gay people are so colorful. I had no idea. We must not have very many back in Florida, 'cause I don't remember anyone looking like this. This is wonderful."

"Welcome to West Hollywood." Lito laughed. "The land of the free and the home of the gay."

"Lito, are you gay?"

"No, no. I am Latino. Latin men are not gay."

"I see." Star nodded as she eyed the numerous Latinos surrounding the car as they inched their way through the intersection. Given the traffic and the size of the vehicle, it was like turning the *Titanic*. "Maybe we could go to the fair for a little bit?"

"Not tonight," Lito insisted. "Miss Jayne said you had an early day tomorrow. You must get ready for your big shoot and I must get you straight home so you can sleep."

"Oh, pooh," she pouted. "I guess getting ready for my big break is not a good reason to complain. But I hate to miss a party. And this looks like a good one." Just then she noticed another limo, making its way along Santa Monica in the opposite direction. Sticking through the roof of the limo was a gaggle of what Star didn't realize were drag queens, waving and blowing kisses to the crowd.

"Oh," Star gasped. "Look at that. Does this car have a sunroof like theirs?"

"You bet." Lito grinned. The roof opened and the sounds of the crowd came flooding into the car.

Star virtually levitated through the open skylight and was soon seated on the roof, blowing kisses of her own. As they passed near to the other limo, one of the "girls" spoke.

"You look great, honey," she shouted to Star.

"Thanks," Star shouted back, startled by how husky the girl's voice was. "So do you all."

"Girl," said one of the others in the neighboring limo, "that is one amazing wig."

"It's not a wig," Star said proudly.

"Oh, girl," the first one said, aghast. "That is *not* one of God's colors."

Star slunk back into the car.

"Lito," Star said, feigning a yawn, "I think it's time to go to the hotel."

"Okay, Miss Star," he called over his shoulder. "We're almost there anyway."

As far as Star could tell, the Bel Age Hotel was as close to perfect as anything could possibly be. Not only was it beautiful, it was literally two blocks from the street fair that she had passed with Lito. Better still, as a guest with *Mann* magazine, she was provided with a junior suite—kind of a room and a half—and treated like visiting royalty. There was even a little refrigerator so she could get her own food and save money while she was staying there. For a girl who'd never stayed anywhere the rooms didn't open directly into the parking lot, it didn't get any better.

As she stood on the balcony gazing down at the

amazing party going on below, Star felt a little strange and lonely. She reached up and touched her hair. She needed to get to a drugstore and buy some color before the shoot on Monday. Sure, there was all weekend to worry about it, but why wait till the last minute?

A mischievous smile crept across her face as she considered venturing out again, but she was too tired, so she resolved to go out in the morning and pick up some hair color as well as some food for the little refrigerator. I'll just lie down for a minute, she told herself as she fell onto the bed. She didn't even turn down the bedspread. And that was the last thing she remembered of her first night in L.A.

It took a moment.

First, there was a lot of pounding. In Star's dream, it was native drums and wild men. Some sort of tribe, indigenous to West Hollywood, was celebrating and Star was presiding over the ritual from the sunroof of Lito's limo. There was also a lot of shouting.

"Star?" a familiar voice called repeatedly. "Star? Are you in there?"

But that was just the WeHo tribe chanting her name. Star closed her eyes tighter, but the natives turned ugly and tied her to a post to do something with her hair.

"Star, open up, we know you're in there."

Startled, she sat up in bed. Who knew she was in here? And where exactly was here? Then she realized that she'd slept in her clothes and had never even turned down the bed. The hotel. Los Angeles.

"Star!"

"Okay, okay," she called, putting her feet on the floor and attempting to stand. "Keep your thong in." She pushed her hair back out of her eyes and took a few uncertain steps to the door.

More pounding. Annoyed, she yanked the door open to get it to stop.

Billy and Skip gasped.

Star screamed for joy.

They just screamed.

"It's you," she said, jumping up and down and hugging them both, her sleepy daze gone in an instant.

"What happened to you?" Billy asked tentatively, reaching out to touch her face. "Is this a rash?"

"What? Oh . . ." She laughed, touching her face and feeling the pattern embossed on her skin. "Blanket face. I slept on the bedspread. What are you guys doing here? This is so great that you came by to see me."

"Didn't Jayne tell you?" Skip said, pushing past her and into the room.

"No," Star said, confused, closing the door behind them.

Billy opened the drapes and the window and Skip got on the phone.

"Hello, yes, we need some coffee up here stat," Skip said, taking Star's chin in his hand and turning her face back and forth under his gaze as he spoke. "And put together some brunch stuff: bread, fruit, quiche, like that. . . . Ummhmm. Three of us," he concluded, hanging up the phone without saying good-bye.

"So Jayne knew you two were coming over today?" Star said, elated to see them.

"She sent us," Billy said, joining them.

"We're here to do your hair and makeup for the shoot," Skip explained.

"But the shoot's not until Monday," Star said with look of confusion.

"Okay. Mostly your hair," Skip admitted.

Billy opened the little refrigerator and took out a can of juice.

"How'd that get in there?" Star wondered aloud as Skip examined her hair. "Better not drink it, Billy. It's not mine. Maybe the last people left it."

Billy did a spit take with the cranberry juice. "Star, darling. It's called a minibar. The hotel stocks it with liquor and mixers and chocolate and then charges you an arm and a leg when you can't resist them. It's the best racket since airport food."

"Well, go easy. I don't have any extra arms and legs," Star said. "Breakfast is going to cost me my food budget for the week."

"Relax, darling," Skip said, dragging a chair in front of the mirror and pulling her into it. "The magazine is paying for it. Live it up."

"Even long-distance calls?" Star asked sheepishly.

"Mmmhmm." Billy nodded. "Want some juice? Or there's a split of champagne in here. You want a mimosa?"

"God, no more champagne ever," Star said, making a cross with her two index fingers to ward him away.

"Too much fun at the Castle last night?" Billy asked, dumping tomato juice into a glass and handing it to her. "We heard about you and Vince."

She started to answer but began coughing as soon as she took the first sip.

"It's a Virgin Mary, honey," Billy said, "take it easy. Best thing in the world for a hangover."

"Ummhmm," Skip said with an air of finality and crossing to his case. "She's going to be the next platinum blonde."

"You think?" Billy said reverently.

Star tried to weigh in but couldn't quite get her breath.

"Oh, yes, most definitely," Skip said, pulling the necessary chemicals from his bag of tricks. Star gasped for breath from the fiery spices. "Jean Harlow, Marilyn Monroe, and now Star Wood Leigh. It's time."

"It is," Billy declared.

"Is it?" was all Star could manage.

Getting her hair just right had taken most of the day on Saturday. Eleven hours spent bleaching, stripping, and toning.

"It's your only hope, darling," Skip had explained. "It's this or shave your head, and we don't have time for it to grow back before the shoot on Monday."

Aside from physical pain, the worst part of the process was the mind-numbing boredom. Skip whipped up a bowl of frothy, purplish blue chemicals that burned like Drano, and then he painted it on her head. And she sat under a dryer with the Drano burning her scalp until they checked and rinsed it. And then they'd do it again. First, they took out all the color, then they put it back in. It took hours, and most of the time was spent waiting for the chemicals to do their job. Only then when the color was perfected could Skip even contemplate the cut.

A couple of hours into it, Star reached her breaking point. "Not again," she wailed, making for the door. "No more. Nothing is worth this."

Skip pulled the electric clippers out from his bag and buzzed them at her, blocking her way.

"Remember, darling," Billy comforted, "the higher the hair, the closer to God."

For revenge she made them let her give them French wraps, "just to calm me down," she said deviously.

And even after her hair was declared "perfection," there was a skin-chaffing couple of hours while Billy perfected her makeup. Star had never been one to wear much makeup, so trying to hold still while Billy was plaguing her with tiny little brushes, painting shadows and highlights, especially around her eyes, was torture. Worse, her tears kept spoiling his work.

"I think just a natural look," Star had suggested.

"The natural look takes at least two hours," Skip grumbled.

In the end, it was a fresh-face look, heavy on the eyeliner.

At last, well after dark, the room strewn with room-service carts, ruined towels, tissues, and enough cotton balls to start a walk-in clinic (not to mention enough chemicals to have the place declared a hazardous-waste dump), the moment had arrived.

"That's it," Billy declared, stepping back to look at his work. "Those are *the* perfect come-fuck-me lips if ever I saw them."

Skip tossed aside his copy of *Vogue,* rose from the sofa, and prepared to find fault. Hand resting thoughtfully on his chin, he paced around her scrutinizing. Star felt like a bug in a jar, trapped and examined. She was sure she'd cry if they tried one more thing. She winced as Skip reached toward her, but held steady as he scrunched and shaped her hair a bit with his hands.

"By George," Skip said, taking her hand and helping her up from the chair, "I think she's got it. I really think she's got it!"

Billy jumped up and down and clapped his hands as Skip turned her slowly to face the mirror.

"Drum roll, please." Skip paused.

Billy complied, taking two combs to an up-turned ice bucket.

"Ladies," Skip said, "I give you Miss Star Wood Leigh."

At first, she could only stare. Then tears came into her eyes.

Billy and Skip exchanged a worried look.

"Oh my God," she said at last. "I . . . I can't believe that's me."

"You were always beautiful, darling," Billy whispered into her ear. "All we did was show it off."

"For eleven hours," Skip scoffed.

"And I think someone has earned a little trip to the pride festival," Billy said playfully. "Oh . . . you can come too if you want, Star."

She laughed.

With her high-fashion head, the boys suggested contrast, picking out some jeans and her Mother's T-shirt to set off the look. "SHUCK ME, SUCK ME,

EAT ME RAW," Billy had exclaimed. "You'll be a hit on the boulevard tonight."

And they'd made a night worthy of their day, not leaving the dance tent a minute before three in the morning. Skip and Billy had forbidden the beer tent for fear of bloating before Monday's shoot, so Star was more exhilarated than exhausted when her newly platinum head hit the pillow.

She laughed aloud, alone in the dark.

Only a few days before she'd hardly ever worn much more than mascara, and then only when she'd felt forced. And her hair had been cut with the sewing scissors as often as not. Yet, there was Skip using her name in the same sentence as Marilyn Monroe.

Laughing was the only thing to do.

Sunday, she was pretty much on her own to explore the surprising contrast of the parade on Santa Monica and the rock 'n' roll venue of the Sunset Strip just a few blocks to the north. She went to Barney's Beanery for lunch, where, according to Billy, everybody went for their last meal. Given the menu offerings, Star thought that not too surprising. "All red meat and roadkill." She shuddered, surprised to find that the L.A. diet was not composed of yogurt, sprouts, and tofu. She chose a small salad, but even then had to ask that it not be served with bacon grease.

Following a map in a brochure she'd found at the hotel, Star walked over to Flores to see where

Jean Harlow had signed the sidewalk and a little farther to see one of the places where Marilyn had supposedly lived. And then home, back down Sunset, to take advantage of the free long distance and a call to her mom.

"Esther?" Lucille had questioned her. "Rick, do we know anyone named Esther? Come to think of it, there did used to be this girl, homely little thing—"

"Okay, Mom, I get it," Star said, laughing and glad of the familiar ribbing.

"So, what do you think so far?" Lucille asked, her motherly guilt duly exacted.

"It's beautiful, Mom," Star said, lying in the big bed and gazing out the windows overlooking the city below. "It's flat like back home, but it has mountains that go right down to the sea. I've met all kind of stars, most of them I never even heard of. And I've got a date with Vince Piccolo."

"Isn't that something," Lucille said with a secret smile. "Where are you two going?"

"I don't know," Star said, kicking her feet into the air. "But who cares? I'll be with Vince Piccolo."

"As long as he treats you good."

There was a long silence. Star crossed and uncrossed her ankles in midair. "I'm scared, Mom."

"Why on earth?" Lucille said, knowing full well.

"Momma, can you believe it? They're letting me be on the cover of their magazine." Star let her legs fall to the bed with a bounce. "I feel so lucky."

"No, darling," Lucille corrected. "It's the other way around. *You* are letting *them* put your picture on the cover of their magazine. You're a beautiful woman. They know what they're doing. They're the lucky ones."

"Thanks, Mom," Star said quietly, still more than a little frightened and glad of her mother's confidence and approval.

"Okay, don't get all weak in the knees," Lucille urged, not wanting to get emotional herself. "And then what happened?"

"Oh, Billy and Skip, the guys I met at Brandi's shoot? They came by yesterday and we spent the whole day *designing my look,*" she said, imitating the way Billy talked in italics sometimes.

"What does that mean?"

"Making me look presentable."

"Don't get smart."

"Well, it means for one thing that my hair is now platinum blonde," she said tentatively, gauging for her mom's reaction before barreling forward. "And I had more makeup on my face in one afternoon then I've worn altogether in my whole life— and that's counting the makeover they gave me at Brandi's shoot."

Lucille asked the million-dollar question: "What are you wearing?"

"A school uniform is all I know," Star said, not sure what exactly that meant.

"Hmmm," Lucille remarked, not really wanting

to think about it too much. "I'm glad about your hair. That other color . . ." She trailed off, making a gasping sound.

"I know."

"So, who all was at the party besides Vince?"

And that had been their conversation until Star was drifting off, tired and distracted enough to sleep on the eve of her big day.

Morning had brought Lito and the limo . . . and dry heaves and coffee.

Turned out that *Mann* magazine headquarters and studios were just down Sunset Boulevard from her hotel; still, protocol demanded that Lito be dispatched to drive her. Star felt kind of silly. It was less than the distance she used to walk to get a cold root beer from the IGA on Front Street back on the key. "This is it?" Star marveled as she realized that she'd already walked by the building several times in her local sightseeing. "I could have walked here from the hotel," she said, bounding out of the back of the limo where Lito had insisted that she ride, locking the front doors and refusing to open them until she got in the back. "I *have* walked here."

"Star?" Sami called as she approached the car. "You're right on time."

"Oh, like I've been able to think about anything else," she said with a little laugh.

"You look amazing. Your hair's great. The color really suits you."

"Thanks! And I'm so excited to get done up again—false eyelashes and everything!" Star said as she allowed herself to be shepherded toward the door. "Oh, how long do you think I'll be? Oh, never mind. Lito," she called, turning back to him. "No telling how long I'll be. I can just walk back to the hotel from here when I'm done."

Lito just shook his head and smiled at her.

"Lito," Star whined. "I can manage. You have to make a living."

Sami peered over Star's shoulder, pointed at him, and mimed a telephone to let him know she'd call when the shoot was over. He nodded and gave Sami the thumbs-up, which Star assumed was for her. Relieved to see him get back in the car, Star blew him a kiss and waved as she allowed Sami to lead her into the studio.

"I hope everything's satisfactory at the Bel Age?" Sami inquired, pushing the UP button and pausing with Star to wait for a car.

"It's nicer than my house." Star giggled wildly.

"Well, good, 'cause I've made arrangements for you to stay on until the end of next week," Sami said, holding the elevator door for her and then following her inside. "I hope that's all right. Mr. Mann wants to meet with you. Peter Rodick called and asked for an appointment—Jayne said lunch only. And Vince called. He wants to take you out to celebrate tonight."

"He does? That's great. Do you think we'll be done in time?"

"Oh, yeah," Sami said, holding the elevator door as it opened onto the studio floor. "I'll call him back and tell him it's okay then?"

"It's so okay."

Star stepped off the elevator and froze. There, framed on the wall ahead of her, was every single cover of every issue of *Mann* magazine since the fifties. Sami kept her brisk pace, chattering away and striding down the hall until she realized that Star was no longer with her; she stood staring at the wall of faces staring back. Sami rushed back to collect her.

"Star," Sami said gently, as if trying to wake her from a sound sleep. "Star, it's this way."

"They're all so beautiful," Star said, awed and intimidated by the company she would soon keep.

"And you're one of them," Sami said, deftly guiding her away from the wall and down a hallway lined with beautifully framed nudes of the women featured in the magazine over the years, photos that did not make Star feel any better.

"And here we are," Sami said, continuing her line of distracting idle chitchat as she ushered her into Studio B.

"Cupcake," Billy said, spotting her from the

coffee station along a far wall of the studio. "Has June turned suddenly cold? You look like you're freezing."

"She's not blue, she's green," Skip snorted, emerging from their office area. "I've got bad news for you, girl. You're going to survive this."

"You must be Star." A gaunt, middle-aged woman approached and seized her hand. The woman was pale, with dramatically bobbed black hair and dressed entirely in black. "I'm Bethany."

"Star this is Bethany," Sami began. "She'll be your stylist today."

No response.

"Star, can you hear us?" Billy said, snapping his fingers near her eyes. "Earth to Star."

"Oh, God," Skip said, "get her in here quick or breakfast will be served again."

Bethany, Sami, and Billy managed to get Star into the toilet off the dressing room just in time. "I'll be right outside this door if you need me for anything," Bethany said maternally.

"I'll be across the street at Ben Frank's having scrambled eggs and bacon," Skip called cruelly, delighting in her panic.

Eventually Star emerged, sheepish, pale, and shaken. "I'm so embarrassed," she said. "I'm sorry to be such an amateur."

"We've had plenty of professional vomiters up here, believe me," Skip said with a teasing little smile. "So, an amateur is kind of refreshing."

"Here's some toothpaste, a toothbrush, and some mouthwash," Bethany offered.

"Thanks," Star said, taking them. "I'm so sorry for all the trouble."

"Please," Bethany said, waving her away. She held open the bag to show Star; it was filled entirely with toothbrushes, toothpaste, and mouthwash. "You think you're the first girl to toss her cookies up here? We're going to get through this, but I want you to know you're going to be nervous and it's okay. Okay?"

"Okay," Star said, smiling and retreating into the bathroom to freshen up.

Star regarded herself in the mirror in the small, featureless room.

"Okay, Papa Jens," she said to her reflection. "This is it. This is me embracing what life offers me. But I gotta tell you, it's scaring the crap out of me. I wish you were here."

"Star," Bethany called, knocking gently on the door. "Are you okay? Ready to get started?"

"Ready or not," Star said to her reflection. "Coming," she answered.

She took a deep breath and opened the door.

"Okay?" Bethany asked solicitously. "Here we go. I want you to try on a few things and then we'll turn you over to Dr. Strangelove over there and his henchman Thong."

"Fuck you, asshole," Skip said, imitating the Terminator's thick Austrian accent.

Star laughed, remembering the line.

"Nice talk," Bethany chuckled, as she held up various articles of clothing, making noises of agreement and dissent to herself. "Okay, try these things on for me." She handed Star a mismatched collection of clothing and toddled her off to the dressing room, where they chose a few items. Bethany gave Star a nice white terry-cloth robe to wear while she got her hair and makeup done.

Soon she was laughing and at ease as Skip and Billy helped her prepare.

"I'm thinking pigtails," Skip said, holding her hair up with two hands. "Very Lolita with that plaid skirt and the school tie."

"That's not a skirt, that's a vest," Star said, a bit jumpy about how little she'd actually tried on.

"It's a scarf," Bethany corrected. "But I'm betting he's going with the cheerleader."

"You're both wrong," a new voice intruded into the conversation. "I thought about it after our meeting and it's the letter jacket."

"Mitch," Bethany said, rising to greet him. "Great to be working with you again. This is Star."

"Star, hi," Mitch Lader said informally. "Good to meet you. Bethany, let's go have a look."

"You betcha," Bethany said, following him back into the dressing room.

"He doesn't like me," Star said under her breath.

"He doesn't know you," Skip said. "He's the

best. That's how all the good ones are, all business, trust me. I'm not nice enough to say good things that aren't true."

"He hardly says good things that are true," Billy said, earning a rap with the back of a hairbrush.

"So, the letter jacket," Skip said, nodding as he regarded her hair. "More rouge and windblown."

"Thunderfuck." Billy nodded.

"What?" Star laughed at the word.

"Like people would like to think they look after great sex," Skip said as he began professionally mussing her hair and spraying it into place.

"Okay," Mitch said, emerging from the dressing room with Bethany and the oversize letter jacket Star had tried on earlier. "So, I think this and the scarf are the way to go. And, boys, as to the look . . ."

"Thunderfuck?" Billy asked.

"You're monster talent, boys, don't ever change," Mitch said, pointing a finger gun at them and firing. "Good to meet you, Star. I'll see you out there. Bethany, come look at that lighting with me, would you? Skip, nice nails by the way. So, effeminate and yet girly."

"Thanks," Skip said, gritting his teeth in a smile and pulling Star's hair surreptitiously.

"You got it," Mitch said, Bethany following him out.

Star felt almost unnoticed and a bit on the outside. The little team was familiar enough with one another to have inside jokes and to guess each other's thoughts and tastes, and for a moment she wished she were back at Mother's. She was glad that all she had to do was stand there. That was shaping up to be challenge enough.

"Okay," Bethany said to Star, all too soon. "It's time. Are you ready?"

"She is," Skip said with one last spritz.

"And I'll do touch-up out there," Billy said, holding up a little sandwich bag he had used to collect lip pencil, Bardot-gauge eye-liner, blush, and a few of the other items out of his vast collection.

"Okay, honey," Bethany said, handing her the jacket. "Put this on."

"This is it?" Star said, a bit horrified. "Jayne said I wouldn't—"

"No, no, honey," she soothed. "You have to trust Bethany. With the scarf and either a football helmet or a pom-pom, you'll be dressed for first communion."

Star regarded the jacket a moment.

"Besides, it's not that kind of magazine," Bethany assured her. "Put the robe on over the top and then we'll get you situated out there."

Star smiled and stepped into the dressing room. This is really it, she thought. I'm really doing this. She let the robe fall to the floor and looked at herself in the mirror. All she could see were a thousand wrongs—the mole, the birthmark, the scar from that time she hit the rocks surfing. What had she been thinking?

"Star?" Bethany's voice came from the other side of the door. "Ready?"

She picked up the jacket and slipped it on. Fortunately, it was several sizes too big; still, she pulled at the waist to try to get it to cover more.

Bethany knocked again.

"I'll be right there," Star called. "Last-minute check."

Slowly, she slipped the robe back over the jacket. One last look in the mirror and then she opened the door. No one was even looking at her as she emerged. Skip gave her hair a quick fluff.

"There," he pronounced. "We discovered you, so don't let us down."

Star smiled weakly.

"Okay then," Bethany said, holding the door. "Right this way."

Billy followed as they made their way into the studio toward a huge piece of white paper hanging from overhead. It was lit so brightly that looking at it hurt.

"Star, hi," Mitch said, looking up from the camera. "Welcome aboard. This is Jens, my assistant. Billy you know. It'll just be the four of us, unless we need Skip, but that's it. Okay?"

"Jens," Star repeated, so stunned by the coincidence that she couldn't really speak. Fortunately, it sounded a lot as if she had said "yes" so no one no-

ticed her catatonia. She had never heard the name
Jens even once other than in reference to her grandfather. It was like some cosmic sign.

Bethany shuffled onto the huge white paper and
helped her off with the robe, while Mitch and Jens
busied themselves elsewhere. Then, using the scarf
and the football helmet, Bethany arranged Star into
a pose, which Mitch checked periodically through
the camera. Bethany was talking to Mitch, who
was speaking with her and the assistant and Billy to
get the shot set.

No one was really talking to Star. They simply
moved her around or arranged her as they did the
costume pieces and the lighting equipment.

"Billy, a little shadow here," Mitch directed,
brushing the right side of his own chest to indicate.

Billy stroked the makeup brush along Star's left
breast. She shivered. "How's that?" Billy asked.

"Better," Mitch said, looking through the camera. "Bethany, let's get the helmet just as far as we
can."

Bethany tugged at Star's elbows, raising the helmet she was holding in front of her crotch. "How's
that?" Bethany asked, not Star, but Mitch.

"More," Mitch said, gesturing up with his hand.
"More, more. Oops, too far. Down a bit. That's it."

Star was mortified. "Can you see?" she asked, a
bit desperate. She felt cold air in all sorts of places
that, even though you couldn't see them, weren't
technically covered.

"Not to worry," Mitch said. "Come have a look, Bethany. I think she should lean on the helmet, it's too big to hold."

Bethany came and looked with him, then walked away nodding. "Good idea," she said. "Jens, can we get a couple of apples over here?"

Apples? Star shuddered.

Jens brought a couple of wooden crates over to where Star was standing, making her even more nervous. Then he knelt down in front of her and slipped the boxes under the edge of the white paper, stacking them up so that there was a raised spot in the paper that served as both backdrop and floor covering.

"Okay," Bethany said, reaching for the helmet. "Let's just put that right here."

Star felt exposed and again began pulling on the gathered waist of the open jacket. She fought back the tears.

"Now," Bethany said, gently guiding her to the helmet, which was facing straight toward the camera. "Lean right here." Bethany placed both of Star's hands on top of the helmet as though she were going to vault over it. Then, efficiently, in the way that a doctor might touch you, she pushed down on Star's now exposed lower back until her chin started to rise. As Star's face came up to eye level with the camera, Bethany stepped back to check her work, strummed her lip with her thumb a moment as she gave Star a critical look, then stepped forward to firmly arrange Star's breasts so that they were only *just* covered by the open jacket and trailing scarf.

"There. How's that Mitch?" Bethany asked, stepping away.

"Beautiful," Mitch said. "I think that's it. All the bases covered."

"Okay, relax, Star," Bethany said. "Just relax. It's going to be great."

"Let's get some Polaroids," Mitch said.

It was too much. Star couldn't contain it any longer. She held the awkward and uncomfortable pose, but she could not stop the tears.

There were a couple of flashes.

"Bethany," Mitch said, pointing at Star and then stepping away.

"Star?" Bethany said quietly as she approached her. "What's up?"

"I need a minute," Star said.

"Sure, okay," Bethany said quietly, then raised her voice to address the room. "We need a little break."

"No problem," Mitch said, already at the coffee table with Jens. "We're running ahead anyway."

Clutching her robe around her, Star rushed from the room.

"Relax, Star, it's going to be great." She just kept hearing it over and over in her head as she got herself into the dressing room, her body wracked with sobs as she slid down the door and sat on the floor behind it.

"Relax, Star, it's going to be great." She heard his voice, felt his breath on her neck, his hands on her.

She had only been twelve years old.

It was an awkward age. Star was a late bloomer and the gymnastics hadn't helped. Other young women like Brandi had curves like a mountain highway, but Star still had the look of a young girl. And because she looked younger, people tended to treat her as if she were younger, especially her mom. It only made her rebel all the more.

Star and her mom had just had a blazing argument about whether she was old enough to go to the movies without an adult, so she'd omitted that part of her plans when she'd asked if she could stay over at Brandi's that weekend. What her mom didn't know wouldn't hurt her.

O.Z. had given Brandi and Star a ride to the Tavernier Towne Theatre on Plantation Key. They were on their own for the afternoon to see a matinee of the new Tom Hanks movie *Big*. Star didn't know it, but Brandi had arranged to meet a guy she had a crush on after the movie. The guy was older, a "client" of her stepfather's. Star wasn't too keen on the idea when Brandi sprang it on her, but when he arrived with a friend in his Porsche, the idea suddenly looked and felt free and glamorously grown-up.

Star couldn't even remember the guy's name or see his face clearly, but his voice . . . she'd never forget.

"Relax, Star, it's going to be great."

They'd gone back to his condo, and Brandi and her friend with the Porsche had gone upstairs. Star had been left alone to play cribbage with the strange man, and it had seemed okay at first.

It started innocently enough. Bringing her a fresh, forbidden, and hence decidedly grown-up rum and Coke, he'd come up behind the chair where she was sitting and rubbed her shoulders.

"You're so tense," he'd said. "How about a massage?"

"I don't know," Star had deferred, starting to feel uncomfortable.

Then she was fighting to keep the straps up on her top as he continued to rub her neck, pushing her forward, onto her stomach. And then she was fighting to stand up as he pulled up her skirt. She remembered the cribbage pieces scattering across the floor as the board fell from the spot in the middle of the couch where they had been playing.

"Relax, Star, it's going to be great," he'd said, lying on top of her, holding her down.

And then he was inside her.

It had been mercifully quick and her screams and "No"s had gone unheeded—by him and everyone else there that night. Star had been too ashamed to say anything when Brandi and her friend came down. She couldn't even tell her mother she had been to the movies, how could she tell her this?

And so it had been a secret, her secret. She never even thought about it anymore, but then that morning, in the studio with those strangers, her clothes still in the dressing room, her body touched and adjusted, it had come back to her.

"Relax, Star, it's going to be great."

She remembered Papa Jens teaching her to relax by regulating her breathing. She tried to focus on only that.

"Al," she said aloud, remembering. That was his name.

Star felt angry and indignant that a man so many years before could make her feel ashamed of herself today, at this, her big moment. She arose from where she was sitting and crossed to the mirror. She dried her eyes carefully with a tissue. Billy would have to touch her up, but she did her best to preserve his work. And then, very deliberately, she took off the robe and hung it up.

Still wearing the letter jacket, she leaned on the back of the chair at the dressing table and regarded herself in the mirror as the camera had in the room next door. A smile spread across her face as she had a good look at what the camera was seeing.

And then, as though she were walking out, she

opened the dressing room door and strolled across the makeup room and back into the studio wearing just the letter jacket.

"Sorry about that," Star said to everyone. "It won't happen again. Billy, I'm going to need a little touch-up please. Mitch? Could you tell me about what we're trying for here? If this picture was in a story, what happened on the page just before?"

"I get you," Mitch said, rising and moving back to the setup. "Well, I think the game is over and you're out with the winning quarterback," he began.

For the next couple of hours Star became a part of the team, not more and not less than the other members, at ease with who she was and what she was there to do. Things went so well that they were able to try a number of different looks, though the letter jacket was the one they went with.

On one break, Skip had gone to get her robe for her as she had simply come back into the makeup room between setups with no costume at all. "Put something over that, would you?" he fussed.

But at the end of the day, they presented her with the letter jacket as she emerged from her dressing room, back in "street drag" as Billy called it.

They applauded her.

"That was varsity work out there," Mitch said, handing her the jacket. "If that's your first shoot, I'll be seeing a lot more of you."

"What didn't you get to see?" Star asked, laughing at her own joke.

As she stood at the elevator, she was proud of herself, proud that soon her cover would be adorning the wall beside the others. She was glad she'd come to Los Angeles, even if this feeling of freedom was all she got.

For Star, it had been like a part she was playing. Like acting out a sexual fantasy. If she thought about it clearly enough in her head, it somehow came across to Mitch's camera. He didn't really have to direct her, he just told her what he was looking for and she was able to make it happen.

No one had been more surprised or pleased than Star. It had been fun and liberating. She could not get back what had been taken from her as a young girl nearly ten years earlier. But she didn't have to give up anything more.

7

some girls

"And right here on these steps is where Katharine Hepburn met Spencer Tracy," Peter said as he squired Star down the steps in front of his office. It was Star's first time on a movie lot and she could not have been more thrilled.

Could life possibly get any better?

There had been nothing but raves on the cover shoot, though she got the greatest sense of personal satisfaction from simply having survived it. That everybody liked the pictures was just the cherry.

Her first date with Vince had been sweet, with the promise of good things to come. He'd taken her out after the shoot to Firmament, a trendy restaurant and bar at the Miro—the hottest hotel on the Sunset Strip that week. He had reserved a private pergola for their little celebration. Star would have called it an arbor with curtains on it, but what did she know? The drapes and jasmine that tented the sofa and cushions that surrounded their table afforded them a privacy that they couldn't ordinarily have had out at a public restaurant. And the view was almost as remarkable as the one she'd first seen at the Castle.

Of course, they'd gotten celebrity treatment, a new and heady experience for Star. But what she liked better than the deference and attention from the superior staff—who anticipated and saw to their every need—was the masterful way that Vince managed it all. He ordered a selection of hors d'oeuvres and dishes for them, selected the wine, the desserts, and the champagne. All Star had to do was show up and sit down.

"Jayne tells me that you're a vegetarian," Vince had said as the first plates were set before them. "So, I've chosen some things that I thought you might like. But please feel free to order something else if it doesn't suit you."

He had actually made the effort to find out what she liked beforehand, just to make her happy. It was an unfamiliar concept for Star and she found it wonderfully overwhelming.

As he fed her stuffed mushroom caps, she

looked deeply into his eyes and thought how easily she could love this man. Beautiful, famous, rich, thoughtful . . . what's not to love?

After dinner she'd slipped off her shoes and snuggled up to him on the sofa overlooking the lights of the city. They had sat like that a while, just enjoying the touch of being so close. Without speaking he brushed back her hair, lifted her face to his, and gently, so gently, brushed his lips to hers. She pressed for more and he withdrew, teasing and drawing her on.

She ran her hand behind his head to draw him in, and he hid his face just where her throat joined her body, his hot breath only encouraging her. Leaning in, her hand found his thigh and she reached for more and found that he was as excited as she felt. But that was it. He deflected her attentions by drawing her into his arms for the kiss she'd been wanting . . . and then he held back, not quite giving it to her.

Star's first taste of him only made her hungry for more.

But instead of giving, he promised.

The rest of their evening in the Firmament was filled with stories of his famous career and the famous people who had inhabited it. In return for her attentiveness, she was asked to his beach place for dinner that Friday. It wasn't what she had wanted, but it had been enough.

A second date with Mr. TV was thus arranged

for later in the week. In the meantime, she was having lunch at a movie studio with Peter, who assured her he was a famous movie producer even though they'd still not quite nailed down what that was. And here they were, walking down the very steps where Hepburn had met Tracy, whoever they were. Star had a vague notion that Hepburn had been in *Breakfast at Tiffany's,* but the only Tracy she knew of was Dick, and he was only a cartoon, wasn't he? So she said nothing and acted impressed, which wasn't hard. She was.

She'd managed to be plenty impressed seeing the studios of her father's favorites *Jeopardy!* and *Wheel of Fortune.* She'd also seen a movie in the making, and the tank where Esther Williams swam her water ballets. Star had never actually seen an Esther Williams movie, just the scenes from *That's Entertainment!,* but she knew who she was because they shared the same name, a fact she did not let on to Peter. "They filmed *Gone With the Wind* here?" she marveled, whirling around and reviewing the lot again. As with most children from the South, she had been taken to *Gone With the Wind* with her history classes several times over the years.

"And *The Wizard of Oz,*" Peter added. "At the same time."

She was speechless.

The place was amazing and beautiful and perfect. It was as much a fantasy world as the movies made there.

It was all like a dream about her life.

"And this is the commissary where Clark Gable got a standing ovation when he returned to work after Carole Lombard's death," Peter said, holding the door for her. "It's named for Rita Hayworth."

"Mr. Rodick," the hostess said, breaking away from what she was doing as she saw them come in the door. "Right this way." She ushered them to his regular table, chosen for its view of the room and from the room.

"So, how'd she die?" Star asked as he held the chair for her.

"Plane crash," Peter said, stunned but smiling at her. It was as though she were a foreigner and he was only just realizing how little English she spoke. He made his way around to his side of the table, scoping out the room to see who was looking. He nodded and smiled, waved and ignored, in keeping with the degree of importance accorded each in that place and that moment by the arcane and Byzantine set of rules with which the celebrity list would be compiled, overturned, and rewritten with the publication of the following week's box-office figures, power lists, and TV shares.

For her own part, Star scanned the room eagerly, looking for anyone she recognized as famous, and finding blessed few.

"Can you believe this room?" Peter said under his breath, leaning near her to speak confidentially.

"There's four of the most powerful people in Hollywood right here."

"Really?" Star looked around again to see if she'd missed anyone. As she turned to look over her shoulder, she came face-to-face with Van Pursens, startling them both.

"Hi, Van," she said almost reflexively.

"Hi?" Van said, not sure where he remembered her from. "The party at the Castle, right?"

"Star," she said, smiling, proud to be remembered. "And do you know Peter Rodick?"

"You're with Peter," Van said knowingly. "Of course you are."

"Van." Peter nodded with a tight smile. Van was still on the nodding list and wasn't officially on the speaking list yet, but Star knew who he was, so he made an exception. "I hear good things about your latest."

"That's great because I'm looking for a distribution deal," Van said, shaking his hand. "Perhaps I should call your office?"

"Perhaps," Peter said—the kiss of death.

"So, you're here with Star," Van said.

"I'm getting a private tour of the back lot," Star said proudly, patting the back of Peter's hand.

"Oh, is that what we're calling it now?" Van said nastily.

Star didn't know what he was talking about, but she knew just what he meant. It was the same tone of voice Adam had always used to make her feel that what she was doing was foolish or unimportant, It worked but she wasn't about to let him see that. She was determined to be nice to him no matter how badly he behaved.

"So, Van, what is your latest?" Star asked, smiling at him.

"It's a little independent about a boxer," Van said, wishing his way out of the conversation.

"Like *Rocky*?" Star asked brightly, trying to get him to talk about it.

"Not much, no," Van said even more irritated by the put-down of his work as derivative.

"Oh," Star said, disappointed by his refusal to talk about it. "Are you in it?"

"No," Van said, forcing a smile that only made it worse. "I directed it," he explained slowly as though the concept might be too much for her.

"That's too bad," Star said with a little pout. "I still remember you best for your martial arts work in *Hip-Hop Cops.*"

Well, that was all he could take. "Peter, if you'll excuse me," he said, barely civil and no longer even looking at Star. He turned and stalked back out of the Hayworth, preferring the more plebeian fair of the chips and sandwiches at the Gower to the shredding from Star's claws.

"What's so funny?" Star asked. Peter had not stopped laughing since Van's departure.

"I wish I could get rid of them all that well." He smiled at her.

"I got rid of him?" she asked, certain only that Van always seemed miffed each time they parted.

"Did you ever," he chortled. "What sounds good to you? The filet is excellent. But they do a nice pounded chicken breast."

"I think maybe just a nice salad," Star said, scanning the menu.

"Oh, come on," Peter urged. "Treat yourself. How about the stuffed pork chops?"

"I don't really eat meat," Star said, trying not to make a thing of it.

"Really," he said under raised brows. And then, in a technique that had earned him a permanent spot on *Premiere*'s top ten, he made a complete about-face with such conviction that you'd never know he hadn't always believed it. "That's really smart. I don't eat a lot of meat myself. Good healthy choice, low cholesterol and fat. You know they do an amazing eggplant Parmesan that you might like."

Star smiled and decided not to mention the cholesterol and fat in the Parmesan. "That does sound good," she agreed. "Eggplant it is."

Her remark turned several heads in the wake of Van's exit.

They ordered and snacked on fresh-baked breads while they waited for the food to come.

"I just keep wondering who else has sat here," Star said, thoughtfully buttering her breadstick. "I mean, what famous star sat in this very chair, you know?"

"I do." Peter smiled, pleased to see that she was enjoying the visit in her own way.

"And it's not just here," she said with an expansive gesture almost overturning her water goblet. "It's the whole city. Everywhere I go. Like, did you know that the Pollo Loco place right down Sunset from where I'm staying is the parking lot that Joni Mitchell is singing about in 'Big Yellow Taxi'? It's like the whole city is famous. I feel famous just being here."

"So, you're enjoying your visit?" Peter asked quietly, leaning in, making it seem as if there were only the two of them alone in the Rita Hayworth Dining Room.

"Yeah, though we'll see how long that lasts now that the vacation is almost over," she said ruefully, biting the end of the tiny baguette.

"Vacation?" Peter asked, pleased just to let her talk.

"It happens back home a lot," Star said with a knowing little smirk. "People come to the Keys or Miami and they have a great time. Who wouldn't? They're in a hotel or are renting a house. There's someone to do the laundry, they eat out every night and get drunk at noon on Wednesday. They think that if they lived there, that's how their life would be. But the truth is, it doesn't really have anything to do with Florida. Anywhere would seem like paradise if they lived there as if they were on vacation. Once you're making a living and paying the rent and doing the laundry and eating leftovers out of your own refrigerator, Miami is the same as Cincinnati. It's not where you live, but how you live there, you know?"

"Do you think anybody knows how smart you are?" Peter asked, a bit knocked out.

"I did okay in school," Star said with a shrug. "They seemed to notice."

"You're very funny," he said with a little laugh that was more like a smile. "So why does your vacation have to end?"

"Well, so far I've been on the all-expenses-paid *Mann* magazine prize package," Star explained, gesturing expressively with the tiny loaf of bread. "But if I want to stay, and I do, it's back to paying the rent and doing the laundry."

"And leftover meat loaf?"

"Leftover eggplant," she corrected with a grin.

"So, what about your 'how you live' philosophy?" he asked, a tiny accusation.

"Oh, don't mistake me. There's nothing wrong with all that stuff. It's what makes the good times the good times. The trick, I think, is to have a good time doing the laundry. If you can do that, the rest is a cinch."

"You're a very wise woman," Peter said a little too seriously.

Star threw her head back and laughed at the very idea.

Peter enjoyed it, even if the laugh felt as if it

were at his expense. Fortunately the food arrived and he was saved from having to explain or even acknowledge the moment, but he knew what he had to do.

"So, Star, um," Peter began as though the idea were just forming in his mind, "how's your lunch?"

"Really good." She nodded, wiping at her mouth with one of the huge white linen napkins. "You were so right about this eggplant."

"It's the cilantro," Peter said knowingly.

"Really? You think?" Star said, taking a bite and thinking about it. "I think it's the fresh basil. But there is cilantro. So, what was it you really wanted to ask me?"

"They'll never see you coming," he said, laughing. "You're the stealth bombshell."

"Thanks," she said with a smile, pleased to be found out. "So what was your question?"

"Just an idea really," he said with a self-deprecating smirk. "I keep a place in town that I don't live in. If it would help out, you could borrow it. Stay there for a while."

"Oh, Peter," Star said, setting her fork down heavily. "Oh my God. That is such a kind offer. I really haven't had the chance to even look for a place, and this way it wouldn't be so desperate. It shouldn't take me too long though. I've got the numbers for a couple of places already, and my friend Billy tells me it's really a renter's market right now."

"Star, don't worry about it," he said almost distractedly, going back to his lunch. "There are plenty enough bullshit things to deal with in this town. Looking for a place to stay doesn't have to be one of them."

"Maybe I shouldn't," Star said, second thoughts catching up with her. "It's such a huge relief not to have to make it work so quickly that I just said yes. But that's too much really."

"Star, come on," he said, waving it off. "I'm never there. It's no imposition. The place just sits there. You think I got to town and nobody helped me? I was in ladies' shoes for God's sake. People helped me. When you succeed, you'll help someone else."

"I don't know . . ."

"Really," he said with an end-of-discussion tone he'd honed in contentious production meetings. "You'll go, you'll try it out. Then if it doesn't work, you can go back to Florida or find somewhere else. Get your career started. Let me do this."

"Okay, but just until I find a place of my own," Star said, finally agreeing. "Thank you." She gave him a quick peck on the cheek.

From his carefully chosen seat, he saw just who was watching. And he smiled like the Mona Lisa posing his silent challenge.

As much as she'd enjoyed the tour of the movie lot and lunch with Peter, as happy as she was about finding a new place to live, and as thrilled as she was over the raves she was getting from the magazine over her cover shots, the big news that week was her date with Vince.

Dinner the night of the shoot had been great, but this was a second date. Were they dating? She squealed as she looked in the mirror and imagined herself living a childhood fantasy. "Am I dating Vince Piccolo?" She had to practice Papa Jens's deep-breathing exercises to calm herself down enough to get the lip liner just the way that she and .Billy had worked it out.

And then Lito had arrived with the car and she had been off to Vince's place in Malibu, back down Sunset Boulevard, this time riding in the back of the limo. It had seemed extravagant not to just take a cab, but Vince had insisted, arranging it through Sami, who had explained that Lito was Star's regular driver.

"I have a regular driver?" Star had asked when Sami called to let her know that Vince had arranged the car for her.

"Has anyone else driven you?" Sami responded playfully.

"Well, no." Star laughed. "I guess when you put it that way. Only it makes me sound like such a star."

"Get used to it."

The road looked strangely familiar. Star was getting to know her way around and was looking forward to getting a car and driving herself again.

Her old Impala, Rusty, was not up to the trip out, so she'd have to find something else soon. Despite having a "regular driver," she was in no way close to being able to afford to take a limo wherever she went.

The sun was closing fast on the water as they reached the end of Sunset and turned north on the Pacific Coast Highway—PCH to the locals.

Malibu City Limits. It seemed almost impossible. One of the most famous cities in the world, yet it seemed more mythical than real. But there she was. And she was not very impressed as she got her first glimpse from the highway. No sign of the beach or the ocean, just houses with no yards backed right up to the curb of a busy highway. Malibu was strangely devoid of the lurid quality of beach resorts on the Atlantic coast, densely overgrown with neon, high-rises, and souvenir T-shirt stores.

It looked surprisingly like the rest of the drive out to the beach through town.

And then they rounded a bend in the road and it was just like in the movies, with broad, sandy beaches and a volatile ocean throwing itself against the rocky shoreline. The sun gilded the water like some cosmic philosopher's stone, silhouetting the dozens of distant surfers black against the golden glare, like shadows dancing on the waves. Her heart swelled and she felt the tears. Could this really be her life?

The gate guard spoke with Lito briefly before waving them through to the strange spectacle that had begun on PCH and continued here, though in greater privacy and better landscaping. Grand though they were, they were still houses elbowing their way to the shore, each so close to the next as to give them the appearance of being one huge labyrinthine structure, one giant beach house running the length of the little residential street.

It was quaint in the way that theme parks are quaint, but too beautiful to be real.

Star half-expected Malibu Barbie and Malibu Ken to step from the door of one of the Malibu dream houses and into their Malibu luxury SUV.

They pulled up to a tall glass spire where Vince stood waiting to open the door for her. He waved Lito off. "Welcome to Malibu," Vince said, taking her hand and lifting her effortlessly out of the car. The kiss was perfect if you were directing the scene, but it was more show than substance. She tried raising herself onto tiptoe to get closer, thinking that distance was the problem, but by the time she got there, Vince had looped his arm around her and was leading her along to the brushed-steel door in the garden wall that served as the front gate.

"Hey, Lito," Vince said, tapping on the front window and pausing as it whirred down. "We won't need you anymore tonight," he said confidently.

Star considered getting back in the car and going back to town.

"Okay, yes sir," Lito said, looking at Star. "And you have the number, Miss Star."

"Thanks," Star said, still a little stunned by Vince's presumption and yet pleased that something—anything—was going to happen between them. She winked at Lito, who looked as apprehensive as she felt. "I'll call you," she said easily. At least that's what she was trying for.

Vince's hand slid down some from the small of her back.

Star waved as she turned, slipping his grasp and making her way into a garden at the foot of the small glass and steel tower that was Vince's beach house. A waterfall tumbled over a collection of local beach rock, forming a stream that cut across the garden before taking a turn around the side of the house and disappearing who knew where. Star paused on the bridge that led to sliding glass front doors. Gazing down, she saw giant goldfish darting around a Lilliputian lagoon, breaking the surface with their opened mouths as if in some silent fishy greeting.

"They're koi," Vince said, closing the gate and catching up to her.

"They seem kind of bold to me," Star said as the huge goldfish rushed forward to greet them.

"Just greedy," Vince chuckled. "I feed them from here. Come on inside," he said, lacing his fingers with hers and guiding her on.

The house was elaborately simple. Sheets of

glass and the slightest possible raw steel framing combined with a series of decks, lofts, winding stairs, and billowing sheer white curtains turned inside into outside and made the Pacific Ocean seem like an extension of the house. The furniture was low and sparse, and the entire place was ablaze with hundreds of candles and several wind-whipped fires, both inside and out.

They stood for a moment in the raised entry-way, overlooking the awe-inspiring scene.

"So, did you forget to pay the power bill?" she asked at last.

Vince only laughed and swept her up into one of his patented beautiful-to-look-at-but-hard-to-remember-no-muss kisses. Star took it in stride, figuring it had nothing to do with her.

For so many years with Adam she had felt responsible for his sexual heat. If he was hot and ready, he was a stud. But if he didn't rise to the occasion, he made no secret that it was her fault. And Adam had been her first real boyfriend.

Star had felt responsible for her rather abrupt introduction to sex. She thought of the experience with Al as forced, but never rape, as if somehow it was her fault for being where she should have known better than to be. After that, Star had moved into a place of denial, making a show of her feigned virginity and swearing oaths to wait until she was nineteen.

The vow had lasted three years until, at fifteen,

Bobby, the cutest boy and best baseball player in the tenth grade, had asked her to her first real boy/girl party. The event was held at the home of Bobby's best friend—one of Buttonwood High's most notorious young wastrels. It turned out to be one of those affairs where word got out that the wastrel's parents were going to be out of town. News of their departure was all that was needed. The party was implied.

Bobby had asked Star to be his date.

Her mom was actually relieved. Her daughter was such a late bloomer and a tomboy, Lucille feared that she would miss all the fun before she realized she could be having it. As she watched Star leaving—in a dress of all things—her hair brushed and pulled back a bit, instead of wild and fresh off the beach, Lucille was thrilled to finally bid her daughter a good-night in the company of a boy who was not wearing a sports uniform.

But Lucille's joy had been short-lived.

The party had been a singular event. Star and Bobby had arrived. Bobby got them each a screwdriver from the absentee parents' bar, then he led Star up to the wastrel's room, where he locked the door, downed his drink, pulled out his erection, and pushed Star down onto the bed. It was over too quickly for Star to find it objectionable. In fact, just the opposite. She was kind of pleased and thought it meant that they were going steady. Even when Bobby tucked himself away, pulled up his jeans, and dashed out to the company of his congratulatory buds, Star beamed proudly as if they were betrothed.

When Star rode her bike twenty-two miles from Arcady Key to see Bobby play baseball in Homestead, she had been bitterly disappointed to find that he hardly seemed to recognize her, let alone pay her any attention. Lucille had sighed sadly in response to Star's tearful call and drove the pickup to Homestead to fetch Star and her bicycle. She had respected Star enough on the way home to simply let her daughter cry it out without questioning her.

"Welcome to dating" was all she'd said.

And then it was Adam. They had always been together. They'd been inseparable as children, always in the same trouble or mud puddle—best buds. Star's rough-and-ready nature and the fact that she had shown no outward signs of impending womanhood had kept them buddies later than they might otherwise have been. By the time that Star's rather abrupt and overzealous puberty had struck, they were so used to each other that it had begun as a matter of course rather than of love or passion.

Their love affair had started more like a circle jerk than any sort of traditional boy/girl thing.

It was as if Adam had looked up one day to find that his best bud had suddenly and without warning turned into a girl. They had seen each other naked often enough over the years, camping out or skinny-dipping, and it had been Adam who had withdrawn at first, becoming shy as his body began to change. Star's girlish frame betrayed nothing of the woman she was about to become. Her slim, fit chassis was like that of a young boy . . . almost. Star's youthful body lulled Adam into an altered sense of security. He'd shared his sexual fantasies with her and, as the two lay in sleeping bags side by side, even his beloved *Mann* centerfolds.

Star found Adam's fascination with sex kind of amusing. Her two experiences had so little to do with sex as to be almost irrelevant, shaping her experience of men more than her attraction to them. Adam didn't seem to be one of them somehow.

One night he had brought a couple of beers along on one of their campouts. Lucille thought Star was at Theresa's, and Adam's folks thought he was out with friends. They had a few beers; got a bit drunk. Emboldened, Adam broke out the magazine and showed Star his erection.

"Come on, touch it," he'd urged.

"Put that away," Star said disgustedly. "I don't want anything to do with your wiener."

"Please, just put your hand around it," Adam pleaded.

"Go to sleep, Adam," Star had said, turning over.

"You can borrow my mountain bike for a week," he'd bargained.

Star rolled over and looked at him with a fury that took some of the starch out of his sail.

"A month," she said at last.

"A month?" he asked incredulously. "No way."

"Okay, then." She turned back over with a smile. "Good night."

Adam switched off the flashlight and the tent filled with the nerve-shattering sound of the cicadas clinging to the palmettos outside.

"Okay. A month then," Adam sighed.

And so their sexual adventures began.

Repulsed at first, Star quickly became fascinated with the mechanics and the hydraulics of it all, the strange feel of his erection in her hand, flesh like velour wrapped around a bird bone. And the improbable outcome of climax—wet and messy and unexpected, as though Silly String had shot out of his ear. Only it wasn't his ear. It had been a kind of revelation for them both, and it had begun with Star's discovery of his body.

At first his bike, various pieces of his clothing, favorite hats, and sporting equipment had found their way into her inventory. But their sexual exploration had quickly become a search for boundaries. Fueled at first by imagination and Adam's paltry magazine collection, Star soon found inspiration in the pages of Henry Miller and D. H. Lawrence. And as her physical sexual maturity caught up with her knowledge and growing technique, they had taken the plunge.

It happened when Adam's parents went out of town for the weekend, and Adam and Star decided to include the VCR as inspiration for their sexual

role-play. Each had chosen a tape at Video Reef, the
local rental store. Too young for adult fare, Adam
had opted for *Porky's* leering look at teenage sexuality. Both had found it dull and surprisingly tame,
given their well-practiced sex games. But Star chose
9½ Weeks, and they finally consummated their sexual relationship well beyond the fine art of mastur-
bation and manipulation they had shared for so
long.

It had taken an entire afternoon to clean up the
kitchen.

It had seemed only logical that they start going
steady after that. Boyfriend and girlfriend.

But their relationship didn't progress much beyond that in the years that followed. They were official, there with each other when the occasion
called for it or desire demanded it. At least their sexual gamesmanship expanded. As a result, Star's
whole idea of sex involved speaking in accents or
dressing up. She kept the Joe Cocker handy, and the
fedora too. Her reenactment of the famous scene
was flawless, and yet she and Adam progressed from
her beloved *9½ Weeks* to develop more and more
original games based on their shared fantasies.

It was fun for a while and then it was just habit.
They didn't grow closer to each other because they
were always pretending to be someone else. So,
while their sex life was physically robust, their personal life never got past the side-by-side sleeping
bags. Sometimes, for lack of greater inspiration,

Adam would simply look over Star's shoulder at the latest *Mann* centerfold always hanging on his living room wall. Or he'd have her read aloud from one of the erotic letters in *Ask a Mann* or the stories in *Mann Talk*. Their only connection was the physical act, working to get themselves off before the fantasy evaporated or the story ended.

It was part of the reason Star had resented those centerfolds in Adam's apartment so much, and the violation of having Marci's pictures added to the collage. Adam made love to his fantasies, not to Star, though for her part she never imagined herself with Adam either.

One of her favorite substitutions was Vince Piccolo. So, finding herself alone with him in his candle-filled sand castle in the real-life fiction of Malibu, California, Star felt light-headed. It was as if she'd stepped through that poster on her bedroom door and into the fantasy itself. She'd imagined herself with Vince dozens of times before. In fact, Adam did a pretty fair Vince Piccolo impersonation. But now Vince Piccolo was for real. The fantasy was the reality and she didn't know exactly how to react.

He led her out onto the deck, where dinner was laid out for them. It looked like a picture out of a magazine. And the taste, even more surprising as it looked almost too beautiful to be real. They worked their way up to champagne and strawberries as the sun melted like butter onto the surface of the Pacific.

Inspired by her memories from her favorite movie, Star rose and sat astride Vince's lap, facing him as she tied her napkin around Vince's eyes. She took a mouthful of her champagne and then pressed her lips to his. At last his tongue darted past her lips and they drank the champagne together. She poured the champagne over parts of her body, then presented herself to be licked clean. First, her fingers . . . then, ripping open her blouse, her shoulders, breasts, and body.

When she took her turn on him with the chocolate sauce, he could hardly control himself, tearing off the blindfold and dragging her to the bedroom. Star was short of breath and ready to be ravished by the movie star of her fantasies. She had already used up most of his staying power and it was over almost as soon as it started. Star didn't look on that as particularly bad news. An early showing to her meant the fun of the time and effort to get to a second event. To Vince it had been a sleeping pill. She started on getting him going again before she realized that he was asleep.

She didn't start laughing in earnest until she was back in Lito's car.

"So, I'm calling him Superman," Star confided to Jayne over her second glass of chardonnay. "Because he's faster than a speeding bullet."

"No sequel, eh?" Jayne managed after a pronounced bout of laughter that had drawn the attention of the dinner crowd at Spago. Jayne had wanted to take Star out to congratulate her on her first cover, and Spago was *the* place to see and be seen. It was kind of a debut. Jayne had even seen to it that the magazine got Star a new outfit for the evening and the full Skip and Billy. "Just a little perk," she'd explained to Star.

The Spago Garden was dominated by hundred-year-old olive trees that had been flown in from Greece. Brushed by a cool ocean breeze, the trees stirred gently, as Tivoli lights, wound into the olive boughs, twinkled overhead. As they sat surrounded by the rich and famous in the garden, Star felt as if she'd snuck in and was going to be found out and asked to leave at any minute. She felt as out of place as one of those olive trees.

"So, what are your plans?" Jayne asked, trying to capture linguini gracefully on her fork.

"I don't know exactly." Star shrugged. "I've got a place to stay for a bit, but that's as far as I've gotten."

"Then you do want to stay on and try to make a go of it here?" Jayne asked, giving up on grace and hoping for the best with a bite of her pasta.

"Yeah." Star nodded thoughtfully, spearing one of her cheese-filled pumpkin ravioli. "It just seems like too good an opportunity to waste."

"I think you're right. I can tell you there's plenty of excitement over your debut on the cover."

"Everyone keeps saying that, but no one has seen the cover yet," Star said, thinking that with Jayne she might get to the bottom of the mystery.

"No one except the people I've shown it to."

"Jayne," Star said with a tone of excitement and accusation. "You didn't. Who?"

"Well," Jayne said as if trying to remember, "the folks at *LADA,* who want to see you in their offices on the lot to read for a guest shot on the show." She pressed a card into Star's hand.

"*LADA!*" Star exclaimed, fighting unsuccessfully for control and once again drawing the attention of those around her. "That's one of my favorite shows. You got me an audition?"

"I showed the casting director your picture," Jayne said firmly. "*You* got the audition."

"Oh, Jayne," Star gushed. "I just can't believe it. Oh my God. What'll I do? I've never auditioned for anything before. I'm not an actress."

"And how many magazine covers did you shoot before this one?" Jayne grinned devilishly.

"Well, none."

"Exactly. And it's already getting you noticed and it's not even out yet."

"I guess," Star agreed, grinning shyly, but proud of herself. "But they're going to expect me to, like, move and stuff."

The rest of the dinner had been Jayne taking time to give Star some advice about the audition, but really about succeeding in Los Angeles; what it took and what it cost. There were some friendly warnings, a few cautionary tales, and some dire predictions, but nothing Jayne said could possibly have dampened Star's spirits.

"*LADA,*" Star exclaimed for about the hundredth time as they stood waiting for the valet to bring around Jayne's Mercedes convertible.

Nearby, just at the edge of the property, a band of photographers, like refugees at the border of a hostile and forbidden land, clamored for admission.

"Hey, Jayne," one of the men called, flashing a quick shot of Star's little previctory dance. "Who you got for us tonight?"

"Here's one of the necessary little evils of success," Jayne said, taking Star's elbow and leading her into the no-man's-land that ran along the unseen boundary.

"Jayne," the photographer mocked, his pride wounded, "is that any way to talk? No one's ever called me little."

"Ladies and gentlemen," Jayne said, dropping Star at the DMZ and stepping back to clear the frame. "I give you *Mann* magazine's October cover girl for this year, Miss Star Wood Leigh. *S-T-A-R W-O-O-D L-E-I-G-H,*" she spelled the name for them as the flashes strobed and blinded Star, who did her best to smile graciously.

"Get a picture now, while you still can."

8

walking on sunshine

The "little place" Peter kept in town turned out to be a nineteen-room starter mansion in Benedict Canyon.

"Isn't that where Sharon Tate was killed?" Star interrupted as Peter tried to give her directions over the phone.

"Now all of a sudden you're an expert on the history of Hollywood?" Peter said, laughing.

"No," Star said, joining in. "I just took this thing called the Grave Line Tour. They take you to all these places where famous people died."

"Lovely," Peter said distastefully.

"Not really, but it may help me find your place."

"Like, turn right at the Beverly Hills Hotel is too tough for you?" Peter joked. "Just give the driver the address. Tell him that Alto is on the right between Hillgrove and Cielo. And, yes, Cielo is the street where Sharon Tate used to live," he concluded, cutting her off. "Anything else?"

"They're sure they caught the people responsible for her death?"

"Twenty-five years ago," Peter said lightly. "Listen, I'm sorry I won't be there, but everyone knows you're coming. Astrid will stop by in the morning to set up a workout schedule with you."

"Astrid?" Star asked, puzzled. "Who is Astrid? And what do you mean everyone?"

"The personal trainer," Peter explained as though it should be obvious. "The house is staffed."

"Staffed?"

"Yeah, you know," Peter said, making light of it. "Cut the lawn, keep the leaves out of the pool, do the dusting, like that."

"The personal trainer?"

"She's great. There's a gym at the house, why waste it? Oh, and feel free to use one of the cars if you need it. Look, I've got to run, but I'll be back late tomorrow. See you then."

Star listened to the dial tone as she doodled a little map to the house. She looked around her beautiful rooms and thought how happy she'd been there, then stepped out onto the balcony to wave good-bye to her wonderful view. She hated to leave, but at least she had a place to stay for the time being. Soon she'd have something permanent. She had one day to move and get settled before her first audition.

She looked in the bathroom, one last check to see if she'd left anything.

The phone rang.

"Hello?" she answered curiously. She'd already spoken with Peter, her mom, and Jayne. Who else would call?

"Miss Leigh?"

"Yes," Star answered, still curious.

"This is the front desk," the young man on the other end of the line introduced himself. "Your car is here."

"My car? I don't really have . . . My regular driver, you mean?"

"That's right," he said cheerfully. "Just wanted to let you know."

"Thanks," Star said, grinning. How had he found out? she wondered. "Tell him I already left."

"We'll let him know."

Two minutes later there was a pounding at her door.

Star opened it to find a much distraught Lito, red-faced and out of breath as though he'd run up the stairs to her room.

"Miss Star," Lito chastised. "That was not very funny. My work with the magazine is very important to me. You should not tease about professional things. What if I'd left?"

"I don't think there was much chance of that happening," Star said with a gentle laugh. "So, Jayne ratted me out, did she? I'm sorry I scared you though."

"Miss Jayne told me," Lito admitted, gathering her bags as he spoke. "But I asked her to. I wanted to say thank you for helping me to get started with the magazine. They're requesting me for all their VIP runs now. So this ride is on me."

"That is so sweet, but you have to stop doing this. I can't afford to pay you and you have to earn a living." Star gave him a little kiss on the cheek and grabbed her purse and a couple of shoulder bags. "But I'm glad you did. It wouldn't have been the same discovering a new place in Los Angeles without you," she said, leading the way out the door.

Peter's place on Alto was one of those high-Spanish-baroque piles that are perhaps the only thing truly indigenous to Los Angeles. The wrought-iron gates opened onto a rambling "fussienda" with so much trim, filigree, and embellishment that it looked like a huge, heavily frosted cake.

"Wow," Star said, a bit surprised by the manicured lawns, the topiary shrubbery, and the sculpture-filled fountain glittering in front of the portico that hung off the front of the house. "If this is the little place he keeps in town, I wonder where he really lives, the White House?" Star said, turning to Lito on the front seat next to her.

As they pulled into the dramatic entranceway, a phalanx of Asian women emerged from the house and formed a line to the car. The most senior of the group opened the back door as the limo came to a stop.

"Hello," Star called, once again alighting from the front and surprising the welcoming committee. "I'm Star Wood Leigh and I'm looking for Peter Rodick's house."

"Miss Leigh," the smartly uniformed woman said, closing the rear door and walking briskly to take Star's offered hand. "Welcome to Valhalla-baloo."

"How's that?" Star asked, shaking the woman's hand.

"Valhallabaloo," the woman repeated. "*Valhalla* is the Viking word for heaven, and a hulla-baloo is a big disturbance, I'm not sure what language. It's the name Mr. Rodick came up with for the house."

"A big disturbance in heaven?" Star smiled. "No self-esteem issues there. I'm Star. I'll be staying here for a few days, but I'm guessing you know that."

"Yes," the spokesmaid said. "I'm Ling, but Mr. Rodick calls me Dinga. These are the other staff, who you'll get to know as you go along. Will you need rooms for your driver?"

"Oh my." Star laughed. "Heavens no. This is

Lito. He's really more like a friend of mine. He drove me up here since I don't have a car."

"There are several in the garage that Mr. Rodick wants for you to use," Dinga said, smiling warmly as she escorted Star up the broad front steps. "Let me show you to your rooms."

Star's "bedroom" consisted of a sitting room, a dressing room, and yet another room with, funnily enough, a bed in it. Her balcony opened over the large formally shaped rectangular pool in the back-yard and a striking view of the city beyond. A bougainvillea-clogged iron staircase wound from the balcony to the patio below.

"I can hardly believe this place," Star said, amazed by it all.

"There are eight other bedrooms to choose from if you'd rather," Dinga said, pausing as she un-packed Star's things.

"No, no, this is fine. I just mean that I can't be-lieve that Peter doesn't even live here."

"This is Mr. Rodick's house," Dinga insisted as if for Star's benefit.

"Valhallabaloo? Oh, yeah, I'm sure this is his house all right."

She spotted the small aqua-blue box with the white satin bow on her pillow. "Oh, Dinga, some-one seems to have left this here," She said, retriev-ing the box and handing it over.

"No, Miss Leigh," Dinga said, refusing it. "It's for you."

"For me?"

"Yes, it's a present from Mr. Rodick."

"A present for moving into his house?"

"That's the last of it, Miss Star," Lito said, dropping off the final bag he'd ferried up the stairs from the car.

"Oh, Lito, thank you for looking after me," Star said, embracing him. "Daisy Duke lost in the big city? What would I have done without you?"

"You call me if you ever need a hand," Lito said, handing her yet another card.

"You know I will," Star said, slipping it into her pocket. "I'm going to miss being driven everywhere, but there are cars here and I do know how to drive. I can get in more exploring this way. And I get to ride in the front seat without an argument."

"You call me to take you to the Academy Awards," Lito said with a wink and a smile.

"Yeah, well, I won't wait till then." Star giggled. "But if that happens, you'll be the guy I call. Good luck, Lito."

"And *buena suerte* to you, Miss Star," he said with a little wave before turning to leave.

Star felt a little sad, not knowing when she'd see him again.

"Miss Star," Dinga said, adopting Lito's name for her. "I'm going to iron these things." She held up an armload of clothes that looked perfectly respectable to Star. "I'll be back to finish your unpacking in a few minutes. It will give you time to freshen up."

"Okay," Star said, amused by the idea of freshening up after the ten-minute ride over from the hotel. "Thanks, Dinga."

Dinga took a little bow as she backed out of the room and closed the door behind her.

Star turned to look around this next stop on her tour of Los Angeles and realized that she was still holding the small turquoise gift box. She sat on a nearby damask chaise to open it.

Tiffany & Co. appeared as she removed the ribbon.

She may have been from Arcady Key, but she knew what Tiffany's was. Inside the gift box was a flat velvet case, buffeted in cotton batting. As Star opened the case, a note fell out into her lap and a small gasp escaped her lips. A diamond tennis bracelet was mounted to the satin inside.

Tentatively, she slipped the bracelet around her wrist and examined the effect as she held her arm up to the sunlight pouring in the nearby windows. It was nice, but maybe too nice? With a heavy sigh, she picked up the note that had fallen into her lap.

Welcome home,

Peter

Astrid was a very exotic name for a decidedly local resident. Fit and blond, she could pass for a recent

Scandinavian import—until she opened her mouth and the Valley Girl came spilling out.

"Star?" Astrid said, coming up behind where she was having breakfast at a table by the pool.

Startled, Star choked on her cereal and coughed in response.

Undaunted, Astrid took Star's hand and pumped it vigorously, taking the cough as her good-morning. "So I'm like the resident trainer here," Astrid said with a gesture that seemed to indicate the pool and the rose garden. "I'm Astrid. Peter said you'd be hanging here for a while and I wanted some face time with you."

Star managed to get her hand away from Astrid and grasp for her juice. She took a sip, but it only made things worse and she began to cough more violently. I can't be choking, she sought to reassure herself. If I'm coughing, doesn't that mean I'm still breathing?

"I've got other outside clients, but I'm totally on call here, you know?" Astrid went on, oblivious. "I'm thinking that we could start out three days a week to begin with and then totally ramp it up if we want or just play it by ear, you know? I see you're up early, and mornings are totally best for me, you know? So, what about around now Monday, Wednesday, and Friday? You think? I mean except for Monday holidays. We can meet Tuesday, Thursday, and Saturday. I know it'll be like kind of off rhythm, but you need a day between workouts and we'll shift your diet so you're ready for it. Oh, and when we do have to meet on Saturdays, it'll have to be at eight fifteen 'cause I've got a long-standing ten-twenty yoga class, you know? Unless of course when Saturday turns out to be the first Saturday of the month, when I have synchronized swimming, so then we'll have to do Tuesday, Wednesday, and Friday. If you're like cool with it?"

Star nodded vigorously, as much in the hope of dislodging the errant raisin as of getting this highly caffeinated woman to shut up.

"So, okay, then we'll meet Monday, Wednesday, and Friday mornings at eight thirty," Astrid confirmed, pounding Star once soundly on the back, accomplished the task and launching the raisin into the pool. "Excellent. I'm totally looking forward to it. See you tomorrow. Later," she finished, dashing out the nearby gate.

There was the thunk of a car door and the sound of an engine coming to life, followed by the crunch of gravel as the car pulled away.

Star laughed weakly as she continued to stare at the gate. Who—or what—was that? Breakfast seemed suddenly less appealing having only just survived it, so she followed to see what was on the other side of the gate.

She passed under an arbor of the purple bougainvillea into a sort of paddock enclosed within high, stuccoed walls that were the same sherbet color as the house itself and topped with

the same frothy white "frosting." The walls were
pierced by two massive wrought-iron gates on one
side and on the other by a series of broad stable
doors that ran along the first floor of a building
that formed the fourth and back wall of the paddock. Above the rough wood was a covered
gallery of still more doors and casement windows,
all heavily shrouded by more of the same
bougainvillea. She assumed that these led to the
staff quarters.

Star crossed the courtyard to the nearest of the
huge rough-hewn doors and stood on tiptoe to peer
through one of a series of small, high windows that
were clearly intended more to let light in than to
display what was inside.

She saw an enormous yellow convertible. It was
the garage. She looked for a way to open the doors
to get a better look. The door was huge and
wouldn't budge, and no handle or hinge was in evidence. As she looked down the row, she saw a
smaller door tucked under the stairway that lead up
to the gallery. The door was unlocked and it led
into a small office, which opened into the vast
garage space. The huge yellow convertible turned
out to be a Rolls-Royce Grand Corniche, though
Star thought it looked like a circus wagon. There
was also a Bentley sedan that looked as if it were
late for a funeral, several other stuffy banker's cars,
an enormous Range Rover, a Cadillac limo that
seemed to be up on blocks, and a cute little Mer-

cedes convertible. It wasn't as fancy as Jayne's, but Star thought it would be just right for her.

Just to be sure, she practiced sitting behind the wheel.

She checked herself out in the rearview mirror. Yes, that was her, but could this really be her life she was living?

"That car looks very good on you."

Startled once more, Star looked up into the eyes of a really fine-looking specimen of a man wiping his hands on a greasy rag. They regarded one another a moment. Star felt short of breath, both from the surprise of seeing him and how naked his stare made her feel.

"I'm sorry," she said, jumping from the car and resisting the urge to run. "I didn't mean to . . . they said I could use one of them and I was just looking."

"And I think that's the one." He nodded, moving nearer, his coveralls rolled down to reveal a well-developed chest barely contained in the ribbed cotton cloth of his tank top. "You must be Star. I'm Marino." He reached for her hand and then took it back. "Sorry, I'm filthy. I was trying to get things ready so you could have your choice this morning. Good to meet you though. Really good."

"Good to meet you," Star said as he drew nearer. Aside from the half-naked men at the gay pride festival, he was the most male thing she had seen since she'd arrived. Star could feel herself re-

acting. A man in coveralls with grease on his hands
was more like home than most anything else she'd
seen so far in Los Angeles.

"This is where Mr. Rodick keeps his old cars, so
mostly they've just been sitting," he explained,
drawing nearer. He was substantially larger than she
was and just being so physically dominated reminded her of her own sexuality, and his. Aside
from being present for Vince's orgasm, her sex life
had been on hold for the three weeks since she'd
touched down at LAX. Marino's eyes ran over her
body with such undisguised heat that she could almost feel it. "Him being out of town and all, he sent
me over to make sure these were in order for you."

"Hasn't he heard of trade-ins?" she marveled.

"Never thought about it." Marino shrugged as
he stood next to her.

"How many cars does he have?"

"'Bout average, considering," he said, slipping
the fingers of each hand beneath the roll of his cov-
erall and the waistband beneath.

Star caught her breath and they stared at each
other silently for a moment.

She saw the muscle of his arm flex just at her
eye level as he shrugged. She wanted to take a bite.
She and Adam had played mechanic and destitute
customer often enough, and she was trying to remember her lines.

"So, which of these has the most comfortable
backseat?" she asked, ad-libbing wildly.

"It'd have to be the Bentley," he answered after a moment's consideration, not looking away. "I mean the Caddy is a limo and all, so there's more room. But for actual comfort it would be the Bentley."

"Which one is that?"

"This one right over here." Marino walked in the direction of the car.

"But you're not sure?" she asked, catching up with him.

"Well, it depends I guess," he answered earnestly. "But, no, I'm not sure."

"Okay, then let's find out." Star took his hand and playfully pulled him toward the Bentley's rear door.

Turned out it was the Bentley.

And Star was singing along with the car radio, the top down on the freshly waxed Mercedes 560SL as she pulled up to the studio gates.

"Walking on sunshine, woe-hoe . . . Hi," she sang to the gate guard, so excited to be where she was and doing what she was doing.

"And don't it feel good," the guard sang along with her.

The two had a laugh as Star turned down the music a bit.

"Love that song," the guard said, grinning, infected with Star's top-of-the-world mood. "Name please?"

"Star Wood Leigh."

"Uh, there it is, *L-e-i-g-h,* Leigh," he said, writing on the hang tag. "Here you go. Now you can park in the lot over there anywhere but the first two rows. The Kelly Building is straight back between the two lions, second on the right."

"Thanks. I've got my first audition today. Wish me luck."

"It doesn't involve singing, does it?"

"No," Star said askance.

"That's good. You should do great."

"You devil." Star giggled, pulling onto the lot.

"Good luck," the guard called after her.

She found a perfect space right near the lions. As she made her way toward the building, Star began repeating the lines from her sides just to make sure she had them by heart.

" 'I don't know who you think you are, but you're in my place now, and in my place we play by my rules,' " she said, trying to sound tough.

" 'Is that supposed to scare me?' " she went on, alarming a passing messenger. " 'Do you think you're the first person to point a gun at me?' "

The messenger spun to look over his shoulder for a gun as Star breezed past him.

" 'You can shoot me, but then you don't get anything you want from me,' " she concluded with conviction as she turned up the walkway to the Kelly Building.

Over and over, she repeated the four lines until

she arrived at the office where she was to report. She took a Papa Jens deep breath and opened the door.

It was all remarkably makeshift-looking. A gate-leg table, some folding chairs, and a beat-up old desk composed the reception area. A young woman looked up from the pages spread in front her on the dilapidated desk.

"May I help you?" she asked, extending her hand as if she expected Star to give her something.

"Hi, Star Wood Leigh," Star said, trying to shake the oddly angled hand.

"Résumé?" the girl said, taking her hand back. "Head shot?"

"No," Star said, puzzled by the girl's odd behavior.

"Are you here for the audition?"

"I think so," Star said, nodding. "For *LADA*?"

"This is the place," the girl at the desk sighed.

"Then, yeah." Star nodded. "The casting director saw my shots for the cover of *Mann* magazine and asked me to come in to read," Star explained quietly, trying not to broadcast the story to the other actors slouching around the nearby catering table.

"So, you're a model who doesn't have a picture of herself?" the young woman asked incredulously.

The door opened and a busty young blonde strode past followed, much to Star's surprised, by Van Pursens.

The two regarded each other a moment.

Star decided to try to start things off on the right foot.

"Van," she said, sounding as pleased as she could. "I'm so glad to see you here. Are you auditioning too?"

"Come inside," Van hissed through gritted teeth.

"Well, Van, there were people here ahead—"

"Get in there," he shouted, holding the door and pointing forcefully.

"Well, okay," Star conceded, moving toward the door. "But I think we should leave this to the people in charge."

Van followed her into the large and largely empty room, with two more gatelegged tables behind which sat a couple of people talking on the phone.

"Come over here a minute," he said, motioning Star toward a far corner of the room.

"I don't want to be rude, Van," Star said, reaching the end of her patience with his abrupt and inexplicable behavior. "I really need to say hello to the people who—"

"Did you call me an eggplant?" Van demanded, his voice quivering with quiet anger.

"What? What are you talking about? An eggplant? Just now?"

"No, not just now," Van said, fighting for control. "The other day, when I ran into you and your daddy at the Hayworth."

"Why would I call you an eggplant?" Star said, cracking up, too amused by the outrageous claim to react to his mistaking Peter for her father. "I mean we don't seem to have hit it off, but I have to tell you I can come up with worse things to call people than fruits and vegetables. Why would you think I called you an eggplant?"

"I saw it in the columns," Van huffed, folding his arms defiantly.

"Columns?" Star asked, completely lost. "I feel like I'm at the Mad Hatter's tea party. Are you just making this stuff up as you go along?"

"You mean to tell me you don't know anything about it?"

"I did have eggplant for lunch that day, excuse the expression."

"You don't even know what it means, do you?"

"Eggplant?" she wailed incredulously.

The people sitting at the tables looked up from their phones, frozen and clearly startled by her use of the word.

"Don't make this any worse than it is," Van said. "I read it in the *Daily Reporter.*"

"Well, I don't even know what the *Daily Reporter* is, but I can tell you this, you're no eggplant. I like eggplant. You're a fruitcake," Star said, her voice rising. "I came here to audition today. I wish you luck on your audition. Now, if you'll excuse me, I'm going back outside and get in line so I can try out for the part. And you can go to hell. I apologize to all of you," she concluded, speaking to the room's other occupants, who had been staring at them, unblinking. "I just want you to know that I am not with this man and I never called him or anyone else an eggplant or a rutabaga or a zucchini."

And with a flourish, Star turned and stormed out of the room.

So much for my good mood she thought. "That is the rudest man in Hollywood," she said under her breath. She tried breathing to calm herself down. The other people in the room stared silently, making her feel worse than ever.

The phone on the girl's desk buzzed. "Yes. . . . Mmmhmm. Oh yeah. Sounded pretty good to me the first time. . . . Okay, but I don't know how you'll top that," she concluded, hanging up the phone. "Miss Leigh? They'll see you now . . . or is it again?"

"But there were people ahead of me," Star said, trying to buy herself some time, and also to try to appease the other actors, who were now staring at her with open animosity.

"Miss Leigh, if you'd please just go on in. They're asking for you."

"This shouldn't take too long," Star said apologetically to the others as she rose to cross to the door. If it was possible, she was even angrier at Van than before. They were going to ask her to leave or just get rid of her as quickly as possible, and it was all his fault. "Thank you," she said to the girl at the front desk as she turned to enter the room she'd only just left.

"Hi, Miss Leigh," said a rather severe-looking woman with Joan Jett hair and makeup. "I'm Rowena, Jayne's friend. I'm so glad you could come in today. I'm the casting director; this is Angie Hardcastle, the creator and EP. And I think you already know Van Pursens, the director."

She'd have cried if she hadn't been so angry. "Hello, Star," he said expressionlessly, saluting her with a folded magazine.

"Okay," Rowena said. She was trying to keep it light and professional, but she really wished she were anywhere else in the world. "Here's what we'd like to do. You and I will read your sides together, and then we'll see where it goes from there, okay?"

"Sure," Star said, the last fume of her good mood evaporating.

"Good, now as I think you know, your character is a madam for a high-tone call-girl service," Rowena said, slipping on her glasses and turning to the Post-it–marked script. "TJ, the lead, is trying to find out who murdered one of your girls, but you don't want to admit that she was working for you. Okay?"

"Mmmhmm," Star said with a weak smile.

"You need a moment?"

"I can't think that a moment will make a difference," Star said, the tears almost coming. "I'm ready when you are."

"Okay," Rowena said, feeling a bit sorry for the girl as she opened the script and began to read. " 'Okay, cut the crap, lady. You can come clean with me or I can shut your operation down right now.' "

" 'I don't know who you think you are, but you're in my place now, and in my place we play by my rules,' " Star said, as if she were speaking to a third-grader she was trying to cajole back into his seat.

The best thing about the reading was that it was brief and at least Star would be out the door soon, or so she thought.

"Thank you," Star said, rising as soon as they got to the end.

"We're not done with you yet," Van said sharply, and then softening. "Miss Leigh."

Star turned to look at him, a deer in the headlights. "Okay," she said, sitting back down.

"You've never done any acting before, right?" Van said harshly.

"No," she said simply.

"Believe me, you've done plenty of acting," Van said with a snort of derisive laughter. "Remember the last time you convinced Peter to buy you something? That bracelet maybe? Remember how you acted all sweet and sexy? Like you'd make it worth his while if he bought you that bracelet? That was acting. And that's also this character. Got it?"

Star went cold; her teeth clenched, her eyes narrowed, and her ears blazed. A strange smile spread across her face. If she'd had a gun, she could have killed Van and then done the reading. "Yeah," she said tartly. "I've got it."

"Read it with me this time then," Van said. "Just like you're trying to use sex to get what you want. You can do that."

"Ready when you are," Star said, sparks flying.

The others in the room ached to be anywhere else.

" 'Okay, cut the crap, lady. You can come clean with me or I can shut your operation down right now,' " Van said snidely.

Star rose slowly and crossed to sit on the table in front of him before speaking, smiling at him, never losing his eye. At the same languid pace, she leaned down so that her face was uncomfortably close to his and, with a throaty little laugh, began.

" 'I don't know who you think you are,' " she said, dragging her index finger along the bridge of his nose and then tapping it twice, " 'but you're in my place now.' " She continued withdrawing her hand, allowing it to rest with the fingertips just touching her right breast as it peeked through the vee at the neck of her blouse. " 'And in my place we play by my rules.' " She allowed the fingers to slip under the edge of the vee.

" 'I can have two marked cars and a couple of

uniforms milling around outside your door. How do you think that will affect business?' "

Star laughed and patted his face. " 'Is that supposed to scare me?' "

" 'I don't care if it gets you off,' " Van said, grabbing her hand and twisting it away. " 'I'd just as soon shoot you as talk to you.' "

Star played up what was in fact just Van taking and holding her hand as though he were hurting her. Tossing her long blond hair out of her face and into his, she submitted to him by pressing herself against him. " 'Do you think you're the first person to point a gun at me?' "

" 'Get away from me,' " Van said, snatching his hand away.

Star slumped across the table. " 'You can shoot me,' " she said, rubbing the spot where Van's holster would be, " 'but then you don't get anything you want from me.' "

The two regarded one another a moment, and then Star sat up, smoothed her clothes primly, and crossed back to get her things. "Thanks for bringing me in," she said, breaking the silence.

"I'm scared of you, lady," Van said with a little grin.

"You nailed that," Rowena agreed, relieved that it was safe to speak again.

"I felt the heat," Angie agreed, just before getting back on the phone.

"Listen," Van said quietly, coming around the

table to walk her to the door. "We can't say it for sure, but someone will call you later today."

"Thanks," Star said numbly, still too stunned from the reversal of the situation to be sure how she felt.

"Here," he said, thrusting the magazine into her hands. "This is the column where you're quoted. And just so you know, *eggplant* . . . it's a racist thing."

"Really," Star said, shocked by the eggplant news and downright flabbergasted to see that something—anything—she'd said had been written about in a magazine. "That's just horrible. Van, I would never . . . I will never order it again."

Van laughed. "It was good work today. I look forward to doing this with you. Truce?" he offered, extending a pinkie.

"Pinkie swear," she said, wrapping her pinkie around his. "Truce."

They shook on it.

The call had beaten her home.

"You got it," Peter shouted, running out the front door into the path of her car. She had to swerve to miss him. "You got the part!" he proclaimed as he lifted her out of the car without opening the door.

She shrieked and threw her arms around his

neck as he spun her around in the air in an impromptu dance of celebration.

"Let's go shopping to celebrate," he said.

"Put me down, Peter," she scolded playfully. "I don't want to spend my money before I've even earned it."

"No." He waved her off. "My treat. We'll have a *Pretty Woman* shopping spree on Rodeo Drive. You should look like the star you are."

"Thank you, Peter, but you've done enough," Star said seriously. "This house, the car, the bracelet . . . I appreciate it all, but, you know, Julia Roberts was a prostitute in *Pretty Woman*. I'm not a prostitute, though I do play one on TV," she said suddenly, shouting with laughter.

The two ended up sitting in the driveway, tears running down their faces. "Okay, that's it, young lady," Peter said, picking her up and putting her back in the passenger's side of the car she'd left at the curb. He hopped in behind the wheel. "You're coming shopping with me, no more arguments."

It really was a lot of fun, once she got past her misgivings.

Peter obviously had a tremendous amount of money and a couple of hours on Rodeo Drive was not going to put much of a dent in it. She did her best to be the voice of moderation, but it was a hopeless task. She was on the playground of the American capitalist glutton. The shoes were too yummy, the dresses too hot, and before you could say American Express, they were on their way back up the hill with the trunk filled with a few thousand dollars' worth of goods. Peter would not let her look at the price of anything or see any of the receipts, but Star knew that some real bank had been left between Wilshire and Little Santa Monica.

"You know what we should do?" Peter said as he drove them back to the house. "We should get all dressed up and go someplace nice for dinner. You been to the Dome yet? Or L'Orangerie?"

"Really, I'd love to, but not tonight," Star said. "I've got Astrid in the morning, and I'm a little worn-out from the day. But thank you, Peter, for all your kindness."

"Sure thing," Peter said, acting casual as he pulled the car up in front of the house. "I've been out of town and I probably need to make an early night of it myself. Rain check?"

"You bet."

"Till then," Peter said, leaning in for a goodnight kiss.

Star saw it coming and turned her head just in time to give it the cheek.

"Okay, and back to one, everybody," the assistant director called.

Star sighed as she retraced the eight steps she had taken four times to get a shot where no one even had any lines. She was truly amazed that the making of this spine-tingling, fast-paced, action-adventure police drama was duller than a slow day at Talon's Nail and Tan Spa. They did everything over and over; first to get it right and then to get it right from five different angles.

Not only was the work slow and repetitive, it made almost no sense. They were shooting all her scenes in one afternoon, starting with her last one. And then seemingly randomly until they had them all. It wasn't a big part, just a dozen or so lines scattered here and there through the one-hour script, but since they went backward and forward, it was hard to keep it in her head what her character knew or didn't know at any given moment. It gave her a new respect for actors.

"And, action," Van called.

Star made her way down the steps, greeted the guy she was just supposed to be seen with in this scene. Though there was no sound and no scripted lines, the two had to create their own scene. And the scene they created had to reflect where they were in the story, how the two characters felt about each other, where they had been before they met, and where they were going afterward. And all without a word of dialogue.

"Hi," he said, opening the car door for her. "If we have to do this fucking scene one more time, I say we steal this car and go to the beach. What do you think?"

"We've been doing this so long I'd forgotten we

were at the beach," Star agreed, nodding seriously as she stepped into the car.

He closed the door, walked around to the other side, started the engine, and pulled it up twenty feet. They got the wave-off and he stopped.

"Perfect," Van called.

"That's a wrap for today, ladies and gentlemen," the AD called, rattling off instructions about call times, props, costumes, and a lot of stuff Star wasn't paying any attention to. It was her last shot. For better or worse, it was done. She'd been less nervous about this than the shoot. She'd worn more clothes for one thing, but she felt more insulated from this. It was more removed from her, less personal.

With the shoot it was just her; here she had a character to hide behind. It was almost like wearing a mask.

"Hey, Star," Jessica, who had played one of the call girls, called to her as she returned her costume. "Some of us are going over to the Gulch after if you want to come."

"Thanks," Star said. "But I've been up and at 'em since six this morning; I'm ready for the last roundup."

"I know what you mean," Jessica said, lowering her voice. "But that guy from the bar-fight scene really wanted to meet you."

"Friend of yours?" Star asked, taking a seat at the makeup mirror beside her.

"We're in class together. His name's Brad." Jessica nodded.

"They're all named Brad?" Star giggled.

Jessica laughed.

"I'm not kidding," Star said. "Watch this. Brad!" she called out.

She got "yeah's" and "hunh's" from four different guys and laughs from Jessica.

"Good work today," Star said, not specifying, and then turned back to Jessica with a superior shrug.

"You got any remover?" Jessica said, giving up.

"Cold cream." Star took it out of her bag and handed it over. "Thanks for trying. Maybe we can meet up another night?"

"You got it." Jessica smiled. "Let me put your number in my cell."

The good-natured camaraderie in the day players' trailer reminded her of the locker room at Mother Pearl's. It made her feel a little blue as she thought how nice it would be if Theresa were there and the two of them could talk or just have a beer at the bar or go over to Randy and Andy's and sit in the hot tub and have a Zax. Or if she could just hug Mutley, she thought as she turned in her jewelry and hand props.

Star wasn't too tired to go to the Gulch, she was too homesick.

"Night, Brad," she said to the prop guy.

"Night," he said genially.

She smiled as she stepped down the metal steps on the front of the trailer.

"You had a good first day," Van said, coming up to her.

"Thanks," she said. "Coming from you, that's a compliment I can really trust."

They laughed.

"We have a truce, remember?" he said, walking along with her as she made her way toward the parking lot.

"Yes, but when does it expire? It's like a cease-fire. Shouldn't there be negotiation toward a more lasting peace?"

"You knock me out," he chuckled. "I tell you what, how about a peace summit on Saturday? What do you think?"

"A summit? That's sounds like a big deal." Star giggled, playing along. "Geneva?"

"Mount Hollywood. I could pick you up around eleven."

"In the morning?"

"Yeah," he said. "Get in a good day's work on—what was it?—that lasting peace."

"How about I meet you somewhere?" Star said, shy of her arrangement and not wanting to have to explain Peter or her living arrangement on a first date.

"The negotiations haven't begun and already you want a compromise." He winced, playing it up as they paused near the little lot where the cast and crew had parked.

"This will give you the advantage when you ask for your first concession," she encouraged him, giving his arm a little punch.

"Good point." He nodded. "You know Quality on Third, near Crescent Heights? We could meet there for an informal breakfast meeting and then move on to the summit."

"I can find it," she said, smiling, charmed by how playful he was when he wasn't fighting with her.

They reached the parking lot. Rather than walk up to the Mercedes and give herself away, Star paused next to an old VW as though looking for her keys.

"Great," he said, surprising her by leaning in for a kiss. More than a peck, but not quite a bushel, it was a very creditable first kiss. "Wear hiking shoes," he said, touching her nose and then turning to leave. "See you then," he called, vaulting into his black SUV and roaring away.

She waved and watched him go.

"Excuse me," a young woman said to Star as she edged by to get into the Volkswagen Star was standing beside.

"Sorry." Star stepped aside and headed for the convertible.

All the songs on the radio seemed sad and she

gave up and switched it off as she turned the car toward home, or what passed for home. It was so grand she couldn't really complain, but it wasn't hers and she'd done nothing about finding a new place.

It had been a really great day, her first time on camera. Acting, she thought with a little laugh at her own expense. She'd known her lines and she hadn't fallen down, so she was calling it a victory. But somehow, because things were so good, it made her feel even more blue. It was because there was nobody to share this perfect day with. She thought of her friends back home, of being able to drive out to the key and spend the night at her parents'. Or take Mutley to the beach for a run.

She got back to Valhallabaloo and left the car out front for Marino to put away.

"Hello," she called from the front door.

No answer.

The table in the front hall groaned with packages and shopping bags all swagged with a banner that said *Congratulations* in glittery script. More extravagance from Peter. She sighed as she peeked in a couple of bags and opened the lids on a box or two. But her heart wasn't in it and she left it on the table and went up to the phone in her room.

Dropping onto the bed, she dialed with her thumb without having to look at the keys.

"Hi, this is Theresa. I'm not home right now—"

Star cut it short and dialed the next.

"Y'ello," her mom's voice cut through the three thousand miles.

"Mom?"

"Hi, Esther," her mom said, still the only person who ever called her by that name. It took Star back to being the little girl who used to be called that.

"How's everybody?"

"Well, now, you know good and well that if something was wrong, I would have called you. Is everything all right?"

"Yeah," Star said without much conviction. "It was a great day. I did my part for *LADA* today, and I just wanted to share it with someone. Made me kind of homesick."

"Homesick?" Her mom chuckled. "For this place? Used to be you were sick of it, now you're sick for it. There's just no pleasing you, child."

"Used to be I could just drive down and remind myself what a little pissant place it was and then be home in time for *Wheel of Fortune,* old woman."

"There's that smart mouth," Lucille said, making a clucking noise with her tongue.

"The one I got from you?"

Lucille laughed, proud of her daughter.

"So, Mom, how about this. You tell me what's so bad about that place since I can't come home tonight and see for myself."

"Oh, lands, where to begin?" her mother said with an expansive sigh. "Let's see. Your father's been on one of his gambling junkets, drunk since last Thursday, which means he's been staying over at that no-account friend's house."

"Dale?"

"Yes, Dale," Lucille said, as though it were a bad taste in her mouth just to name him. "Anyways, that means I've had myself a little vacation as there's only me to cook for and the house stays clean without me having to clean it. It's like magic how clean this house is when there's no one here."

"How about Hank?"

"Honestly, Star, I haven't seen him since the day you left for California," Lucille said, realizing it as she said it. "In fact, I've heard less from him than from you. Isn't that the way? If you were still here, I probably wouldn't see you till Thanksgiving or hear from you, but since you're so far away, we talk most every day."

"I guess," Star said, knowing that there was truth in it. "But you know I'd be home to see Mutley."

"Oh, God, Star, that dog has taken to doing the cutest thing," Lucille said, reminded. "I keep meaning to tell you, but we're usually talking about what famous person or knockout thing has happened to you and I always forget."

"So what is it, Mom?"

"He has put together a little collection of your old clothes and taken to sleeping on them—I guess 'cause they smell like you—with one of those vulgar T-shirts from Mother's, 'Beat me, fuck me, make me write bad checks,' or whatever it is that they say on them."

" 'Shuck me, suck me, eat me raw,' " Star corrected her, laughing.

"Yeah, that's it," Lucille agreed, going on with it. "Anyways, he's got one of those on the top of the pile, the one you wore to the party right before you left. I guess he misses you."

"Oh, Mom," Star said as the tears came.

"Now don't get yourself all in a twist about it," her mother comforted in her own prickly way. "You're not missing anything here, and Mutley will be wagging his tail on the porch come your next visit. Hell, nothing's changed here since hurricane Andrew came through. So you just hang in there, sweetie. We'll all be here come Christmas or whenever you make it back."

"Thanks, Mom," Star said, still sniffling. "I'll talk to you tomorrow."

"Get some rest. And congratulations on your first day as a movie star."

"Thanks, Mom," Star said with a little laugh. If Mom only knew how far she was from being a star.

She hung up the phone and snuggled with one of the dozen or so pillows heaped on the bed and pretended it was her beloved Mutley. She was just drifting off when the phone beside her bed rang.

She sat up and looked at it. That phone had never rung before. Star was uncertain whether she should pick it up, so she let it ring. Eventually it quit and she turned back over. There was a knock on her door.

"Miss Star?" Dinga said, opening the door just a smidge. "Telephone for you. Mr. Rodick."

"Thanks, Dinga." Star rolled over and grabbed blindly for it. "Hello? Peter?"

"How's my Star?" he asked brightly. "Did you get your surprise?"

"Surprise?" Star yawned. "It looked more like Christmas. I thought there was some strange local holiday I'd missed."

"Only your first day on the set of your first production. I'm sorry I didn't get over to the set to say hi, but it's been one of those days. I thought a few surprises would make up for it."

"Peter," she said, knowing the discussion was pointless. "It's too extravagant. You can't keep doing this."

"Oh, it's just a few trinkets," he said, making light of it. "Believe me, it does more to make me happy than it ever could you. So I'm really doing it for me."

"So, get yourself something," Star said, throwing herself back onto the heap of pillows.

"Look around you," Peter chortled. "I take plenty good care of me."

"Can't argue with that."

"Listen, let's go out and celebrate," Peter said, abruptly changing the subject. "I'm meeting some people—Ovitz, Bart, Lansing, a couple of others—

and I thought you should come. Big names. People you should meet."

"Not tonight, Peter. I'm too tired. I'm already in bed. Astrid wore me out this morning and then the shoot this afternoon. I think I'm just going to have a swim and make an early night of it. But thanks for thinking of me."

"Oh, okay, then have a good night," Peter said, stung but determined not to show it. Not a man to be easily discouraged, he had never gone after something he didn't get. Star was next on his list. The truth was, part of what made her attractive was that she would not be easily added. But he'd find the way to her heart, he always did.

9

bohemian rhapsody

Star awoke with a start. She looked around, startled, a moment's confusion, before remembering she was in her room at Peter's. It was early and the gray light of an overcast L.A.morning seeped in around the drapes. It was a coastal layer, a local phenomenon that took away any sense of time. The light had the same quality whether it was 7 a.m. or noon.

She'd been having an awful dream. Stuck in this long hallway, unable to find an open door, she just kept trying door after door as she made her way along the endless corridor that stretched on infinitely before her and behind her. As she continued frantically down the hallway, she was pursued by a hideous, mournful wailing, like ghosts from a bad horror movie.

As she lay in bed coming around, she became aware that she could still hear the strange wailing. Sleep left her completely as the adrenaline rush of terror seized her. She thought of calling the police, but what would she tell them? Peter? No, she didn't want him over here. Her mom? She'd never hear the end of it, and there was nothing her mom could do from Florida.

She resolved to take the situation in hand and see for herself. Resolutely she tossed aside the covers and stepped from the bed. An old oversize, hooded sweatshirt lay across a nearby chair. She pulled it on so that she wouldn't have to face the poltergeist in just the panties and camisole she had been sleeping in.

Cautiously she approached the door, the noise growing a bit louder with each step. She carefully eased the door open a crack; determining that the apparition was not in the sitting room, she rushed to grab the poker. Finding the fireplace tool heavy and unwieldy and figuring it was just big enough for the specter to seize it from her and beat her to death with, she chose instead a really nasty-looking candlestick from the mantel. It was solid, she could get a good grip on it, and she'd never really liked it anyway.

The banshee wail rose to a new high and Star cried out softly, startled by the impending horror. If only she knew a priest to call. Feeling like Drew Barrymore in the opening scene of *Scream,* she eased toward the door to confront the awaiting ghoul. She grasped the doorknob firmly and, summoning all her courage, snatched the door open and drew back the awful candleholder, prepared to do her worst.

Nothing.

There was a moment of silence and Star breathed a sigh of relief, thinking that she'd had a narrow escape from her terrible fate when, suddenly, the caterwauling resumed in a new and more terrifying trip up and down the scale. Rather than paralyzing her, the fear swept her up and into a courageous charge. She thundered down the stairs in the direction of the hellish howling, stormed through the kitchen, and with the determination of the marines and a bloodcurdling howl of her own flung open the door and leaped inside.

Chaos and screams.

Dinga and a couple of the other household staff were terrified by Star's shrieking intrusion into the laundry room and disbursed, the laundry they'd been folding flying through the air as they ran howling in all directions, out the back door, into the servants' dining room and beyond. Of course, this only scared Star worse and she screamed louder, dropped the candlestick, and beat a hasty retreat back into the kitchen.

Star's screaming brought a similar reaction from the staff who'd barricaded themselves in the butler's pantry.

And the staff's bloodcurdling screams brought more screams from Star, who was trying to hide behind the cabinet door near where she'd collapsed, her legs unable or unwilling to support her any farther, and Dinga caught up with her.

"Miss Star, are you all right?" Dinga asked, breathless from the screaming and the running and just generally being frightened out of her wits.

"Oh my God, Dinga," Star said, sitting on the tile floor and leaning against the cabinets. "You guys scared the hell out of me. What was that noise?"

"What noise?"

"I can't describe it," Star said, still panting. "It was like a cat in the washing machine."

"*Lakmé*," Dinga answered with a little laugh.

"What is that? Some kind of religious rite?"

"It's an opera by Delibes," Dinga said, grinning. "We were practicing the 'Flower Duet,' though admittedly there were more than two of us. If we scared you, perhaps we need more practice."

"No, it just sounded so eerie," Star said, beginning to laugh at it all as the relief coursed through her. "Was it in your native language?"

That was all Dinga needed as she began to laugh too.

They had a good laugh together and the little

troupe even reunited to give an encore performance for their audience of one. Star agreed that it was quite lovely when you knew what it was.

"What does it mean?" Star asked, applauding them.

"Well," Dinga said thoughtfully as she put on the kettle for tea. "Literally, Mallika is pointing out the flowers and the swans to Lakmé, who is sad and worried. But, I think it means to enjoy the beauty of life while you can. The flowers bloom only for a short time."

" 'Gather ye rosebuds while ye may'?" Star asked.

"Exactly," Dinga said, taking down the tea things and beginning the ritual. "I like that. Is it a poem or a song you know?"

"I don't know," Star said with a sad smile. "Just something my grandfather always used to say to me. Sorry about scaring you."

"As am I," Dinga said, seating the lid on the tea ball and dropping it into the teapot.

"Thanks for the song," Star said over her shoulder as she left.

She tried to get back to sleep, but it was no use. The whole thing had only made her feel worse. She missed home; she missed her grandfather; she felt lost and alone. Who could she turn to? Depend on? She was scared of a lot more than just eerie noises. That she felt so on her own made her long for some sense of security, somewhere in her life. She'd never

really known the feeling of stability. Her parents
were good to her but they were as precarious as she
was. Adam had come to be as much a threat as a
source of comfort. And her friends usually de-
pended on her to be the strong one.

She took a long shower and tried to celebrate all
the good things in her life: the beautiful marble fit-
tings of the enormous bathroom, the luxurious
comforts of the house at her disposal, the wonderful bath stuff she'd gotten on her shopping trip with
Peter, the little secret dreams she'd never dared to
hope would really come true, suddenly coming to
life all around her.

She was going to be on the cover of *Mann* magazine. She was going to be on *LADA*. She was
going on a date with Stormy from *Hip-Hop Cops*.
She'd been on a date with Vince Piccolo . . . oops,
too far. Her mantra crashed again and she was
back to just feeling alone. As she made her way out
to her favorite table by the pool with her bowl of
granola and soy milk, the dark mood returned and
she began the mantra again.

She took a bite and chewed ruminatively as she
tried to bolster her spirits.

Mutley nuzzled at the hand in her lap and she
reached out to stroke his head.

"Mutley," she screamed, leaping to her feet so
suddenly that she spilled the cereal, upset her chair,
and frightened Mutley so badly that he began to
bark ferociously at the offending chair. "Oh my

God, it's you," she said, dropping to her knees and throwing her arms around his neck. Tears came and the two of them rolled around on the massive rocks that made up the jigsaw of the patio.

As she looked up from the cool stones where she lay with Mutley, she saw Peter standing under the arbor by the gate to the motor court. He had a deeply satisfied smile on his face as he watched Star and Mutley tumble around on the broad blue slabs of slate.

It was as if she saw him in a whole new way, as if he had magically been transformed into a new person. Perhaps what she could really see, or wanted so very much to see, was how much he cared for her. Not that he wanted something from her, but that he wanted to see to it that she was happy, that she was taken care of, that that was what he truly wanted. And in that instant, it made her love him.

Star bounded to where he stood by the gate, his arms folded, content. She leaped into his arms, almost knocking him off-balance, he was so unprepared for her sudden show of affection.

"You wonderful man," she said, covering his face with dozens of little kisses. Mutley circled them, barking, demanding that he not be left out.

Peter only stood there with Star in his arms supporting her as she climbed over him. He was pleased—amazed even—by the outcome of such a simple act.

At last, Star's celebration died down and she stopped. Leaning back from him while still in his arms, she looked into his eyes as they regarded one another in that moment as though for the first time.

"Thank you, you darling man," Star said, stroking his face. "My heart's desire. I don't know how you knew, but you knew."

"You see," he said quietly. "I told you I got far more out of giving little gifts than it ever cost me. I'm just glad I got the chance to see you this happy. Thank you."

She could resist him no more, and as she leaned in to kiss him, somewhere inside the house Dinga and her ensemble again struck up the "Flower Duet" from *Lakmé*. Only this time it sounded more like the voices of angels.

Without another word, Peter carried her up the winding iron stairs that led to the balcony off her room. It was all he did to push the moment. As he sank with her onto the sofa in the little sitting room, she began to hurry through the things she knew would inflame him and move them on to more. But he stopped her each time she tried to rush.

As she tried to unbutton his shirt, he took and held her hand—not forcefully but lovingly. As she ground her body into his, he rolled them over so that they were just barely touching. Then he began to stroke her body all over, gently and with kisses.

Her frustration served as tinder to her excitement and she fought him for control. The more she fought, the more control she gave him. She dug her nails into his back and drew him to her, and he took her wrists and held them above her head against the mattress as he nipped at her T-shirt-covered nipples. She raised her face hungrily to his and he buried his face in the nape of her neck, breathing into her ear with such intensity that it was like an electric current, running through her writhing body.

As she wound her legs around his waist and drew herself up to him in her excitement, he withdrew, sliding down to bury his face between her legs. And as his tongue made contact, she joined the soprano line of the "Flower Duet" echoing up from the floor below.

In the way that he had persisted in searching for presents to make her smile, he made love, seeking to bring her more and more pleasure. It was endless foreplay. It was the part of *9½ Weeks* that Adam never got. It was like torture, interminable, unendurable, exquisite torture as he searched her body, tasting, flicking, tickling, touching, to see how it made her react and then acting on her like an apothecary's full stock of aphrodisiacs. It took twenty minutes for him to remove her clothes, but that twenty minutes was better than most of the sex she'd ever had.

By the time he penetrated her, Star's whole body ached for it as if she had no will left, no resistance, just complete and utter surrender. Even then, he took his time bringing her near, then pausing to draw her back from the abyss before driving her to the edge again. At last, when she thought she could stand it no longer, he sensed her readiness and followed her over. It seemed to last forever as the strained notes of the aria trailed up and concluded in concert with their own activity.

As the final notes rang out, the two fell gasping on Star's still made but much disarranged bed.

"Wow," Star said at last with a husky little laugh. "I never knew how much I liked opera."

Somehow Mutley's arrival changed things. Star felt at home and at ease and the idea of looking for another place to live abated for the time being. The presents continued to arrive, but Star felt less pressured by them. For his part, Peter wisely kept to his own space and allowed Star hers, leaving after lunch on the day they made love and not returning for two days.

For her part, Star began to live her life in Los Angeles, truly enjoying it for the first time. She called Billy and met him for lunch at a little French bistro near the magazine's offices at Sunset Plaza. She began to take her training sessions with Astrid seriously, learning to enjoy the mechanized workouts that were replacing her beloved volleyball and bodysurfing. She helped Marino "wax" her car.

She took long drives up the coast with the top down and just reveled in where she was. And she relaxed as she stopped refusing the wonderful gifts that had been presented to her. It might well have been a fool's paradise, but it was still paradise and she was gathering all the rosebuds she could lay hands to.

On the day before her date with Van, he phoned to ask if she'd consider meeting him at the studio as he had a looping session.

"Is that like a sewing circle?" she teased. "Are you making a rug?"

"Ha-ha, very funny," Van said flatly. "Do you really not know?"

"No clue," she admitted breezily, always glad to learn more.

"Looping is the way you put the voices back in scenes where the sound is bad. Actors come in and lip-synch as they watch their own performances. If it's done right, you can't tell the difference."

"It's where it doesn't sound like their voice is really coming out of their mouths," she said, getting it.

"You really can't tell," he said emphatically.

"Oh, you can always tell," she said casually.

"Okay, I'm glad I told you about that," he said, not wanting to get into another of their little disagreements on the eve of their first date. "So, what do you say you meet me there, hang out, and as soon as it's over, we'll move on to our summit."

"So, still hiking boots?" she asked, wanting to change with their plans.

"Oh, yeah, same summit, but maybe a different breakfast venue. We'll see. Sometimes these things go on a while and sometimes they're done in a take or two."

"Fine with me," she said, still really pleased to be able to tell Theresa that she was going out with "Stormy."

Given the "hiking boots" instruction, Star decided to break out the tomboy drag. It felt good to be in a pair of reasonably respectable but still beat-up jean shorts, a comfy sport-sleeved tee, and a pair of well-worn hiking boots. She pinned her hair up haphazardly and wore just enough makeup to avoid getting the look that said "Is something wrong, dear?"

She got Marino to give her a ride to the studio so that she wouldn't have to explain the car. She made her way up to the gate on foot.

"Hello, sunshine," her singing-partner/gate-guard said to her as she arrived at the lot midmorning. "Where's your car?"

"Oh, I rode in with a friend. I'm meeting Van Pursens. Do you know where he is today?"

"He's in the Griffith Building, all the way down and to the left." He pointed in the general direction.

The lot was like some small medieval town where winding footpaths had been paved, but there

was no plan or order to it. As a result, following
the guard's directions, she had found herself at a
two-story, white clapboard building with dark
green wood shutters and galleries. It looked a lot
like old military barracks.

No official building name was in evidence, but
since it was in fact all the way down and all the
way to the left, insofar as that was possible without
actually jumping the wall and leaving the lot, she
figured it must be the place. She stepped into the
first-floor hallway to ask after Van's whereabouts.

"Well, it's about time," said a handsome-
looking woman who made her sweater and jeans
seem like an Armani suit just by the way she wore
them.

"I'm sorry," Star said because of the familiar
tone, assuming they had met on the *LADA* set, as
she followed her down the hallway. "I got a little
lost trying to find the building and wasn't even sure
this was it. There's no sign outside."

"Yeah, they just repainted and they haven't put
the DeMille sign back outside," the woman said,
pausing outside an office door and directing Star inside.

"DeMille?" Star said following, uncertain of
where she was or was supposed to be. "I thought it
was Griffith? Anyway, it's nice of you to wait out
there for me."

"It was worth it," the lady said, handing Star a
clipboard. "You're perfect for this. I love that you

came in costume. Look, we've already got your stuff, so just fill this out so we know how to get in touch." There was a flash and then a Polaroid.

"I'm sorry," Star said, "I think I'm in the wrong place. I think you have the wrong person. I'm here to meet Van Pursens for breakfast or possibly lunch."

"What you do with your personal life is your own problem," the lady said with a knowing smirk. "This is an audition for *Hammer Time*. And I'd really like to put you on tape. I think you're what the producers are looking for, that's why I assumed you were here for this when I saw you in the hallway."

"Well, I don't know," Star said, not quite sure what to think and too surprised to be nervous about it. "What does it involve?"

"Just read a few lines on camera. I'm Camille, by the way. Sorry for the confusion, but I really do think you'd be perfect for this. Have you done any acting?"

"I just did my first guest shot this past week," Star said, so swept up in the moment that she allowed herself to be led in front of the small video camera in what was clearly an unoccupied office. Hmmm, *Hammer Time*? She figured it must be a music video or something. How hard could it be? "What the hell," she said.

"There's the spirit," Camille said, pointing to the cue cards her assistant was holding up. "When I tell you to go, just say your name, count to five, and then read these cards."

"Okay," Star said, thinking that sounded easy enough.

"Great," Camille said, taking a seat. The cameraman nodded at her. "Go."

"Hi, my name is Star Wood Leigh," Star said, smiling into the camera. "One, two, three, four . . ."

"You counted?" Van shrieked with laughter and pounded on the steering wheel of his obligatory black SUV. "You actually counted? That's perfect. You are a pearl of great price."

"She said count to five," Star insisted, still part of the joke at her own expense. "So I did. She said it wouldn't be hard."

"But it was?"

"Well, it was harder than that," was all she could manage.

Laughter precluded saying much else for a bit. It was nice just to be in the car together and laughing on what was left of a beautiful Southern California morning.

"So," Van said, finally able to get his breath enough to speak. "Do you think you got it?"

It was one of those kinds of laughs that just keeps feeding on itself like wildfire in dry brush. If they looked at one another or spoke at all, they lost

it again. They made a genuine effort to try to quell
the blaze, but the embers wouldn't die out.

They laughed all the way up La Cienega from
Venice to Sunset Boulevard and then down to Fair-
fax, until they pulled into the tiny parking lot for
Bristol Farms, where they laughed for a bit while
they waited for a space to open up. It always
amazed Star that in such a huge place with so much
space and so many cars, Los Angeles had done so
little to create parking spaces.

"Is this where you want to have breakfast?"
Star said, stepping out of the enormous vehicle.
How silly she thought these big gas guzzlers were.
Van was a single man and it wasn't like he worked
construction, so most of the massive thing was
never occupied. And everyone had one. "How can
you tell which one is yours?" Star asked, looking at
the vehicle as she waited at the curb nearby for
Van.

"That," he said, pointing at the vanity plate
with his key-chain remote and signaling to engage
the alarm. The car emitted a little two-note tone
that sounded like a greeting from R2-D2.

"Big 1," Star said, reading the license plate.
"What does that mean?"

Van turned and grinned lasciviously at her as he
walked backward into the plate-glass wall by the
store's front doors.

"Guys," Star said, getting it. She rolled her eyes
as she opened the door in his face and went inside

without him. "What is this place?" she asked, pointedly changing the subject.

"It's a grocery store." He shrugged, making his way through the cramped aisles of the little store to the deli counter in the back. "Morning. Pursens," he said to the lady behind the counter. "Picking up."

"Morning," the lady said brightly as she went to look for his order.

"What are we picking up?" Star asked, catching up with him. "I'm pretty hungry."

"Grab a piece of fruit to eat in the car," he said, nodding. "It'll be a bit before we get to lunch."

"What happened to breakfast?" she said playfully as she looked around for the greengrocer's section.

"You had that big audition," he said, pointing the way.

That was all he had to say. The mention of the forbidden topic cracked them up again. They laughed through the rest of the transaction, causing some raised eyebrows and comments about their visit.

"That's a beautiful picnic basket," Star said as Van loaded his purchase into the cavernous rear compartment of the SUV. "Good thing you brought the big car so there's room."

"Funny," he said, vaulting gracefully behind the wheel. "They do a great job of them. This is the place to come for a picnic basket when you're going to a concert at the Hollywood Bowl."

"Oh, I haven't been there yet," she said wistfully, remembering pictures that she'd seen of the famous massive half-shell–shaped concert stage. "It always looks so glamorous."

"I guess it is." Van nodded. "I grew up with music. My father is a musician and I've been there a lot over the years. I take it for granted, but it is a beautiful, kind of old-fashioned place."

"So is that where we're going?"

"Today?" Van shook his head. "No. But as soon as I get back and find out what tickets are available, you bet."

"Pretty confident."

"I have a good feeling about today." He reached over and brushed the back of her hand with the back of his. "I haven't laughed that hard on a first date since . . . well . . . ever. I mean, during the date, not after."

They laughed again.

They talked easily with each other as they made their way to Griffith Park and up to the observatory, where, to Star's amazement, they were actually able to park.

"Is this where we're going?" Star asked, marveling at the famous building. "This is where they made that old movie with that actor who died in the car crash and what's her name who played Gypsy Rose Lee."

"It is, but it's not where we're going," he said, grabbing his backpack and the picnic basket and striking out in the opposite direction. "So, of all those people, you remember the one you've proba- bly never seen? Why's that?"

"Who?"

"Gypsy Rose Lee."

"Oh. I guess because she was a stripper and she became really famous," Star said with a shrug. "You know? Like the most famous strip- per ever."

"I guess that is unusual," he agreed as they made their way along the tree-shrouded approach road, then up into the hills.

"Yeah, it's like she was just famous for being who she was, not for what she did," Star said with a little smile. "Where are we going?"

"Why, to the only place we could possibly go for a Hollywood summit," he said with a knowing smile.

It was a good solid hike on a pretty rough trail. Star loved it. She'd been looking at these mountains from a distance since her arrival. And here it all was, dusty and scratchy and aromatic. It kind of amazed her that there was so much undeveloped land in the middle of such an overdeveloped place. And she was from south Florida, so she knew from overdeveloped.

They seemed to be making their way to a grove of massive TV antennas that sprouted hideously from the crown of the hill they were climbing. The air was close and still as they made their way up toward the disgraced peak. Strange noises and rustling leaves nearby gave her the willies.

"I'm pretty hungry," she pointed out.

"It's worth the wait," he said. "We're almost there."

At last, they crested the ridge and began their descent. They were on the ocean side of the hill, and the air that had been cut off from them on the other side hit strong and cool. Star felt exhilarated and refreshed, but it wasn't just the fresh air and the view. It was the excitement of spotting their destination: the HOLLYWOOD sign.

Or rather from their perspective:

"It's perfect!" she shouted, jumping up and down and clapping as she ran past him down the trail.

"Hey, now, wait up," he called. And the race was on. Star actually beat him to the sign, but Van kept going, rounding the *H* and disappearing into the sage below.

"Come back here," she called, following him and finding herself on a narrow ledge above a fairly steep drop-off. She slowed down and edged around the end of the sign only to find herself in the thick of some fairly dense brush. "Hello?" she called out.

As if in answer, music drifted through the sage toward her. She followed the sound and emerged in a small clearing enclosed by the dense brush with the sign looming overhead. During their brief separation, Van had spread a cloth on the relatively flat ground, cranked up the boom box he'd had in his backpack, and retrieved the wine and two glasses from the picnic basket.

"*Et voilà*," he said in welcome, pouring two glasses and offering her one.

"This is pretty great," she said with a little thrill to her voice. "What beautiful music."

" 'Rhapsody in Blue.' I'm glad you like it. May I have this dance?" He extended his hand gracefully in her direction.

She answered with a silly little bow and stepped up to him, thinking that he was only kidding. Instead, as the music swelled, he swept her up into his arms and led her around the clearing in a spontaneous and enthusiastic dance, sometimes Fred and Ginger, sometimes wild and free. She was usually a little self-conscious about dancing, but there was something liberating about Van, and Star lost herself in his enthusiasm.

As they danced, they danced with greater and greater abandon. The disc was filled with an eclectic collection of music, the rhythm of each wilder and more sensuous than the last. Van tore off his shirt and then his shoes, dancing barefoot on the massive smooth boulder that made up the floor of most of the little clearing. Caught up in the moment, Star followed suit until the two were dancing in their underwear. When they collapsed onto one of the blankets gulping breath, they rolled easily into one another's arms, the music continuing to accompany their abandon.

"Oh my God," she gasped, shivering involuntarily in anticipation. "That really is a big one."

He flicked his exceptionally long tongue at her, gave her an eyebrow wave, and turned in profile. "You should see what I can do with it."

"Is that what I should see?"

He smiled and stroked her face with the backs of his fingers.

Reaching up, she took his hand and guided one of his fingers to her lips. She kissed and then suckled on the finger until, unable to control himself any longer, he took her into his arms.

The kiss was electric. Star's toes curled and she ran her fingers through his hair, drawing him nearer for more.

Running his hands up her back, he dispensed with her bra with a practiced ease. His kisses ranged lower and lower on her body. The talented tongue found her exuberant nipples, teasing and torturing each until she cried out, her voice echoing in the hills around them.

Van clapped his hand over her mouth urgently and the two froze.

There was a hollow clicking sound, then suddenly, almost right on top of them, a tour group on horseback came riding by only a few feet away.

"Erected in 1923 at a cost of twenty-one thousand dollars as a real estate promotion," the tour guide droned, and the group ambled past. "The HOLLYWOOD sign originally read HOLLYWOOD-

LAND, the name of the development it was intended to promote. Its home on the side of Mount Cahuenga is today insured by a private trust and revered as a national monument."

The voices and noises receded into echo as the group passed them by unaware.

Hearing the sound, she became suddenly, deliciously aware that they were outside. She was naked, or nearly, outside. It was as exhilarating as the long fingers that were sneaking under the waistband of her panties. She kicked up her legs in response, sliding the brief, skimpy garment down her legs and kicking it away with her feet, never to be seen again.

"Shhh," Van stuttered in between hiccups of laughter.

She howled a girlish, laughing howl and dove onto Van greedily, tearing away his boxers and taking him into her mouth in a gulp.

His echoes joined hers.

"Oh, God, yes," he moaned, tangling his fingers in her hair.

When he could stand it no longer, he lifted her face to his. They kissed intensely for a moment before he finished reversing their positions. He filled his hands with her and then emptied them and filled them again as he explored her body. He scooped her up into his palms, literally lifting her off the ground and raising her, facing him, onto his shoulders. He rose to stand with her resting there, then drove that skilled and titled tongue home.

She simply screamed.

Almost losing her balance, she grasped his head to keep from falling as he backed her up to lean against the leg of the giant *H* above them. She writhed against the gleaming white facade, pounding her head against it and calling out to the city below as he brought her to bliss again and again.

When at last he let her body slide down between him and the sign, lowering her onto the seat of his passion, she gave herself gladly and gratefully at last.

Hooray for Hollywood.

"I'll never be able to look at that sign the same way," she said, looking back over her shoulder as they made their way down the hill.

"That's one of my favorite places," he said. "I love being naked outdoors and to be in such a public place and still in such privacy, perfect. Think of how many people looked up at that sign while we were up there."

"We'll have to go hiking again," she said with an evil little laugh.

"I grew up here, so I know all the best places," he said conspiratorially. "And I was serious about that concert at the Hollywood Bowl. I'd really like to take you there, though I'm afraid we'll have to keep our clothes on."

"Drag," she said with a little laugh. "I like the liberation, but I'm not an exhibitionist."

"Where can I drop you? Is your car still back at the studio?"

"No, I got a ride," she said, realizing the limits of her deception. Marino had delivered her to the studio so Van wouldn't see Peter's car and she wouldn't have to explain it. But he was going to see Peter's house and that was going to be much harder to explain. "I'm off Benedict Canyon," she said casually. After the afternoon they'd spent, it wouldn't be a problem, she assured herself.

"Benedict? Great," he said, turning the car off Vermont onto Sunset. "Right on the way."

"Yeah," she said sheepishly, looking out the window. "I'm borrowing a friend's place." She looked out the window and asked questions about the sights along the way. Some of them Van knew about, but most of them he had no clue.

"People who live here don't really know anything beyond the rash generalizations," Van explained. "L.A. is so big that we decide what certain areas of the city are like—what they are about—so then we don't have to think about them. The most any of us see of the areas where we don't live is what we can see from the freeway. Here we are," he said, turning onto Benedict Canyon. "Where do I go?"

"Up ahead, on Alto. It's the first right past the third light."

Winding their way up the hill, Van began to look around, a bit confused by the surroundings. By the time Star pointed out the gates, he was downright curious.

"Right here," she said, pointing at the gates.

"This is your house?" Van asked, pulling up.

"Nice, huh?"

"It's a palace. Is it yours?"

"No, I borrowed it," she explained, gathering up her things.

"Borrowed it? From who?"

"Peter Rodick," she said, tucking her bra into her purse. She hadn't had the heart to put it back on. "He loaned it to me while I find a place."

"How's that coming?" Van asked, a tone of sarcasm creeping into his voice.

"How's what coming?" she asked, looking up from her purse.

"Finding a place."

"Oh, well, it's only been a week, but I haven't had a chance to look really," she answered blithely, oblivious of his mood shift. She leaned across for a good-bye kiss to go with their great afternoon.

"Do you have a room of your own?"

"What's that supposed to mean?" she said, pulling back.

"I mean, what are the terms of this loan?" he asked, his voice twisting into ugly.

Star drew back to slap his face, but he caught her hand.

"Hey, hey, hey, little wildcat," he said, setting her back in her seat. "Claws in."

"I will if you will," she said, pulling her wrist from his grasp.

"I just meant—"

"You just thought that I was fucking him for my room and board? Is that all? Well, let me ask you something, Van, what if I was? I'm not, he doesn't even live here, but what if I was? Would that make you better than me? Would it be okay for you to make me feel bad about what I was doing? What happened to all your talk of freedom and liberation this afternoon?"

"Are you through?" he asked after she was quiet for a minute.

"Yes," she said, kicking open her door. "I believe I am."

"Star," he called after her, exasperated. He got out of the car and got in between her and the keypad to open the gates. "Star, listen to me. Don't you see what's going on? Don't you see what he wants? He's just using you to get what he wants."

"He's not like that," she said, hot tears of anger coursing down her face with what mascara she hadn't sweated off during their athletic afternoon together. "He's kind and generous and unselfish. Qualities you wouldn't understand."

"I wouldn't understand?"

"No, one afternoon together and you already think you own me."

"Oh, really? So he expects nothing from you?"

"Not a thing. He says that doing things and giving me gifts makes him happy."

"He's turning you into a lapdog," Van said, stepping aside so she could punch in the code to open the gates. "Listen," he went on calmly as the gates sprang to life and slowly began to open. "Think what you want of me, but, Star, this is a trap and all this is just bait. If you stay here, you'll forget to go get a life of your own. This one is just too easy. And soon you'll belong to him just like this place and everything else. If you're in love with him great, but if you're just in love with all this . . . ."

Star turned angrily away and stalked up the drive.

"I had a great time today," Van called after her.

She never looked back. As she made her way across the lawn, she heard him start the engine, turn, and drive away.

It had been such a great afternoon. How dare he ruin it with such mean-spirited and petty accusations? By the time she got to the house she was too angry to cry. She flung open the massive door and stormed across the front hall to the stairs.

"Star? Is that you?" Peter called from somewhere in the back of the house.

"Hi, Peter," she called back, continuing her ascent.

"Where have you been?" His voice got nearer.

"Out for a hike," she said, slowing down.

"Where? Alone?" Peter demanded, coming into the hall below her.

"The HOLLYWOOD sign," she said, stopping and turning to look at him. "And, no, I was with a friend. We had a little picnic."

"Who? What friend?"

She only looked at him. Once again he was changing before her eyes.

"None of my business?" he asked, a playful tone to his voice, but not his manner or his questions. "You really should let someone know where you're going. Something could happen. And I had plans for us. I was trying to put together a dinner with some friends tonight and thought you'd like to go shop for something special to wear."

"Are you trying to trap me?" she demanded.

"Trap you?" he asked, confused.

"No, I guess it's too late for that. They have to feed the animals at the zoo."

"What are you talking about?"

"Nothing," she said with a weary and defeated smile. "I'm sorry about this afternoon. I'm too pooped to go out tonight. But thanks."

"No problem, sweetie," he said easily. "Get some rest. We'll do it some other time."

She nodded and turned to go but stopped near the top of the stairs and called back to him, "Peter?"

"Yes," he answered, returning to the hallway.

"I really appreciate you letting me stay here. It's very kind of you."

"Sure thing," Peter said with a dismissive little laugh.

"See you around." She turned and went back upstairs.

"Hello, Billy?"

"Hi, darling," he said, cradling the phone as he sorted transparencies on the light table in his office. "What a flawless surprise. To what do I owe the honor?"

"I kind of need to talk to you," she said, twisting the phone cord nervously.

"Why don't you meet me for lunch? My treat. I'd love to see you and you could stop by and see the picture we're using for the cover."

"Sure," she said, distracted. "That sounds great."

"Is everything okay?" Billy asked, detecting the off tone to her voice.

"The big stuff is great, Billy," she said, brightening a bit for his benefit.

"But the small stuff's got you down?"

"What time?" she asked, smiling despite herself.

"Come now. Nothing's doing around here."

"Well, I've got a workout," she said, letting the cord unfurl. "So about eleven thirty?"

"Perfection."

It was nearly eleven o'clock by the time Star made her way out to get the car, Peter's car. She felt guilty even taking it out that afternoon, but it would have to do.

"Why so down?" Marino asked, looking out from under the hood of a Range Rover Star didn't recognize with a suggestive smile that she knew only too well.

"Oh, nothing," she said distractedly. "Only, would you know where I could buy a car?"

"More than likely," he said with a little puff of surprised laughter. "What kind of car are you looking for?"

"Well, I think it's going to be more what I can afford than what I want," Star said, raising her shoulders in doubt. "I'll know soon."

"I'm sure we can work something out," he said with a teasing grin.

"No, I really want to pay for it," she said, shaking a finger at him.

"Yes, ma'am." He saluted, then winked.

She smiled and blew him a kiss as she dropped herself behind the wheel of the car.

It was a beautiful day and Star was soon pulling into one of the lots at Sunset Plaza, near the magazine offices. It was one of the most successful spots in Los Angeles, sort of a chic little shopping village. But it wasn't the chic that made it a success. It was the parking. Huge, open lots supported a booming business, and it made Star wonder why almost nowhere else in this city got that. The truly bizarre thing about Sunset Plaza though was that the spectacular view of the city was given over to the parking lot. The parking lot was on the Sunset ridge side. The shops and chic little restaurants were all pressed up to the loud, noisy, smelly street.

She smiled as she walked past. Already, she'd come to love this strange city, even with its growing list of quirks.

"Hello," she called tentatively, opening the door to Studio B where she'd had her shoot so recently and where Billy and Skip had their "office."

"Star," Billy called, delighted to see her as he came to the makeup-room door. "Come in and see your pictures."

"Okay, sure." Her pictures really weren't a source of much curiosity for her. She couldn't really see the point of what she thought of them. But she looked to be polite to Billy.

"Here you are," he said, holding up a large color blowup of Star, poised to leap over a football helmet wearing only an open varsity letter jacket and just the hint of a smile.

"I always look older than I think I'm going to." Star said, curious at the effect. "But everybody likes it, right?"

"Old?" Billy cackled. "You think you look *old*? And that's your whole reaction to this photo of you that's going to be on the cover of a national magazine?"

"You did a very good job," she said, squeezing his hand reassuringly. "I look great."

"But?" he said, holding on to her hand.

"Well, it just seems to me that my opinion is the least important one," Star said with a shrug. "If everyone else likes it, then this is a good picture. If I don't like it, well, at the end of the day, who cares?"

"I do," he said gently.

"And I think I look great." Star sat in one of the makeup chairs. "God, it was worth coming to L.A. just to get my hair color fixed. But if I'm happy and no one else is, then it doesn't really count, does it?"

"You're more than meets the eye, you know that?" Billy said, bussing her on the cheek. "Let's go get something to eat."

"Great, I'm starving." Star leaped up. "I haven't had breakfast yet.

"So what did you need to talk to me about?" Billy asked, leading the way as they headed out of the studio to the elevators.

"I need your advice about finding a place to live." Star pressed the button.

"You're kidding?" he said with a little laugh. "My friend Monica just called me yesterday to tell me she was looking for a roommate. You two would be perfect. She's a model too. And she's been in the business here long enough that she could give you a tip or two. Where have you been living?"

The elevator arrived and they stepped in.

"Well, I'll tell you." Star began her tale as the elevator doors closed.

The story took all of lunch, during which Billy really only said "Oh my God" and gasped a lot. Afterward Billy called his friend Monica, who was looking at a place in a nearby building.

"It's on Sweetzer, just a couple of blocks from here," Billy said, hanging up the phone. "You can see the place and meet her."

"Okay, sure," Star agreed numbly. "I guess I really screwed up, huh?"

"Don't be silly. He offered to let you stay at his place until you found a place of your own, and so now you'll find a place of your own. Come on, I've got a good feeling about this."

"Where are you going?" Skip demanded, passing them as they left the studio.

"Location scouting," Billy said with a raised eyebrow that Skip recognized.

"You don't usually take a woman with you for that," Skip called after them snidely.

"Bitch," Billy and Star said together.

"The rumor is that it used to be Marlene Dietrich's," the old woman who managed the building explained. "But you never know for sure about these things."

"It's beautiful," Star said, looking around, amazed by the quaint old apartment.

"It's ancient," Billy warned.

"Hello," a young woman's voice echoed through the empty apartment.

"Monica," Billy called back. "The floor collapsed and we're trapped in the basement."

"Oh, Billy, don't be such a spoilsport," Monica said, meeting them halfway as they emerged from the hallway that connected the bedrooms to the large front room. "It's quaint, it's lovely, it's historic—"

"It's cheap," the old woman added.

"And the price is right," Monica continued, putting the best spin on it. "Hi, I'm Monica, you must be Star. What do you think?"

"I think it's beautiful," Star said again, peering through the creaky, old casement and the wisteria vines that shrouded it. "I love this old-fashioned courtyard. It's just like *Melrose Place* without the pool."

"Or the plumbing, heat, or air-conditioning," Billy pointed out.

"Do you take pets?" Star asked.

"I think it comes with pets," Billy said, looking around suspiciously.

The old lady nodded.

"We'll take it," Star said.

They filled out the papers and worked out the money. What with the deposit and first and last months' rent, Star wasn't left much to work with, but she was able to cover it. She had her own place in the big city. The downside was she only had a little over $500 for a car; thank goodness for Marino.

"It's not much," he said, introducing her. "But it will get you around and I can work on it as you can afford to have things done."

"Are you kidding?" Star said, looking at the beat-up little Honda. "You should see what I've been driving most of my life. Let's take it for a spin." She reached out to grab the handle, pulled the door partly open, and it snapped shut again. She repeated the operation—twice—before she realized that Marino was laughing.

"What is so funny? What's the matter with this door?"

"Here," he said, still chuckling. "Allow me." He reached in through the window and detached the bungee cord that was holding the door shut, and it swung open.

"The engine works, right?" Star asked, looking Marino in the eye.

"I got it here, didn't I?"

"It seems sacrilegious to have this car in this motor court," Star said, looking around sadly at the grand surroundings she was leaving behind. "I gotta go pack." She handed Marino the cash. "Thanks for helping me out with this." She raised up on tiptoe and gave him a peck on the cheek and then turned to go.

"Let me know when you're ready," he called. "I'll help you with your things."

"Not much to get," Star said, turning back toward him. "But thanks, I will."

Star packed the few meager belongings she'd brought from Arcady Key and set the few pieces of mismatched luggage outside the door to her room. Carefully, she arranged all the jewelry and clothes and gifts that Peter had given her, as much to see everything one last time as to make it clear that she hadn't taken anything.

She started out, but turned back at the door for one last look.

Mutley, who loved riding in a car above all things, dashed out the door with a chorus of joyous barks and then, when Star didn't follow, came back to check on her. As if sensing her mood, he nudged her hand with his head. It made her smile a bit and she stroked his ears.

She wasn't alone and she was striking out on her own in Los Angeles for the first time. It was scary, but it was also kind of exciting. It was, after all, what she'd come here to do.

"Come on, Mutley," she called. "Time to go home."

10

more, more, more

Mutley loved his new home. He was particularly fond of running and sliding on the hardwood floor in the big, empty living room. Billy loaned Star a futon and a few odds and ends, but for the most part, the new apartment still looked uninhabited even after the girls had moved in.

The old lady who ran the place had a huge, ancient, ill-tempered cat named Mr. Whiskers, who presided over the courtyard each day from one of the large wicker chairs on their shared front porch. It was Mutley's delight to dash out the front door and give Mr. Whiskers a good workout, upsetting flowerpots, furniture, and the residents' blood pressure as they turned the courtyard into the Melrose Place 500. Far from being an innocent victim, Mr. Whiskers took perverse delight in tormenting Mutley, wandering languidly along the windowsills outside Star's apartment to attract his attention and getting him worked up for their next few laps around the courtyard.

Mutley wasn't the only one making new friends.

Monica was turning out to be an interesting addition to Star's life. She had been around the business for a few years, long enough to accumulate some experience, as well as a rather jaded patina. Her beauty was unexceptional but more than adequate to the task of neutralizing the bitterness that might have made a lesser woman unattractive. Anywhere else in the world, Monica would have been extraordinary. But in the tiny, inwardly focused world of young Hollywood, she was merely expected. No more than the obligatory gym bag over her shoulder, pilot script tucked under her arm, and cell phone plastered constantly to the side of her perfectly sculptured head. Her mild cynicism made a nice balance for Star's inexperience and optimism. That, combined with her spending almost every night at her boyfriend's apartment—if for no other reason than that he had furniture—made her an ideal roommate.

It was the best of times and the worst of times. Money was tight and Star was no longer living in mansions and cavorting with the rich and famous. Even so, she gloried in a sense of happiness and freedom each day. This was why she'd come to Hollywood. She had her own place. She'd done her first two jobs. The sky was the limit. She felt real and alive. Sitting on the washer waiting on the rinse cycle at the Laundromat on Fountain Avenue, surrounded by the acting students from the school next door running lines and rehearsing scenes amidst the fluff and fold, was more exhilarating than all the trips to Rodeo Drive. She felt a part of the dreams that fueled the city. It made her feel that anything was possible.

And when her head got too high in the clouds, a crack from Monica could put her feet back on the pavement they were both pounding.

"You see that girl?" Monica said, pointing out a bit player in a show the girls were watching on a TV Billy had "liberated" from Skip. "She gives great head."

"How would you know?" Star laughed, tossing a couple of popcorn kernels in comment.

"I don't, but I know the casting director for this show," she smirked. "You'll want to watch out for him."

Star laughed, but she remembered his name.

If she'd had to describe the difference between life on Alto and Sweetzer, it would have been that she no long felt like a spectator. It was more like she was in the game.

Always good with her money, Star had set aside more than a month's worth of estimated expenses from her earnings. With the $40 of weekly grocery money she had allotted, she struck out for the neighborhood Mayfair Market, part of a local chain of small grocery stores. After loading up with a nice selection of toilet paper, tuna, ramen, peanut butter, dog food, and a chew toy for Mutley, she still had a few dollars left over for impulse buys.

It was the highlight of her day, she thought ruefully. The vacation was most definitely over. Her arrival in Los Angeles had been so high glam that Star felt just a little sad as she patrolled the aisles of Mayfair trying to find herself a treat. The Tiffany tennis bracelets and lunches at The Ivy of only a few days before were quite the contrast to finding no treats at Mayfair Market in her price range. She wheeled the cart to the register and joined the line. As she waited, Star leaned against the plastic-coated handle on the back of the shopping cart and scanned the covers of the glamour and fashion rags displayed on the side of the checkout stand. *Vogue* was in her impulse-buy price range, but it was way too depressing to be considered a treat. It's not fun to buy a fashion magazine when you can't afford any of the fashions, she thought to herself, smiling.

Star continued to scan the covers as she progressed in line, watching the selection decline from magazines to tabloids. It was the picture that caught her attention first. It was a picture of her, with Van. It was a picture of her on the cover of the *Informer*. And it was terrible. The headline read, "Drunk and Disorderly," along with the caption "Stormy and Blond Gal Pal Trash Local Market in Drunken Spree." It was from the parking lot at Bristol Farms.

"Ma'am?" the checker said to her. "Ma'am, are you ready?"

Star looked up, startled, suddenly aware that she was in line at the grocery store.

"Sorry," she said, pushing the cart forward. Unbelievable. It was simply unbelievable. She'd have been outraged if she hadn't been so shocked. She wanted to read the article but didn't want to be seen reading the scummy paper at all, let alone an issue with her own picture on the cover. Should she buy it? What would people think? Had anyone else noticed? Had she been noticed? Was everyone looking at her? Was there going to be a picture of her in another publication of her reading the other tabloid? She looked around for cameras and became keenly aware of the security cams mounted in the ceiling.

"Ma'am?" the checker asked again. "Do you want to get that?"

"Hmmm?" Star said, looking up and realizing she still had the paper in her hand. "Oh, yeah. I guess I'd better. Otherwise I'll never know what happened."

The checker took the tabloid and rang it without reaction or comment, though she did give Star a bit of look for the flaky remark.

Finally, when the groceries were bagged and Star had her precious change, she fled the store as much to avoid possible new photographs as to get home and read the article. The phone was ringing and Mutley was barking a friendly welcome as Star wrestled with the groceries and keys. As she got the door open a crack, Mutley wedged himself through and came flying out, knocking Star aside, to engage Mr. Whiskers in a tempest of flying wicker and begonias. The two took off on their circuit around the courtyard on both upper and lower levels, and Star tried to retrieve the bag of dog food she'd dropped during the charge.

"Mutley," Star called as she ran for the phone, abandoning the scattered groceries. "Hello?" she said, grabbing the cordless from its charger on the kitchen cabinet, dashing back into the fray.

"Now, I thought you'd gone out there to be on the cover of *Mann* magazine, so imagine my surprise when I go to get my hair done today and I see you're on the cover of quite a different publication."

"Hello, Mother, hang on." Star clutched the phone to her chest. "Mutley, come here right this minute. Mutley! Mom, could I call you back? The dog is on the roof."

"Will that be in the papers too or should I go turn on the news?"

"Mom, it didn't happen, okay? Mutley...
Mom, I'll call you back."

She clicked off the phone, righted a small table
that had been upset in the high-speed pursuit, and
daintily set the phone on it before running to
Mutley's rescue. Mr. Whiskers sat leisurely cleaning his paws on a nearby overturned chair. Mutley,
on the other hand, had been tricked onto the roof,
where he was stranded. Mr. Whiskers had led the
dog on a merry chase around and around the
courtyard—sometimes on ground level and sometimes up the stairs and onto the second-floor
gallery. As the pursuit continued, Mutley had become more focused on his quarry than on where
he was going. So, on the way up the stairs for the
third or fourth time, Mutley had followed when
Mr. Whiskers had detoured onto the adjacent low-
hanging eve of the roof. Up and over the pitch he'd
followed the cat, narrowly avoiding a fall on the
other side by screeching to a stop perilously near
the edge as Mr. Whiskers leaped to the safety of a
nearby tree.

Mutley went berserk as he watched Mr.
Whiskers stroll across the courtyard, but could not
manage to retrace his steps as Mr. W took a seat in
full and unobstructed view of Mutley's perch.

"How in the world did you get up here?" Star
cajoled, climbing the stairs to the point where they
intersected the roof and patting the shingles to attract Mutley over to safety. For his part, Mutley

would get near her, and then Mr. Whiskers would yawn or stretch and Mutley would run back across to the edge to bark again. It took Star quite a while to coax him over, and even then it was no small undertaking to get the big, hairy beast down off the roof, more or less against his will as it involved pulling him down onto the landing over a precipitous fifteen-foot drop.

Of course, the instant Mutley's paws touched the boards that made up the stairs, the race was on again, and Mr. Whiskers rose to his feet just as the old lady opened her door to see what was going on. Mr. Whiskers darted between the old woman's legs, and as she spun to see where he'd gone, Mutley took the reverse route into the house. Star could hear yowling and crashes along with the old woman's screams emanating from inside. She sighed and crossed down to help as the phone began to ring again.

Irate over the hideous photograph, the complete lies that the paper had told about her, Mutley's insanity over the neighbor's cat, not to mention that she'd gone from living in a palace to living in an empty apartment—now her mother was calling again. She let it ring and attempted to make the rescue. As if to make matters worse, just as Star got near the door to the old woman's apartment, it opened and the manic pets hurtled out and then into Star's open door.

She sighed, crossed over, and closed the door.

There was plenty of food on the porch and nothing inside that they could hurt. The phone continued to ring.

"Listen, you," Star said, answering, "I told you I'd call you back."

"Is this Star Wood Leigh?" asked a tentative voice on the other end.

"Yes," Star said irritably.

"Hi, it's Camille . . . from *Hammer Time?*"

"Oh, right, hi," Star said, rattled and even more irritated by the cosmic timing. "Sorry about that. Thought you were my mother."

"Okay," Camille said without prejudice. "I'm not. Listen, I think you've got it. The producers want to see you and they're not calling in anyone else."

By the end of the day Star was a wreck and a mess. The meeting with the producers had been nerve-wracking and inconclusive at best, the groceries were still scattered on the front stoop, and she'd never gotten to call her mother back. When she opened her front door, Mr. Whiskers shot out past her, though on the plus side, Mutley was asleep on the floor in front of the empty fireplace.

As she gathered up the groceries to bring them inside, she rattled the bag of dog food and Mutley ran to his bowl in the kitchen, where he waited for her as she made her way inside. She smiled at him despite the chaos, dialing the phone as she filled his food and water dishes.

"Hello," her father's voice crackled through the line.

"Hi, Daddy, it's me," Star said, boosting herself up onto the kitchen counter to talk more comfortably.

"Well, if it isn't my daughter the celebrity," Rick chortled. "The cover of the *Informer*? You have arrived."

"Oh, Dad," she moaned, leaning back and knocking her head on the kitchen cabinets behind her. "Gross."

"They don't put pictures of nobodies on the cover of that magazine," he said with great authority.

"Unless the nobody in question is drunk and disorderly at the grocery store with somebody famous," Star wailed.

"Rick? Is that Star?" she heard her mother in the background. "Give me that phone. Star? Is that you? What on earth?"

"Mom, I was not drunk at the grocery store," Star began, defending herself before she'd said hello. "We were just laughing. You remember it was after that audition where I counted out loud and we were totally cracked up over it. I told you about it."

"So, are you two serious?"

"Mom, I only had one date with him. You know that," Star said with a sad sigh.

"So, you haven't broken up with Vince Piccolo?"

"Superman? Remember? We only went out a couple of times. But it was over before it started, remember? Mom, it's all made up. I went to the grocery store. That much is true. But that's it."

"It says you two bought a basket of wine while you were there," Lucille accused.

"A basket of wine?" Star asked sarcastically. "Does that even sound reasonable? 'Hello, I'd like to buy a basket of wine, please.' We got a picnic basket and it had a bottle of wine in it. I drank half a glass and I don't think he had that much. And the point is we hadn't had any wine at the time the paper says we were drunk and disorderly at that grocery store. It was eleven o'clock in the morning."

"Be that as it may, young lady," Lucille said, stepping up onto her soapbox with her prepared speech, "I do not care how they do things in the big city of Los Angeles, I do not approve of going out and making a drunken spectacle of yourself in public. Do you understand me?"

"Yes, Mom," Star said with a little smile. It may have sounded like fussing, but Star knew only too well that this was how her mom said "I love you."

"And I am sorry to hear that you've broken it off with Vince," Lucille added on a conciliatory note.

"Mom, you remember why I call him Superman right?" Star asked a bit incredulously.

"I do, and I know that that can be a blessing after you get a little older and the bloom is off the rose, if you take my meaning," Lucille said, managing to make it sound prim.

"I'm hanging up now," Star said, then remembered. "Oh, and I had an audition today so it looks like I might be on this new show called *Hammer Time*."

"Never heard of it," Lucille sniffed. "But good luck with that."

"Thanks, Mom. I'll give Vince your regrets if I ever see him again."

"And no more public spectacles," Lucille shouted as Star hung up the phone.

Mutley was at the back door waiting; Star got the leash and took him out for a brief walk up and down the alley outside.

"We'll take a longer walk later," she promised as she dragged him up the back steps. "First it's my turn. And I hear that big bathtub calling my name."

As Star submerged into a tub full of fragrant bubbles, she marveled at the day she was having and chuckled to herself. If I had known L.A. was like this, I'd have come sooner. "What's next?" she said aloud.

The words were hardly out of her mouth when the door burst open and Mutley, Monica, and Billy burst in with Monica's boyfriend, Phil. All three had copies of the front page of the *Informer* pinned to their chests and were flashing small disposable cameras at her.

"Oh my God!" Star squealed, sinking farther beneath the bubbles.

"There you are," Billy said.

"Our very own tabloid queen," Monica said.

"Get out of here, all of you," Star said, trying to sound stern but really only laughing. She settled for throwing a wet sponge in Billy's direction.

"Okay, we're going," Billy said, retreating. "But hurry up. We're going to a party at Randy Pizarro's."

"Randy Pizarro?" Star called after them, but once the door was closed, there was no further information from outside. She rushed through her regime and toweled herself off, anxious to find out the details. Randy Pizarro was one of the biggest action-adventure movie stars in the world, and in spite of her mood Star could hardly resist a chance to meet him, let alone go to a party at his house. He'd started out with what was supposed to be a small movie he made himself. It had been a huge hit, won him an Academy Award, and made him a star. He was *the* rags-to-riches Hollywood story. He wasn't too hard to look at either.

Of course, the three were waiting outside the bathroom door, cameras trained and ready to go as soon as she got out. Star did her "I vant to be alone" bit, playing it up to the hilt, then opening her towel long enough to flash them before running into her room and slamming the door.

"Put on a little black cocktail dress and get out here so I can do your hair and makeup," Billy called in.

"I don't have a little black cocktail dress," she called back.

"Check your closet, sister," he shouted back.

There it was, the perfect little black cocktail dress in just her size, hanging in her closet with a couple pairs of jeans and a few random items of clothing in what was far from a complete wardrobe. There was a note pinned to it.

My darling Star—
  In moments like these, always remember what Mae West said: "I'd rather be looked over than overlooked."
                              Your number one fan,
                                        Billy

In fairly short order and after more than half a glass of wine, her hair and makeup were divine. Billy and Star, Phil and Monica, arrived to a poolful of stares, covert and otherwise. Making their way from the main entrance through to the courtyard of Randy Pizarro's Italianate Bel Air mansion, they met with an interesting mix of pool party and high fashion with bikini-clad women and men in and around the pool and haute-couture–clad celebs and wannabes orbiting.

Second to the last place she wanted to be was at

a party that night. She felt exposed and violated and paranoid after such a public splashing. But the last place she wanted to be was alone at home when friends who would go to such trouble to cheer her up were at a party. She was glad she'd come if only to be with them.

"The liquor's free," Monica said, grabbing Phil's arm. "We're going to find the bar."

"We'll bring you back something from our expedition," Phil said as Monica dragged him away.

"What a house," Billy whispered as they entered.

"Is it solid gold, do you suppose?" Star said offhand, looking around in amazement.

Billy lost it, shrieking with girlish laughter that made it clear to all who were interested that while he and Star may have arrived together, they were definitely not *together*.

Plenty were interested.

"It is the pushiest, most vulgar thing I ever saw," Billy hissed, recovering slightly. "And I am beginning to believe that you are the most unintentional wit of our age."

"Sometimes I just have no idea what you are talking about," Star said, smiling and shaking her head at Billy, who only laughed harder.

"Hello," the deep, smooth voice broke in. "Welcome."

Star turned to find herself looking directly into the eyes of *the* Randy Pizarro.

"Oh, God . . . I mean, hello, Mr. Pizarro," Star managed.

"Please, call me Rand," he said, extending his arm to her. "Let me get you something to drink, introduce you to a few people."

"Thank you, Rand," Star said, testing the name as she took his arm. "This is my friend—"

"Billy and I need no introductions," Randy said, patting Billy warmly on the back. "I may not remember the names of all the actors I work with, but I remember the people who've made me look good, and no one makes you look better than Billy."

"Thanks, Rand," Billy said with a little smirk, never having been invited to call him anything but Mr. Pizarro.

"So, Billy," Rand said, escorting them across the courtyard and into a large dining room where the bar was set up along with the food, "do you really hate the new house?"

"Rand," Billy said, really pushing it, "I can't find the words."

"I think it looks like a Cuban bordello during Batista," Rand said with a little laugh.

"Whorehouse of the Caribbean." Billy giggled, nodding. "Like a ride at Disneyland."

Star couldn't help but laugh.

"My mother decorated it," Rand said. "It used to be a pretty nice house. I'm going to make her live here. I'm moving out right after the party."

"That'll teach her," Billy said, more impressed with Rand than he'd ever been on the set.

"What'll you have to drink?" Rand said, turning his considerable focus on Star.

"Something Caribbean," Star suggested.

"*Très* Cuba libres," Rand said in his smoothest continental.

"Make mine diet," Star asked. "I don't know how to say that in Spanish."

"That's okay," the bartender said wryly. "I don't speak it."

"Diet for me too," Billy put in.

"So, how about a tour?" Rand suggested once Star had her drink in hand.

Billy gave her a questioning look that Star very much appreciated and understood. She winked.

"You know," Billy said with a nod and a smile to let Star know he'd gotten the best-girlfriend signal, "I'm going to take a pass on the tour, but I'll meet up with you guys back by the pool a little later."

"Enjoy," Rand said graciously to Billy, pleased that his old friend had gotten the best-bud signal that he wanted to be alone with Star.

The house was jaw-dropping even if it was about as subtle as Donald Trump. In many ways, it was the perfect house for Rand. He too lacked a certain finesse in his work and in his personal life.

And so when they'd made their way to the master bedroom, rather than bother with the niceties of seduction he cut right to the chase.

"Babe," he said giving her a demonstrative pat, "you've got a world class ass."

Then he tackled Star onto the huge round bed without any more warning or encouragement. It became more a wrestling match than lovemaking.

"What are you doing?" Star demanded, struggling to evade his grasp.

"I thought you were as turned on as I was," he said, trying to gain some traction.

"What made you think that?" Star grunted, prying his grip loose long enough to get onto her knees and scuttle across the massive mattress.

"We'd be perfect for each other," he panted, diving in and catching her by the legs, clutching them to his chest with both arms. "Come on, baby, you could be my number one girl. I could set you up."

"Number one?" Star said, trying to kick her way free. "What does that mean exactly? Is there a number two girl? How many are there?"

"I could take care of you," he insisted. "Really help you out."

"It would really help me out if you let me go," Star said, managing to roll over and get a grip on his ear.

"Ow, ow, ow, ow," he cried out, letting her go momentarily in his surprise.

It was all Star needed. She darted out of his grasp and out of the room. She dashed down the hallway, and remembering a powder room from the tour, she rounded the corner and ducked in, locking the door behind her. She listened intently at the door. Nothing but the gentle sound of running water.

"Buona sera."

The deep voice scared her and she cried out, turning to see who else was in the room. Even though he stood facing away and only looked at her over his shoulder, she could tell that she was sharing the room with a devastatingly handsome man. "I'm sorry," she hissed, realizing and turning away. "I'm hiding from someone."

"Veramente," he said, finishing up and flushing.

"Do you speak English?"

"But of course," he said, tucking himself away and zipping up. He turned to offer his hand. "I'm Antony Cravatta, *a vostra disposizional.*"

Star looked at his hand and then back up at his face.

"Oh, *scusami,* excuse me," Antony said, turning to the basin to wash his hands. "So, who are you hiding from?"

"The host," Star said, looking over his shoulder to check herself in the mirror.

"Most unfortunate. Why did you come to his party if you are trying to avoid him?"

"I'd never met him until tonight," Star said, sitting on the vanity beside the sink. "I mean he's a big deal, so I thought it would be . . . less awful."

"Awful?"

"I prefer my calamari *fritti.*"

He laughed.

"That's it," she said with a shrug. "That's all my Italian."

"I'm sorry," Antony said, sitting beside her.

"Me too. I only came to try and cheer myself up."

"Well, then by all means, you should have a good time at the party tonight," Antony said, rising and offering his hand once again.

"What did you have in mind?" she asked skeptically.

"I think there's calamari *fritti* downstairs," he said, standing solid, holding his hand steady. "And there's a band in the back, so maybe dancing. And you don't seem to have a drink. Campari and soda is vile but refreshing."

She laughed and, taking his hand, allowed herself to be led back downstairs.

Antony turned out to be a fellow starving actor, there for free food and a good time. Star found him not only great to look at, but a lot of fun to be around. He seemed only politely interested in her. It made her feel more at ease than she had in a long while.

"What happened to 'Rand'?" Billy whispered in her ear when Antony stepped away to get them drinks. "And where did you find this one?"

"I left Rand in his bed upstairs, and I found this one in his bathroom." She giggled at how delightfully dreadful that sounded. "God, don't tell the *Informer,* I'll get my own issue."

"Yeah, at this rate you might become famous before anyone knows who you are," Billy said, miming turning a key near his mouth. "My lips are sealed, but you *must* call me tomorrow and give me the dirt."

"Deal," Star said as she spotted Antony heading their way. "Or maybe the day after?"

The party was a turning point for Star. She left with whom she wanted. It was her choice, and really the first time in her life that had ever happened. It was also the first time she'd ever realized she had a choice. Rand had apologized for his behavior and called as well as sending bushels of flowers, but it had only come to friendship.

Antony or "Ant," as Star had taken to calling him, was another story. He was fun and he seemed to "get her" well enough. He sold himself to her on their first night together.

Monica had gone to Phil's, so Ant brought her home. They talked easily together as they walked Mutley, and then he brought her back to the house. She enjoyed his company and was already thinking that she'd like to see more of him, but it was the sex that sealed the deal. Ant was no fan of foreplay. It just didn't interest him. On the plus side, he didn't expect any either. When they returned to her apartment, he followed her inside, grabbed her, and kissed her good.

"Wanna fuck?" he asked, and that's just what he meant.

"Un-huh," Star said. She did and she liked the direct approach. Even with Adam and all their time together, it had never been that easy. But it was easy for Ant.

He picked her up and carried her to bed. At first she thought it was going to be wham bam, later, babe. He dropped her onto the bed and ripped off his clothes. He was hard and ready to go, pulling off her clothes without ceremony when she went too slow.

And then it was on.

Her legs slid up his arms as he leaned in and he was inside her.

It was a good, vigorous screwing, practiced, workmanly, reasonably accomplished, but as is so often the case with a quick start, the finish came sooner than Star would have liked.

But then an amazing thing happened.

Slowing his pace, Ant leaned near her ear. "Did you?" he whispered elliptically.

"Not yet," she answered, startled by the question no one had ever asked her.

And he just kept going.

Three times that night. Without stopping. "Okay?" he asked.

"Ummmhmmm," she moaned dreamily. It had

been far more than three times for her. In private she called him Everiser after that battery bunny that just keeps going and going. He was not the most imaginative lover, but like a favorite dildo, he was always ready to go and willing to keep at it until she was satisfied.

The sex wasn't memorable, but it was sex and it was a time in her life when Star needed to limit the hassles. Ant was the perfect partner for that. For the same reason he wasn't memorable in bed, he was the right man for right then in Star's life—he never thought of anyone but himself. It was perfect. Star never had to worry about how her life was affecting him because he never noticed she had one. He wasn't mean-spirited about it, he was just too pretty to notice anything beyond his own reflection. She frequently found him serenading himself in the mirror. Star adored him. He adored Star. They looked great together. And they stayed out of each other's way.

What took first place in her life was the result of her accidental audition. Camille had called her two days after the party.

"Star, hi, it's Camille."

"Hi," Star answered warily. Money was tight and a steady job was just what she needed.

"Who's your agent?"

"I don't know yet," Star admitted candidly.

"You should get one or a lawyer," Camille said. "Because you've got an offer to negotiate."

"Oh my God!" Star said, jumping up and down on the bed. "I got it? I got the part?"

"They want to make you an offer," Camille confirmed.

"Well, give me a few minutes to get an agent, will you? And I'll call you back."

"Sure, or I can hook you up with someone, but do call me today, because they're ready to move. The pilot got picked up and the show's going to be a midseason replacement, so they want to start shooting next week."

"Oh my God!" Star jumped up and down on the bed again.

In response to her obvious enthusiasm, Ant got up and, dragging a pillow and a blanket from the bed, went in search of another spot to sleep, never once asking her about the call then or later.

It was the perfect match.

Star may have sounded overjoyed on the phone, but the call had created a new worry. She already had the part, now she needed an agent? As with movie producers, Star had a hard time figuring out what exactly agents did. All she really knew was what Monica had told her: "An agent is someone who feels entitled to a percentage of what you earn for a job they refused to help you get."

What was true was that Star did not know what making a deal for a television show involved. She didn't even know how to get an agent. And then it hit her. It was time to make contact with the mother ship.

"*Mann* magazine, Jayne Hersfield's office, Sami Rankin speaking, my I help you?"

"Hey, Sami. Do you have to say all that every time you answer the phone?" Star asked playfully.

"Only on the days when I want to keep working here," Sami said, good-natured about the ribbing. Both women knew Jayne would sooner give up her real right hand. "What can I help you with, Star?"

"I'm wondering if Jayne knows any good agents. I've got an offer to do a TV show and I need someone to negotiate the deal."

"You know, Star," Sami said after a moment's stunned silence, "I'll try not to be surprised when you call here next week to let us know that the board has unanimously acclaimed you the new publisher."

"God, I hope not," Star said with a derisive little laugh. "All I know about magazines is how to make them into collages and Christmas decorations."

"Congratulations on the show, by the way," Sami said with a laugh. "Let me get Jayne for you."

On hold for a minute, Star sang along with the Andrea True Connection while she waited for Jayne to pick up.

"More, more, more, how do you like it? How do you like it? More, more, more . . . how do you like your love?"

"Star," Jayne said. "You must be psychic. I was just going to have Sami call and set up an appointment. We need to talk. What's this about a television show?"

Jayne had always been a lifeline for Star. She was glad to have such a great mentor to turn to as she figured things out. Once again, Jayne came through, promising to get her old friend Ian Pestin to call. For her part, Star made a date for later that week to meet Jayne and Mars at the Castle, and to stay on for a workout with Jayne, later that week.

"Hello," Star said, answering her phone a few minutes later.

"Hold for Ian," a pinched female voice said. There was a loud click and silence.

"Hello?" Star said again, unsure what the caller had said. "Hello?"

"Ian Pestin," said a distracted baritone voice. The caller then covered the mouthpiece and shouted, "Who the fuck am I talking to?" There was some muffled conversation that Star could not make out. She considered hanging up, but curiosity kept her on the line.

"You're Jayne Hersfield's friend, right?" Ian demanded, coming back on the line.

"I'd like to think so," Star said, too stunned to be offended by the man's tone.

"I'll bet," Ian snorted. "I'm only doing this as a favor for Jayne. I don't take new clients and I don't take people at your level. But for Jayne . . . you'll let her know. Copy?"

"What?"

"So here's how we'll do it. You'll talk to my girl, she'll get your information and the name of the person on the show I need to talk to, blah, blah, blah. I'll do the deal and she'll call you when it's time to sign. Copy?"

"What girl?"

"You talk to her, not me. Copy?"

There was a click and she was on hold again.

And she had her first agent.

Hammer Time was a half-hour sitcom, a send-up of the ubiquitous home-makeover programs that had become so popular as a way of marrying thinly veiled DIY product-placement infomercials with low-budget entertainment. *Hammer Time* was about the life of a family man who hosted such a show. Star was cast as the most naked of all product-placement tools, the sexy *Hammer Time* girl. Her character was there to help push the products because of how she looked in a T-shirt, not unlike her job at Mother Pearl's. What appealed to Star was that, like the rest of the show, her character was about making fun of hiring girls in tiny T-shirts to sell products to men.

Bottom line, though, was that she was hired because of how she looked in that T-shirt.

Allen Thames had created the show and was playing the lead. Star and he hit it off right away.

He was clear about why she was there without making her feel degraded for it. Better still, he was far too involved with his work to make her feel that he was interested in her for any other reason than her contribution to the show.

"You must be Star," Allen said, approaching her on her first day of work. "I'm Allen."

"Hi, Allen," Star said, taking his hand. Allen was the only person Star had ever met who had a memorable handshake. He got a hold of her and she did her best to hang on.

"I gotta tell you that audition tape was one of the funniest things I ever saw. We didn't even consider anyone else," Allen said, laughing again as he continued to shake her by the hand. "That is exactly what we're looking for. And we'll buy the outfit you had on and make it your costume. Just add a tool belt and it's perfect. I'm looking forward to working with you." And he was gone, leaving Star vibrating. With most people, a handshake was a form of greeting. With Allen, it was a full-contact sport.

His energy and enthusiasm were infectious and Star was soon enjoying her new job.

She also found that she liked the show's half-hour comedy format. It was very different from her experience on *LADA*. For one thing, there was a live audience. For another, because they shot the whole show together, not in bits and pieces, she had a much better sense of what she was doing. It was more taxing than *LADA,* but she had a much better sense of what she was doing. Plus, it was funny.

They were well under way on the first episode when Star stopped by the Castle for her meeting with Jayne and Mars.

"Hi, Starlet." Mars greeted her as she arrived at the appointed time. "Come on in and sit down." He ushered her into his private study. "Can I get you something?"

"A root beer would be great. I'm supposed to have a workout with Jayne after and the sugar will get me through it."

"I'll see what we can do," he said, dialing. "Root beer . . . and how about bringing up a pot of coffee and things. . . . Great." He hung up and regarded his protégé a moment, sitting not behind the desk but in the chair across from her. "Why so tired?" he asked, cocking his head and looking her over.

"Oh, I'm blowing the candle at both ends," Star said with a sigh.

Mars laughed good-naturedly.

"I'm starting this new TV show, which is so exciting. And I'm trying not to miss anything. My new roommate and her boyfriend have been opening my eyes to a whole new side of Hollywood. And this guy I've been seeing—he's trying to get started as an actor—so I'm spending a lot of time with him and his friends, because I sort of am too."

"This new guy, he treats you good?" Mars asked, eyebrows raised, very paternal.

"Yeah." Star couldn't help but smile at Marsten Mann, noted libertine, taking such a protective tone. "He could be more romantic, but I don't really have time for romance anyway."

"Is it serious?"

"No, not really. It's fun, but it's just for now."

"Good," he said, pleased and nodding. "Now's the time for fun. You can get serious later."

"You'll let me know?" Star teased.

"Count on it," he said, taking the joke but not really kidding.

"Hello," Jayne said, knocking on the door as she opened it. "Sorry to be late."

"It gave us a chance to catch up," Marsten said, glossing it.

The drinks followed Jayne in and they all got settled.

"So, Star," Jayne said seriously, "good to see you."

"Yeah," Star agreed. "It seems like longer than it's been. So much has happened."

"Yes, you're really picking up speed," Jayne agreed, nodding.

"That's kind of why we wanted to talk to you," Mars took it up. "We want to work with you again."

"Your issue is out and we can't keep it on the stands," Jayne said. "Lots of response from the subscribers. You're a hit."

"Thanks," Star said, smiling, more relieved than she was letting on. "I'm really glad to hear that."

"So, we want to take it to the next level," Mars said, looking at her intently.

"We think you're MannBait material." Jayne nodded, agreeing.

"We want you to do the gatefold," Mars confirmed.

"What's that?" Star asked, confused. " 'Gatefold'?"

"Oh." Mars chuckled. "It's the centerfold. We don't actually call it that. I'm not sure where that term came from exactly. But we'd like for you to be Miss March."

"I don't know what to say," Star said at last. "I'm so surprised. I know that the process takes a lot of steps and . . . well, I haven't taken any of them."

"Even so," Mars said, "we'd like you to consider it. Think about it; talk it over with your manager. Jayne tells me you're working with Ian? Let us know. But we consider you part of the family here, Starlet. And I'd really like for you to do it."

"Thanks," Star said. "How soon do I need to let you know?"

"Jayne will let you know about all that," Mars said, rising to let them know it was time to leave. "You two are going to use the gym?"

"Yeah," Jayne said. "I need to get in a few laps at least."

"Ask my wife to join you," Marsten said, escorting the two to the door. "I bet Angel would like someone to work out with. And, Starlet, there's a party coming up for Halloween, I expect you to be here."

"Thanks, I'd love it." She grinned, still overwhelmed by their offer.

The mood pervaded Star's workout. She was distracted and unfocused.

"Okay, Star, what's going on with you?" Jayne demanded when Star tripped on the treadmill.

"I've just got my head unscrewed," Star said, managing to right herself before she fell and switching the machine off. "It's the *MannBait* offer."

"So, what do you think?" Angel, a former gatefold herself, asked Star.

"Well," Star said, looking down at her body, "I think I've got some pretty stiff competition."

"What are you talking about?" Jayne asked, switching off her treadmill and coming to rest next to Star.

"The cover was one thing, but I'm obviously going to have to spend every free minute I've got in the gym."

"You're in great shape," Jayne said, puzzled.

"But my shape isn't as great as some of those other models," Star said, throwing back her shoulders. "I can get a bra that lifts and separates, but I need one that divides and conquers to stand next to those other girls. And I don't get to wear a bra in the gatefold."

"Oh, Star." Angel laughed, as she too gave up on her aerobic work and hopped off the StairMaster. "You're doing just fine, but if you want what those other girls have, you can do just what they did. Buy it."

"What?" Star asked, truly not sure what Angel meant.

"They're called implants, darling," Jayne said, still laughing.

"But I thought those girls were all, you know . . ." Star cupped both hands out from her own ample bosom.

"Well, they are," Jayne answered her elliptical question. "They're not defying nature, just helping it along."

"They were all girls to begin with," Angel said with a raucous laugh as she took a running leap into the pool.

"So far." Jayne laughed as she and Star made their way to the pool at a more leisurely pace.

"Implants?" Star said, pausing to look in a mirror along the way. "What do you think? Should I?"

"Star, we made the offer as is," Jayne said, pausing and catching Star's eye in the mirror. "You do what you want. I think plastic surgery should be about feeling better about yourself. So just know that we're fine either way."

"Do you know someone?" Star asked as they neared the water's edge. "A doctor, I mean."

"I can have Sami set up an appointment with

someone good. Go in and find out about it. Then you can decide."

Star perked up. "Get me a consultation," she joked. "Stat!"

The Beverly Hills Medical Arts Building was more akin to an Ian Schrager hotel than any medical offices Star had ever seen. The valet parking was especially interesting what with the Honda and bungee cords holding the doors shut. The valets didn't know what to make of it.

The place felt more like an art museum than an outpatient surgery center. The lobby atrium was open to skylights four stories above. The scenic glass elevator ascended inside a silent waterfall that emptied into an infinity pool in the lobby. It all gave her a serious case of the giggles. She thought it far more likely that she'd find a piano player and strolling hors d'oeuvres than medical professionals on the fourth floor.

As she made her way up to the Center for Cosmetic Medicine, her giggleitis got worse. It was the kind of giggles that you get in a junior high school class when the teacher refers to galoshes as rubbers. It was immature and she knew it. But she was nervous, and the harder she tried not to giggle, the worse it got.

She took a Papa Jens deep breath and tried to take herself in hand. With a little "Here goes" she opened the sandblasted green-glass door. Two X-ray-thin Beverly Hills housewives raised their bandaged faces from their *Architectural Digest*s to look at her. Unnerved, Star couldn't tell from their facial expressions what they were thinking. She smiled and went to the brushed-steel Regency writing desk, where she was greeted by a woman dressed more like a flight attendant than any nurse Star had ever come across.

"Hi, I'm Star Wood Leigh." Star lowered her sunglasses and peered over the tops. A little giggle escaped, but she stopped it. "Sorry. I have an appointment."

"Yes," the young lady said, looking at Star with a similar absence of expression. "Barry will be right with you. I'll let him know you're here."

"Barry is a doctor, right?" Star asked. Another little giggle.

The young lady inclined her head but Star couldn't really read her. No one seemed to have any facial expressions in this place. Little did she know that people came here to have their facial expressions removed.

Just then, a nearby mahogany panel slid open and a perfectly manicured man emerged. He was wearing a suit that looked as though it had been stitched on his body and was escorting a young woman with a bandage across the bridge of her nose, and what was left of two black eyes.

Star looked up and met the bruised eyes.

"That's it," the woman with the broken nose exclaimed, looking straight at Star. "Those are perfect. Those are exactly what I want." She marched straight over to where Star stood, pointing at and, at one point, actually touching Star's breasts. "Which ones did you get?" the woman demanded.

The giggles were irrepressible. "I got the Hyytianen-Leigh models," Star managed between bouts of maniacal giggles.

"I've never heard of those, but they're marvelous," the woman said, getting *way* too close a look.

"I'll tell my parents you said so," Star squeaked. "Those are their last names. I'm sorry . . . but these were factory-installed."

"Oh," the woman said, looking up from Star's cleavage and into her eyes. The look was one of hurt and betrayal.

Star took a step backward. "Maybe I'd better go," she said to the girl at the desk. "Tell Dr. Barry I couldn't wait."

"I'm Barry," the impeccably dressed man said, stepping forward to her rescue. "Gail, take Miss Hyytianen-Leigh back to my office, would you?"

Star was so impressed that he got the name right that instead of arguing she followed Gail through the mahogany sliding panel, which scooched aside with a hydraulic *Star Trek* swoosh. They entered a hallway of backlit white-glass panels that looked like the scene from the end of *2001: A Space*

Odyssey. Star had never really understood all the fuss about the movie, but it made a cool doctor's office, she thought, giggling wildly.

Gail brought her a lemon Perrier as she took a seat in a surprisingly comfortable shell chair. She'd managed to calm herself down some by the time Barry returned.

"Hi," Barry said easily, taking her hand with one of his and patting it in a sort of sympathetic greeting. "I'm sorry about that. We pack their noses with cocaine, so there's really no telling what the nose jobs will say."

If he was trying to help her stop giggling, that was definitely not the way to do it.

"Nervous?"

She could only nod.

"Well," he said playfully, taking a seat behind the folded glass that was his desk, "there is nothing you could say, show me, ask, or want that I have not already seen, heard, or done. Giggling is not that unusual. So giggle away, I don't mind. But you can tell me or ask me anything. It's just between us."

"Thank you," Star said, settling down. The freedom to giggle took away the necessity for the moment.

"So, what did you want to talk about today?"

"Breast implants," Star said with a little shrug.

"Oh," Barry said, only a bit surprised. "Well, there are a number of options. Let's have a look, shall we?"

"Sure," Star said, pulling her T-shirt over her head.

"Well, okay, we can start with that," Barry said, pulling a Sharpie from his inside coat pocket and grabbing a hand mirror as he rolled his chair nearer. "Yes, very nice. Good formation." He held each in his hand as though weighing it.

"Yes, we'll have several options," he began, uncapping the Sharpie and handing Star the mirror so she could see what he was doing. "We can cut here and go in like so. Or here and go in like this. And then, depending on the implant you choose, nipple-placement options vary."

He rose and crossed to remove a tray from a drawer in a nearby cabinet and brought it over. "Here are some of your options." He set the tray full of liquid-filled pillows in front of her.

Star lost it.

"Honest to God, Theresa," Star said into the phone from where she lay on her borrowed futon, "nipple placement. I can decide."

"I had no idea they worked like that," Theresa replied with a case of long-distance giggles from their old apartment in Florida.

"Apparently they're like pasties, you can just stick 'em on wherever you want," Star said, laughing wildly.

"So you could have them put them on your forehead?" Theresa asked, breathless.

"Then they'd really be headlights," Star said, dissolving again, tears in her eyes. "Anyway, it would be the first time a guy looked me in the eye since I was sixteen."

They just laughed for a bit, unable to speak, enjoying the company.

She and Theresa had shared it all. There was only one thing Star had never told her, but she knew that she could if she needed to. She wasn't ready to tell Lucille because her mom was required to tell her she was perfect just the way she was, and Star wasn't sure she could handle it if she didn't. Plus, Star wasn't ready to talk about the gatefold idea with her parents. That's what had started the whole implant adventure in the first place, so the stories were inseparable.

"Star," Theresa said with that here-it-comes tone. "You know, you got a pretty great set. It took you long enough, but there they are. They got you the job at Mother's. They got you the standing ovation at the Dolphins game. They got you the job with Zax. And they got you on the cover of *Mann* magazine. What makes you think you need more?"

"I don't guess I do need more. It's just, well, it's the whole idea of being compared to those other girls who've been in the center of the magazine. It's like trying to do the best job of the job I've been offered, you know?"

"Would it make you feel better about yourself?"

Star was quiet for such a long time that Theresa spoke.

"Star? Are you still there?"

"Yeah, I'm still here," Star sighed. "I'm just thinking about that. I don't know that it'll make me feel better about myself. I feel pretty good about myself right now. More confident maybe?"

"Well, then you should do it."

"Really?"

"As long as it's not about making you feel okay about yourself, 'cause I don't think that can come from the outside," Theresa said, thinking aloud. "And you know what they say: tits and ass can't get you jobs unless they're yours."

With little more than a couple of girlish giggles, it was decided.

Once the decision was made, the biggest issue was the cost.

"So what did you decide?" Jayne asked, broaching the subject in a call to discuss scheduling the shoot.

"Well, I'd like to do it, but it turns out I can barely afford the consultation," Star said laughingly. "I wonder if I could get $250 for drawing on people with magic marker? Short of standing on Wilshire and San Vicente with a paper cup and a sign that says WILL WORK FOR BOOBS, it's the only way I'll be able to afford them."

"Hmm. You know what Star," Jayne said, with an inscrutable tone. "I think I may have a solution for you there."

"Like?"

"Well, Peter has told me to call if you need a hand with anything."

"Oh . . . no, I don't think so," Star said hesitantly. "I want to do it, but Peter? No, I don't think so."

"Look Star, reality check," Jayne said, bottomlining it. "This is a way for you to do this if you want. You think about, but Peter can easily help you with this. It's your decision."

In her anesthetized sleep following the procedure, Star dreamed that everyone she knew was filing past her as she lay topless in a coffin. After a moment's musing, each would take out a Sharpie and sign them.

When Peter took his turn and began to write "pay to the order of," she forced herself to wake up.

"Too creepy," she moaned. Her mouth was dry. Why was she so sore? "Oh, yeah," she said, realizing and raising her head slightly to have her first look. A look of alarm spread over her face. She reached down to her waist and tugged on the formless hospital gown to get a better look. Finally, she could contain it no more, and the shout came up from her diaphragm and echoed through the Center for Cosmetic Medicine.

"That's it?!"

11

hollywood nights

It was something Star had never wanted to do. She hadn't expected to be asked, not so soon anyway. But her time had come earlier than expected, and everyone she trusted assured her that however questionable it seemed, it was the right thing to do. And so after a lot of soul-searching and a sleepless night, she'd agreed to do the interview.

Hammer Time had succeeded beyond anyone's wildest expectations, rocketing from unknown midseason replacement to the top of the ratings.

Perhaps the biggest surprise of the surprise hit had been the phenomenal success of one of the least known of the show's cast members—Star. The show centered around Allen's character. Star's part as the *Hammer Time* Girl was the smallest on the show, never even involving her in the plot or action in any real way. Yet when she came out each week in her tight T-Shirt, tiny shorts, and work boots to introduce the tool of the week, the reaction had been anything but small.

The ratings soared heavenward and Star was given a lot of the credit.

"I'm really just the most expensive prop on the show," Star had said in an offhand remark to a reporter from *TV Guide,* on the set to interview Allen, only to see it blown up under a picture of her on the cover of the magazine.

"It's really not true," Allen had said in his typical good-natured way when later asked about the quote. "We have very expensive props on the show."

Star's debut as Miss March was gasoline on the fire.

They'd done the shoot as soon as she was healed. In fact, the doctor took out her stitches in one of the guest bathrooms at the Castle when both were up for movie night. Her implants may have been a disappointment to Star, but they were an inspiration to readers everywhere.

In tribute to her name, Jayne and the boys had come up with the idea of painting white stars strategically all over Star's body. Like icing drizzled on a Danish, they only made her perfectly sculpted form that much more tempting. The hardest part had been having Billy paint the stars on each of her nipples.

"Oh my God," Star screamed out as the tiny sable hairs of Billy's brush nettled her areola. "Billy, that's amazing. Can you come by the house later?"

"No, this is as close as I ever want to get to one of these." Billy giggled. "But you can keep the brush," he suggested, dabbing on a bit more.

"Oh, that's like chocolate," Star moaned. "I'm not just keeping that brush, I'm naming it."

She'd come a long way in a short time from that first nervous shoot.

And the effect was as irresistible as the subject. People who only knew her as the *Hammer Time* Girl suddenly knew her name.

Even Ian, her reluctant manager had finally realized that she was getting noticed. In addition to taking credit for discovering "His Star," as he now referred to her, he had begun to capitalize on the boost in attention and actually, well, manage.

"The iron doesn't get any hotter than this, darling," he'd said in his smoker's wheeze over the phone. "This interview could really put you on the map."

Star kind of thought that Allen's show being a hit had put her on the map, but it was the first time Ian had ever called her directly, so she figured it must be important.

"Her name's Barbara Rose Kopetski. She's the top reporter at *Entertainment Journal*," he said grandly, getting the name of the magazine wrong. "It doesn't get any bigger than this."

Star had been reluctant, but the day arrived and she was trying to make room for Barbara Rose amidst the astonishing number of bouquets and mementos that had begun arriving the day after the show first aired.

"God," Barbara Rose said. "This place looks like Rudolph Valentino's funeral."

"There could be a body in here," Star said with a shrug.

"There could be two," Barbara Rose said, moving a massive spray of roses and lilies so that she could sit down. "All this foliage would hide the corpses and the smell."

"We've actually started sending the overflow directly to the Children's Hospital at Cedar Sinai," Star said with a little smile. "You know, brighten up their days too. I keep my favorites and of course the notes. We wouldn't want the kiddies to see some of those."

"No, I guess not," Barbara Rose acknowledged, writing furiously in her notepad. "So, Star, tell me a little bit about how you got started in the business. Were there lots of grueling auditions?"

"No, not really," Star said with a nervous laugh. "I haven't had to audition much. I guess I just slept with the right people."

"I see," Barbara Rose said, breaking her pencil and scrambling in her purse for another. "Anyone I might know?"

"Oh, Barbara Rose, I'm kidding," Star said with a little wave. "If anything, I've managed to sleep with all the wrong people. Or I slept with the right ones . . . but only after they could have done me some good."

Barbara Rose emitted a shrill noise that might have been laughter. She savored each word, laboring to get it all down, and wondered if there was a Pulitzer for entertainment journalism. Star was having quite a good time. Barbara Rose seemed to have a great sense of humor and was easy to talk to. For her part, Star just tried to be herself, as Billy and Skip and Monica and Ian and Jayne and Allen and pretty much everyone she'd talked to about the interview had recommended.

"Well, Star," Barbara Rose said, looking up, "I've got to ask you. You don't have to answer me, but after the MannBait spread, all America wants to know. Are they real?" She made a little gesture to indicate just what she was talking about.

"God, no," Star said, laughing uproariously. "As a matter of fact, though, I was a little disappointed with them. I'm still wearing the same-size bras as before; they're just a little more snug."

Barbara Rose smiled, a blissed-out glaze spreading across her face. And she knew this was why she had become a journalist.

"I'll say."

To say the least, it was a firestorm.

When Barbara Rose's column hit newsstands, people who had never heard of the *Hammer Time* Girl or perused a copy of *Mann* magazine knew the name Star Wood Leigh. And they knew it in 142 languages around the world. *Mann* magazine, always popular, had to go into reprint to keep up with the demand for the March issue. And the *Hammer Time* ratings, always chart-topping, became stratospheric.

"They tuned in to see Star's boobs and they never tuned out," Allen was quoted. "Either Star has some really great boobs or it's actually a pretty good show. And who cares either way?"

Star slept her way to the top. Star sends rejected bouquets to sick children. Star's boobs are IMPLANTS. It was that last headline that seemed to get the most coverage. A special feature in one magazine focused just on who might possibly be the mystery donor who paid for them. Suddenly she'd gone from curiosity to news. She was variously dubbed scandalous, vapid, immoral, superficial, and courageous. She was called a victim, a martyr, and a hero. But she was never ignored. If she went out, it was reported. If she was seen in the company of someone famous, it was reported. If she went out to do the grocery shopping, it was reported. And most often, she didn't have to do anything at all. She was usually as surprised as everyone else to read her latest press. It seemed only a matter of time before Elvis and space aliens were involved.

The effect on Star's life was immediate and pronounced. She had to get a new phone number. She and Ant actually got a place together out at the beach to get away from the prying eyes of the suddenly insatiable media. There were stories about her leading a life she'd only ever dreamed of in publications she'd never even heard of and languages she couldn't speak. Most remarkable of all, her manager actually started taking her calls.

Perhaps the rudest surprise of all came from an unexpected source.

"Star, it's Jayne," she said, catching Star on the *Hammer Time* set. "I need to talk to you."

"What?" Star asked, alarmed. "What's wrong?"

"Well, it's about the doctor bill," Jayne said.

"What does Peter want?"

"He says he doesn't remember agreeing to pay for them," Jayne said.

"What? I can't believe that," Star gasped. "You talked to him, didn't he agree?"

"He says he doesn't remember," Jayne sighed. "He did say that if you'd like to come to dinner with him he'll bring his check book."

"Fuck him!" Star said, enraged. "And not in a good way."

"We could take it out of your check," Jayne suggested.

"So how much do I owe you for doing the gatefold?" Star laughed.

One day, at the end of rehearsal, Star was making her way back to her dressing room when Allen called to her from the door at the end of the hall.

"Star." He stood silhouetted in the doorway, wearing a mischievous smile and a plush white robe.

"Hey, Allen, what's up?" she said, passing her own door and taking a couple of steps toward his.

He dropped the robe and kicked it into his dressing room.

Star stopped where she was, uncertain how to react.

Allen smiled, extended his hands by his sides, and slowly turned so she got the whole 360. "There," he said as he came to face her again. "I just thought it was only fair."

And with a grin, he closed his dressing room door.

She could only laugh. "Not bad, Allen," she said to herself as she returned to her dressing room. "Not bad at all."

Star's life had changed. She had always received a healthy share of men's attention, but as the presses rolled and the concocted versions of her took hold in the public's imagination, men began to react like car-

toon characters driven mad by some magical and irresistible scent. They'd follow her through stores,
stare at her unflinchingly in restaurants, and wait by
her car in parking lots just to watch her get inside.
Surprisingly few actually spoke to her.

In meeting Ant, she had realized she had a
choice. Suddenly, she discovered, her choice included almost everyone she saw. She was still officially "with" Ant, but the offers were hard to miss.

Ant's life had changed too. Overnight he had gone
from being one-half of "Who's that cute couple?" to
"Who's that cute guy with Star Wood Leigh?" and finally, fatally, to "Are you Mr. Leigh?"

"That would be Star's father," he had replied
with good humor, but it was the writing on the
wall.

Star could sense the change from that remark
on, but she knew the end had come one night soon
after at a party at the Castle. It was a "Rites of
Spring" party and the place was lousy with nymphs
clad only in a few flowers and a diaphanous drape
or two. Star had chosen a stunning little bikini
made of what looked to be leaves, which she wore
with a sarong tied around her waist.

Ant wore "jams" she'd found for him, fig-leaf
appliqués on transparent mesh. They were quite the
couple stepping out of Star's shiny new Jeep. She'd
considered calling Lito, but the weather had been
unseasonably hot and the drafty Jeep seemed the
perfect choice.

They were the center of attention from the instant they arrived. Maybe it was the heat, maybe it was the full moon, but Star couldn't remember ever being touched as much as she was that evening. A hand at the small of her back that trailed down just a bit too low. An expressive finger that teased just at the top of a breast to make a point. Her hands were held, her hair was stroked, and she was hugged and kissed senseless. Or maybe it was the wine.

There was plenty of that. In keeping with the bacchanal theme, the whole place was pocked with flowing white tents and ablaze with torches. Trays of food were heaped with fresh fruits, roasted meats, and ripe exotic cheeses, but there was no silverware. The guests ate with their hands and licked each other's fingers.

Of course, as was always the case at Castle parties, the women outnumbered the men three to one. A gang of the girls held an unofficial orgasm race in the Jacuzzi. Each girl took a jet and the crowd decided whether she was faking it.

What men were there were either exceptional, exceptionally beautiful, or both. There was an imported tennis star, more noted for his temperament than his record, who kept disappearing into the caves behind the lagoon with a different nymph about every half hour. A major movie star whose recent and ugly divorce had been splashed all over the papers was drinking instant margaritas, lying on his back as a couple of the resident beauties poured tequila and margarita mix into his open mouth. And neither man's behavior stood out from the general tone of the debauched and decadent evening.

The party went late. Most of the "big names" had left, and Marsten and Angel were holding court over coffee and desserts in the main drawing room inside.

Outside in the wild night air, those who remained were nocturnal creatures, stalking the night, preying on one another, reveling in the darkness.

Star and Ant had gone their separate ways—not unusual for the two at a party. Star was sitting with her feet in the lagoon near the backyard waterfall as she talked with a really hot Calvin Klein model who was wearing only the underwear he was famous for modeling and who kept picking at Star's leaves.

The lagoon with its waterfall and grotto was perhaps the most famous sight at the Castle. That night it had been filled with lilies and beautiful naked women. The more traditional pool furniture had been removed and been replaced with heaps of cushions and suspicious-looking benches. The full moon and the palm trees overhead gave the spot an air of exotic mystery. As with the grounds, there was only torchlight and the moon. As the flames licked the water, it was only just possible to glimpse couples pressed dangerously close to one another shimmering in the momentary light, locked in a passionate embrace, then disappearing back into the darkness and the water.

More than one couple had left the lagoon for the relative privacy of the secretive and mysterious grotto to consummate what they'd started on the shores of the lagoon.

"The way you look at the camera," Calvin Boxer Briefs was saying to her, his voice thick with wine and passion, "it's like you're looking right at me. I wish I could do that. I could get an exclusive if I could get that. How do you do it?"

"Well, I kind of get someone in mind and then I see them just past the camera," she explained, running her finger dangerously close to the Calvin on his waistband. His perfectly sculpted body was so tempting and touchable. She didn't go farther than that tantalizing waistband, but she didn't keep her hands to herself.

"Star," she heard Ant call her, and looked up. "Star? There you are. We've been looking everywhere for you," he said, approaching with a buxom nymph in tow. "Star, this is Bambina. We were just talking and she's got implants too. But I don't think they feel the same as yours do. Here, feel," he said, taking her hand and placing it on Bambina's breast.

It started so innocently that she didn't even think of it at first. She felt the warmth of the flesh through the thin fabric as she tested and probed the breast before her. Bambina sat down next to her and let her legs dangle in the lagoon, leaning back at first and enjoying the attention and the gentle feel of Star's hands on her breasts.

Star touched her own breast to compare. Her willful nipples, always a little peaked, leapt to high beam. When Bambina reached out and began to rub Star's breast, the comparison was forgotten. Ant, who had sat down behind Bambina, leaned forward and nuzzled her neck. His eyes locked with Star's and silently asked permission. Or was it forgiveness? He slid his hands around Bambina and pulled aside the drape, exposing her breasts to the full moon. Calvin responded by tugging at the tie at Star's neck with his teeth.

As the few leaves that had been concealing Star's famous duo fell aside, Bambina leaned forward and buried her face in them.

Star threw her head back, falling against the model's firm, warm chest as she cried out short, guttural sounds of pleasure and surprise. The noise and activity were a spark to those nearby, and several girls dropped their bikini tops and blouses and slipped into the water. Star felt hands and wet flesh rubbing against her legs as she and Bambina were pulled into the water of the lagoon. As they came to rest on a ledge a few feet beneath the water's surface, Bambina covered Star's mouth with hers. Star did not resist. She felt the tongue probe gently and then more forcefully into her mouth. Bambina began to massage Star's breasts, increasing the pressure. Under the water, Star's hand found the twist of fabric that was tied around Bambina's waist. Her fingers slipped under the wet fabric and inside, then inside Bambina, who drew back and gasped for breath.

"More," she hissed as Star slipped in a second finger. "More." She knew what she was doing, Star thought, with a mischievous smile. With boys, it was guesswork, though she had become a really good guesser. With another girl, she thought with a little laugh . . . well, she knew what she liked.

Inspired by Star's dexterity, Bambina leaned down to one of Star's nipples, nibbling, biting, teasing. Star threw her head back and looked up at the heavens as she cried out again. Her head fell to one side and she watched two girls she didn't know go down on each other at poolside. She was wondering what that would be like when, as though reading her mind, someone swam up between her legs and began to nibble at the leaves there.

Star felt herself being lifted out of the water by a couple of women, who began to massage her body with a bottle of baby oil that had appeared from who knows where. As she lay writhing on a pile of cushions someone had dragged over. Star no longer knew or cared who was touching her or whom she was touching, caught up in the pure pleasure of the moment, the warm spring night and the madness of the full moon.

At one point, she looked over and saw Ant and Bambina kissing as she and Bambina had been kissing only moments before. Again, Ant gave her that beseeching look, and she realized that he was asking not for forgiveness or permission but only for her response. She smiled and blew him a kiss as she felt her bikini bottoms slip away.

A warm, loving smile spread across his face, he took Bambina by the hand, and the two disappeared beyond the hedge into the shadows. As quickly as they were gone, Star forgot them as a skilled tongue flicked between her thighs at just the right depth and intensity to make Star scream. This was an area where Ant had no interest and less talent, and she'd missed it so much.

"Poor Bambina," she said, laughing as she thought of it.

The foreplay went on until Star could stand it no more and she slithered out of the mouths and arms and legs only to be forgotten as soon as she stepped away. She found her top and the sarong, but there was no sign of her bottoms, which didn't seem all that important. She tied the sarong around her waist and merely carried the top in her hand as she made her way the short distance to one of the pool houses to freshen up.

Along one side of the lagoon, running perpendicular to the house, was a row of little, shake-shingled huts, partly concealed from both the lagoon and the main house by clumps of lush tropical plants. Each of the half dozen or so huts offered a small sitting room and a bath with tub and shower. Cleverly hinged louvered shutters formed the walls of the huts and could be raised to make them into open-air shelters or closed for a more private poolside experience.

Star opened one of the louvered cabana doors and stepped inside. Candlelight flickered over the flowers that filled the sweetly scented room. Star picked up a fluffy towel to dry off a bit just as the door opened.

"Occupied?" asked her boxer-brief–clad model.

"Preoccupied?" Star asked, surveying the relief map of the front of his close-fitting briefs.

"I enjoyed the show." He shrugged, stepping in and pulling the door closed behind him.

"I see that. I enjoyed being watched." She put her hand over her mouth at the admission.

"I could leave the door open," he suggested.

"Don't lock it," Star said with a naughty grin.

"I didn't." He pressed himself against her as she backed up to the broad cabinet next to the sink.

"We shouldn't," she said, turning her head aside, but not pulling away, enjoying the feeling of his size and his hardness against her.

"If we don't, someone else will," he said, driving his tongue into her ear.

She gasped as he lifted her to sit on the sink and then turned to take his tongue in her mouth. Her hand found its way into the Y-front, and she grasped his erection like a handle to draw him nearer as she pulled it through the opening. He parted the sarong, which fell away easily, and they pressed themselves together so tightly it was as if they were fused into one.

His lips pressed against hers as he impatiently tried to gain entrance, driving her wild. Fortunately, they were at the Castle and condoms were as ubiquitous there as beautiful women. He fumbled with the packet and she took it away from him. She tore open the pouch with her teeth and made a delicious torture of slipping the little cap over his second head and then slowly, excruciatingly, rolling it down over his erection. By the time she was done, he couldn't stand the wait an instant longer. Her cries ushered in the season they were there to celebrate.

She and Ant had made love that night when they got home and it had been more spirited than usual, but it was never the same after that. Once she had given her assent, it was an invitation to the end. They never really broke up. It was far more interesting than that. But there was never a moment's animosity or a hurt feeling or a cross word.

The next step in their breakup involved a persistent producer, an enormous coincidence, and national television.

As Star's profile grew, so did the professional offers she received. She did guest shots and walk-ons on a number of shows. She became a sought-after guest for the talk shows, both established and merely strident, enjoying both. Movie offers started to come her way, but none caught her eye. And her modeling career was crackling, allowing her to pick and choose assignments.

Mostly though, she said no.

It was simply not possible to satisfy all the requests for her time. Ian rode herd on the majority of offers, but there were other avenues of approach, and Star found herself receiving scripts and pitches from waiters, store clerks, and of course network executives to stagehands on the set. One such offer came to her through one of her buddies on the set of *Hammer Time*. Engel was one of the production assistants and "way" cute. Star discovered as she got to know him that he was an inveterate surfer who did production work purely as a means of keeping himself in long boards and Sex Wax.

In fact, it was Engel's love of surfing that had inspired Star's renewed interest. Tedious hours on the set working brought them together, but their mutual love of the beach made them friends. They were able to escape the confines of the sunless cavern of the studio by hanging out at the craft-services table and talking about favorite beaches, and debating the merits of the Atlantic versus the Pacific while they ate all the "healthy" snacks.

They were together off set too. He not only helped her select her first board, but spent time beside her in the water, helping her to master it. Their friendship was easy and natural. So, when Engel approached her with a script by a lifeguard buddy and asked if she'd mind reading it, she could hardly say no. But reading it was all she did.

To Engel's credit, he did not bring it up again. The same could not be said of his lifeguard bud or the former soap star who'd signed on to play the lead and produce the proposed one-hour drama series, *Lifeguards, Inc.* They were relentless. They called Ian, who said no. They called Drea, the talent agent Ian had brought on to field and manage such requests, and she said no. They sent messages to Star in flowers, candies, bottles, bathing suits, suntan oil, T-shirts, and once even written in the icing of a cake. She referred the myriad and imaginative requests to Ian, who referred them to Drea, who said no.

Finally, Engel stopped by her dressing room. "Dude," he said, looking her square in the eye, "please go meet with the *Lifeguards, Inc.* folks. I'm sorry I got you into this, but they're totally riding me about it and I'm starting to lose my balance."

"God, what do they want?" she said, shaking her head.

"You," Engel said simply.

So, for no better reason than to get Engel's friends to leave them both alone, and with the worst possible attitude about it, Star took her precious afternoon off and drove to Santa Monica for an audition. She came straight from the studio and the contrast could not have been more dramatic. The weather was cooler and the "set" was the Pacific Ocean, also the site of the production offices. The job would require spending the day at the beach.

Her resolve began eroding as soon as she got out of the car.

"Heads up," someone shouted just in time. A Frisbee came flying straight at her head. She dropped her purse, fielded, and relayed it to the next person. "Sorry about that," the guy who'd warned her off said, jogging over to her. "You must be Star. I'm Stan Merman, Engel's friend. Glad you could come out today. You're pretty handy with a Frisbee."

"I grew up on the beach," Star said, gathering up her things with Stan's help. "It goes with the territory."

"You any good at volleyball?" he asked playfully.

"Florida state champion, four years running," she said proudly.

"What position?"

"Setter."

He gave a low whistle in response. "That's about all I need to know." He stood up, brushing some of the sand off his baggy khaki shorts. "There's the corporate volleyball court," he said, pointing to the net and brightly colored boundaries staked into the sand around it.

"Do you want to hear me read?" Star asked, righting herself.

"Can you?"

"Yeah."

"You read the script?"

"I read part of it all the way through."

"Seems good to me."

"Do you want to tell me about the part?"

"Look, I figure if we got you here, you're in if you want to be as far as we're concerned. We'll work out your part."

"Just like that?"

"Well, no. First I'd want you to meet everyone and maybe play some V-ball, see how we get along?"

"Sounds great."

"Hi." It was the Frisbee guy. If you called central casting and asked for tall, dark, and handsome, this was the guy they'd send. Perhaps that's how he'd landed the lead on *The Days of Our Youth*, the soap opera Star's mom had watched when she didn't have the day shift.

"You're Bass Porter," Star said, recognizing him by his character name from sick days when she'd watched with her mom.

"I used to be, but I got better," he said genially. "You've got a good arm there."

"Star, this is Foster Streithope," Stan said, introducing her. "He'll be playing the lead in the piece and your boss on the show."

"It's good to meet you," Star said, amazed that Foster looked exactly as he had when she was home sick with strep throat in seventh grade.

She met a few of the crew, played a little volleyball; they even talked about the show, but not much. What Stan and Foster talked about was what they wanted to do and how they wanted to do it. They wanted the show to be fun and easy, a good excuse for getting paid for spending their days at the beach.

"It sounds great, it really does," Star said, genuinely intrigued. "But I'm already on a show. And I've got a contract."

"We'll shoot around it," Stan said.

"I don't have a lot of experience."

"I don't have any." Stan laughed. "I did used to be a lifeguard though. We'll learn together."

"I can swim," Star conceded.

"That's most of it," Stan said.

"Hmm. Let me see what I can do." Star knew she'd do whatever she had to do. It was just too good to pass up. Besides, the *Hammer Time* gig wasn't so demanding. She was already doing something extra almost every week. "Call my manager tomorrow. I'll talk to him."

Hammer Time was picked up for a full season. *Lifeguards, Inc.* was scheduled to premiere in the fall. So, Star began double duty almost immediately. Allen had been open to the idea. He didn't want to change the magic formula and no one wanted to lose her or her press. Star was glad to stay on. It was a small part, but it paid more than *Lifeguards*.

On the first day of shooting *Lifeguards*, Star realized she and Ant were no longer together.

She arrived on the set bright and early.

Stan met her and was bringing her up to speed in preparation for the afternoon's shoot. They had tried her in two-piece bathing suits, but had settled on a simple, well-cut one-piece for all the female regulars, deeming them "more businesslike."

"Just like Miss America," Star pronounced, trying it on.

Costumed and ready, she made her way over from her trailer to the "offices" for a table read prior to rehearsing and shooting.

"Uh . . . hi, Star," Ant greeted her in the door, clad in the show's signature navy blue trunks and the requisite tan.

"Ant?" she said, more than a little surprised. "Are you on this show?"

"Yeah, huh," he said, equally startled. "Are you?"

There was a moment of tension and then laughter. It was all they could do. It was over, and if they hadn't realized before that they'd drifted apart, they knew now. It was that simple. The shoot was fun and easy, like playing in the sand. And Ant got his own place later that week.

It was a good time, but there was a lot of hard

work. Star started the week off on *Hammer Time,* and then on Wednesday she started a second work-week on *Lifeguards, Inc.* The *Lifeguard* days were particularly grueling. It was bad enough they started with a 5 a.m. makeup call, but Star was loyal to Billy and Skip, so that meant she was at their house at 3 a.m.

It had taken a lot of pleading to get them to agree to the arrangement, but she thought the results were worth it.

"They keep saying they want me to look more natural," Star said, yawning, on her first visit.

"Too late." Skip sniped, combing out her hair.

"It's great of you to be over here at Billy's so early," Star said, patting his hand.

"Yeah, isn't it," he said with an odd laugh.

"I'm actually thinking it's a mixed blessing that he comes home every night," Billy said, handing her a cup of strong French-roast coffee.

"You two? Really?"

"Who else would put up with him?" they both said at the same time.

Eventually, when Star's falling asleep on the set got to be a problem, Stan found out about the arrangement and worked it out so that Billy and Skip could be on the set and Star could sleep in until 3 a.m. and come in at five.

But rather than solving a problem, it created a whole new set.

Skip was content to hang out in the makeup

trailer and gossip and drink coffee, but Billy was on set with Star to do touch-ups and more than a little mothering.

One particularly challenging shot required Star to "dolphin" across some waves to rescue a swimmer. The surf was particularly rough that day and gave her slight frame a beating. At the end of the first take, her hair was thrashed, her makeup was history, and her eyelashes were hanging off her face. Billy collected them and marched over to the director, holding out his hand.

"You see this?" he shouted, pointing to the two wisps of soggy hair on his palm. "That's all that's left of her."

Billy's watchful and vocal presence had a number of effects. Star looked great and her shots were calculated to keep it that way. When a scene wasn't working, the joke on the set got to be "Hmmm, I think it needs more eyeliner."

It was the beginning of an unimaginably good time in Star's life. She was working incredibly hard, earning more than she'd ever imagined, and enjoying *all* the new men in her life. With Ant gone and her new, mostly fictional, tabloid reputation preceding her, her sex life began to live up to the legend.

There were other perks too, or at least Star thought so. She was able to lavish gifts on those she cared about and help out the people she really wanted to.

There were gifts for family and friends and contributions to causes. In the tradition of her own anonymous donor, Star paid for Theresa to have implants of her own, flying her out for the operation and hooking her up with Barry. But, what she liked best was just being able to get that perfect something for someone she knew.

On one such impulse, she flew Theresa out for a long weekend, and the two went to a tennis tournament in San Diego as guests of Helmut Kreiger, a tennis star Theresa had always swooned over but had never gotten closer to than her portable TV. Not only did they get to sit in Helmut's box, but they also had lunch with him. Sadly the lunch was with him and his fiancée.

To make up for it, Star took Theresa out for a night at a local strip club, Duncan's Fife, to ease the pain. To Star's credit she did ask the concierge at their hotel for an all-male strip club.

"Hi," Star said to the man behind the bullet-proof glass at the front of the tiny and not very accommodating lobby. "When's the next show?"

"Uh, well, the show's continuous from two p.m. to two a.m." the front man said, not blinking at all.

"Great," Star said with a playful giggle. "Two please."

"Okay, ladies," the guy said with a shrug. "That'll be forty bucks."

Star forked it over and looped her arm through Theresa's.

"I don't know about this," Theresa said, pulling away.

"Oh, come on. One drink."

The door buzzed and Star pushed it open.

Glare from the stage blotted out the darkened room, and the two friends squinted their way to the bar as they eyed the long-haired Fabio wannabe in the distended, leopard posing pouch.

"Whattaya got with an umbrella in it?" Star asked the shirtless guy behind the bar.

"Star," Theresa said as her eyes adjusted. "Star."

"You want peach or melon?" Star answered.

"Um, Star. There are no women here."

"No, it's all male strippers," Star explained patiently. "Melon or peach?"

"Peach," Theresa said. "What I mean, Star, is that there are no women here at all."

The bartender gave them a little smile and nod. "You're the first."

"Tonight?"

"Ever."

"Cool," Star intoned.

"Two peach daiquiris?" the bartender confirmed.

"Make 'em doubles," Star ordered, eyeing Theresa's uncertain expression and runner stance.

"Star," Theresa pleaded, trying to drag her back to the door.

"Don't worry. I've got a lot of experience with this. Some of my best friends are gay."

"Who?" Theresa demanded. "We know all the same people."

"Not anymore," Star said, passing her a daiquiri and dragging her to a table near the stage.

"Honey, that's amazing," said the occupant of a nearby table. "You look just like Star Wood Leigh."

"Doesn't she," Theresa said, realizing the evening's potential for the first time.

"I'm telling you," their admirer said. "They look so real."

"But they're not," Star said with a little shimmy, enjoying the joke at her own expense.

"Well, actually, hers are bigger," one of the occupants of another nearby table said with a superior tone and knowingly raised eyebrow. "And the hair's a little dark. Star's hair is almost white. Just a hint of gold."

"Not very convincing, huh?" Star said, sticking out her bottom lip.

"Oh, don't pay any attention," the naysayer's companion scoffed. "He's just jealous. He's too tall to go as Star. You're almost exactly the right height. Arthur, we all saw that disastrous mess you made of yourself at Mardi Gras."

"I'm not too tall," Arthur said indignantly, then pointed an accusing finger at Star. "She's too short."

"You're Star Wood Leigh, aren't you?" another young man asked, approaching their table backed by a group of friends, who leaned forward to hear her answer.

"Oh my God, you *are* Star Wood Leigh," the original accuser said, putting his face down on the table.

As the focus of the room shifted from the stage to Star, the long-haired dancer brought his act to Star in hopes of regaining the room. When, even leaping off the stage and dancing on her table did not catch the crowd's attention, he leaned down and offered his hand to Star.

It was a sensation. Star had never danced at a strip club, but between the sexual fantasy life she shared with Adam, palling around with Randy and Andy and the guys, and her appreciation for Kim Bassinger's performance in *9½ Weeks*, she could work a pole with the best of them.

She and "Fabio" whipped the crowd into a lather, dancing way too close to one another, then teasing the crowd with little flashes of "forbidden" flesh. Star loved it. It was like having the dance floor all to yourself. There were screams of appreciation, and when she took a moment to catch her breath and acknowledge her new fans, she saw Theresa, standing and cheering with the rest of their little group.

It was one of those moments when Star saw the perfect something that she could get a friend, and she went for it.

Fixing Theresa with her gaze, she danced over to the edge of the stage and extended her hand to

Theresa, who shook her head violently and backed away.

"Come on, boys," Star shouted in a throaty voice, tossing her wild mane of hair seductively.

As Star beckoned her with a single finger, Theresa found herself lifted off the ground and placed gently on the stage. Star and her partner in grinds each took one of Theresa's hands and dragged her to the middle of the stage. With Star in front and the stripper behind her, Theresa never stood a chance.

Putting his arms around her from behind, the stripper ground his hips into Theresa's ass, gyrating her hips with his own as he ran his hands up and down her body. For her part, Star untucked and un-buttoned Theresa's blouse, tying it at the waist and leaving a single button fastened to keep Theresa's secrets.

Between the insistent beat of the music and the encouragement of the crowd, it wasn't long before Theresa was dancing with abandon as another star in the show. And then other strippers were dancing with them. And then it was two in the morning.

Star and Theresa danced with the strippers until closing time.

When they finally made their way back to the hotel, they were too keyed up to go to bed, so instead they put on their nighties and got ready to raid the minibar.

"God, Star," Theresa said as she followed her

down the hallway to get ice. "That was like the most fun I've ever had in my whole life."

"Yeah, it's been like this since I got here." Star shrugged, scooping ice into the bucket from their room. "I mean, I still have to work plenty hard, but I'm having so much more fun than before."

"Maybe I should move to California," Theresa speculated as they toddled back down the hall to their room.

"Well, you could always stay with me while you get started."

"I don't know." Theresa folded her arms and shifted from one foot to the other, a little chilly as they stood outside the door. "It's so far from home and it's not the same for me as it was for you."

"No, it would be great," Star encouraged, excited by the idea. "Just like when we were together in Miami."

"Well, the job's going really well right now," Theresa said, giving her newly expanded decolletage a little shimmy. "The girls have really boosted tips. Maybe next year, if I can save enough. Though it is so far from home and everyone. I worry about mom more these days."

"It is a long way. But it's like Mama says, I didn't go home all that often when I lived close."

"I guess," Theresa said, rubbing her bare arms. "Star, could you unlock the door?"

"I don't have the key," Star said, a little surprised.

"Well, I don't have it," Theresa said defensively.

"Well, I asked you to bring it," Star insisted. "Right when we were leaving, I said, 'I've got the ice bucket, bring the key, will you?'"

"Oh, that's what you said." Theresa frowned. "I thought you said, 'I've got the ice bucket, come with me, will you?' So I did."

"Thanks," Star said, laughing.

"Now what?"

"I don't know; wait for the maid to come by?"

"It's three in the morning. We should go down to the front desk."

"We can't go down to the front desk dressed like this."

"Why?"

"For the same reason that my last bad-hair day got featured on *Entertainment Tonight*. Do you know there was speculation that I had a drug problem over that?"

"Don't exaggerate."

"It's true. I was out of shampoo. I was at the store buying some when they took the picture. My mother called to see if I was going into rehab."

"Could you ladies hold it down?" asked the handsome but sleepy-looking man from the suite across the hall. He leaned into the hall wearing nothing but a pair of black silk boxers.

"Oh, my hero," Star said, throwing open her arms and approaching him with such bravado and determination that he backed up and closed the door a bit. "Thank God you've come along. My friend and I are locked out of our room. Can we come in and call the front desk?"

"I'm not sure. This some kind of trick? Did a reporter send you? Or a teammate?" he asked suspiciously.

"Are you really afraid of us?" Theresa asked, a little put off.

"A little, yeah. I play pro baseball. You'd be surprised the lengths some people will go to for a story."

"Brother, don't I know it," Star said, leaning on the door he was holding. "That's why I'm afraid to go down to the front desk to get a key."

"You're that tool girl who was in *Mann* magazine. I'm Armando Villarreal. I just came out here to play shortstop for the Padres."

"So can we use the phone, Armada?" Star asked, having no idea who he was but glad of the thaw in neighbor relations.

"Call me Mando. Sure, come on in." He swung the door open and backed out of the way.

"Watch out, Star." Theresa giggled. "I think he's packing."

"So, Mando, we were just getting ready to have a few drinks," Star said with an eye to making it up to Theresa yet, after two swings and two misses.

"I don't know," Mando said, hanging back as Star made her way over to the phone.

"By the way, this is my best friend, Theresa. She's a huge baseball fan."

Theresa knew little or nothing about baseball and shot Star a nasty look.

"Really? Who are your favorite teams?" Mando asked as Star called the front desk.

"Well, the Marlins are sort of the home team," Theresa said with a little shrug, knowing just enough to get by with the customers at Mother's.

"I used to play with them before I was traded to San Diego," Mando said, amused by the obvious little ruse.

"Okay, so I don't really know all that much about baseball," Theresa confided while Star continued to try to convince the desk clerk that she was who she was, that she could not come down, and that the manager should come *up* to their floor.

"For your information, I'd like to ask a question," Star said authoritatively into the phone.

"So why did your friend tell me that you were such a baseball fan?"

"She's just trying to make it up to me because Helmut Kreiger is engaged."

"Were you seeing him?" Mando asked, still a little fuzzy from being so recently woken up.

"No, I'd never met him. But I always thought he was babe-a-licious. So she flew me out to meet him 'cause she was going to the tournament as his guest. Turns out, he's engaged. And to tell you the truth, I'm seeing someone back home, but I didn't have the heart to tell her since she'd gone to so much trouble."

Mando smiled. "She is a very good friend."

"Tell me about it," Theresa said quietly. "She even tried to take me out to see some male strippers to cheer me up, but it turned out to be a gay bar."

Mando laughed.

"We had a great time though," Theresa said, laughing a bit herself. "Honestly, I think I could have a good time with her at a bus terminal."

"So you're seeing someone, eh? How about your friend?"

Theresa just smiled and shook her head.

"Well, that's that," Star said, hanging up the phone. "The night manager will be up to ID me in a minute, and then maybe he'll let us back in our room. I'm glad to see you two are getting along so well. Maybe we could start the party over here and then go hit our minibar when this one is dead?"

Theresa and Mando smiled at her.

Star spent a little while trying to get them together, unaware that her every effort on her friend's behalf only charmed him more.

When the manager came to let the girls back into their own room, Mando finished off his second glass of orange juice, made his apologies, and bid them good-night.

"I'm sorry, Ter," Star said with a little pout as the door closed behind him. "I've struck out all weekend trying to fix you up."

"It's okay, Star," Theresa said, shaking her head

at her friend, "I've just started seeing this guy back in Miami anyway."

"Oh my God, you dog," Star said, grabbing a pillow and pounding her. "I can't believe you didn't tell me."

The two sat up talking about Theresa's new beau until they passed out in the parlor of their suite, waking only just in time to get it together and get Theresa to the airport. Star dropped her friend off and got on the road for home. But news of her holiday reached home before she did.

Headlines blared "Star Appears at Strip Club" and "Star Caught in Hotel Orgy with Mad Mando Villareal."

"Big weekend?" Allen grinned as they sat down to read the week's episode.

"Sounds like it, huh?" Star said disgustedly. "It just makes me feel like hiding in my house and never going out again."

"I know what you mean," Allen said, taking a seat and leafing through the new pages. "When Sally and I were having some problems a couple of years ago, the press made it sound like I'd tried to kill her or something."

"Yeah, and look what they did to Princess Di," Star said, rolling her eyes.

"She really made the most of it though, didn't she?" Allen said, nodding.

"What do you mean?"

"Well, she knew the press would look wherever

she stood, so she went and stood in front of stuff that she wanted people to see. Land mines, AIDS patients, charities, like that. The trouble is we want them to look when we want them to look, but we don't want them to look when we don't want them to look. I guess you can't have it both ways."

"I'd rather be looked over than overlooked," Star said, smiling, as she remembered the note from Billy.

"Yeah, I guess that's true."

A smile spread across her face as it hit her. Her mom had always told her that no matter how dark the day, it was never so dark you couldn't see a blessing if you were willing to look for one. Star saw the blessing.

Mike Dean
President
Brotherhood for Animals Gaining
Legal Equality
B.A.G.L.E.
11912 Park Avenue
New York, New York 10021

Dear President Dean,
     I am very much concerned about animal rights and welfare. I have done what I could all of my life. When I was a young girl, my father was out of work in his chosen profession and

worked briefly on a commercial turkey farm. As both of my parents worked, I had to go with my father to the farm several times and saw firsthand at an early age the cruel and unusual conditions present on the farm, of which I am sure you are more than aware.

My work for animal rights and my vegetarian diet began almost immediately. Back then, the best I could do was roll pennies, rescue strays, and volunteer at local shelters. But times have changed and I think I am in a position where I may be able to help focus attention on the work of B.A.G.L.E.

Please feel free to contact me at your convenience at the address or phone numbers below. (I trust that you will keep both between us.) I look forward to helping B.A.G.L.E. in any way that I can.

Sincerely,

[signature]

It was the beginning of a long and happy friendship between Star and B.A.G.L.E. But best of all, it changed the way that she looked at every harsh video, nasty picture, and ugly headline about her, for a while at least.

"This is for the animals," she said to herself each time. It made it hurt a little less.

"Hello, Star. This is Mando Villarreal. We met in San Diego recently and I read in the newspaper that we're dating. It sounded like a good idea to me so I got your number from your friend Theresa. She said it must have been you who wrote her name and phone number on the pad by the phone in my hotel room, and that it was only fair that she give me yours. I hope you don't mind. Anyway, give me a call if you—"

" Mando?" Star said, picking up the phone by her bed. "Sorry, I was just screening calls in my sleep."

"In your sleep?"

"I started to hear you talking to me in my dream, and then as I woke up, I realized it was the answering machine."

"Hi," he said, at a loss for more.

"Hi. Sorry about all the articles and stuff."

"I'm not. I think it sounds like a lot of fun."

"Yeah?" she asked sleepily.

"And just so you know, it's already boosted my stock. So, I guess I'm asking for you to save me from becoming a terrible liar, because if it keeps up, I'm going to have to start bragging. But if you went out with me, then it wouldn't have to be a lie."

"You're cute."

"Listen, I'm going to be in Los Angeles for a couple of games next week. You wanna?"

"Well, we can't have you turn into a liar, can we? And to tell you the truth, I've already been doing a little bragging myself."

"You want to come to the game?"

"Only if I can come in the locker room." She giggled.

"I'll see what I can do about a pass," he said, chuckling. "I've got games Thursday to Saturday and I don't have to leave L.A. until Monday."

"I've got work Thursday and Friday, but Saturday's good, I think."

"Yeah, Saturday's an afternoon game, so that works."

"I'm going back to sleep now," she said, her voice already husky with the return of sleep.

"Come to the stadium, I'll meet you after the game. Sweet dreams."

In the ensuing week, Star had full shoots for both shows, so she needed the little rest she did get. She started with the standard fare at *Hammer Time*. The part was fun, but the table read wasn't much more challenging for Star than the actual performance. *Hammer Time* was well under way, and by Tuesday, she was done until they shot in front of an audience at the end of the week. Wednesday was the table read for *Lifeguards*. She had looked over the script but hadn't really noticed the upcoming episode would include a new recurring character, a professional surfer.

Her interest level changed when she got to the set for the read.

"Star," Stan called to her as she entered the offices and made her way to get coffee before heading into the conference room for the read. "I want you to meet someone. Star this is Rufus Forrest. He'll be joining us on a semiregular basis to play the part of Salty Keller."

"The championship surfer?" Star said, recognizing him.

"Well, not in this episode," Stan began, but Star's tractor beam had locked on to Rufus and she was no longer aware that Stan was talking. Or in the room. Or her executive producer.

"I'm so glad to meet you," Star said sincerely. "Your win at Pipeline last year was awesome."

"Thanks," Rufus said shyly. "Call me Ruf. My mom calls me Rufus. My friends call me Ruf."

"I know," Star said, completely melting in the icy-blue gaze of his eyes. "I just didn't want to act like I already was."

"Well, I'm kind of an admirer of yours too," he said with a naughty grin that she got. "So, I'd be honored. Do you surf?"

"Just starting," Star said as they made their way into the conference room, leaving Stan behind with a bemused expression.

"Great, we'll have to go off sometime when it's up," Rufus suggested.

"You know, that's just what I was hoping," Star said with a naughty grin of her own.

"Alright, Foster," the director called as they prepared to get the shot. "You see the boat capsize, you grab your floater and run toward the water, past the camera. Let's get this one. We're losing the light. And we need more seagulls. Where's the cracker whacker?"

The cracker whacker had come to be a job title, but it was actually a device crafted from a tennis-ball pitcher by the scenic department. The purpose was to "fire" crackers in a specific area to attract the resident seagulls into the shot. There was not much in the way of scenery to work with. The ocean, the sand, the stunning cast, and the occasional flotation device were in most of every shot. Seagulls dressed up the shot and gave a little more movement.

Once the gulls were in place, the shoot was ready to proceed.

"Okay, and action. See the boat," the director called out. "Now see it capsize. And run through the gulls."

Stan's focus drifted off. It was the third time on this shot. He thought the director had a crush on Foster, but then so did Foster, so they'd have a lot to talk about. As Star's gaze drifted, it fell on the trailers that served as dressing rooms, since the whole show was one long outdoor-location shoot.

"What the hell?" he said almost to himself, both puzzled and alarmed.

Star's trailer was rocking. Violently. Slowly at first and then picking up speed, it started to roll. "Uh-oh. Hey, Engel," he yelled to his old buddy who'd jumped the *Hammer Time* ship to come work at the beach. Stan pointed at Star's trailer, still rocking and rolling and picking up speed as it headed across the parking lot toward the offices. Mutley stuck his head out the window contentedly, always his favorite way to ride.

"Holy shit," Engel said, breaking into a run. "Is anyone in there?"

"I don't know," Stan said, bolting.

As others spotted the trailer, the crew more or less dropped what they were doing and pursued the trailer rocking and rolling across the lot. Foster, the director, and the camera guys kept working, oblivious to the mayhem.

Despite everyone's best efforts, they were only able to divert the trailer from hitting the parked cars, but it still collided with the side of the small building that housed the production offices, smashing out the glass front door and coming to rest in the heavy ficus hedge like Dorothy landing on the Wicked Witch.

More bizarre still was that the rocking did not

stop. In fact, after impact it increased in intensity, slamming the trailer into the side of the building again and again.

Trying the door, they found that it was locked, and there was a general hubbub as people spread out to look for Star. The search changed quickly to panic when Star's strangled cries were heard from inside the trailer. They pounded on the locked door of the trailer. Someone was dispatched for a crowbar to pry the metal door open.

"Star!" Stan shouted in to her. "Are you alright? Star, can you hear me?"

At first, the only reply was from Mutley, who barked a greeting from his post at the window.

"Star, are you in there?" Stan shouted again, genuinely concerned for her welfare and wondering if the thing could explode or something.

"Just a minute," she sang out cheerfully.

"Are you okay?" Stan asked, genuinely confused.

"Well, sure I am," Star said, coming to the door, followed by Ruf. "Why wouldn't I be? Ruf and I were just . . . running our lines."

"Star," Stan said, trying not to laugh in her face and failing miserably. "You and Ruf don't have any scenes together."

"We don't?" Star said, still not sure exactly what had happened, but pretty sure she had been caught.

The next day, when she got to work, in addition

to finding that her trailer had been securely anchored and chocked, a new sign was on her door beneath the star and her name.

IF THIS TRAILER'S ROCKING, DON'T COME KNOCKING.

12

life in the fast lane

"Star Shows More Than Team Spirit in Dodger Locker Room."

The headline was typical of the kind of press Star had been getting since *Lifeguards, Inc.* had hit the airwaves that fall. And there was more. Ian had been forced to file a lawsuit to win back the right to Star's name from an Internet porn site that had staked out StarWoodLeigh.com. Astrid, her personal trainer from her days with Peter, was selling her "Star Wood Leigh Fitness Program," taking credit for Star's amazing transformation—though she wasn't saying what Star had been transformed from.

Brandi had made the cover of the tabs for a full month with her lesbian love story "I Was Star's High School Sweetheart," and more of Star's used underwear was turning up on eBay than in her laundry basket.

Star's life was the subject of constant scrutiny and comment. Her every move was reported and she was feeling the heat. Even her "I'm doing it for the animals" mantra was having limited success in staying her ever-impending nervous breakdown.

So the locker-room story was par for the course . . . except for one little problem. It was true.

Star's love life was even hotter than her career, and that was saying something because her career was on fire. With Ruf living in Florida, flying in only for the odd episode and what he called "the occasional special occasion," and Mando on the road with his team much of the time, Star had the best of all possible worlds. Two great regular dates and the option to play the field.

The press was always blowing things out of proportion, though. They made it sound as if Star were in the Dodger locker room with the whole team. While she had to admit that actually sounded pretty hot, it wasn't practical. What had happened was that Star had been teasing Mando about the locker room and the team showers and the dugout since they had started dating. And that's all it had been, up until the week Mando was in town for that doubleheader against the Dodgers. Mando had accompanied her to a party at the Castle, where he'd met an executive at Fox News Corp, the same company that owned the Dodgers. The two had become close enough that Mando was able to ask him for a favor—an after-hours visit to the Dodgers locker room with his girlfriend. Star hadn't even known where they were going.

"It's a surprise," Mando had said, tying the blindfold around her eyes in the back of the limo. He'd actually carried Star in the team entrance, leaving Lito with the car just outside. That had been their downfall. A sports photographer who'd come by late to get a couple of night shots for a feature on Dodger Stadium spotted Star's "regular" driver and called it in to the pool.

Oblivious to their detection, Mando and Star were making the most of their time together. The location was incidental, but only to them.

By the time they were naked and frolicking in the showers, the secret was out and the press was in; they caught the two of them soaping each other in some interesting places. In fact, Mando was just about ready to slide into home when the first flash went off. The photos were good, but if the press had arrived just half an hour earlier, they'd have gotten some shots of Mando, not only up at bat, but hitting one out of the park from the bench in front of Eric Karros's locker. As it was, the shower shots could have been taken anywhere. Star and

Mando were forced to barricade themselves in the manager's office until Mando could raise his friend at Fox to have the reporters ejected. The invading hordes had made off with their clothes, so Star had to wear Mike Piazza's jersey, and Mando a terry-cloth robe, to get out to the car.

Fame had its price. It may have gained them entrance into the locker room, but it had also brought the press, a plague of locusts to ruin their erotic picnic.

And all of it on the eve of the opening of her new club, Ka Mano. In truth, it wasn't really her club. Her financial investment had been minimal. The club's main backers had involved her more for her sizable assets than for her deep pockets.

The evening was to be an elaborate toga party with a Roman-orgy theme. A cross between the innocent hijinks of a fraternity kegger and the hedonism of a Roman orgy, the idea for the toga party had been inspired by the many theme parties Star had enjoyed at the Castle. In fact she'd suggested it herself. "This way everybody will be much closer to naked," Star pointed out in an interview she'd given before the Dodger Stadium fiasco. "You can't help but be up to something when you're only wearing a sheet."

So, the bar was wrapped in grape vines, the guests were hand-fed grapes, and there wasn't a vestal virgin in sight. The controversy over the locker room incident along with the who's-who guest list turned the opening of Ka Mano into Circus Maximus. To make matters worse, Star was going to have to face it alone. Mando was back on the road and Ruf was surfing in competition in Australia.

Or maybe it was just as well.

Dating both men had proved to be a delicate balancing act. Neither relationship was serious, but it would have been difficult if both had wanted to come to the opening. Star was getting tired of juggling, and both men had expressed interest in something more permanent. The real question was, was she ready to settle down? She was having a great time, but a part of her, a small but growing part, ached for the peace and quiet of married life and an end to the relentless scandals and splashy tabloid headlines.

"Are you ready to go, Miss Star?" Lito called from the living room where he'd been cooling his heels while Billy and Skip, already in tunics and laurels, put the finishing touches on Star's elaborately draped toga and her vine-and-flower-filled chignon.

"Almost," she called before turning to Billy, giggling. "God I just can't think with all this hair."

"Now hold still."

"Hurry up," Star countered.

"You own the place," Skip snorted. "You can be as late as you want."

"Hardly," Star said with a snort of laughter. "I'm just the name on the door, not the money in the bank."

"I thought you were an investor in this?" Skip asked as he adjusted his wreath in the mirror beside her.

"I have a little money in it," Star said, trying not to move. "But the big investors approached me to help promote the place."

"So you get extra shares for your name?" Skip said, sitting down and catching her eyes in the mirror as they talked.

"Okay, that's got it," Billy said, then shouted. "We're done Lito. Ten minutes."

"Thanks, doña Bill," Lito called back.

"That's nice," Billy said as they snickered at him.

"That sounds like a good deal," Skip said, ignoring Billy.

"We'll see," Star said with a roll of her eyes as she rose and admired the effect in the mirror. "Every scheme that Ian and Drea and their cronies come up with seems like a good idea at the time, but I've yet to make any money that didn't involve me working my ass off."

"Or showing it off," Skip suggested.

"Bitch," Star said, laughing. "Yeah, that too. Well, I may be headed to the poorhouse, but at least I look amazing." She kissed near their faces to avoid mussing their work. "Is there any chance that

I can go to the bathroom in this getup? Or do I
have to hold it in till after the party?"

The evening was already living up to its reputation
by the time they arrived: searchlights, red carpets,
limos—and a throng of celebrities. Not to mention
the photographers and news crews. Enough press
to cover a small invasion choked traffic on La
Cienega, heralding the epic event.

Looking around, Star was gratified by how far
she had come in such a short time. Not so much by
the hype, as by her friends. Marsten and Angel
Mann were there along with Jayne and, of course,
Sami, who was taking care of them all. Vince arrived with his latest arm decoration, the star of
Sunset Place. It was her third nighttime soap, but
probably her last as an ingenue. Peter Rodick was
there with his famous ex, the well-known singer
Judy Maxwell. And of course the cast, crew, and
executives from both *Hammer Time* and *Lifeguards, Inc.* were there too. Van Pursens had come
in with Alisha Chapeau, another former child actor
who had apparently given up on acting, though
Star suspected that had happened before she got
out of the business. Still, she was a fellow *Mann*
magazine poser, so who was Star to judge? Even
Ant had brought someone, Bambina from that
memorable night at the Castle.

"Let them eat cheesecake," she proclaimed, officially kicking off the festivities as she broke a bottle of her favorite bubbly on one of the columns by the front door. Star smiled, posing for the benefit of the cameras and the publicists who'd planned it.

With three exes in shadow and no date, Star started hitting the Cristal as soon as she was through the door and done with the red carpet. Then it was on to shooters with Billy and Skip.

Swimming through the famous people filling up what was turning into a very successful opening, she spotted rock icon Michael Stetson, lead singer of the band Belladonna, who had arrived with an entourage of groupies, hangers-on, and enough other functionaries to put an Eastern potentate to shame.

Star caught his eye through the surrounding crowds and they exchanged a sly smile. She was struck by how beautiful his eyes were. And then, as quickly as the little window opened, it closed again and he was lost from view. When the kamikaze slammers and Cristal chasers didn't do the trick, Star took to the dance floor to blow her brains out with the music. She found herself drawn into the orbit of Tommie Thoms, the rap singer turned model, who was breaking into the movies. Clad only in a leather gladiator's skirt, he was definitely the best-looking thing on the dance floor. Like Star, he was famous for his body; and yet she'd read or heard almost nothing about him outside of his work. She wondered how he kept his private life so private. He hadn't even come with a date to the party. Only his habitual costar Jefferson Day, another of Hollywood's most eligible bachelors.

As Tommie and Star worked the dance floor, he handed her a little bottle of liquid. "Just take a sniff," he shouted over the music.

"Is it drugs?" she asked, dubious of his directions.

"No, it's actually deodorizer," Tommie said, laughing.

"Okay." Star popped the top and took a tiny sniff. It smelled bleachy. She really didn't get it.

"Here," Tommie said, laughing and taking the bottle from her. "Like this." He popped the top and took two deep sniffs, snapped it shut, and passed it back to her, though he was so lost in the music that he no longer seemed to notice that she was there.

Star took the bottle and, mimicking his demonstration, found herself suddenly somewhere between passing out and climaxing. The music felt louder and warmer somehow, and she was swept up into the rhythm, dancing as though she were alone in the room, and yet acutely aware of the crush of warm bodies around her.

All that mattered was the music, the dance, and her body.

The feeling was short-lived—the intensity began to fade almost immediately—but the sensation was remarkable. It was like getting a booster shot of awareness of what her body already felt. Apparently she had been too caught up in the press, the guests, and the catering to notice what she was really feeling.

As the dance subsided, she realized that Tommie was across the room. Turning back to the party, she found herself looking into those beautiful eyes.

"Hi," Michael said.

"Hi," she said, not looking away.

"Nice party."

"Thanks."

"Wouldn't it be great if everyone was naked?"

"Not really." Star shrugged. "It's the wrapping paper and decorations that make all that junk under the dead tree into Christmas."

"You're pretty smart for a girl who looks so good with her clothes off."

"How do you look without yours?"

"Want to find out?"

"Sure." Star laughed.

"Okay." He raised his toga, put it over her head, then slipped his own head underneath.

"You're not wearing any underwear," Star observed.

"Everyone's naked under their clothes, what's the point?"

"For me it's self-preservation. If these got loose on the dance floor, people could get hurt."

Their behavior was bizarre for only a moment, then people began dancing and writhing together under their togas. The place started to look like a highly animated KKK meeting.

"I've got a suite at the St. James," Michael said, a statement of fact.

Star slipped out from under Michael's toga, and the two slipped out of the party, almost unnoticed—unless you counted the hundreds of photographers and video cameras out front.

Star told Lito to wait on Skip and Billy and then take the rest of the night off. Then she climbed into the back of Michael's limo. As soon as the door was closed, he pulled his toga over his head and began tugging at the golden rope that cinched the waist of Star's. They began tearing at each other's clothes. Since they were both wearing what was basically just a drape, it didn't take much. Michael was a kisser, Star realized with pleasure, and he fell on her at once, driving his tongue into her mouth with an intensity that made Star long for things to come. He ground his body into hers with the same commitment as he kissed. The feel of his erection, pinned between them, set her writhing so that they fell off the seat onto the floor where they remained for a bit, just enjoying the motion of the car and the friction of their two bodies together.

Then, as suddenly as he had fallen on her, he withdrew his mouth from hers and began sampling the rest of her, licking her face, probing her ears, biting her nipples. Lifting her up and turning her away, he pressed her naked flesh against the fortuitously tinted windows, as he dove between her legs and drove his insistent tongue into her, both in front and behind.

"Now," she screamed, fighting him for what she wanted, needed, had to have.

As the limo cruised the crowded streets of West Hollywood, the two made love, shielded from view only by a trick of the light and the tint of the windows. The feel of the leather seats against Star's naked skin was a toe-curling new sensation. Michael was a skilled lover, licking, sucking, tasting, nuzzling . . . even so, his considerable talents could not compare to the thrill of the near exposure to the crowds that surrounded the car as they made their way down the crush of the Sunset Strip. As the limo pulled up to the hotel, they scrambled to put their togas back on. It didn't seem to matter that they weren't wearing their own, and Star didn't bother with panties as they dashed across the lobby of the posh old hotel and dove into a waiting elevator.

"I can't wait to get up to the room," Star said, running her hand firmly across his vacu-formed chest.

"Right, then," he said, pounding the STOP button solidly with his fist. As the car abruptly ground to a halt, they sank to the floor.

Once again, the thrill of discovery inspired her and she took him in her mouth with a passion, urging him to an orgasm he was fighting a losing battle to delay. His shouts alarmed guests passing the elevator on the floors they were stopped between, but by the time the proper authorities had been alerted, the elevator was moving again and Star and Michael were well on their way to his suite.

"You play nasty," Michael said.

"I can play rough too," Star said, smacking his ass through the thin material of his toga, then running to avoid reprisal.

"Has Star Wood Leigh Sold Her Soul to Rock and Roll?" one headline asked.

Pictures of Star and Michael were everywhere, and for good reason. They were everywhere together. Ruf and Mando were both athletes, and there was definitely something to be said for that, but Michael was an out-of-control thrill seeker and ready to play at Star's level from the first night.

Unlike Adam so many years ago, Michael wasn't content to live off fantasies and porn stories, he wanted to live it or never mind.

Their sex life became a tour of the city. Star had even considered writing a feature for *L.A. Magazine* on the subject.

On one occasion Michael had followed her into the ladies' room at one of the city's ritziest restaurants, locking the door and screwing her with such ferocity that they broke one of the spindly Louis Quatorze vanity chairs Star had been braced against.

On another occasion they actually got caught by an assistant stage manager who came to give them a ten-minute warning in the greenroom of a national talk show on which they were making a joint appearance. He brought her to orgasm under the table-cloth at a lifetime achievements awards dinner for some ancient rock star, and she gave him a hand job under an outdoor table at a poorly lit bistro they both liked a great deal. One night Michael filled his bedroom with lights, video screens, and a camera.

"I don't know about this," she had said when she saw the setup. "You can leave a mark, just not a record."

"Relax," he'd said. "There's no film in the camera."

Placated, she'd agreed. More than that, she realized she loved making love surrounded by images of themselves making love.

But one of Star's favorite sessions of all took place in a stall of a crowded men's room at a Las Vegas casino. It reminded her of her beloved *9½ Weeks*. Star was sated. She loved being with Michael. He made her feel complete and completely satisfied. Life seemed a little flavorless when he left on tour. But she was amazed how much more energy she had for *Hammer Time* and *Lifeguards, Inc.*

"I think he's the one," Star confided in Theresa one night on the phone when a pint of Häagen-Dazs wasn't enough.

"What about Rufus? And Mando?" Theresa reminded her. "They're such sweet guys. Michael may be fun, but he's too wild."

"You don't even know him," Star sighed. "He's so sweet and I miss him so much."

"Well, you've got some time coming up. Why not surprise him at his next stop on the concert tour? It shouldn't be too hard, and he must be missing you too."

"That's a great idea," Star said, missing Theresa's subplot entirely. "It's just an airplane ticket and a couple of hours and I'm in—" She paused as she ran her finger down his itinerary. "Dallas, Texas."

"Nothing bad could happen there."

"What?"

"Nothing," Theresa said. "Bon voyage."

The presidential suite at the Dallas Palais was so large that it actually had a private staff, separate from the rest of the hotel. The marble entry, replete with museum-quality sculpture and a hand-carved Italian fountain, opened into a cavernous main salon large enough to accommodate two massive fireplaces, two separate sitting areas, and a concert grand piano. The salon opened onto a private roof garden big enough for a pool and a cabana and backed with a stunning view of the broad, flat city forty-two stories below.

But Star didn't notice any of these things when she sneaked in with a cold bottle of Cristal and a passkey.

"I want it to be a surprise," she explained to the man at the front desk.

"Oh, it will be," the clerk said, nodding.

What she noticed first was the two naked women making out in the fountain in the foyer.

"Michael?" Star asked the two. One of the women pointed toward the salon without looking up from what she was doing.

"Michael," she said again.

He was sprawled on the floor in front of one of the huge fireplaces. Propped up on pillows, he was making out with a stunning Latina while getting head from a couple of women who were making out with each other, his erection trapped between their lips. Michael absently stroked their hair as they took turns going down on him. On the sofa next to them two men were blowing each other, one six and one nine.

Star's breath caught in her throat as she looked around the room, out to the pool, and garden beyond. Michael's little grouping was the least of it. There were boy couples and girl couples and boy/girl couples and little cluster fucks where you couldn't tell who was doing what to whom. It was all so casual, as if they were making idle chitchat at a cocktail party.

She was excited by what she saw, but she was

also a little overwhelmed. Michael was capable of playing at her level, but was she in his league?

"Star," Michael called out to her, noticing her standing at the door. "You're here," he said, delighted, gesturing for her to come nearer. "Now it will be a perfect party."

Mesmerized, she drew nearer. He'd had no other reaction to her arrival beyond the social niceties with which one might greet any party guest. The fact that he was getting a blowjob from two women while making out with another in a roomful of naked people having full-on sex with each other, did not even color his tone of voice. He didn't appear caught or ashamed and was genuinely delighted to see her, a fact that became even more apparent as she reached him and he pulled her down, his lips nipping hungrily at hers, his mouth prying her mouth open as his tongue slipped urgently inside.

Hands, she had no idea whose, anxiously stripped away her clothes and one of the guys from the sofa joined by one of the young women began to nurse at her nipples as the young woman who'd been making out with Michael, her mouth free, went down on Star.

Star made little gasping moans that were lost in Michael's hungry mouth as the skilled Latina hit the spot. She drove her tongue into Michael's mouth as he began to move to enter her. The woman went down on Michael and Star alternately before she suited Michael up and guided his erection into Star.

As Star and Michael began to writhe against each other one of the guys from the sofa brought his erect member to Star's mouth. At first she flicked her tongue tentatively against the strange erection as Michael urged her on. But as Michael drove more deeply into her and her own passion rose, she engulfed the engorged organ with abandon. And then they changed places and she went down on Michael with the young man inside of her. And then they changed yet again as she went down on the young man, and Michael screwed the Latina as she went down on Star. And then Michael was on the other side of the room with other people and Star was still having sex, but she no longer had any idea with whom.

It was complete and total abandon. It was scary, in a new way. It was as though she'd been having sex à la carte all her life and suddenly discovered the all-you-can-eat buffet.

But in the end, she felt an unfathomable loneliness.

She wasn't sure where Michael was. She wasn't sure *who* Michael was.

She managed to find her clothes and tried to get them back on, though she was discouraged by those around her. Eventually she went out into the front hall, which had been abandoned by its two denizens. She got dressed in the company of the statues, and left.

As she closed the door, Star knew that she would

not see Michael again. Not that she was hurt or ashamed or sorry about what had happened. It had been an amazing experience with peaks of white-hot pleasure. But she realized that with Michael it would never be about the two of them being together. He had been glad to see her, then he'd moved on to other people at the party.

She liked à la carte and he liked the buffet.

Star was a little sad when she got back home, but the whole thing had sharpened her appreciation of what she had with Ruf and Mando. Maybe it was time to make a decision. Both were away, and frankly she was enjoying the break. Theresa had come out for another visit, and Star was looking forward to wrapping up the season on both shows and going away for a fashion shoot that Ian had set up for her in Cabo.

They were having girls' night out at Ka Mano the first time she saw him.

"Here's to being single," Star said, raising her glass. "No men tonight and definitely no rock stars ever."

They toasted.

"I think everybody should drink to that," Star said, calling the waiter over and instructing him to take a kamikaze shooter to everyone.

"Star," Theresa cautioned, "that's a little extravagant."

"I get a huge bar tab here every month." Star shrugged. "They want me to entertain here. Either that or become a serious alcoholic."

When the waiter signaled to Star that the drinks had been delivered, she rose to her feet, lifting her glass above her head. "To no men and no rock stars ever," she said, vaulting her glass skyward before downing it. Her voice was lost in the loud crush, but everyone got the gesture and drank with her.

And then she saw him.

Jimi Deed, keyboard player for Fools Brigade, a rock band with a worse reputation than Michael's. He looked at her with the devil's eyes and she quickly turned away.

"Oh my God," she said to Theresa. "It's like I'm cursed."

"What is it?" Theresa asked, concerned.

"It's Jimi Deed," Star hissed.

"Who?" Theresa asked, looking around.

"Jimi Deed," Star said again, louder this time, unaware that he was now standing right beside her.

"At your service," he said, leaning down and licking the side of her face.

Star shivered.

"Oh, God," Theresa said, disgusted. "Get lost."

Jimi laughed and took a seat on their table. "Not until you give me your phone number," he said, lying back across the table, propping himself on his elbow.

Star and Theresa got up and walked away.

"Hey," Jimi shouted. "Why'd you buy me a drink if you didn't want to meet me?"

"I bought everyone a drink!"

"What's your phone number?" he said, jumping to his feet and running after them. When he caught up, he got in Star's face.

"I. Do. Not. Want. To. Go. Out. With. You." Star enunciated each word clearly.

"So what was up with that toast?"

"We were drinking to no more rock stars," Star said, pushing past him.

"I'm the last one you'll ever need," he said, vaulting up and grabbing the two arms of the large overhead chandelier and swinging on it like a trapeze. "Check it out and see for sure."

The bouncers took over, and following a rather comic struggle in which Jimi wrapped his legs around the neck of one of the bouncers, they managed to pry him down and escort him to the door.

"Ask him what you'll be missing," Jimi shouted to her from the door, indicating the bouncer he'd had his legs around.

"Why do they always think that's the deal breaker?" Theresa said, laughing in spite of herself.

"You tell 'em you're not interested," Star said, laughing along and doing her best impersonation, "and they say, 'Well, baby, maybe you'd be interested if you knew what I was serving.' Like it's something other than tube steak."

"Like theirs is the only one." Theresa guffawed.

"Well, it's given them so much pleasure over the years, they can't imagine that it won't do the same for you," Star said, signaling the bartender for another round for the two of them.

"Are you trying to get me drunk?"

"Too late," Star answered, glad that Lito was outside waiting for them.

Theresa only laughed.

"I will say I've had pretty good dick karma so far," Star said. "No big disappointments, so to speak."

Theresa fell off her barstool as the drinks arrived. It cracked Star up so badly that she fell off too.

Despite Star's fervor, clarity, and even good diction, that night at Ka Mano was not the last time she heard from Jimi Deed. He managed to get her number and called repeatedly, leaving messages, playing her songs, and generally driving her crazy.

She changed her number.

He shaved her name into his hair and made a big deal of being photographed in the press, starting the rumor mill working in his favor. The more she denied the rumors, the more the press asked. He sent her an intimate picture of himself revealing a new tattoo of her name, just along his pelvic bone. When she didn't respond, he tugged down the right side of his pants on the red carpet at a movie opening, sharing his obsession with a hungry world.

He even sent over a song he had recorded about his dick.

"Oh, my penis has a first name, it's *L-A-R-G-E*.

"Oh, my penis has a second name, it's *F-U-C-K* me—"

That's as far as she got before she shut it off and tossed it out the window.

Finally, she tried talking to him.

He had managed to get her phone number once again, and she heard his voice on the answering machine and picked it up.

"Okay, listen to me, Jimi Deed," Star said hotly. "I don't know what *part* of no you don't understand, but the answer is no. I don't want to go out with you. No. It's a complete sentence. No. I'm seeing somebody and I think it may be serious and I don't want to go out with you."

"Not that fruit Michael Stetson," Jimi snorted derisively.

"No, it's not Michael, and I'll thank you not to use those kinds of slurs around me," Star said primly. "But it is serious and it is none of your business. And the answer is no."

"You should go out with me once, just to be sure."

"No. No. No," Star yelled into the phone.

"Is that your final answer?"

She hung up.

She really did want to get serious. If she were married, this kind of nonsense would stop. She sighed. Was it Ruf? Was it Mando? The only thing she knew for sure, it wasn't Jimi.

Jimi was not the only crank caller in her life; he was just the most creative.

Steph Golden had made himself famous producing music videos. But he'd worked with all the greats and had won all the awards he could and was ready for a career change. He was angling to become a movie mogul. To do that he'd bought the rights to *Hy Voltz,* a popular action-adventure comic-book heroine, and he figured on starting himself a movie franchise. The way he saw it, Star was the key to making that happen.

She was still not sure about the movie thing. She was just finishing her first season of *Lifeguards,* and that was as close to acting as she'd ever come. Movies scared her. They were big and so your mistakes were big. She wasn't ready to make that leap. So when Steph had approached Ian about the idea, Star had overruled him and passed on it. That had not slowed Steph down; he just kept throwing larger sums at her while messengering her one-sheet movie posters featuring Star's image in the lead role.

"We'll premiere the whole idea at Cannes," he pleaded in one of his many phone calls to her.

"Cannes? What can?"

"The Cannes film festival, in the south of France?"

"Europe, France? Well, I have always wanted to go to Europe."

But that was as far as it went. She was still ambivalent about the whole idea.

So, what with wrapping up the first full season of two television shows, trying to keep what she had with both Ruf and Mando working long distance, and the relentless barrage from Jimi and Steph, she was slowly going out of her mind.

The whole thing came to a head on the final day of shooting for *Lifeguards*. The episode centered on Star's character, so her preparation had been heavier than usual. On the plus side, she had already completed the last episode of *Hammer Time*. She was leaving the next day for a two-week shoot in Cabo, which would include a lot of downtime, of which she was in sore need. And she had made arrangements to fly straight from Cabo to visit Ruf at his family's place outside Palm Beach in Florida, and then later to spend some time with Mando in Jamaica to try to make up her mind.

On the downside, when she got to work that day, she found that not only had Jimi spray-painted a rather graphic love poem on her trailer, but somehow Steph had gotten inside to leave her a leatherbound copy of his script, diamond-studded with her name. "Oh, Mutley," she said, collapsing into her makeup chair. "What are we going to do with these two?"

She managed to get ready and get her head together. "Okay, Mutley," she said, giving him a hug and then locking him inside her dressing room. "You guard the trailer. Don't let any lunatics inside."

It was a perfect day on the set and Star realized what a great job she had. She was working with one of her favorite directors from the season. She had a lot of scenes with Ant, and they worked really well together, something they hadn't gotten to do a lot of during the season. They were easy together, good friends who had parted well and amiably. Their characters were flirting with romance, and their personal history brought some real heat to their more romantic scenes.

"That's a wrap," the director called on the last shot of the last day.

"Good work, everyone," Stan shouted over the din of applause. "Have a great summer. Let's do this again next fall." There was more applause and an announcement that the wrap party would begin in the conference room in half an hour.

Star grabbed her things and made her way toward the trailers as they started to strike the camera, props, and set pieces.

"Star?" Engel said curiously as they passed each other. "What are you doing here? I thought you were in your trailer."

"Not yet," Star said cheerfully. "Why?"

"Look," Engel said, turning and pointing.

Star darkened when she saw the rocking trailer.
"Mutley," she cried.

It was a phenomenon that Star had never actually gotten to observe, though with two athletes for
boyfriends she'd heard the jokes. And, of course,
there was the sign on her door. This time the trailer
looked as though it was having its own personal
8.0 quake.

"God, my dog is in there," she said, dropping
her things and running for the trailer and her
beloved Mutley.

"Star, wait," Engel called after her. "Let me get
some security or something to go with you."

But it was too late. Star was not about to wait
to find out what all the wild barking was about.

She took the three steps in one leap and
snatched the door open.

Steph and Jimi looked up at her from where
they had been grappling with one another on the
floor of her destroyed dressing room.

"This guy was in your trailer," Jimi said, pointing an accusing finger in Steph's face, which he bit.
Jimi screamed and rolled off Steph.

"I found this nut job in your trailer," Steph said,
jumping to his feet as he tried to get in one more
kick. Jimi caught Steph's foot and pulled it out
from under him, causing Steph to fall on top
of him.

"You're both right," Star said through clenched
teeth in a voice so demonically possessed that Mut-

ley stopped barking and ran under the daybed. "You are both nuts and you both broke into my trailer."

"Well, I was just trying to defend you," Jimi began heroically.

"He was smelling your things," Steph tried to shout over the top of him.

"Shut up," Star screamed. "Both of you. Now, gentlemen, listen slowly. Here's how it's going to be. I'm going to my wrap party, and then I'm going home and get a much needed and well-earned good night's sleep, during which time I will get no strange deliveries or crazy phone messages or anything else. Then tomorrow I'm going to Cabo for work."

"Without me?" Jimi demanded.

"Yes, without you! And if I see you or hear from you the entire time I'm there, our deal is off."

"And the script?" Steph ventured.

"I'm taking a copy with me to read while I'm gone, and you will not try to find out what I think of it before I get back. And that will be more than a month away."

"And you! When I get back, I will go out on one date with you. Just to shut you the hell up. No promises and no sex, I don't care how big it is. Do you both understand me?"

Jimi and Steph nodded.

"Good, now get the hell out of my trailer, and don't either of you try to contact me again before you hear from me," Star said, following as the two scrambled to their feet and, pushing and shoving, made their way out the door. Star realized that every grip and teamster and would-be tough guy was behind her giving force to her words (not to mention pretty much the entire cast), but she was proud of herself nonetheless. She'd been bossed around by men for most of her life, and she'd taken a stand about what she wanted.

She had a choice and she was making it.

It was a pride she still felt as she later described the scene in a phone call to Theresa, as Star lay in a tub full of gardenia-scented bubbles in her candle-filled bathroom, overlooking sunset on the Pacific.

"Oh, God," Theresa said. "You agreed to go out with Jimi Deed? And a movie?"

"I agreed to spend one measly day with Jimi and to read that movie guy's comic-book script," Star said, stressing the terms of the agreements. "It'll keep Jimi happy for a while and give me something to read by the pool. It'll help me sleep and won't be habit-forming."

Theresa laughed in spite of her concern. She'd watched the Michael Stetson episode with genuine concern. These guys were too wild and Star was too willing to go along for the ride. It was the same story as with Brandi or the stray dogs or the birds with the broken wings. Star's heart was in the right place, it was just too soft for her own good. She trusted and loved too easily, and Theresa didn't want to see her hurt.

"Well, the main thing is for you to get some much needed rest," she said. "Two weeks in Cabo, then out here to visit Rufus, and down to Jamaica for a holiday with Mando. No worries, no Hollywood, and no rock stars. Promise me?"

"Promise you what?" Star asked, drizzling suds and warm water over her flesh. She wrung out a huge sea sponge, then propped it behind her head.

"Promise me that you'll think about it, that you'll give some serious thought to calling this whole deal off?" Theresa said, getting herself worked up.

"Oh, calm down, Theresa," Star said, waving her champagne flute grandly. "I promise I'll call you when I get there. But really, I don't think you have anything to worry about. You're taking this way too seriously. It's one date and a movie about a comic-book character, what could possibly happen?"

"What could possibly happen?" Theresa demanded incredulously. "Look at your track record. What hasn't happened?"

"Since when did you get to be the relationship expert?" Star began, warming to the argument.

"I'm worried about you," Theresa said, trying to control herself. "Just go down there and get some rest, clear your head, and then call me and we'll talk about it."

"Why is everyone trying to tell me what to do?"

"I'm not trying to tell you—"

"If you think about it long enough, there's a reason not to do everything. That's why you're there and I'm here."

"Star?" Theresa said, shocked. "You don't know what you're saying."

"I'm not a child and stop treating me like one," Star shouted, slamming down the phone.

"Oh, God," she moaned. "What have I done?" She and Theresa had not had an argument in the fifteen years since they'd become best friends. But Star knew she wasn't really angry at Theresa. There were just too many people with too many opinions about how she should live her life. The blowup at the trailer had been her declaration of independence, but now what?

The phone rang.

Star regarded it a moment and, with a sigh, sank beneath the bubbles.

Simon & Schuster
proudly presents

Star Struck
Pamela Anderson

Available in hardcover
from Atria Books

Turn the page for a preview of
Star Struck . . .

1

you shook me all
night long

Why do my nipples hurt? was
Star's first thought as she woke from a
strangely deep sleep, her hands gliding
along her naked body to the tender
nipples that had awakened her. She winced as she
made contact, realizing only belatedly that she was
naked. Star tried to open her eyes but couldn't; the
room was too bright. She raised her hand to shield
her view, only to be blinded by a huge diamond
ring that hadn't been on her finger when she went
to sleep.

When had she gone to sleep? And where?

Stretching, Star reached up to push back her

hair as she tried to get her bearings and she struck herself on the forehead with the chrome handle of the Colt .45 she was holding in her right hand. She screamed and fell off the dresser on which she'd been perched. The gun went off, taking out a glass table top that shattered into four-carat chunks of safety glass.

Star stared at the revolver in her hand. She'd never even touched a gun before, but here she was, naked except for a pair of Gucci boots, a strange diamond ring, and a gun welded to her hand.

What the hell was going on?

Why did everything feel so strange? So blurry?

She was hungry but didn't have an appetite. Her skin felt alive, vibrating gently against her every nerve ending. The sun was so bright she could hardly see and the carpet was so soft it tickled her bare ass where she sat, puzzled, on the floor.

Looking around, Star was relieved to see that she was still in her hotel room in Cabo. Well, what was left of her hotel room. Pictures had been torn off the wall and defaced; cushions from the chairs and sofa had been built into a fort in the middle of the room; tables were stacked to the ceiling; and dozens of empty Cristal bottles, scattered everywhere, prompted her to wonder if the damages would be covered under the "incidentals" clause in her modeling contract.

As she further surveyed the damage, Star noticed the unmade bed that was a confusion of sheets, pillows, and strangely chosen items from around the room—a candlestick, an ice bucket, and a selection of well-placed objets d'art. Condoms, some used, some blown up like balloons, also littered the space. "Well, I'm glad we played safe," she said with a little laugh, swatting one of the oddly shaped balloons out of her way. That's when she saw the tiny video camera and a few dozen tapes strewn across the coffee table, along with the remnants of several lines of cocaine. How odd, Star reflected. I don't do drugs. I wonder who's been here? Her musings turned to panic as she saw a pair of bare feet sticking out from beneath the tangle of Frette sheets, next to a blender that must have been taken from the room's wet bar. Actually, the blender was working double duty because its cord had been used to bind the mysterious pair of ankles to the bedposts.

A modern-day Goldilocks, Star crept closer. Who are these feet attached to? And what are they doing in my bed? Tentatively, she reached out and touched a big toe with the barrel of the gun. A small, strangled cry escaped her throat as the toe responded, wiggling as if to get away from the cold steel barrel. Star put her hand over her mouth, felt the strange diamond against her cheek, and pulled it away.

She felt so naked.

Well, aside from the boots and the ring, she

was naked. But it wasn't just that she didn't have any clothes on. She felt vulnerable—raw and exposed. Try as she might, she could not remember what had happened last night, could not remember how she'd wound up asleep on the dresser, and could not guess who this might be in her bed. She stood frozen for a minute, listening to the muffled cries coming from under the sheets.

Star made her way around the bed looking for clues to identify the stranger. She found nothing. It was a man; that much was clear from the rather sizable tent pole raised under the sheets. But who? Surely, she would remember an erection like that, she thought with a playful giggle, reaching out and giving the massive morning wood a tap. The moans changed, a different tone now, at least an octave lower.

Finally, she could stand it no longer. She reached for the hem of the crumpled sheet, ready to expose the identity of the well-endowed stranger . . . but then her phone rang, startling her as it played its version of "You Shook Me All Night Long."

Star pulled back, oddly frightened by the old AC/DC song that had shattered the silence.

Should she answer it?

The phone rang again. It echoed in the room and in her head.

Would it seem suspicious not to answer it?

It rang.

And rang.

What time was it anyway?

Taking a deep breath, Star answered it.

"Hello?" she said softly, moving away from the body in the bed.

"Star? Honey, is that you?"

"Who is this?"

"It's Rufus," the caller said with a startled laugh.

She considered the information for a moment. Everything seemed so strange. She felt dizzy and medicated.

"Your boyfriend?" he said, when she didn't answer, an edge in his voice.

"Hi, baby, I'm sorry," she said, scratching her nose with the gun. "I just woke up and I'm not feeling right."

"Not feeling right?" he said, curious at her strange choice of words. "What do you mean, 'not feeling right'? And why are you whispering?"

"Are you working for the CIA?" she asked sharply, closing the bathroom door behind her.

"What?"

"Well, I just thought, what with the third degree you were interrogating me," she snapped.

"I'm sorry," he said gently. "You just seem so strange."

"Well, I feel strange," she continued. "Isn't that what I've been trying to tell you?"

"Is everything all right?" he asked, genuinely confused.

"I'll have to get back to you when I know, but thanks for your concern." Star clicked off the phone, regarding it irritably for a moment before dropping it into the toilet.

Her captive was waiting patiently for her when she returned to the bed.

"What did I do last night?" she asked herself.

And then, with a child's impatience on Christmas morning, she tore off the sheet and found herself staring into the face of the rock-and-roll musician Jimi Deed, bound, gagged, and tied to her bed. Star hadn't seen Jimi since she threw him out of her trailer back on the California set of her TV show, Lifeguards, Inc. The only way she'd been able to convince him to leave had been to agree to go out with him when she got back from Cabo, though he'd called persistently and threatened to follow her. She was still in Cabo, and yet here he was.

"What are you doing here?" she demanded, unconsciously waving the gun at him.

Jimi winced, crying out in fear as the barrel of the shiny pistol passed near his nose.

"Oh, sorry about that," she said, embarrassed and apologetic, although continuing to wave the gun around. "It's not mine," she explained. "I'm not sure how it got here. For that matter, I'm not sure how you got here. I'm not really a gun person; I don't even know how it works, really. I mean, I guess you just pull on . . ."

And with that, the room was suddenly and violently filled with feathers raining down like the first snow of the season. Jimi screamed through his gag and writhed wildly on the bed, his head next to the blackened remains of the pillow she'd shot out from under him. She looked like an angel with a .45.

"Oh . . . I'm so very sorry," she said, putting the gun on the bedside table. "You don't look too dangerous. Well not most of you, anyway," she said, lifting the sheet for a peek under the big tent he was pitching. She gave a low appreciative whistle. "Looks like you've got a bigger pistol than me."

Jimi struggled vainly against his bonds, startling Star. She dropped the sheet, frightened, but soon realized that he was no threat to her in his present condition.

"So how did you wind up here?" she said, sitting down beside him.

Jimi made some rather defiant noises through his gag.

"Oh, right, the gag," she said, knocking herself in the forehead with the heel of her hand. "My bad. Now, no screaming. I doubt anyone would hear you or, judging from this room, care. But I've got a really bad hangover from all this champagne, so, shhh."

Star unbuckled the very professional ballgag that was in his mouth, allowing him to spit out the orange ball.

"What the fuck?" he demanded.

"What do you mean?" Star said, rising. "And what the hell are you doing in my hotel room?"

"I'm tied to the bed and you've got a gun," he said. "Two plus two."

"When did you get here?" she asked, still puzzled. "What happened last night?"

"I've been here for three days," he said. "Last night just made it clear I should have left after two. Or killed you. Now will you let me go? I was supposed to be somewhere last night."

"You've been here with me for three days?" Star asked, not really paying much attention to what he'd said after that. "How is that possible?"

"Are you going to let me go?"

"I don't know. Do you promise not to tell anyone about all this?"

"I promise I'll visit you in Mexican jail," Jimi snarled, straining at his bonds.

"Now you have to promise me that you won't get me in trouble," Star said, rising, alarmed by his belligerent attitude even in his present circumstances.

"Are you fucking kidding me?" he said with a snort of laughter. "You kidnapped me and tied me up at gunpoint."

"Oh that's ridiculous," Star said, laughing. "I've never had to tie a man up, unless he wanted me to."

"Well, it seemed hot at first," Jimi admitted,

doing what he could to shrug. "But then you wouldn't let me go, and that's kidnapping."

"You seem pretty glad to see me this morning," she said, reaching out and playfully tweaking the persistent erection, tenting the sheets in front of him. "Maybe we could work something out."

"Work something out?"

"Well, used to be you wanted to date me pretty bad, as I remember."

"That was before I married you and you tied me up and kidnapped me!" he roared. "Now all I want to do is see you behind bars."

"M-m-m-married?" Star stuttered. "I'm married?"

"Since yesterday."

"My mom is definitely not going to approve of this."

"She was pretty pissed," Jimi laughed.

"She was here?"

"No, you called her to tell her," Jimi nodded smugly.

"Oh my God."

"What else happened? How did you get here?"

"You really don't remember, do you?"

Star only shook her head in answer.

"I'll make you a deal," Jimi said. "You untie me and let me go to the bathroom, and I'll tell you what happened."

"No, I don't think I can trust you yet."

"We're married," Jimi said with a touch of self-righteousness.

She looked at him.

"Okay, so that doesn't count for much," he agreed. "But I really do have to pee."

She looked around the room and found the solution—an ice bucket, filled with slush and an up-ended bottle of Cristal. She arose from the bed where she'd been sitting, grabbed the bucket, and, marching out onto the balcony of her top-floor rooms, dumped the contents down the combined heights of the high-rise hotel and the steep cliffs on which it sat, into the Pacific, hundreds of feet below.

Leaving the French windows open, she walked back to the bed where he lay and pulled back the sheets.

"I can't believe I don't remember this," she said, taking his cock in her hand and guiding it into the ice bucket.

"You can't be serious!" he snarled.

"Roll over as much as you can," Star said playfully. "It's time for a little game of fireman and hose."

"Fuck you."

"Suit yourself," she shrugged, taking the bucket away.

"I'll piss right here," he said defiantly.

"And you'll lie in it," she said, folding her arms under her naked breasts.

"Mother fuck," he said, turning his hips as much toward her as he could, bound to the bed as he was.

"Oh, you want the bucket back now?"

"Just put it over here."

"Say please."

"Please," he said through gritted teeth.

Once again she took his cock in her hand and guided it into the bucket.

"Wow," she observed, looking at the almost-full bucket.

"Well, I've been tied up since last night."

"Okay then . . ." Returning from the bathroom where she'd emptied the bucket, Star took a seat on the bed, legs folded Indian style beside Jimi's naked body. "So, tell me what happened."

"You didn't untie me," he said, turning his head away.

"Tell me," she said, reaching out and toying with his now deflated cock.

"No," he said. "Cut it out."

"Tell me," she coaxed, stroking him back to erection.

He shook his head violently from side to side.

"Come on," she said, stroking harder.

"Get the fuck off of me," he protested.

"If you tell."

"Fuck you."

Laughing, she grabbed some hand cream from the bedside table and slathered it onto her hands and his erection. Mercilessly she began again, stroking and stroking until his balls tightened and he neared the brink. Abruptly she stopped and let him subside. As his orgasm faded she resumed her tease, stroking, sucking, and riding him near to orgasm. Again and again she played, always stopping just before he finished, until he was screaming and begging for release.

"Please, please, now," he pleaded as she rode him once more to the edge.

"Will you tell?" she asked, slowing down and letting him subside again.

"No, fuck you!" he spat.

"Okay, then," she said, climbing off. She spotted the video camera on the coffee table and brought it back with her. "Smile for the camera," she said, straddling him once more. She taped the two of them as best she could from her position astride him. She was driving him slowly mad, and enjoying every minute of it.

"I'll do it, I'll do it, I'll do anything, just don't fucking stop!" he screamed as she brought him to the brink once more.

"How can I believe you?" she asked, turning to film his answer.

"I don't know," he said. "I give you my word."

"I must have tied you up for a reason," she said. "I'm not sure about your word. Tell me something that I can use against you if you go back on your promise. Something nobody else knows."

"I was involved in a hit-and-run accident a couple of years back."

"You're a rock star," she scoffed. "That's like a rite of passage. What else?"

"I used to pay for studio time by screwing the woman who ran the recording studio."

"You've probably been bragging about that one for years," she said dismissively, picking up the pace and riding him harder. "Tell me real secrets."

"I used to take tap and ballet classes in high school," he blurted out, desperate. "And I was really good. My mom has recital pictures in her living room."

"That's the stuff," she said, bearing down. She had managed to get herself off a few times in the process, but managed to score one more off of her captive before he lost it and erupted, screaming and writhing in his relief.

She fell to one side and they lay panting next to each other for a bit.

"You raped me," he said.

"Raped you? Me?" she said, rewinding the tape and playing it back for him in the viewfinder.

"Please, please, now," his voice rang out. "Oh fuck yeah."

"Yeah, you sound like a rape victim," she said, giving him a swat. "Now, tell me the story.